Shadow Patriots

Forge Books by Lucia St. Clair Robson

Ghost Warrior
Shadow Patriots

Shadow Patriots

Lucia St. Clair Robson

A TOM DOHERTY ASSOCIATES BOOK
NEW YORK

SHADOW PATRIOTS

This book is printed on acid-free paper.

Map by Mark Stein

Edited by Robert Gleason

A Forge Book
Published by Tom Doherty Associates, LLC
175 Fifth Avenue
New York, NY 10010

www.tor.com

Forge® is a registered trademark of Tom Doherty Associates, LLC.

Library of Congress Cataloging-in-Publication Data

Robson, Lucia St. Clair.
    Shadow patriots / Lucia St. Clair Robson.—1st ed.
      p. cm.
    ISBN 0-765-30550-X
    EAN 978-0765-30550-3
    1. Philadelphia (Pa.)—History—Revolution, 1775–1783—Fiction. 2. Brothers and sisters—Fiction. 3. Quaker women—Fiction. 4. Women spies—Fiction. I. Title.

PS3568.O3185S47 2005
813'.54—dc22

                                                                    2004062878

First Edition: May 2005

Printed in the United States of America

0 9 8 7 6 5 4 3 2 1

This one is for Ginny Stibolt,
dear friend, inspiration, and an all-around good scout.

I want to add a special dedication
to the men and women of our country's armed forces,
who, since 1776, have sacrificed their own lives and liberties to protect ours.

Acknowledgments

Those who preserve our historical sites are national treasures. Some who helped with this story are Ken Moss and Sheena Brown at the Morris-Jumel Mansion in New York City. Connie Clark, docent at Raynham Hall Museum in Oyster Bay, New York, shared her knowledge of the Townsend house's history and her experiences with its not-so-corporeal residents.

William Lange, ranger, and Ed Buck, interpreter, at Valley Forge National Historical Park possess an awesome amount of information. Also at the park, intern Chris Glassburn helped answer nagging questions about eighteenth-century military and medical arcana.

Ellen Nielsen and Jim Romer suggested resources for information about the Quaker religion. The Friends Historical Library at Swarthmore College in Pennsylvania cleared up puzzlement about Quaker speech patterns.

Thanks to Kerstin and Annika Ebsen and their father, Ragnar, of Uetersen, Germany, who searched old books for examples of eighteenth-century German expressions. Mathilde Krug Smallwood was kind enough to go over the German phrases I used and correct my errors.

I appreciate the help of David Eccles on questions of weaponry. Special thanks also to Joseph Vallely and Dean Avery for their encouragement and suggestions.

As always, I am deeply grateful to my literary agent, Virginia Barber, who has encouraged and abetted me all these years. Uncountable thanks, Ginger, and wagonloads of affection.

Our acts our angels are, for good or ill,
Our fatal shadows that walk by us still.

—John Fletcher (1579–1625), *An Honest Man's Fortune*

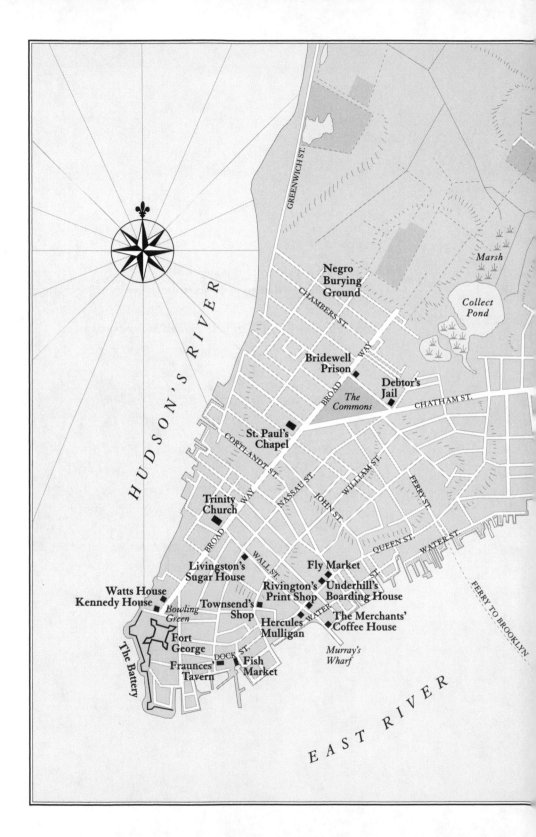

GREENWICH ST.

HUDSON'S RIVER

Marsh

Negro
Burying
Ground

Collect
Pond

CHAMBERS ST.

BROAD WAY

Bridewell
Prison

The
Commons

Debtor's
Jail

CHATHAM ST.

St. Paul's
Chapel

CORTLANDT ST.

NASSAU ST.

WILLIAM ST.

JOHN ST.

FERRY ST.

Trinity
Church

BROAD WAY

QUEEN ST.

WATER ST.

FERRY TO BROOKLYN

Livingston's
Sugar House

WALL ST.

Fly Market

ST.

Watts House
Kennedy House

Rivington's
Print Shop

Underhill's
Boarding House

Bowling
Green

Townsend's
Shop

Hercules
Mulligan

WATER

The Merchants'
Coffee House

Fort
George

Murray's
Wharf

The Battery

DOCK ST.

Fraunces'
Tavern

Fish
Market

EAST RIVER

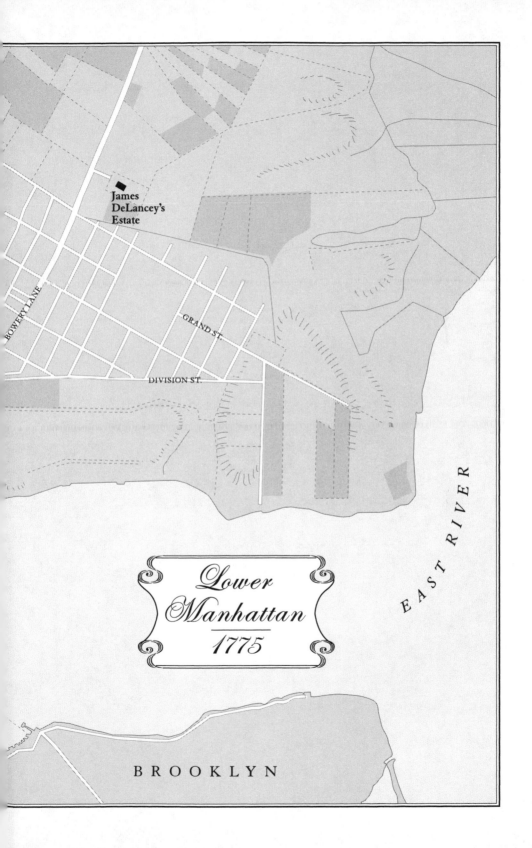

James
DeLancey's
Estate

BOWERY LANE

GRAND ST.

DIVISION ST.

EAST RIVER

Lower
Manhattan
1775

BROOKLYN

GENERAL WASHINGTON'S OTHER AIDES WERE CURIOUS ABOUT what Captain Alexander Hamilton was doing, but they did not glance at him, hunched over a desk in a far corner. Their goose-quill pens quivered as they filled out requisitions, wrote reports, and transcribed directives. They had hung their dark blue jackets over the backs of their chairs and rolled up their shirtsleeves. August of 1779 was not as hot here in the highlands of West Point as elsewhere in New York, but the room was small and the air stifling.

Usually Hamilton would be decoding the Culpers' latest letters in Washington's office upstairs, but the commander in chief had had another attack of rheumatism. The surgeon was up there now, bleeding and blistering him. Hamilton poured sand on the fresh ink to dry it. He shook the sand into a pot, rolled up the letters, and tied them with a blue ribbon. He surveyed the tabletop to make sure he had left nothing behind that would get Samuel Culper, Jr., and Samuel Culper, Sr., hanged if seen by the wrong eyes. He didn't like to think that a traitor might be in this room, but they lurked everywhere else, so why not here?

He headed for the door, dodging chairs and tables, and the sprawl of black boots and portly cuspidors. He avoided the sabers, plumed helmets, and a banjo dangling from the chair backs. He reached the hallway and took the narrow stairs two at a time. Halfway up he stood aside to let the surgeon pass on his way down, with his basin of blood in one hand and his lancet and blistering iron in the other.

Hamilton found Washington sitting with his breeches rolled up, his feet propped on a stool, and his knees bloody. Martha Washington knelt beside him, wrapping strips of cloth around a muslin poultice to hold it in place over the sores. The Washingtons' alliance mystified Alex. The general was so tall and imposing in his perfectly tailored uniform that if people noticed he wasn't handsome, they soon forgot it. He had an aloof air that attracted women of all sorts, yet he loved his plump, plain little wife with a solemn passion.

Martha wiped her hands on her apron and spread out the leftover muslin. She put the makings of her poultice—the packet of flour and the soothing herbs, the mortar and pestle—into the middle of it. She tied the four corners together and picked up the bundle, along with her kettle of hot water.

"George spends too many nights sleeping in the cold and damp." She gave Alexander a beseeching look, as if her husband's favorite aide could help her George more than the surgeon could.

"There's nothing to be done about it, my dear," Washington said, "except to send the British packing once and for all time."

"And then we can return home." She laid a hand for a long instant on his shoulder before she left the room.

After her full skirts cleared the door Washington turned to Hamilton. "You should get you a wife, Alex."

"It is my most earnest desire, sir, as soon as we send the bloodybacks packing." Hamilton was more than handsome. He had the brooding appeal of a puppy with an injured soul. Women purred around him wherever his commander established headquarters.

"Socrates was right, you know. 'By all means marry.'"

Hamilton knew the reference. "'If you get a good wife, you will become happy; if you get a bad one, you will become a philosopher.'"

"I have got a good wife, which may be why I am not a philosopher." Washington winked at him.

"Philosophers don't win wars, sir." Hamilton set the roll of letters on the general's desk. "Speaking of marriage, did you hear of the country woman who signed for ownership of a cow?"

"Can't say as I have."

"The seller asked, 'How is it you made a circle instead of an *X*?' The woman said, 'Oh, I got married again and changed my name.'"

Washington's chuckle cheered Alex. The general had so few occasions for laughter.

Washington slid the ribbon off the parchment. "The latest from the Culpers?"

"Yes, sir. One of Major Tallmadge's dragoons just arrived in a lather with them. The top one is dated the fifteenth of this month. It arrived expeditiously, given the distance their correspondence must cover."

"They're using Tallmadge's new numerical code, I see." Washington unlocked his desk drawer and took out a small notebook with columns of entries written in Major Benjamin Tallmadge's neat hand.

He read the letter silently, his finger moving along the lines of script. The finger stopped at the sentence that read, "I intend to visit 727 before long and think by the assistance of a 355 of my acquaintance shall be able to out wit them all."

Washington looked up. "Seven-two-seven stands for New York, but what is 355?"

"It means 'lady,' sir.

"Who is she?"

"We don't know."

"That's good." Washington stared at the number 355 as though he could see in it some image of this mysterious lady, what she looked like, if she was highborn or servant class. "The less we know about her the better."

One

Wherein Robert Townsend sees more than he cares to;
a tailor named Hercules spills the peas

AS THE WOMAN WRESTLED HER VAST HAT BRIM, TOWERING
wig, and seven yards of hoopskirt out of the carriage, Robert Townsend
saw the calamity coming. He should have shouted a warning, but he
couldn't believe the goat would maintain a collision course on the crowded
street. The wooden soles of the woman's high clogs reached the cobblestones. She gave her hoop a swing to one side, like a flagship dipping its
colors upon arriving at anchor.

With perfect timing the goat ran under the lifted section of skirt and
caught his horns on the hoop. The maiden screamed. The goat bleated.
Passersby stopped to gawk.

The more she tried to shake him out of her clothes, the more his horns
tangled in the folds of the velvet, and the greater the number of people
cheering him on. She tottered on her high shoes, then toppled backward.
Her skirt and petticoats, held aloft by the hoop, formed an arch above her.
To no one's surprise and everyone's amusement, she wore nothing underneath. Rob was probably the only one embarrassed by the view. He
turned away and headed for the dockside tailor shop of his friend Hercules Mulligan.

June of 1776 had settled like kettle steam on New York City. The stagnant sewers in the middle of the narrow streets demanded cat-agile footwork, knee-high boots, and an inferior sense of smell. Loose cobblestones made the streets even more treacherous. Benjamin Franklin said it best: "You can always tell a New Yorker by his gait, like a parrot on a mahogany table."

The city fathers had persuaded New Yorkers to dump their garbage into the streets instead of leaving it to fester in their dooryards and cellars. The theory was that what the pigs, chickens, goats, dogs, cats, rats, and crows didn't eat, the rains would wash into the Hudson and the East River for the outgoing tide to transport. That was the theory. In practice, servants dumped more slop in the streets than the animals could eat. The rain washed more of it into the rivers than they could carry out to sea. Much of the garbage ended up here at the lowest end of Manhattan Island. The mixture formed a scum-covered swamp around the maze of wharves jutting into the East River. In exile aboard one of the five British ships anchored offshore, Governor Tryon could smell the city as well as see it.

Rob Townsend had watched the Continental Army straggle into the city four months ago, but this was not his fight. He was a Quaker, and he swore loyalty to no one but God. As purchasing agent for his father's store on Long Island, Rob continued to go to the docks every day.

Before the rebel army arrived, most of those loyal to King George had begged, borrowed, or stolen every vehicle they could find. Horses and hand carts disappeared under trunks and sacks, spinets, mattresses, and the portraits of ancestors staring morosely from sumptuous gilt frames. Thousands had fled north up the Post Road, crossed the Harlem River over King's Bridge, and scattered into Connecticut. Others had loaded skiffs to the foundering point and rowed across the Hudson River to New Jersey. Many had crowded onto the ferry going to the hamlet of Brooklyn and dispersed into the Long Island countryside.

The loyalists who stayed behind pretended to side with the rebels. If they were good at deception they avoided having the Sons of Liberty ride them around town on a fence rail that rendered their testicles unserviceable. People might be uncertain about which side of the political fence rail they preferred, but no one wanted to straddle it. New Yorkers had become adept at spying and lying, informing, avenging, and dissembling.

The city took on the look of a garrison town. Drums rattled the window panes. Soldiers crowded the narrow streets. Wagons, caissons, and artillery carriages loosened the cobblestones that had held firm thus far.

The first to venture back into business were the strumpets in the district known as the Holy Ground near St. Paul's Chapel. Taverns and gaming houses multiplied. Shopkeepers took the shutters off their windows and trebled their prices.

During the day the docks teemed with stevedores unloading supplies and ammunition. At night sloops and catboats ghosted out of New York's creeks and coves and smuggled provisions to the five British ships anchored out of artillery range. With oars muffled, British sailors came ashore looking for love and a tailor. They carried parcels and messages for Rob's friend, Hercules Mulligan. The word among them was that in a city of traitors, ingrates, rogues, roughs, and rebels, Hercules Mulligan remained loyal to the king. The parcels contained uniforms. The messages listed body measurements. No man wanted to fight a war in badly fitting breeches.

Hercules Mulligan's parents knew what they were doing when they named him. He stood taller than a pie safe, and almost as wide. His round face ended in a square chin that curved out like the butt of a carpenter's adz. He looked as though he should be felling oaks or carrying bales up a gangplank. Instead, with a bristle of pins in his mouth and the basting needle lost among the rugged promontories of his fingers, he circled the mayor of New York and the coat he was altering.

Mulligan always gave Mayor David Matthews wide seams because he knew he would be letting them out soon. Matthews liked to rub his paunch and announce that he was expanding his horizon. Mulligan wondered when the mayor had last seen his own feet, hidden below his equator like two sloops in the southern latitudes.

Mayor Matthews flinched when a pin stuck him. "I say, my good fellow, have a care."

"Beggin' your pardon, squire." Mulligan was deft at his craft, but now and then he liked to jab Matthews. He said he wanted to deflate him a little.

Rivulets of sweat, whitened by the flour used to powder Matthews's horsehair wig, ran down the sides of his face. The mayor lowered his voice to share a confidence.

"I hear that Mr. Washington has fathered a brat on his washerwoman's daughter."

Mulligan mumbled around the pins. "Has he now?"

"Yes. And I have it from reliable sources that he is in such reduced circumstances he has sold his brass buttons and must hold his trousers up with twine, like one of his darkies back in Virginia."

"The rebel army reminds me of a bird a gentleman killed." Mulligan's brogue grew more pronounced whenever he told a story. "His sarvant looked the bird up and down and said, 'By my soul, darlin', it was not worth the powder and shot, for the dear little thing would have died in the fall.'" He topped off the mayor's glass of whiskey.

Mayor Matthews laughed so hard that flour drifted from his wig onto his sloping shoulders. He had downed a lot of whiskey. If Mulligan had held up a candle, the mayor's breath would have set his own nose hair on fire.

"My good fellow, we shall need neither powder nor shot to bring down a certain treasonous bird."

"Will it be done with a snare then, your honor?"

"A snare, yes, indeed." He snorted merrily. "Our agents have bought several of Washington's own guardsmen. They were quick to accept the offer. The lads have not been paid since spring."

"Money is like muck," Hercules observed. "Not good except it be spread around."

"I myself was rowed out in the dead of night to see Governor Tryon, and he gave me the sum of one hundred pounds sterling to bribe them."

Mulligan wondered how much of that money Matthews had pocketed. He decided to overcharge him more than usual.

"So Washington's own life guards will kidnap him?"

"That's what they think. We told them that Lord Howe wants him captured so he can stand trial for treason." The mayor lowered his voice. "But he's slippery, he is. He could slip the noose. With the guards in our pay, a loyalist in the household could season his favorite dish with rat poison."

"What is his favorite dish?"

"Peas and lettuce stewed in butter and garnished with ham. The cook always serves him peas on Sunday."

The sun was squatting atop the city's westernmost roofs when the mayor held his glass aloft in a toast to King George and Sir William

Howe, the king's commander in chief in the colonies. He hugged Mulligan, tears spangling his bulging blueberry eyes. The sweat and flour had dried like delta mud in the creases radiating out from them.

With his wig riding low on his forehead Matthews set a zigzag course for the door, as though tacking into a headwind.

"Pease porridge hot," he warbled as he tottered off down the crowded street. "Pease porridge cold. Pease porridge in the pot, nine days old."

Hercules went to the door hoping to witness Matthews break an ankle on the cobblestones. Instead he saw Rob approaching.

Rob followed Hercules inside. "The shipment of shagreen and baise arrived."

Hercules surveyed Rob's rumpled coat, with broad tails that reached the tarnished buttons at the knees of his faded brown breeches. His chestnut hair was unpowdered, pulled back, and tied with a string.

"Those Quaker duds are the color of mud, lad. Why do you not commission me to fashion you a bang-up costume from that shagreen?"

Rob shrugged. They had had this conversation before. "I think the cloth will be snapped up soon. I myself have bespoken six bolts."

"I shall call on the ship's captain tomorrow." Hercules tucked a pewter whiskey flask into the waist of his breeches. He put his tinderbox in his old wide-brimmed felt hat and settled it like a bird on the nest of his red hair. "I'm going to look for Alex at the Drunken Duck. Will you be coming along?"

"You do not need a flask and a tinderbox to drink at the Duck. You must be off on a piece of business."

Hercules raised a conspiratorial eyebrow, an invitation to join him.

Rob shook his head. "I will not entangle myself in your adventures."

"Ah yes. Those Quaker scruples." Hercules picked up a lantern, sauntered out after Rob, and locked the door behind him.

Rob set off for his lodgings nearby, and Hercules headed for Broad Way. He wished he had heard of the plot earlier. General Washington and his big white horse had visited the neighborhood this morning. Crowds had followed, eager for a glimpse of him. People had thrown flowers from the windows instead of the usual chamber pot contents.

Washington was taller than Mulligan, six feet three inches at least. He wore a buff-and-blue coat with gold epaulettes, a red waistcoat, and buckskin breeches that fit him as snug as chamois gloves on a card sharp. The general had tipped his tricorn hat to the cheering throng like a king on a royal progress.

Mulligan wasn't surprised that Washington had come here to shop. New York artisans made everything, from silk hose to soup tureens, and the general seemed determined to leave nothing for other customers. The shop boys loaded the general's wagon with army tents and camp stools. Servants staggered under packages of crockery, glassware, linens, bolts of cloth, and sewing notions for Mrs. Washington. So much for the rumor about the American commander in chief selling his trouser buttons to make ends meet.

Mulligan knew what was in the general's parcels because he made it his business to know everything that went on in town. Information passed along to the right people earned him an extra guinea now and then. He also knew where he would find the general. He and Mrs. Washington had taken up residence in the vacated country house of a loyalist. It was three miles north, in the wilds of the rural village of Greenwich. Once Hercules passed Chambers Street he would follow the narrow track among fields, streams, ponds, bogs, hills, forested ravines, and limestone outcrops. He could save himself the trip if he found his good friend and the general's favorite aide, Captain Alexander Hamilton.

The sun was setting behind the shops and three-story townhouses when Mulligan walked up Broad Way, climbing over the barricades the rebels had thrown up. Soldiers had moved into the mansions abandoned by their Tory owners. Mayor Matthews called General Washington's army "the dirtiest people on the continent." For once the mayor was right. They propped their mud-caked boots on the velvet sofas, and chopped up the oak paneling and mahogany banisters for their cook fires.

"'Od's ballocks! Leave off, you bottle-arsed rascal."

Mulligan heard Man-O-War Nance before he rounded a corner and saw the scuffle. The officer of the day and his detachment were trying to quell the disorder. New York's flocks of prostitutes had flourished with the arrival of the soldiers. New England's Puritan sons seemed particularly eager to make up for lost time when it came to wanton women and whiskey.

"Damn your blood." The big blonde balked as the captain prodded her along with his musket. She spotted Mulligan. "Hercules, me darlin', tell this brute that I am yer own dearly beloved, and no whore at all."

Mulligan grinned. "I ne'er laid peeps on the trull before."

"May God strike ye for a liar, ye shitten rogue." Nance pried a cobblestone from the street and heaved it at him.

Mulligan blew her a kiss. The soldiers herded the women across the weed-grown common toward the provost prison. Mulligan turned left onto Beekman Street and headed for the Drunken Duck.

Alexander Hamilton had lived with Hercules's family before British regulars and the highly irregular American militiamen took potshots at each other at Lexington a year ago. Hercules knew where he would most likely find Alex.

Alex Hamilton said that so many bastards drank at the Drunken Duck they did not mind one more. He said it with a West Indies lilt, and a smile that did not extend north of his mouth. He knew about the sly asides and the slanderous jests concerning his mother.

Two

Wherein King George loses his head; the East River sprouts a forest;
Sir Billy dallies

NO CELEBRATION WAS COMPLETE IN NEW YORK WITHOUT A riot. No riot was complete without Hercules Mulligan. The celebration of July 9, 1776, proved no exception.

Hercules waved at Rob Townsend as he strode past with fifes, drums, and a torch-toting mob hallooing behind him. The fifes were playing the ancient Dutch harvest song that began, "Yanker dudel doodle down." It was a sprightly tune and must have set a fast pace for the turnip pluckers of old. The British had adapted it to make fun of the Americans, but they had turned it into an anthem.

"A perpetual itch to King George!" Hercules bellowed.

"Down with the king," the rabble replied. "Death to tyrants."

New Yorkers didn't require much reason to celebrate, but today they had a good one. Several hours earlier George Washington had assembled his army into a hollow square on the common. Rob had joined the civilians gathered there. Washington rode to the center of the square, and as if on cue, gunmetal clouds slid across the sun. Thunder rumbled a drum roll. A gust of wind blew the general's cloak around him and riffled the plume in his hat.

Captain Hamilton had stood in his stirrups and unrolled the parchment that had just arrived from Philadelphia. He shouted into the wind and the people in front relayed the words to those farther back.

" 'When in the course of human events it becomes necessary for one people to dissolve the political bonds which have connected them with another . . .' "

Rob had thought himself immune to political rhetoric, but tears were streaming down his face when Hamilton reached the end of the document. " '. . . with a firm reliance on the protection of Divine Providence, we mutually pledge to each other our lives, our fortunes, and our sacred honor.' "

America had declared itself a sovereign nation. Everyone stood in silence until the first large rain drops splattered on their hats, and then they cheered. Rob shouted until he was hoarse.

Washington and his escort wheeled and cantered away through a driving rain and a blizzard of hats flung into the air. The rank and file marched away in formation. The townspeople scattered for shelter. In New York the nearest shelter was always a tavern.

By the time the rain stopped they were primed for the riot segment of the festivities. Hercules suggested paying their respects to King George's leaden likeness. With axes, ropes, and chisels the mob headed for the bowling green near the water at the far end of Broad Way. On the way they encountered a loyalist who must have been drunker than they were because he shouted, "God bless King George." They stripped him naked and dragged him, face down, across the wet cobblestones.

As Rob watched him being hauled past he pitied him but not much. He was an Irishman named William Cunningham. Two years ago he had arrived with a shipload of indentured servants so starved and sickly that many died. The Liberty Boys had set the survivors free. Cunningham had swaggered from one tavern to another ever since, damning the rogues who had stolen his goods.

Rob followed the crowd to where King George, larger than life, surveyed his fractious subjects from atop a lead horse on a marble pedestal. Even in friendlier times people had ridiculed the statue since the sculptor forgot to include stirrups. With a roar the mob toppled their sovereign, hacked him up, and dismembered his horse too. Waving body parts, they started merrily back up Broad Way.

"Rob Townsend!"

Benjamin Tallmadge was twenty-two, the same age as Rob. He was average in height, compact of body, lean of face, careful with money, efficient with time, and frugal with emotion. He looked like the schoolteacher he had been until a month ago when he accepted a commission as captain in the Connecticut Regulars.

"When did you get to New York, Ben?" Rob asked.

"In time to see them hang that sergeant of the life guard for trying to poison the commander in chief's peas."

A man standing behind Ben sneezed once, then three more times. Ben hauled him forward.

"This is my classmate, Nathan Hale. Nat, meet Rob Townsend. Rob's an old friend from Oyster Bay."

Hale tried to observe the amenities, but he sneezed again.

"Are you well?" asked Rob.

Nathan blew his nose. "We are quartered in the old snuff mill on Bowery Lane. The powder has gotten into our clothes."

"Nat knows Latin to admiration." Benjamin started walking toward the docks, and Rob and Nathan fell in beside him. "When he accepted a commission with Knowlton's Rangers, he left bereft the ladies of his Latin class. He tried to teach them declensions when conjugation was what they desired."

Nathan's face lit with the shy smile that had inspired twenty girls to attend his instruction in Latin and Greek each morning at 6:30.

The three men walked to the end of the dock and stared at the British war fleet that filled the harbor and the sound beyond. The full moon's light illuminated so many masts they looked like a forest of pine trees. The thousands of cannons all seemed to be pointed at New York.

"Good Lord." Nathan Hale had not seen the masts until now.

"They dropped anchor eleven days ago, and still no stir amongst the British."

Benjamin folded his arms across his chest and stared at the warships. "I wonder what Sir Billy is up to."

He should have wondered whom Sir William Howe was up to.

AS GENERAL WILLIAM HOWE STUDIED HIS CARDS ABOVE THE tabletop he felt Elizabeth Loring's silk stocking–clad toes slide up his left shin to his white linen knee breeches and then along his inner thigh. They stroked his shaft and tickled his stones. His lads, as Mrs. Loring called them, sat up and took notice.

He hooked a finger under the high collar of his scarlet coat to pull it away from his neck. The collar itched him already in Staten Island's August heat, and now that bare-arsed cherub, Eros, was stoking the fire. Howe imagined sucking on Mrs. Loring's rosebud toes. He imagined kissing the arch of her instep, the undulations of ankle, calf, back of knee, and inner thigh. He imagined draping her silk skirts and petticoats over his head like a tent and burying his face in the nosegay of her fragrant blond fur.

Mrs. Joshua Loring, Howe's opponent in this three-hand, cutthroat variety of euchre, gave no indication that her toes had strayed. She sipped her brandy and dabbed her handkerchief at the seed pearls of perspiration adorning her full, rosy upper lip. She knitted eyebrows as pale and feathery as chick's down, and studied her cards. Howe concentrated on quelling the uprising in his trousers.

"Your Excellency." Captain John André rapped the table with his knuckles. "I say, General, show us what you have there."

Howe's cheeks turned red. Mrs. Loring threw her head back and let loose a glissando of merry brays. She laughed so hard she shook powdered curls from the heights of her hairdo. Her laughter tested the palisade of whalebone stays struggling to hold her endowments in check. Her breasts jounced so energetically that they almost popped out of her low-cut dress again. Howe and his lads were disappointed when they didn't.

Howe laid out his cards and Mrs. Loring gave a shout of triumph. She withdrew her foot from Howe's groin and leaned across the table to rake the heap of coins into her lap. Howe tossed an extra shilling into the chasm between those abundant breasts.

Eliza's breasts always reminded William Howe of mid-ocean swells in a sea of milk. He woke up each morning with his palm riding their crests. All day he anticipated falling asleep with a hand cupped over at least one of them. He preferred the left one because under it he could feel the steady beat of a heart unperturbed by indecision, guilt, or regrets.

Howe glanced at twenty-three-year-old John André. Captain André was devilishly handsome, and Howe worried that he might cause defection among Mrs. Loring's affections. But if her toes had attacked anyone else this evening, her victim would have been as unable to concentrate as Howe was. Instead she had ceded most of the games. She had tumbled two hundred guineas into debt so far.

Howe would settle her accounts of course. He hadn't had to sell his commission to defray his gambling debts like a lot of officers, but at the end of the evening he would be poorer by what he had lost to her and what she had lost to everyone else.

It was a small price to pay. Mrs. Loring often quoted chapter eight, verse fifteen of Ecclesiastes. "A man hath no better thing under the sun than to eat, and to drink, and to be merry." Giving her brute of a husband the lucrative post of commissary of prisons in exchange for his lovely rib was the best bargain Howe ever made.

A young subaltern made his way through the dancing flock of red coats and silk taffeta dresses in the next room. He stood in the doorway and surveyed the officers and ladies intent on their games of Pharaoh, brag, and whist, then he headed for Howe. He halted in a click of polished boot heels and the rattle of sabre fittings. He held out a letter and saluted with such vigor that Howe thought he might give himself a concussion.

Howe broke the seal, read it, and refolded it. He stuffed it into his coat, winked at Eliza Loring, and dealt the cards.

Captain André raised one eyebrow. "Washington's reply?"

"Yes."

"He hasn't changed his mind then about accepting a pardon?"

"No. He persists in the delusion that the rebels are the injured parties."

"Cheeky devils, those Jonathans."

Mrs. Loring broke in. "Washington told Sir William that the Americans have done nothing wrong, and have no need of pardon."

"Done nothing wrong!" John André's finely arched eyebrows rose only slightly. With André even umbrage was genteel. "Treason, impertinence, attacks on His Majesty's appointed officials, and the murder of his soldiers seem wrong to me."

This message from General Washington repeated what the man himself had told Howe under a flag of truce. In return for laying down their weapons, General Howe had offered the rebels pardons. He had done it in spite of that treasonous claptrap they had been reading up and down the countryside, that Declaration of Independency. What an impudent, ill-written, wretched composition that was. It had resulted in the Americans cashiering the royal governers of all thirteen colonies. That left Sir William and his brother, Richard "Black Dick" Howe, admiral of the British fleet, as the king's sole authorities here.

Sir William Howe was a tall man, but during talks under the white flag, Washington had gazed down at him with that Caesar-addressing-the-Romans look of his. He said Americans would not be slaves to unjust laws and tariffs. Who was he to lecture about slavery, with those shackled Ethiopes on his plantation in Virginia? He was as hypocritical as that skirt-chasing old goat Dr. Franklin and the supercilious little prig John Adams.

Still, Howe didn't want to go to war with him. Fifteen years ago, he had fought the French alongside Lieutenant Washington and many of the American officers who now opposed him.

Besides, William Howe was a Whig. He held with those who wanted to limit the king's power and expand the role of parliament. He hated the prospect of killing other Englishmen, and he deeply resented the fact that these misguided hotheads left him no choice.

At forty-seven William Howe had long legs, heavy thighs, wide hips, and narrow shoulders. He moved with the deliberate grace of an over-weight wading bird. He was indulgent with his men, and more so with himself. His passion for sugar had cost him some teeth, and his cheeks had sunken to occupy the space they left behind. He had heavily lidded eyes, a pout of a mouth, and the puffy features of a man born to wealth and adept at squandering it.

His appearance was deceiving. Inside that dissolute package lurked a sharp intellect and an iron courage, but even without them Howe could not lose this conflict. Thirty-two thousand British soldiers and German merce-naries were bivouacked here on Staten Island. They were well armed, well supplied, and well trained. They could whip the American rabble in time to celebrate Christmas.

Brooklyn Heights would be a perfect staging area for the campaign to snuff out this little rebellion. While General Howe's troops attacked on land, Admiral Black Dick Howe's gunships would bombard the Americans from the East River.

Mrs. Loring could always tell when military affairs were distracting Howe from what mattered. What mattered was her. She leaned across the table. "I understand that the scullery maid caught Squire Dobbes taking a flourish in the pantry with his cook. Word of it has gotten abroad."

André fanned himself with his cards. "Is that the same cook who's so ugly she frightens cockroaches?"

"The very one. When the squire's friends made sport of him, he replied," here Eliza harumphed and hawked and growled a passable imitation of the squire, "'I have a good constitution and do not yet, I thank heaven, have to resort to beauty to whet my appetite.'"

Howe rocked back in his chair and roared laughter. Eliza Loring was a tonic, she was. Howe had planned to write up the order tonight to attack Long Island, but he decided to tarry a while longer with Mrs. Loring. The Americans had waited six weeks to be whipped. A few more days wouldn't matter.

Taran-tara, he thought. We shall have a jolly fine fox hunt in Brooklyn.

Three

Wherein an ill wind blows some good; Washington flings his hat;
Howe fumes while New York burns; Nathan's shoes betray him

IN THE NOISE AND CONFUSION OF BATTLE, CARRYING KING George's finger in his pocket struck Captain Benjamin Tallmadge as a bad idea. He couldn't say why. Maybe he thought it might tempt fate to visit on the American troops more calamity than it had already.

One of his men had kept this piece of the king's statue for good luck, but last night a bolt of lightning had charred him like beef on a spit. It had also fused three pennies to the finger. Benjamin intended to see that the dead soldier's belongings reached his family, but this one would not.

He reined his horse around and heaved the lump of lead as far as he could. It arced upward and vanished into the blue fog of gunpowder smoke in the low-lying field below him. Beyond the field lay the Gowanus marsh that Benjamin and his horse had just swum across, along with the fleeing remnants of George Washington's army.

Still dripping muddy water, his big black horse continued to labor up the slope toward the earthworks along Brooklyn's heights. The Americans' campsite lay beyond the hundred-foot-high ridge, on the narrow strip of land between it and the East River. When he reached it, Benjamin watered the gelding and picketed him where he could graze. A cold gust blew icy needles of rain slantwise onto his face. Benjamin was too weary to curse it.

Long after nightfall men staggered in, their uniforms heavy with mud. They carried the wounded on litters or on their backs. The able-bodied kept watch, standing knee-deep in water in the trenches along the top of the ridge. The rest pulled their sodden blankets over them and slept wrapped around their muskets in an attempt to keep them dry.

At dawn Benjamin looked down from his post and saw the British tents not more than six hundred yards away. On the river behind him, hundreds of enemy warships were trying to maneuver into position. If the wind changed direction, they could set up a rain of cannon fire on the exposed American encampment.

With little sleep, no food or shelter from the cold rain, and no dry powder to defend themselves, Benjamin and the others waited all day for Sir Billy Howe to resume the fighting. The British could easily kill or capture half the American army and most of its high-ranking officers. The war would be over. Less than two months after it was signed, the Declaration of Independency would be nothing but scraps of paper. But General Howe had had enough of slaughter. He assumed his soldiers and his brother's ships could surround the Americans and force them to surrender without further bloodshed. He was wrong.

ALL NIGHT BENJAMIN HEARD WHISPERED COMMANDS AND THE muted tread of boots as one unit after another abandoned the heights. As dawn approached he feared his men would be all alone when the sun rose. Finally a corporal relayed the order to retreat as silently as possible.

Benjamin led his men down the slope to the quiet chaos at the Brooklyn ferry landing. Whale boats and sloops emerged from the thick fog and men from Massachussets leaped out and pulled them ashore, lifting the hulls so they would not grate on the gravel. Since nightfall the Marblehead Mariners had manned the oars. With oarlocks muffled and rags wrapped around their bloody hands they had ferried thousands of troops past the British fleet and across a mile of open water.

In silence men lined up around foundered boats, broken equipment, and cannons bogged in the mud. They loaded their wounded aboard and what supplies they could salvage. In a flash of lightning Benjamin saw Washington's familiar profile, mounted on his old white horse and watching

from a hill. Wrapped in one cloak of midnight blue wool and another of
fog, he supervised the retreat.

He should have gone on ahead, but Benjamin remembered what he had
said before this battle. He had ridden along the lines and shouted so they
could hear him above the wind. "I have two pistols loaded. If I see any man
turn his back today, I will shoot him through, but I will not ask any man to
go further than I do. I will fight so long as I have a leg or an arm."

Benjamin picketed his horse and scratched his ears by way of farewell.
He found his friend Nat Hale, and the two of them boarded one of the few
remaining boats. When they saw General Washington climb into the last
one, they knew he would be in good hands. The Mariner's leader, John
Glover, had charge of that boat. Glover was a shoemaker, and he stoically
ignored the wags who observed that he gave his awl for his country.

The Marblehead men pushed off and the shoreline vanished behind the
gray curtain of mist. The British now occupied all of Long Island. Benjamin wondered what would become of his family in Setauket. The town
had plenty of Tories who would do them ill at the first opportunity.

He thought bitterly of something else the commander in chief had said.
"The fate of unborn millions will now depend on the courage and conduct
of this army. We have therefore resolved to conquer or die." He had not
said they would conquer or run.

One by one the hulls of the British men-of-war emerged from the fog
and loomed over them. Benjamin lost count of how many they passed,
bucketing alongside them under the bristle of cannons. Squalls kicked up
whitecaps, and the whaleboat rolled and pitched. Nathan leaned over the
gunwhale and retched as quietly as he could, but the contrary winds had
kept Black Dick Howe from maneuvering his ships into firing position.
The fog and rain had hidden the army's retreat.

Benjamin resolved, if he made it to the other side, to find a scow and return for his horse. The sun would be about to rise then, but the big gelding
was a fine animal and worth the risk. Benjamin thought it likely that if he
escaped with his life, the horse and a rusty musket would be his only remaining possessions.

When the British charged into battle two days ago, their buglars had
played the call to the hounds, as though setting out on a fox hunt. They did
it to taunt the rebels. Benjamin figured if he went back for his horse, he

might get a look at the expressions on their faces when they discovered that six or seven thousand American foxes had escaped the Redcoats.

BENJAMIN AND HIS COMPANY HEADED NORTH ALONG THE post road toward Harlem Heights. Thousands of civilians crowded the road, fleeing the British invasion that was sure to come. Trudging among them Washington's army straggled for miles. Benjamin urged his big black into a canter to catch up with a group of Knowlton's Rangers in their green jackets.

"Lieutenant, have you seen Captain Hale?"

The lieutenant beckoned him aside and lowered his voice. "The colonel told us someone was needed to go among the British on Long Island and learn of their plans."

"You mean to act as an intelligenser?"

"Yes. He asked would I go. I told him I was willing to fight the bloody-backs, but as for going among them to be taken and hung up like a dog, I would not."

"Did Captain Hale agree to do it?"

The lieutenant shrugged. "When he left the next day, he was wearing his schoolmaster clothes."

"Does he even know we're abandoning New York?"

"Probably not." The lieutenant's look made it plain that he didn't think well of anyone who would lower himself to spy.

With dread heavy in his chest Benjamin rejoined his men. Nathan had a passle of Tory relatives who might betray him, and he was too honest, too open-hearted to deceive anyone.

The army woke up the next morning to stare into the mouths of eighty-six cannons on five British frigates. Sailors had positioned swivel guns in the rigging so they could fire down into the American trenches. British light infantry clambered down the netting on the hulls. In their red coats they looked to Benjamin like blood dripping off the ships' sides. They stood erect on the barges while sailors rowed them toward shore. Soon the river teemed with them.

When the ships fired a broadside, the Americans bolted. Benjamin rode among them, shouting at them to turn and make a stand. He might as well have ordered the wind to shift. As they ran they threw off camp baskets and haversacks, hats, cartridge boxes, blankets, coats, even muskets. Benjamin was relieved to see General Washington galloping toward them. He could turn them if anyone could.

"Take the walls," Washington shouted. "Take the cornfields."

He had no more effect than Benjamin.

"You damned mutinous hounds!" He stood in the stirrups and made the air smoke with his oaths. When the soldiers continued to run past him he yanked off his hat and hurled it.

Benjamin could hear what he said. Everyone could.

"Are these the sorry sons of bitches with whom I am to defend America?"

DOGS ALWAYS BARKED IN NEW YORK, ESPECIALLY AT NIGHT. one dog would start and the others would join in. The chorus would sing with point, counterpoint, stacatto, and fugue until dawn when the rattle of milk wagons and produce carts, the cries of the fishmongers, and the tattoo of horses' hooves drowned them out.

Robert Townsend usually slept through the nightly chorus, but now the dogs woke him up. These past two nights he had slept like a flounder anyway, with one eye open. September nineteenth, the day after the British took over, red-coated soldiers had painted "GR" for "Georgius Rex" in large black letters on houses that belonged to the patriots who had fled the city. Already bedding and red jackets were spread on the roofs to air. High black boots were set out on the sills to dry after the rains of the past week. Those buildings not suitable for officers' quarters were designated as stables, chicken coops, arsenals, storage houses, and lodging for the officers' doxies. The soldiers had wasted little time plundering the city, and broken glass added to the hazards in the streets.

No one had evicted Rob though. Maybe his small room in the garret escaped their attention, or maybe it was too hot and dingy for even a lowly ensign to occupy. The dogs' barking became more frantic, and an old nursery rhyme went through Rob's head. "Tell tale, tit, your tongue shall be split, and all the dogs in the town shall have a piece of it."

Then he smelled smoke and heard distant shouts mingled with the barking. When he pushed open the shutters, a dry wind blew in, carrying the odor of burning wood and a low roar like a distant waterfall. He saw a golden glow against the sky to the south.

He yanked his breeches from the peg and pulled them on. He pried up a loose floorboard and took out the small bag of silver coins underneath. He wondered why he heard no church bells ringing a warning, then he remembered that the rebels took them to make cannons.

The glow at the window brightened like the sun rising. Rob could hear the roar increase and then a series of cracks, like gunfire. Had the Americans decided to attack?

Pulling on his shirt and coat, Rob ran into the street. Above the old wooden tenements to the south, the flames leaped upward as though intent on setting the sky on fire. The detonations sounded closer, as the resin in the old pine timbers exploded. Men, women, and children pelted past.

"Where is it?" Rob shouted.

Someone bothered to reply. "Everywhere."

The neighing of horses and the crash of their hooves against stall doors drew Rob to the stable. He found Hercules Mulligan there with his wife and two children. While Rob drove the horses out into the street, Hercules hitched the biggest one to a cart and heaved Alice and the children into it. He pulled feed sacks from a heap of them and soaked them in the water barrel.

He handed them to Alice. "Put these over your head and the little ones." He turned to Rob. "Make haste, man."

"But this isn't our wagon."

"For the love of Jesus, Mary, and all the saints, step up. We shall sort it out with God later."

Rob held on with both hands as the wagon careened across the cobblestones. When the arsenal at the battery blew up, the explosion lifted the wheels off the street. Hercules drove through a rain of fire and flaming timbers. The heat created a vortex that blew sparks and cinders into the cart and left smoking black holes. In the wagonbed, Alice Mulligan alternated between screams and prayers.

Around them fled dogs and rats and squealing pigs. People ran with their clothes aflame. Broken glass and goods lay strewn everywhere. Rob saw the furtive shadows of looters. On a side street they passed a man hanging by his heels from a tavern sign. His throat had been cut and a blackened torch stuck into the waistband of his trousers.

"An arsonist," Hercules shouted. "May he burn in hell."

They drove up Broad Way through a tunnel of flaming elm trees. As they passed the Holy Ground, the women ran alongside cajoling for a ride. When some of them tried to climb aboard, Hercules's wife, still screaming, beat at them with her statue of the Virgin.

Hercules drove north until a group of red-coated soldiers with lanterns barred his way.

"God save you kindly, sergeant," Hercules said.

"State your name and business."

"I'm Hercules Mulligan, clothier to British gentry. Our home is destroyed and we must beg a roof and crust from kin in Westchester."

"Are you a loyal subject of His Majesty, King George?"

"As loyal as the day is long. The rebels burned my house and shop around my ears, lad. They near murdered my wife and tykes. Why should I wish them aught but bad cess?"

"Be off, then."

"He's a liar, Sergeant." William Cunningham angled out of the darkness. July's drag across the cobblestones had scarred his face, and bits of black gravel were still imbedded in his cheek. "He led the devil's spawn who broke up the king's statue."

Hercules selected his most ingenuous smile. "Pay him no mind, Sergeant. He owes me money and means to shirk payment."

The sergeant wasn't amused. "Get down from the cart."

If Hercules had been alone he would have run. "Am I taken, then?"

"You are." The sergeant turned to Rob. "What of you?"

Cunningham spoke before Rob could. "His name's Townsend. I know him from the docks. He's one of the Quaking sect, and not a troublemaker."

"And what of my family?" asked Hercules.

"They may continue."

Hercules handed the reins to Rob. "Will you drive Alice and the little ones to Mamaroneck, my friend?"

"I will."

"God bless you."

Alice recovered her usual calm even though her dark hair was singed and her face covered with soot. "What will they do to you?"

"Nought, I'm sure. I'll eat the king's bread and sausages for a day or two, and then I'll join you."

He stood on the wheel's hub so he could kiss his boys, and then he jumped down. Rob flicked the reins and the horse started. The darkness swallowed them and the sound of hoofs faded.

Hercules muttered at Cunningham as he held out his wrists for the manacles. "Damned onion-eating, whiskey-wasting, bog-Irish hypocrite. God will see to you, mark me."

Cunningham smirked.

"Where would you be taking me?" Hercules asked the sergeant.

"The provost prison."

"Is it standing then?"

"The fire passed it by."

Hercules laughed. "Isn't that the way of feckless luck though, to level the town and leave the clink.

"Here's a funnier jest." Cunningham's smirk widened. "They have appointed me provost. I shall be your jailer, boyo."

HOWE PICKED UP A VASE AND HEAVED IT AGAINST THE WALL. When he stalked outside, his aides discreetly faded from sight. The Beekmans' mansion stood on a bluff with a clear view of the billows of black smoke rising from the city below. The rising sun made a yellow smudge behind it.

Only ten days ago Howe had entertained a peace delegation at his headquarters on Staten Island. Benjamin Franklin and John Adams were the worst of the traitors, but Howe had wined and dined them. Over brandy that night Howe had hung his heart out like laundry on the line.

"Should America fall," he had said, "I should feel and lament it like the loss of a brother."

Franklin had raised his glass and said with that impish smile of his, "We will do our utmost to save your lordship that mortification."

Howe still smarted from Franklin and Adams's rebuff of his peace offer. And now this.

Major André coughed softly. Howe whirled and with his sword slashed the head off a topiary lion.

"God damn them!"

"No doubt He will, sir."

"I had a gentleman's agreement with Washington. We did not set fire to Boston last year, and they were not to destroy New York." Howe paced to the end of the veranda and back. His face had darkened to the color of a ripe love apple. "Hell's belt buckle, I even gave them time to evacuate the city. The ungrateful curs."

Major André knew how the other officers felt about Howe's generosity to his enemy, but he kept silent.

Howe had been more than generous. Some said he'd gone soft in the head. Appalled by the thousands of dead and wounded Americans in the fields and swamps around the village of Brooklyn, he had pulled his men back. Then that damned Virginia planter had sneaked them out from under his nose. No doubt Washington and his officers were having a good laugh about it, and about this too. How was the British army to winter in a city reduced to charred rubble?

Howe finally realized that André had probably come for a reason. "What is it, Major?"

"The guards have a man who claims to be a schoolmaster named Nathan Hale. However, he had drawings of our defenses and artillery placements hidden in his shoes. He had written the specifications in Latin." André arched an eyebrow in amusement. "Perhaps he thought us too ignorant to translate them."

"I take it he's a soldier, and no schoolteacher at all."

"I believe he's both, Your Excellency. Once the drawings appeared he confessed, but he lectured us as though we were schoolboys. He said he thought it the duty of every good officer to obey any orders given him by his commander in chief."

"An officer, is he? No matter. He'll hang anyway. Send for Cunningham to do the honors.

"When, sir?"

Howe glared at the smoke still rising from the devastation below. "Now, goddamn it."

Four

*Wherein Kate Darby encounters a spectre; a well-traveled rock makes
one more journey; the Darbys acquire houseguests*

SEVENTEEN-YEAR-OLD KATE DARBY FINISHED DELIVERING
food and clothing to a poor family by the docks and set out for home at twilight. Mosquitoes swarmed here at Philadelphia's waterfront, and in spite
of the stifling heat she wrapped her cloak around her. Wooden houses
hunched over the narrow street, and Kate was concentrating on easing past
a snarling cur when she heard trouble coming. She couldn't see the mob
yet, but she could tell it was angry. Mobs usually were.

The last time happy people formed a crowd in Philadelphia was a little
more than a year ago, on July fourth of 1776. That was when the rebels
read their Declaration of Independence aloud, and paraded merrily through
the streets all day. Even then some of them had gone on a rampage that
night, shouting threats at the loyalists who cowered behind the barred
doors of their mansions along Second Street.

Kate and her family considered themselves neither rebels nor Tories,
but they had bolted their doors too. As Quakers they would not take an
oath of loyalty. That made them traitors as far as those who called themselves patriots were concerned. Congress had declared members of the
Quaker religion to be "disaffected to the American cause" and had arrested
many of them.

Kate stepped into the deeper shadows of a doorway. She held her empty basket in front of her, a flimsy shield at best. She smelled the odor of lard-fried cabbage filtering through the cracks in the door at her back. The shouting grew louder. Currents of torchlight flowed around the corner and along the tenement walls toward Kate. She pressed against the door and felt the splinters catch at her cape.

The first of the throng passed, and then the main body. In the center of the press four men carried the fence rail. Astride it with his wrists tied to it and his legs bound together under it was a naked figure covered from crown to heels with ship's tar and goose down. Kate smelled burnt flesh and hair.

The rail rider never stopped wailing. Kate knew she could do nothing for him except pray to God to spare him. Quakers believed that every man contained the seed of God inside him, but such cruelty made her doubt that.

"Come along, miss," one of the revelers shouted. "He's a rich Tory, he is. Plenty of swag to take from his house before we make a whopping great bonfire of it."

A Tory was a person loyal to the king, and it had become the worst of epithets. It had been hurled at her from time to time but more often at her father.

Her father.

Kate left her basket in the doorway.

"Here she comes. A true daughter of Liberty." The mob stopped taunting their victim long enough to give three "Huzzahs."

Kate slid sideways through the press, trying to keep her feet from under their heavy boots. The crowd shoved her this way and that, but she was too tightly hemmed in to fall down. She pushed through until she reached the man on the rail. The sight of him made her gag. The skin had peeled away where the tar had burned through it. Bloody patches gleamed among the black pitch and pale feathers. The tar and feathers made a hideous mask of his face.

"Who are you?" she shouted.

He did not answer, but he turned to stare at her as the mob bore him away. His eyes were those of someone enduring the unendurable.

"Are you my father?" she shouted. But no one heard her.

She set out at a trot for home. With forty thousand inhabitants,

Philadelphia was second only to London in the western world. The wooden tenements gave way to mansions of brick and stone. Carriages rattled along wide streets paved with cobblestones, flanked by brick walks, and shaded by mulberries and poplars.

She stopped to catch her breath when she saw her family's three-story brick house. The sun's last rays glinted on the glass panes in the high windows. The fourteen-year-old servant, Lizzie, let her in. Lizzie swore that one of her ancestors was an Ethiope king, another was an Indian princess, and one had arrived on the Mayflower. For all that, her African lineage predominated.

Through the doorways on either side of the front hall Kate could see the moss green velvet curtains hanging from the stuccoed ceiling to the oaken floor. When she and her younger brother, Seth, were children they had hidden behind them in games of hide-and-seek. The glass-fronted cupboards still sheltered the family's silver plates and tankards, the porringers, salvers, teapots, and candlesticks. The tables, chests, and cupboards and the big secretary where her father kept his account books dozed in the gathering dusk.

"Is my father well?" she asked Lizzie.

Lizzie knew that Quakers didn't use titles like madam or mistress, but she refused to be party to such social heresy.

"Surely he is, Miss Kate. He and young Master Seth are gone to the docks, looking after his ship just arrived from Jamaica. Your mother is in the kitchen."

Lizzie had a lot more to say but Kate's knees went wobbly and she sat on the first step of the broad flow of stairs. She put her face in her trembling hands and wept with relief.

"Are you well, miss?"

"Aye, Lizzie." She looked up and smiled. "I'm very well."

THE FAMILY WAS EATING BREAKFAST IN THE PARLOR WHEN Aaron Darby made his announcement.

"I've made arrangements with the captain of the *Nautilus*. When he returns this winter Seth will sail with him and oversee the factory in Jamaica for the next five years." Aaron Darby didn't look up from his porridge, so he didn't see the distraught look on Lizzie's face. He didn't see his son stiffen.

"I can clerk in the store here and sell goods on consignment." At fourteen Seth stood taller than his father, and had a broad chest and muscular shoulders and arms. Cook said he must have found them on an ash bin because he certainly hadn't developed them from honest labor. Cook said the boy did the sleeping for the whole family.

"At thy age Richard Morris had made ten thousand pounds sterling as a factor in Curaçao. By the time he turned twenty-five he was the half owner of a sloop."

"Probably the rear half," Seth muttered.

A cobblestone crashed through the parlor window. A noisy flock of glass shards, glittering in the early morning sunlight, followed it. A cool September breeze blew through the opening.

Lizzie screamed and threw up her hands, flinging the pot over her shoulder. The pot hit the wall and the porridge splattered. The rock landed on the plank floor and rolled to a stop near Kate, who stood with her spoon poised at her mouth. Cook hurried in from the kitchen, her misaligned eyes, one green and one blue, looking more demented than usual. They all stared at the stone as though expecting it to either explode or demand breakfast.

Before its last two careers as a cobblestone and missile, it had probably served as ballast. Maybe it had rolled around in the hold of one of Aaron Darby's own ships. Maybe it had sailed the triangular route from the wharves at the end of Market Street to the West Indies, then to Bristol or London, and back to Philadelphia. If so, it was a well-traveled piece of granite.

Seth and Kate, their mother, and Lizzie all waited for Aaron Darby to speak first. Even Cook deferred to him, a privilege that only he, God, and King George enjoyed. Aaron looked like a chunk of granite rough-chiseled into a man's shape. He had tied his hair, the color of spun pewter, into a club at the nape of his neck. His iron gray eyes and forward thrust of a jaw gave him a pugnacious air out of keeping with his belief in a faith that held nonviolence as a basic tenet.

"I shall go to the glazier's shop, God willing." Aaron pushed back his chair and stood up. "Seth, take the silver plate to the niche behind the chimney in the great room. Kate, put the good linens in the chest in the root cellar. Rachel, thee must hide the books in the wood box."

As soon as he was out of hearing Cook shook her ladle at Lizzie, who was staring at Seth. Seth was staring back.

"Don't stand there looking like a cat let out of a basket, you bird-witted girl. Clean up the porridge."

Seth walked to the window. Hefting the rock in his hand he looked up and down the empty street.

"I reckon the patriots were getting in their last licks." He tossed the stone out through the broken pane.

In a great show of fifes, drums, and polished muskets, with spruce sprigs in their hatbands and the new flag of red, white, and blue flapping overhead, the American army had marched through Philadelphia and out the other side. Those who supported the rebellion had packed up and fled after them. Men had hauled chairs and desks and crates of the Continental Congress's documents out of the State House. They had loaded them onto dray wagons and hustled away. They reminded Kate of rats in a rush to leave a ship that was taking on alarming amounts of brine.

Quakers did not concern themselves with armies, but what if the British army decided to concern itself with them? Kate knew about armies. She had read Raleigh's *History of the World*. What if General Howe decided to sack Philadelphia in revenge for that fire in New York last year?

"Will the English soldiers harm us?" Kate asked what all of them were thinking.

Seth turned to face them. The morning sun glinting on his red hair made it look like his head was on fire. "When the British attacked at Lexington they proved they will kill us if we do not defend ourselves."

"God will defend us, Seth," Rachel Darby said. "We do not take up arms."

Kate's mother was tall and slender. Delicate bones defined strong lines of jaw, nose, and cheeks, but a pernicious illness bruised the skin around her gray blue eyes. Her hair was the color of old copper and she wore it wound into a knot at the nape of a graceful neck. Except for the dark bruises around her eyes and the gray in her hair, Kate resembled her.

Seth pulled a pamphlet from the back of his trousers. Thomas Paine's essay called "Common Sense" had sold more copies than there were people in the colonies. Seth shook it to get their attention.

" 'The summer soldier and the sunshine patriot will, in this crisis, shrink from the service of their country; but he that stands it now deserves the love and thanks of man and woman.' "

"Oh, Seth, give it over." Kate had heard him recite Paine's essay until she knew it by heart.

"Thomas Paine is right about one thing, these are indeed times that try men's souls." Rachel Darby gave Seth a mother's look. "Do not imperil thine own soul with thoughts of going to war."

When she left to discuss the day's marketing with Cook, Seth raised his fist and shouted, " 'Tyranny, like hell, is not easily conquered.' "

Kate took several long breaths to calm the anger welling up in her. She could not do Seth violence, but she wished Cook would box his ears. Seventeen years of lectures on the virtues of an even temper might have taken tenuous root in Kate, but they had not thrived. Her brother often irritated her until she felt rage radiating down from her dark red hair like heat from a fire.

Once when she was much younger she had used her mother's sewing scissors to rid herself of the red hair she considered the source of her impious anger. Cook had thrown up her hands in horror. Her father had scolded her, but her mother had held her close. Her mother had understood.

Kate jumped when someone pounded on the front door, but Lizzie opened it and called out, "It's only Stork Withers."

Ned Withers kissed her on the cheek. "My compliments to you too, lovely Lizzie."

Ned was two years older than Seth. He was almost as tall, and about half as wide. He walked with the lurching gait that inspired Lizzie's name for him. He was in what Cook would call a lather.

"The Redcoats have reached the town. William Howe's whore and ten thousand New York jezabels have come with them."

KATE HAD NEVER SEEN COOK THIS EXCITED. IN FACT, KATE had never seen Cook excited at all. Angry and indignant, yes, but not excited.

When panniers were in fashion to extend women's skirts out on each side, Cook did not need to wear them. She resembled one of those dolls weighted at the base so they bounced back when pushed over. She said her swivel eyes were an advantage for a cook. She could keep one on the pot and the other up the chimney. They made her look as if she would run amok with a carving knife at any moment. Yet here she was waving a small Union Jack, making little cricket leaps, and shouting "Long live the King." Kate was astonished.

Since the British had shown no inclination to sack and pillage, Kate had joined Cook and Lizzie in the crowd lining the street. Women waved hand-sewn flags. Old men, reeking of camphor, had squeezed into their fifteen-year-old British uniforms left from the French War. The rumble of artillery carriages and ammunition caissons sounded like the thunder of an approaching storm. Kate and Lizzie held hands for reassurance.

The first ranks of soldiers marched to the slow beat of the drums. Their brass glinted in the sunlight. Their eyes looked straight ahead, their muskets rode on their shoulders; they were as perfectly aligned as wind-up toys. Unlike the American army every one of them had shoes and a bright new uniform.

That night Kate dreamed of marching feet and the big wheels of artillery carriages rumbling over the cobblestones. She dreamed of caparisoned horses, of bayonets, swords, and guns, red coats and sashes. She dreamed of brass buttons like twinkling stars, and the swaying gold fringe of epaulets. And they were all chasing her.

The next morning she and Lizzie were dusting in the parlor when the knock came at the front door. Kate opened it, took two steps back, and stumbled into Lizzie. Lizzie let out a small yelp and collapsed into a faint. Kate had a feeling she was shamming, and she wanted to prod her with her toe. She looked from Lizzie to the British officer standing in the doorway, then beyond him to the yard filling with soldiers, horses, wagons, and heaps of baggage.

"Your servant, ladies." The officer swept his hat in a wide curve as he bent into a courtly bow. "Forgive us if we've alarmed you. We mean neither you nor your family any harm."

Lizzie regained her feet and Kate heard her gasp. Kate couldn't blame her. She was fairly certain she had never seen a man as handsome as the young captain. When he smiled he flashed teeth as white and perfectly straight as a newly painted picket fence. The warmth in his luminscent brown eyes made her feel as though she were the only person of consequence in his world.

"My name is John André, Aide-de-Camp to General Charles Grey." André gestured to the tall man standing in the yard.

Grey turned toward them and his eyes chilled what warmth André had created. Smallpox had left his face as rough as a wasp's nest. He owned the hardest eyes Kate had ever seen, like chips of flint.

"And may I ask your name, miss?" André said.

Kate swiveled her attention back to the captain.

"Kate. Kate Darby."

"Miss Darby, if in future I should forget your name, it is because I am certain that someone as lovely as you will be changing it soon, and so I did not commit it to memory."

Lizzie giggled, and Kate couldn't think of anything remotely clever to say.

"The general and I will be billeting here should we find the house suitable." André looked over Kate's shoulder, taking in the walls laid in yellow milk paint, the plaster ceiling with its frescoes of fruit and flowers, the large paintings of landscapes in heavy gilt frames, the broad marble stairs. "I venture to say the general will find the accommodations quite to his liking."

He winked at her. Kate feared that between Captain André's charm and General Grey's menace she would swoon and fill the spot that Lizzie had warmed on the floor.

Five

Wherein Kate meets a resurrectionist; Seth keeps his ear to the floor;
a sewing kit has something to say

KATE WATCHED THE ENSIGN PAINT "GREY" ON THE FRONT
door of her house. He was shorter than she and plumper. In his canvas cov-
eralls he looked like a kettle in a tea cozy. He was a year older than Kate,
and at least as shy. She liked to speak to him because his cheeks turned pink
when she did. She had never had that affect on a man and it amused her.

"James, why are you doing that?"

He jerked around, startled. "Captain André instructed me to mark your
house so no other officers will bother you in search of lodgings."

They both watched a tall, cadaverous man approach. The bottoms of
his breeches hung slack below his knees. His hose sagged around his
skinny ankles. His faded black coat had patches at the elbows. The outer
corner of his ash-colored left eye and the left half of his thick lips drooped.

"Good day, Birdwhistle," said James.

"Is André in?"

"Wait in the parlor."

"Any spies or deserters discovered?" The expression of hope looked out
of place in his case-hardened eyes. "Any hangings scheduled?"

"None that I know of."

Birdwhistle knickered like a horse welcoming his oats. "Perhaps there will be soon, eh?"

"We can always hope," James said dryly.

Kate watched him disappear inside. "Hangings?"

"Old habits die hard." With great care James added "y" to "Grey," and put the brush into the can of paint. He didn't seem to mind keeping Tunis Birdwhistle waiting inside. "In England he was a resurrectionist."

"What's that?"

"They're coves who steal cadavers for the students at the surgeons' schools. They frequent hangings and follow funeral processions so they can dig the bodies up in the black of night. They receive five pounds sterling for each stiff they deliver."

"Is that legal?"

"Of course not. Birdwhistle says he stuffed corpses into herring barrels and tea chests to avoid detection. Imagine a housewife opening a tea chest and discovering someone's Uncle Charlie?" James chuckled. "I suspect that Birdwhistle wants to practice his old trade here."

"I trust he has found a more suitable way to keep body and soul together."

James laughed again. "Keeping body and soul together was never his aim, Miss Darby."

WITH A GLASS JAR IN HAND KATE PROWLED THE NARROW corridor of the attic, searching the rafters for spiders for Cook. The creatures formed the base of Cook's remedy for crop sickness, the after-effects of overindulgence. General Grey and Captain André were masters at overindulgence.

Kate had gotten used to the sound of men's voices under her feet. General Grey and his staff took over most of the lower two floors of the house, but Kate didn't mind moving to the servants' quarters under the eaves. The December wind blew in around the frames of the small windows, but the British liked their fires much hotter than Aaron Darby, and heat radiated from the brick chimney that formed one wall of the room Kate shared with Lizzie.

Kate had always liked the attic. As a child she had explored its crannies and hidey-holes. The British officers disapproved of keeping company with servants, but here Kate could spend her time with Lizzie and Cook, who always made her laugh. She also found the places on the back stairs where she might catch glimpses of John André.

As she passed the room that Seth shared with the gardener she glanced in. Seth was lying on his stomach on the floor with one side of his head pressed against the boards.

"Is thee ill, brother?"

He leaped to his feet. "Nay."

Through the cracks between the boards Kate heard the murmur of men's voices below. "Seth, thee was eavesdropping!"

"I was only curious.

"'Tis dishonorable and if they catch thee, 'twill go hard with thee."

Actually Seth had surprised Kate these past two months. When the family joined André and Grey for dinner Seth was civil and attentive. He joined in the conversation and he asked questions. Maybe he would turn into something other than the scapegrace that Cook predicted.

Kate started down the hall toward the back stairs, but Seth called to her. "The Shippen snippet brought another invitation for thee."

"Again?" Kate thought it odd that Peggy Shippen would come herself instead of sending a servant.

"I think her motive is not a sudden fondness for thee, but for a certain aide-de-camp." Seth pointed to the floorboards and the mumble of men's voices below it.

The tic of jealousy surprised Kate. She had never experienced it before. "Did Mother tell her again that Friends do not attend parties?"

"She did but the chit seems disinclined to take no for an answer."

Disinclined? When did Seth start using words like that? Maybe the officers' genteel manners were sticking to him.

Kate went to the kitchen to deliver the spiders and pick up the market basket that Cook had packed. She put her arms through the woven straps, hoisted it onto her back, and set out for the Bettering House on Spruce.

It was a two-story brick building with towers at each end. Kate's family and the others in their Quaker meeting had donated most of the money to build it. It gave shelter, food, clothing, and schooling to the city's destitute, and provided work for the able-bodied. The British had billeted men on the ground floor, and Kate feared the soldiers were having a bad influence on the women. They were having a bad influence elsewhere too.

The women who followed the army from New York must not have sufficed. Notices had begun to appear in the newspapers alongside those advertising for runaway wives and servants. Sergeants and enlisted men were seeking agreeable women for mutually advantageous domestic arrangements. Cook said that vice was creeping into Philadelphia like the old serpent in the Garden.

On the way home Kate stopped at the guardhouse on Little Dock Street and looked through the iron paling fence. Ten or twelve rebel soldiers in their tattered blue uniforms were digging grass from the frozen ground with sticks or their bare hands. One called to her.

"Good day to you, miss."

"God keep you."

He was very thin and hardly older than Seth. He looked as though he craved a kind word or a smile.

"Do they pay you to clear the weeds from the yard?"

"No, miss." He held up the clump of grass. "We eat them."

"Do they not feed you?"

"Not enough to notice, miss."

The guard started toward them and Kate backed away. "May God bless you."

"God bless you and yours, miss."

Kate hurried around the corner to the Darraghs' house on Second Street. The Darraghs belonged to her Quaker Meeting and she knew Lydia would help her. Two officers in bright red coats leaned their elbows on the railing of the second-floor gallery. They touched the brims of their hats as Kate approached.

Lydia Darragh had a distant cousin on General William Howe's staff. She had prevailed on him to ask that men not be quartered there. The general had agreed in exchange for the use of their parlor for meetings. He and his officers spent more time here than at their headquarters in the tavern across the street.

When Lydia opened the door, the smell of baking bread floated out past her. She was a plump partridge of a woman. She had a small beak of a nose, a pointed chin, ruddy cheeks, a broad smile, and a Dublin brogue.

She held her tall, white linen cap so a gust wouldn't carry it away.

"Come out of the wind, child." She led Kate to the kitchen and the kettle of simmering chicken soup and mulled apple cider.

"I would speak to William Howe," Kate said. "Can thy cousin arrange it?"

"What about?"

"The American prisoners. They aren't getting enough to eat."

"Hardly anyone is, child. Foragers from both armies are scouring the countryside. They leave little for the likes of us."

"I hear that Howe is a reasonable man. He must not know the prisoners are starving."

"We'll take food and clothing there directly." Lydia smiled but she seemed nervous. Lydia was not the nervous type.

Maybe she was worried about her oldest son, Charles. He had joined the Second Pennsylvania regiment of the Continental Army and had been read out of the Quakers' Meeting for it. He had fought in the disasterous battles of Brandywine and Germantown. He had narrowly escaped death at Paoli when British soldiers sneaked into their encampment at night and bayoneted them in their blankets. The officer who led them was General Grey, the same man who made small talk at the Darby's supper table.

Now Charles and the Second Pennsylvanians were bivouacked twelve miles north of the city. Everyone assumed Howe would attack them if he could leave Mrs. Loring's company long enough.

"Kate, hold this sack for me."

Kate held the sack open and Lydia scooped flour into it. She tied that one off and filled two more, leaving the barrel almost empty. Kate helped her haul the sacks to the root cellar. Then Lydia shoveled golden brown loaves from the oven built into the fireplace.

The aroma drew the two officers into the kitchen, and a third one who had joined them. John André bowed to Kate. He made her heart skip as always.

"Ah, Miss Darby, you have come down from your aerie in the attic and into the light of day. If you hadn't such enchanting eyes, I would say you were kin to those swift and silent creatures of the night, the bats."

"Fie on you, John." Lydia flapped her apron at him, "Don't embarrass the girl."

Lydia handed them bowls of soup and they ate standing at the high kitchen table. While André waited for his soup to cool, he took a dry-pencil and a folded piece of parchment from his pocket. He unfolded the paper and glanced at Kate while he sketched.

"What think you of this war, Miss Darby?"

"I think it a dreadful thing to fight and kill folks."

"That it is."

"Will I find my cousin at headquarters this morning?" asked Lydia.

"Captain Barrington? I should think so," said André. "May I be of assistance?"

Lydia tilted the flour barrel so André could see that it was almost empty. "I would request a pass to go to the mill in Frankford."

Kate started to say that there was plenty of flour in the root cellar but she didn't. Lydia hadn't said she was out of flour. She had only let John André come to that conclusion.

Lydia had never mentioned to the British that she had a son in the American army. Maybe she wanted to visit him at his camp beyond Frankford Mills. Maybe she wanted to convince him to leave the army and come home.

The three officers rose and bowed. Before he left, John André handed the paper to Kate. He had sketched a good likeness of her. Across the bottom he had written, "For KD from her most fervent admirer, JA."

Lydia looked at it over Kate's shoulder. "Pay him no mind, Katie. He's a rake, and rakes will make hay. Don't be letting your father see it. You had best use it to start the morning fire."

Kate turned the parchment over. In elaborate caligraphy on the other side was an invitation to one of Peggy Shippen's parties. Kate wrapped the drawing in her kerchief and slid it into the pocket of her apron. She knew Lydia was right, but she had no intention of burning it.

WIDOW NEUSS AGREED WITH BENJAMIN FRANKLIN THAT there is no good living where there is no good drinking. She kept the Rising Sun Tavern five miles north of Philadelphia. Her customers, with their tongues tucked in their cheeks along with their snuff, call her Mother Nice. If Mother Nice had gone to sea she would have run a tight ship. People got drunk soberly in her establishment, or not at all. And while they were at it, they could enjoy a tolerably good meal for sixpence.

Colonel Elias Boudinot, George Washington's commissary officer, was no fool. Whenever he went into the countryside in search of provisions he lodged at the Rising Sun rather than in a drafty tent. He was sitting at his usual table near the fire and stowing roast pork, sauerkraut, and beer into his hold when a woman pushed open the door and let in the cold wind.

She was short and stout and wrapped from brows to bunions in a shawl and a frayed woolen coat that must have belonged to her husband. She was quite unremarkable until she headed for Colonel Boudinot's table. The cold air had turned her nose as red as a turnip top. Fatigue clouded her eyes. She pushed her shawl off her head, revealing pale brown hair pulled tightly back into a knot.

"I have heard that members of George Washington's staff quarter here."

"The reports are true, madam." Boudinot spread his arms to show he was a member of that staff. "How may I be of assistance?"

She held up a flour sack. "I'm going to the mill at Frankford and I need a pass to get through the American lines."

"Pleased to be of service, madam." Boudinot called for a pen, ink, paper, and sand, and wrote out the pass.

As he handed it to her Lydia pressed a cloth needle case into his hand. Boudinot untied it and looked through the pockets with their needles, thimble, and spools of thread. "What is this?" He pulled out a small tube of paper and unrolled it.

The message was terse. General Howe was leaving Philadelphia the next morning with five thousand men, thirteen artillery pieces, and pontoon wagons for fording the river. His destination, the writer speculated, was most likely the American encampment at White Marsh.

Boudinot looked up and saw that she was gone. If she had been there he would have thanked her and not mentioned that Washington had already received the information. A Quaker boy in Philadelphia had delivered it to one of the agents left behind when the American troops abandoned the city. The boy claimed to have overheard it from General Grey himself.

Boudinot figured the least he could do was offer her a ride. He retrieved his hat and coat and hurried out. He looked up and down the lonely country road, but the woman was nowhere in sight.

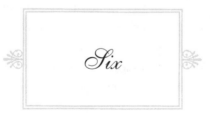

Wherein Kate delivers a better mousetrap; Philadelphia takes Howe;
the young women contract scarlet fever; Seth bolts

PEGGY SHIPPEN WAS MORE THAN BEAUTIFUL AND PRIVILEGED.
She was tenacious. Kate suspected that Peggy wanted to befriend her so
she could see more of Captain André at the Darby residence, although
Cook observed that she was already seeing more of him than was decent.
When invitations wouldn't lure Kate to her house, Peggy tried another
strategem.

That was how Kate came to be struggling along Third Street, trying to
keep the wind from blowing her and her burden sideways into the shop
boys, clerks, and servants hurrying home in the twilight. The wrapping of
muslin and twine contained what looked like a domed birdcage made of
slats of whale bone. It was a mousetrap of sorts, but designed to keep ro-
dents out rather than in. It fit over a person's hairdo while asleep, so mice
and rats could not eat the powdering of flour.

When Miss Shippen sent a servant to order the wig cage from Aaron
Darby's store, she had insisted that Kate show her how to use it. Kate didn't
mind going out even though night was coming on, the wind was cold, and
the not-a-mouse-trap unwieldy. Joy was in the air, and Kate held her face
up into it as though it were a warm spring breeze.

Philadelphia had never seen a giddier Christmas season. Balls took place every Wednesday. Flyers advertising concerts and theatricals papered walls and fences. Kate agreed with Dr. Franklin's comment when the news of the British occupation reached him in France. "Howe hasn't taken Philadelphia," he said, "Philadelphia has taken Howe."

Gleaming carriages rattled past with their matching teams of horses. Now and then they stopped and women cocooned in colorful cloaks stepped down, helped by officers in long-tailed red coats. Atop their wigs the women wore hats so wide Kate wondered how they managed to shut the carriage doors.

Kate hoped to see the most famous resident of Philadelphia, Sir William Howe, with the most infamous one on his arm, the woman people called the Sultana. As Kate walked along, she hummed the ditty that was the rage. She caught herself at it and stopped abruptly. Her people might read her out of the Meeting for a song like this.

Sir William he, as snug as a flea
Lay all this time a-snoring;
Nor dreamed of harm, as he lay warm
In bed with Mrs. Loring.

Kate passed the Shippen's front door and went around to the delivery entrance. The kitchen was a hurricane of shouting and scurrying, with flying cleavers and ladles and a thunder of pounding and slicing. Foothills of pots and platters clattered as the scullery maids scrubbed them.

When Kate asked where she should take the package, a red-faced maid pointed her mop at the back stairs, barely visible through the fog of steam. On the way to them Kate passed an open doorway and saw the remains of a banquet. From the debris it looked as if the roast pigs, beef, chickens, and pheasants had put up a fight. No wonder food was scarce in the rest of the city.

She went up the servants' stairs and was looking for someone to take the wig cage when Edward Shippen wandered toward her. He walked with a backward tilt to balance a stomach as round as a kettle drum. He seemed to be lost in his own house, but Kate wasn't surprised. He always looked bemused these days.

Edward Shippen tried to stay neutral in this fray by refusing to hold public office while the British occupied Philadelphia. Cook said Squire Shippen couldn't decide if he was a patriot putting on a show for the British, or a loyalist afraid of what the rebels would do if they got their hands on him. The dilemma kept him dangling from a tenterhook of anxiety.

His daughter didn't help. Cook said Peggy Shippen was as high-strung as one of Dr. Franklin's kites in a lightning storm. Cook added that Miss Shippen was going through her father's fortune like a sharp knife through soft cheese.

"Ah, miss, how do you do?" Edward Shippen boomed.

"Very well, and thank God for it." Kate was amused that he couldn't remember her name even though he and her father did business together.

"And what have you there?" he asked.

"A device for periwigs."

"Ah, yes. Peggy told me of it." He hurried off, holding it out in front of him like a wet dog.

Kate was about to leave when she heard the military band start, and she peeked around the corner. The wide hallway swirled with candlelight and music and the shimmer of silk and brocade gowns lustrous as oil on water. The sight stunned Kate. An evening's entertainment at her house consisted of reading aloud from the Bible, or Plutarch's *Lives*.

So this was what John André called "the little society of Third and Fourth Avenues." Kate was appalled at the extravagance, but her foot wasn't. It tapped in time to the jig.

Taffetas rustled as laughing couples progressed down the double line in time to the music. The women hiked their skirts up through their pocket holes to leave their feet and ankles free to dance, though how they could even walk in those high heels mystified Kate.

She realized that Lizzie might be right when she said that Peggy Shippen had her sights set on a rich husband. Her lavish parties attracted plenty of candidates in their scarlet coats, gold braid, and high collars. British officers were wealthy. They had to be. The commission for a colonel of the horse guards cost five thousand five hundred pounds, and a major, four thousand three hundred pounds. Even a lowly ensign like James paid four hundred pounds for the privilege of his rank.

Kate backed up to sneak out the way she came and bumped into John André.

"How delightful to see you here, Miss Darby."

"Good evening, John." She started to excuse herself and flee, but Peggy Shippen appeared as though André were a beacon that could be seen for miles.

Her wig was decorated with ribbon cockades and swags striped in the red and white of the British flag. A model of Admiral Richard Howe's flagship, fully rigged, rode the waves on top, and a small Union Jack stood straight out from the mast. Her blue silk lustring dress was trimmed with red and white. The neckline swooped so low and the corset stays pushed her breasts up so high that Kate wanted to throw her shawl over the front of her.

Peggy was small and delicate, with delft blue eyes, a poppy bud of a mouth, cream-smooth skin, and cascades of fine blond hair tucked under her wig. She made Kate feel awkward, and shabby. The dancing had stopped and Kate knew that people were staring at her.

"Welcome, Kate." Peggy beamed in triumph. She had finally netted the elusive Quaker. "And Captain André, how good of you to attend our humble gathering." Peggy took André's elbow in one hand and Kate's arm in the other. Her grip was strong for someone so light and airy. "And aren't you the lucky one to share your roof with the handsomest captain in the British army."

Kate started to protest that she hardly saw John André, but she realized that Peggy wasn't interested in anything she said.

"We girls have all contracted scarlet fever, Kate." Peggy waved a pale arm, encompassing the roomful of red coats. "Come meet these marvelous men. You don't want your twentieth year to find you a spinster."

That stung. "I'm no older than you, Peggy. I won't be twenty for three more years."

But Peggy had shifted her attention back to André. "That homeliest of fellows, General Lee, asked me if I knew a cure for love. I told him the best cure was he himself." She raised her voice so Lee could hear her, and he angled over, followed by two dogs as large as half-grown bears.

Charles Lee was tall and bony, all knees, elbows, and warts. Greasy strands of graying hair had escaped his queue and dangled next to his long face. His filthy collar stood out from his skinny neck.

Kate had heard André and Grey complain about Lee. The British had thought him the only American general they had to fear. When they captured him they threw such a party they even got his horse drunk. He had proved remarkably cooperative in lecturing his captors on how to win their war against the rebels. In fact, he had talked Howe into coming to Philadelphia instead of going to General Burgoyne's aid at Ticonderoga. But he was slovenly and coarse, and by now everyone had grown sick of him.

They were all relieved when the Americans captured a British general in bed with a pair of doxies. They were hoping that an exchange could be arranged soon. To tell the truth, they would have exchanged Lee for the doxies.

Lee jackknifed into a bow. "Ah, Miss Shippen, I shall adopt Lord Chesterfield's opinion on the subject of physical love."

"And what is that, General Lee?"

"That the pleasure is momentary, the position ridiculous, and the expense damnable." Lee laughed like he was coughing up a hairball.

Peggy rolled her eyes and sailed off on André's arm without a backward glance, leaving Kate confused by the unfamiliar emotion of jealousy. She struggled with the urge to stride after Peggy and knock her wig off.

As she headed for the back stairs a young woman came giggling past her, running so fast on her high-heeled shoes that she almost bowled Kate over. An officer trotted after her shouting that he must have her garter for his regimental colors. He chased her into a room and slammed the door. Kate caught a glimpse of someone else backed up against a wall under the stairwell with her petticoats around her waist and a red coat swimming up through them. Kate hurried out into the night.

SETH RAISED THE SASH SLOWLY SO IT WOULDN'T SQUEAK IN the frame. He stuck his rucksack and rifle through the opening and lowered them on a rope to the shed roof below.

Behind him Lizzie stood shivering in her flannel nightgown. He put his arms around her and kissed her one more time. She pressed against him and through his heavy coat he could feel her shaking with grief. He stroked her wiry hair, then pulled her close to warm her, and to hold her for what might be the last time in a long while.

"Enlistment is only for six months," he murmured. "And Charles Darragh says they will grant me a furlough soon. I shall see you then." He tilted her head back and wiped the tears away with his handkerchief.

"Six months is forever."

"It's not as long as five years in Jamaica as Father's factor."

"I'll come with you. Women go to war with their men."

The idea had its appeal but Seth shook his head. How could he explain to her that he had to do this alone? He could not confess that he would have left even if his father never intended to send him to Jamaica. He could not tell her that the longing to join the fight for liberty was greater than his desire to be with her.

"I shall see how things are in camp," he said, "and send for you later. In the meantime I'll write you every day."

He kissed her one more time. And then again. And a third time for luck. He climbed out the window, and Lizzie made a resolution to ask Mistress Kate to teach her to read.

WHEN KATE REACHED HOME SHE WENT TO THE REAR DOOR. As she passed through the side yard she saw a figure emerge from a third-story window. Silhouetted against the moonlit sky he climbed down the vines clinging to the house and jumped lightly to the roof of the shed.

Seth must have had another argument with their father about going to Jamaica. He intended to sulk on the shed roof as he had when he was a child. Kate started to tell him he would freeze, but decided against calling attention to her own infraction. The cold would drive him inside soon enough.

Kate hoped she could sneak up to her room without her father discovering how long she had tarried at the Shippens', but she wasn't surprised to see him waiting at the top of the staircase. The candle he held illuminated the angular lines of his cheeks and jaw but left his eyes lost in dark shadows. She didn't have to see his eyes to know he was angry.

She didn't consider lying to him. Even if she were capable of deception she knew she couldn't fool him. Before she could say anything he held out a piece of paper. It was the drawing John André had made of her. Lydia Darragh had been right. She should have burned it.

Aaron Darby rattled it at her, or maybe he was so angry that his hand shook. "Tomorrow thee will pack a trunk. Thee will ride with Joseph to the summerhouse."

Kate wanted to protest that this was December and the summerhouse was drafty. She wanted to say that she would feel lost and lonely without her mother and Lizzie, Cook, and even Seth. She wanted to say that she couldn't bear the thought of not seeing John André, and she would miss teasing James, the shy ensign. She wanted to say that she loved the music at Peggy Shippen's ball, and she longed to hear it again.

What she said was, "Yes, Father."

Seven

Wherein Seth has a rude awakening,
meets a madman, and finds an old friend

BY THE TIME SETH REACHED THE HAMLET OF SWEDE'S FORD, his plan no longer seemed a good idea. By midday the sky had darkened to cast-iron and the muddy ruts of the road had frozen. Seth's wool stockings had slunk down in folds under his insteps and his shoes had rubbed the skin off his heels. The roll of blankets tied high on his back demanded constant adjusting, the strap of his hunting rifle gouged a furrow in his shoulder, and his rucksack grew heavier with each step.

He wished he'd left his favorite books at home. He wished he hadn't eaten all of his bread and sausages before he reached the two-mile post. And the men would laugh at him for bringing a tin footwarmer.

No matter. The discomfort was temporary. He would collect rations from the Continental Army, along with the enlistment shilling. They would issue him a uniform and a proper soldier's kit. He would have adventures. He would defend liberty. He would see his friend Charles Darragh again.

He trudged past the cottages with their wind-scoured kitchen gardens, skeletal well-sweeps, rooting pigs, foothills of cord wood, and irritable dogs. He was daydreaming about what he would buy with the shilling when he saw the thirty-seven inhabitants of Swede's Ford gathered at the crossroads beyond the last house. He heard the rattle of drums and he broke into a jog. He arrived out of breath, fearful that he would miss the army's passing.

He needn't have worried. The procession stretched in both directions as far as he could see. Some of the men tried to keep in step with the drums, but most of them concentrated on maintaining their footing in the deep, frozen ruts of the road.

Those with no shoes or stockings had wrapped their feet in rags. Some companies had uniforms of their commanders' own design and purchase. A few men wore the moth-eaten red uniform coats and tricorns stored in trunks since they'd fought alongside the British in the war with the French.

Some wore homespun smocks, knee breeches, stockings, and manure-caked boots. Others had on moccasins, leather leggings, and thigh-length wool coats. They wore their felt hats with the wide brims flopping, or caught up at one side, both sides, or front or rear.

Those with no coats had wrapped their blankets around them. Those with no blankets used grain sacks. Those with no grain sacks crossed their arms over their chests and shivered.

Seth turned to a boy he recognized from summers spent at his family's house near Swede's Ford.

"Has the Second Pennsylvania passed yet?"

"Naw. Just a boodle of Yankees."

"Too many whey-faced, onion-eating Yankees, if you ask me," added a woman.

"Yankees will pinch a penny 'til it squeals," said the man next to her.

The men of the Massachusetts regiment had encountered that attitude before. They started singing "Yankee Doodle" as they approached the crossroad.

First we'll take a pinch of snuff
And then a drink of water,
And then we'll say "How do you do,"
And that's a Yankee's supper.

There were a hundred more verses, most of them vulgar. Everyone joined the chorus. The nine thousand soldiers trudged past for hours. They looked more like refugees than an army. The fifes and drums sounded like a dirge.

The folk of Swede's Ford drifted back to their hearths and their simmering kettles of stew or soup. By late afternoon blood from soldiers' bare feet gleamed crimson on the new-fallen snow, and Seth was pacing back and forth to keep his own fingers and toes from freezing. He saw some of the men jump fences, and sneak away into the bare woods and cornfield stubble. He had a feeling they wouldn't come back. He didn't blame them.

As night approached he began to despair. Maybe Charles Darragh was dead. Maybe the American army would keep retreating southward, losing men as it went until it had frittered away to nothing.

Seth considered giving up what looked like a fool's enterprise. He had about decided to seek shelter at his family's house a couple miles away when the Pennsylvania troops appeared through the swirling snowflakes. They looked as bedraggled as the rest, but Seth knew them by the weapons they carried, Pennsylvania muskets and rifles like his.

Seth walked along the shivering line, asking if anyone had seen Charles Darragh. Some shook their heads. Many never raised their eyes from the ground ahead of them.

Seth blocked the path of a big horse ridden by a formidable-looking individual in a black felt hat with the wide brim cocked up at the back. A turkey feather as long as Seth's forearm dangled from the hatband. He looked like he'd be more at ease on the deck of a pirate ship than on a horse. His heavy frame was swathed in a slate-blue surtout coat, with only muddy boots visible at the bottom of it. He looked old to Seth, thirty-five at least.

Seth thought the man might ride him down, but he stopped the horse so close that Seth could feel the steamy heat of the animal's breath on his face. He put his hands up to warm them there and grinned at the officer.

"I'm looking for Charles Darragh."

"Lieutenant Darragh?" The officer nodded toward the rear. "He's with Captain Frazor's company."

"I thank you." Seth started to leave, but the man reined his horse sideways to block him.

"Are you a patriot?"

"I'm as warm a patriot as any."

"If patriotism could keep us warm, we would feel no want for fire-wood." A smile twitched the corners of his wide mouth. "The army can use a strapping lad like yourself. Do you intend to enlist?"

"I reckon to snuff a little gunpowder before I'm through."

"So you've imbibed the prevailing mania for liberty and the rights of man, have you?"

"I reckon I have."

The officer nodded at Seth's rifle. "Do you know the handling of that long piece?"

"I can hit a grouse on the wing or a rabbit high-tailing."

"How old are you?"

Seth should have expected that question, but he hadn't. He was used to people assuming he was older than his years. He glanced at a passing drummer boy who was probably his age, but whose mucous-caked nose barely reached Seth's shoulder. Seth had already decided that he would not carry a clumsy drum, nor a dainty twig of a fife.

"I want to be a soldier."

"Commendable. Now answer my question."

Seth knew the officer's keen blue gaze could detect the tussle between truth and falsehood in his eyes. "I'm fourteen."

The officer leaned down from his horse. "I won't tell if you don't." He winked.

"Thank you." Seth started to leave.

"I won't tell, that is, if you join my Second Pennsylvanians."

"And whom should I ask for . . . sir?" Quakers didn't use honorifics, but Seth knew he had better get used to it.

"Wayne. General Anthony Wayne." He leaned closer as if sharing a secret. "My boys call me Mad Anthony."

Anthony Wayne. Seth almost blurted out that he had heard of the bayoneting of General Wayne's sleeping men at Paoli. He almost admitted that Charles Grey, the British general who perpetrated that atrocity, lodged with his family. He almost apologized for not being smart enough to overhear the plans and warn the Americans.

"I'll remember, sir." Seth thought he should salute, but he didn't know how. He gave a small wave of his hand, turned, and walked away.

When he glanced over his shoulder he saw Wayne sitting with one solid leg over the pommel, watching him. Seth smiled to himself. Unlike at home someone here appreciated him. It didn't matter that men called that someone Mad.

He dodged through the exhausted men who paid no more attention to him than if he were a sparrow looking for crumbs. He finally spotted Charles leading a gaunt dappled gray. The man in the saddle lay with his cheek against the horse's neck. His head was wrapped in bloody rags.

Lieutenant Darragh wore a slate-blue wool coat like Colonel Wayne and a yellow cockade on his hat, but not much else distinguished him as an officer. He was thinner than a year ago when Seth had last seen him, and he looked far older than nineteen.

Charles clapped him on the shoulder. "Does thee bring news from home?"

"I bring news and a recruit."

"Is thee joining the fray then?"

"I am." Seth nodded at the man on Charles's horse. "Has the army encountered the enemy recently?"

"No. Pettiford here was chopping down a Tory's apple tree to get the pippins at the top. His axhead came loose and flew straight toward heaven. He looked up to see where it went. He's lucky it only took his ear off on its way down. He bled a lot, but that was yesterday. I think he's shamming now." Charles poked the man's shoulder with the butt of his pikestaff. "Are you shamming, Private Pettiford?"

"No, lieutenant," the man mumbled into the horse's mane. "I swear to God, I ain't."

"It was easier to let him ride my horse than to persuade men to carry him." Charles's sigh was the only indication that he might be discouraged. "What did thy parents say about thee going to war?"

"I sneaked away and went to thy house. I climbed the chestnut outside the room where thy brother sleeps."

"Skinning in the window." Charles chuckled. "Like when we were lads."

"I stayed the night with thy family, though no one mentioned my presence to thy father. Thy mother walked backwards to bring me blankets and food, so she could truly say she hadn't seen me." Seth reached up to pat the blanket roll. "One of these is for thee."

"Is my family well?"

"Yes, though inconvenienced with the Redcoats roosting in the house. Thy sisters have gone to stay with thy aunt and uncle in Germantown."

"How is life in Philadelphia?"

"The Redcoats are fops and drunkards. We could take Philadelphia like a fox raiding a hen coop."

"Then we would be cooped up ourselves, wouldn't we, and the British prowling the countryside like foxes."

"Where are we going then?"

"The valley where Isaac Potts's old iron forge stood, before the lobster-backs destroyed it."

"That's only half a day's ride from Philadelphia." Seth waved an arm to encompass the brown fields. "We'll have to compete with British foragers, and they've already picked this country clean."

"The Old Man knows what he's doing."

"Where is he?"

"Washington? He's gone ahead to scout our wintering place."

"Thy mother sent thee wool stockings, and jars of pickled onions and gooseberry jam."

"Why didn't thee say so first off?" Charles handed Seth the reins and started rifling through the rucksack.

"Books! That's first rate! And a footwarmer! I would give my commission for one of these." He held up the long-handled metal pan with its perforated lid. "Keep this close or someone will pinch it."

"Do soldiers steal?"

"Does a chicken lack lips?" Charles gave him a pitying look. "The Old Man has had some of the worst thieves flogged but they steal anyway. I've suffered enough want these past months to consider thievery myself."

"Take it," Seth said.

"I couldn't."

" 'Tis thine."

Charles grinned and put the warming pan into his saddlebag. He dipped his fingers into the jar and fished out the small onions. He offered the jar to Seth, but he shook his head. He could see that Charles had not eaten pickled onions, or much of anything else, in a long time. Ignoring the growls of his own stomach, Seth watched Charles devour them all.

Then Charles upended the jar and drank the vinegar, water, sugar, ginger, mustard, and celery seeds they had been swimming in.

Seth thought of the barren countryside he had walked through. He thought of the thousands of men who had passed by here today. He wondered what they all would eat in the months to come. Where would they sleep? How would they keep warm? Then he put those questions out of his mind.

He had found the army. He had found his friend. A mad general said he would do for a soldier. All in all, it had been a good day. He would worry about tomorrow when the rooster announced its arrival.

IN THE TWELVE YEARS KATE HAD KNOWN THE YOUNGEST Darragh boy, she had often thought that if he pursued useful ventures as doggedly as he bedeviled her, he might amount to something. Mandy, the housekeeper of the country estate, rested one lean, coffee-colored hand on the butt of the ax. She put the other one up to shield her eyes so she could watch him approach from out of the watery glare of the early morning sun. "I wonder what brings young John Darragh this way."

"Mayhap he made so much mischief in Philadelphia," grumbled Kate, "that the British threatened to hang him."

Spikes of black hair stuck out from under John's knit cap. His stockings had snags as usual, and the knees of his breeches had worn almost through. He waved his arm in greeting.

"Does thee think to tarry with us, sprat?" Kate called to him. "If so, thee can sleep in the barn."

"I cannot stay. I'm on my way to see Charles and Seth."

"Seth is at home." In fact, Kate was angry with him for going off to sulk the night before she left and not returning in time to bid her good-bye. She was miffed at him for being comfortable in Philadelphia.

"He and Charles are with the Continentals at Valley Forge."

"If thee is playing a prank on me I shall twist thy mule's ears."

An early morning sleet had soaked the old coat John wore and he shivered.

"Come inside, child, before you catch your death." Mandy shooed him through the kitchen door.

She tried to take John's coat to dry it, but he refused to part with it. He stood so close to the big fire that the old wool steamed.

"Thee stinks like a wet spaniel." Kate held her nose. "Tell the truth for thee knows that God loves not a liar."

"I'm not lying. Seth spent the night at our house then left to join the Continentals the same day thee came here."

"Has thee seen him? Is he well?"

"I have not seen him, but my brother sent word that they are all in want of food and clothing. I dared not carry much. If Redcoat patrols stop me they will suspect me of supplying the Americans."

"We'll ride Samuel." Kate started plotting. "We'll wear extra shirts and stockings and coats so we won't arouse suspicion by carrying them. We'll hide bags of cornmeal and salted pork underneath."

"We?" John glared at her. "I'll not go to the patriots' camp with a girl in tow."

"Stay here then."

"You mustn't go, Miss Kate," said Mandy. "It's dangerous."

"Seth is cold and hungry. I will go."

And Father, she thought, is not here to say nay.

Eight

Wherein cow boys come calling;
John Darragh's buttons have something to hide

KATE WAS LEADING THE BIG PLOW HORSE, SAMUEL, FROM THE barn when she heard hoofbeats on the road beyond the oak-lined lane. In the best of times visitors seldom came to the countryhouse in December. These were not the best of times.

Kate tried to hurry, but she felt like a loaded barrow slogging through deep sand. Over her gray wool frock she had put on one linen and two wool shirts, two sleeveless waistcoats, and two heavy wool greatcoats. She wore a pair of brogans that belonged to Joseph, Mandy's husband and the steward of the family's summer estate. Four pairs of stockings filled the shoes, but they jutted so far past her toes that she tripped over them.

She led the horse through the kitchen door and past John Darragh, Mandy, and Joseph, who sat on a stool with his broken ankle propped on a chunk of firewood. The horse's hooves clattered on the plank floor.

"Cow boys," Kate said. "A lot of them."

Mandy collected the pewter pieces and buried them under the ashes of the fireplace. John wiped the muddy, hoof-shaped footprints from the floor. People referred to British foraging parties as cow boys, and everyone dreaded them. Beef on the hoof was their main objective, but they didn't

limit themselves to cattle. Joseph came back with the old musket, and Kate
held up a hand.

"Let them take what they will, Joseph. They must eat too and God will
keep us." She grabbed an apple from the basket of them and tugged the
horse toward the small room just off the kitchen. She lured Samuel inside
with the apple and shoved his rump around so she could squeeze in with
him. "Move the hutch in front of the door."

The horse sidled into the bed then backed into the big trunk. Mandy
tossed the bag of British coins inside. Kate closed the door and heard the
scrape of the tall cupboard sliding in front of it. Then she heard the clatter and shouts of men and horses, sheep, hogs, and cattle milling in the
dooryard.

Kate rubbed Samuel's ears to quiet him. Her breath sounded like a gale
to her, and her heart could have kept time for the militia on muster day.
Samuel's steamy body filled the room and pressed her against the thin
plank door. Men's voices and the heavy tread of boots filled the kitchen.
They sounded inches away. Kate prayed to God that John Darragh would
have the sense to keep his treasonous opinions to himself.

She heard the scrape of barrels being slid across the floor, and the clatter
of pots and pans thrown into sacks. She heard stomping too, as though the
foragers were testing the floorboards, looking for hollow spaces where
valuables could be hidden.

"We're here to requisition provisions for His Majesty's troops." The
man's westcountry accent was so broad that Kate could hardly understand
him. "Present this chit at General Howe's headquarters for payment."

"The good people of this house are loyal to the king," said Joseph.

"Then they will not mind providing for His Majesty's soldiers."

"His Majesty's soldiers are thirsty," someone added. "Where do you
keep the hard cider?"

"Surely you would not take the food that we need to live through the
winter," Mandy said.

"Your master looks a rich cull. He won't let you starve."

Kate had brought Samuel here so the men wouldn't take him. She
hadn't thought about herself, so the next question surprised her.

"And would you be having a sister, lad?"

"Two of them." John's voice held steady. "But they are not here."

Kate sat on her heels between Samuel's legs to make herself smaller. An eternity passed before the men left and she heard the hutch being pushed away. She led Samuel to the kitchen door and peered through the crack in it. The yard outside was empty. Even the flock of hens had vanished, tied to the soldiers' pommels no doubt.

"They took the cow and the hogs," Mandy said. "They took the butter, the cider, the corn. They even stole the chamber pot."

She didn't say that they might have taken Kate too but everyone knew it. Mandy held up a belt woven of yarn and Joseph's oldest knee breeches, mostly patches.

"Put these on, child."

Kate went back into the side room and stuffed her skirts inside the breeches. She tied the belt to hold it up, and put the shirts and coats and waistcoats back on. When she came out, Mandy tied her dark red hair into a boy's queue then pulled Joseph's knit cap over Kate's head.

"Thee is uglier as a boy than as a girl," John said good-naturedly, "and fat too."

Kate held her tongue. For years she had pretended he didn't exist. That still seemed the best policy.

"John and I will return tonight. Tomorrow at the latest."

"Stay here, Miss Kate," said Joseph. "I'll take the goods to the boys soon as I can ride."

"I have to see Seth. I have to convince him to come home."

"It's dangerous to go among those men. And it's not fittin'. You know what your father would say."

"He would say that Seth has made his bed and now must lie in it. But we can't let him go hungry, can we, Joseph?"

"It's Christmas. Think how the sight of Master Seth's dear sister will cheer him." Mandy brown eyes sparkled with tears. "I saved something from those rogues." She moved her skirts aside to reveal a sack of persimmons and apples underneath. "Tell him to come away from there, Miss Kate. Tell him he's a man of peace, like his father. He don't belong among soldiers."

"I will." Kate packed the fruit into wicker panniers, and John carried them outside to tie them across Samuel's back.

As Kate settled behind John on the horse, her heart raced. Never mind British patrols, foraging parties, bandits, and the American rabble. What terrified Kate was her father's wrath when he learned of this.

JOHN WAS EXCESSIVELY CHEERFUL FOR SOMEONE CARRYING what the British would consider contraband. He hummed and whistled and sang as Samuel placed his loaf-sized hoofs on the peaks and plateaus of the road's ruts. When the British patrol stopped them, the sergeant wanted to know why two boys rode out on a plow horse on a bitter winter's morning the day before Christmas. John answered his questions cheerfully and as mendaciously as the worst sinner ever created. Kate was appalled.

The sergeant took apples and persimmons for each of the men as toll, he said, for this stretch of pike. He waved them forward with a "Happy Christmas, lads." Then a private pointed to Kate's brogans jutting from Samuel's sides like coachmen's steps.

"If the lad grows into those feet he'll be taller than a steeple."

"My brother's weak in the head but stout." John tapped his head with his finger. "Pap figures to hitch him to the plow come spring." The soldiers laughed.

They were the last people Kate and John saw. Abandoned wagons, their axles broken by the deep ruts, were the only sign that folk inhabited this once-prosperous country. The bare hills and forests brooded under a leaden sky. When they came to the iron forge for which the valley was named, John stopped humming. The brick smokestack stood sentinel over the ruins of the workers' cottages, the store, the school, the blacksmith shop, the sawmill, and the furnace itself. It was the first of war's devastation that they had seen.

From there they followed the percussion of axes and the crash of falling trees. The American encampment sprawled across a wind-swept hillside bounded on three sides by two creeks and a bend of the Schuylkill River. Hundreds of women and children shared the soldiers' huts, or they would when there were huts to share.

John reined the horse to a halt in front of the brawniest of them. She wore a flour sack for a shawl and had pinned her skirts to an unseemly height. Under the floppy brim of a man's black felt hat, her face was dark with dirt and smoke. A corncob pipe jutted from the corner of her mouth.

"Can you say where the Second Pennsylvania is?" John asked.

"I can." She grinned.

John waited a few beats. "Will you tell us?"

"I will."

Another silence. Kate was cold. She was nervous. She was impatient. But John pulled his leg up, angled it across the saddle, and rested his elbow on his knee.

"Will you tell us now?"

"I will." She looked like this was the most fun she had had all day. She pointed with her chin. "Over yonder." When John reined Samuel in that direction she called after him. "If you lads need anything ask for Mary Ludwig Hayes."

The engineers had marked out the arrangement of huts by companies, battalions, and brigades, but their efforts looked more like wreckage than construction. The temporary quarters of dugouts, lean-tos, and tents were hard to distinguish from the heaps of rubbish. No one had completed the first log hut, and the soldiers dragged the timbers across the survey lines, churning the ground into icy mud. The engineers swore at the soldiers and the soldiers swore back. Kate heard enough swearing to last her a lifetime.

As Samuel plodded among the rows of half-raised shelters a soldier ran past wearing only a scrap of blanket tied around his waist. Kate looked the other way and found herself staring at two more just as naked. Kate smelled a lot of odors, but not the aroma of meat cooking.

They found Charles Darragh, Seth, and several others lined up with their shoulders under the log they were lifting into place.

"Ready," Charles called out. "Heave."

The men raised the log and seated it into the notches cut in the ends of the one below. They didn't have to lift it far. The hut's walls stood only two courses high. John was not impressed.

"Is that all thee has raised in two weeks' time, brother?"

Charles swatted at him with his hat.

"Axes are so scarce we must gnaw the trees with our teeth like beavers." Seth glanced at Kate. "Who is thy friend?"

"She's not my friend, nor thine either. Just a bothersome sister."

"Katie?"

"God's blessings on thee, Seth." Kate ventured out from behind the horse, as shy as if she were greeting a stranger. In a way, she was.

Seth had grown thinner. The planes of his cheekbones, jaw, and nose had sharpened. He was dirtier and more ragged than when he was small and their father would lower him down the chimney to clean it.

Seth hugged her, something he had not done since he was five. "How fares Mother? And how did thee persuade Father to let thee come here?"

"They are well, and Father doesn't know. I was at the summerhouse when John brought word that thee had absconded."

"And Joseph and Mandy?"

"They are well enough, though Joseph broke his ankle chasing the cow."

John held up the saddlebags. "Mandy sent persimmons for the Christmas feast."

Charles and Seth carried the baskets through the opening in the low walls and Seth's hut mates crowded after them. They squatted with their backs against the logs and fell on the fruit like starving wolves on the steaming carcass of a deer.

Kate took off the extra coats, waistcoats, shirts, and scarves and laid them over the top log of the wall. She set the stockings and brogans next to them. She put on her own stockings and shoes and shook out her skirts. She took the saddle off Samuel and retrieved the blankets under it.

Seth ran his fingers over the blankets and the clothes. His hands were cut and scarred, and his palms had blisters upon blisters.

"A happy Christmas this." He smiled up at her. "I thank God, and I thank thee, Kate."

"Thee is thinner, Seth, and more serious."

Seth waved a hand at the camp. "This would make a philosopher of a donkey. We eat firecake and stews made of weeds and leaves."

"Firecake?"

"A little flour mixed with water and cooked on a flat stone."

"But Father says there is food and clothing a-plenty in the storehouses in Philadelphia and Lancaster."

"The roads are too bad for wagons to pass. And merchants and farmers spurn Continental money for hard English currency. Or they ask prices dear beyond all reason."

Kate came to the point. "Return home with me, Seth."

"I will not be a sunshine patriot."

"Quakers do not fight."

"I will." A look came into his eyes that Kate had never seen before. "God means us to be free. And I will fight to my last breath for liberty."

Then he glanced over Kate's shoulder and she turned around to see Charles Darragh cutting the buttons off his brother's coat. He took them apart and pried tiny pieces of paper from under the wool cloth that covered them.

"What is that?"

John beamed. "Intelligence."

Charles unfolded the papers and made a rumpled stack of them.

"Intelligence!" Kate turned to John in astonishment. "Thee is an intelligenser?"

"What's that?"

"A spy."

"Nothing like it." He looked offended. "Mother only put her ear to the floor above the parlor where the officers meet. Father wrote it in cypher and Mother sewed the papers into the buttons. If thee sews the cloth back on them I can wear the coat home."

"Spying is deceitful. How could thy mother do such a thing."

"She feared for Charles's life. But she never lied to anyone."

"Has anyone inquired after Seth?" Charles asked John.

"Cook said that John André asked Aaron Darby about him."

"What did Aaron tell him?"

"He said he didn't know where his son was, but he trusted he was in God's care."

Charles gathered the reports and left for the tent of General Washington's aide, Alexander Hamilton.

Kate turned on John. "The British would have hung thee had they discovered what was in those buttons."

"But they didn't catch us."

Us? Kate hadn't thought about the us in this. Would they have hung her too?

Nine

*Wherein Benjamin's goose isn't cooked; Kate puts her eggs
in one basket; a jovial fraud arrives*

EVEN IF MAJOR BENJAMIN TALLMADGE WERE THE GRINNING
sort, which he wasn't, he shouldn't have been grinning now, but he was.
He sat on his big black gelding at the crossroads and grinned at the four
godawful chasms of mud and destruction leading to it. A scarcity of wagons and a quorum of bad roads were only two of the reasons that grain
rotted in barns and wool uniforms mildewed in the clothier general's store-
house in Lancaster. Other reasons included ineptitude and greed.

Greed was incurable, but at least the ineptitude might be remedied. General Washington had appointed young Nathanael Green as quartermaster
general. Green was a Quaker, or rather he used to be. Brigadier generals
didn't fit into the Friends' scheme of things. They had read him out of their
Meeting, but Green still possessed their virtues of thrift, efficiency, organiza-
tion, and honesty. But that wasn't why Benjamin grinned.

No matter what miracles the quartermaster general might accomplish in
the future, Benjamin had taken care of himself today. His prize hung
lashed by her skinny yellow shins behind the saddle. She hissed and honked
and flapped her six-foot wingspan against Ben's back, but no caress would
have felt better.

By late February of 1778 Benjamin Tallmadge hoped for an early spring, but he knew he wouldn't get it. He'd hoped for a lot of other things that winter—dry stockings, a flea-free bed, and one of his mother's apricot tarts, but he hadn't received any of them. What he'd most hoped for was a Christmas goose, the skin honey-brown and crisp, the grease hot and savory in his mouth, the flesh moist and tender.

Ben had dreamed about that goose the way a lonely man would dream of an amiable woman. Instead, his Christmas feast consisted of roasted turnips and a drumstick from one of the five gaunt chickens shared with the twenty officers of General Washington's mess. The drumstick came with a generous serving of guilt because Ben knew the soldiers had less.

Now he had procured a fat goose. He had found her tethered in a farmer's woodshed. The farmer had carried on as though Benjamin proposed abducting his daughter. Ben told the man he could sell the goose or he could donate her to the cause of liberty, and here she was, riding pillion behind him.

He scanned the brown hills for a British patrol or the rest of his foraging party. He saw instead a woman rounding the curve in the road with head lowered and skirts lifted out of the mud. He waited for her. The purpose of this excursion was to collect supplies for the commissary general, but Ben kept an eye out for anyone who might carry intelligence. If this woman was a spy, he wanted to find out which side was paying her.

When she came closer he realized she was the sister of young Seth Darby. Benjamin didn't doubt Seth's patriotism, but he could not be sure of hers. If the Darby family's loyalties were divided, they wouldn't be the first. More than one rebel in a loyalist household had sneaked out information to the Americans, but the jig could also be danced in reverse.

Ben knew that General Washington employed scores of double agents. He sent them so the British would receive his falsified reports from various sources, making them more credible. General Howe's intelligence officers could be using this young woman the same way.

She looked harmless enough. She wore a plain, gray wool dress under the old coat. Fine wisps of hair, red-gold as a ripe persimmon blew from under her black felt hat. Her face was narrow, a trifle long, with a light peppering of freckles across the nose. Her blue-green eyes held a startled, tentative look, like a deer about to bolt. She carried on her back a market basket of oak splits with straps of woven grass.

Ben touched the brim of his hat and raised his voice to be heard over the goose. "Good morrow to you, Miss Darby. My name is Benjamin Tallmadge. I am acquainted with your brother."

"Good morrow, Benjamin, and may God keep you."

He reached for the basket. "I shall carry that to the commander in chief and save you the long walk to the encampment."

The change that came over her surprised him. Her mouth set in a defiant line and those meek eyes flashed. Ben had seen the same look on Seth's face from time to time when someone crossed him.

"I am taking these eggs to my brother." Her voice was much firmer than Benjamin expected. "George Washington may find his own."

"May he now?" Benjamin laughed. "Then I wish you Godspeed, Miss Darby. Your brother is part of a foraging party. You'll find him on the far side of that ridge." He tipped his hat and turned his horse toward home, or at least the canvas folding cot jammed into the tiny room he shared with ten other officers on Washington's staff.

He hadn't gone far when seven of his men appeared on the ridge and waved. Ben looked over his shoulder and saw a dozen British dragoons crest the hill, their red jackets bright against the gray sky. They swarmed down the slope, and Benjamin's company set out to greet them.

And there stood the Darby girl, caught in the middle. She swiveled left, then right, then turned all the way around, looking in vain for a place to hide. Benjamin couldn't leave her in the cross fire, and if she did carry information in that basket, he couldn't let it fall into British hands.

He galloped back to where she stood, frozen in terror. He realized that he could not carry her and the goose. Muttering an oath, he cut the thong around the goose's feet. Her wings had been clipped so she tumbled to the ground, shook her ruffled feathers, and waddled away. Benjamin stretched out his hand to Kate. She shrugged out of the basket straps and held them with one hand. She extended the other so he could pull her up to sit sideways in front of him.

Holding the reins around her, Benjamin spurred his horse. Pistol shots whined past them and he felt the breeze of a ball tickle his earlobe. The Darby girl clung to the gelding's mane.

Benjamin leaped his horse over Seth who was stretched out on his stomach, his rifle barrel steadied on a rock. When the regulars came into range

Seth and the others opened fired. Ben primed and loaded his musket, but this was the sort of fight where the rifles' greater range paid off. After a few potshots the British decided to call it a day.

The Darby girl jumped down with the basket still upright. Her hand shook when she pulled back the cloth and inspected the contents.

"I packed them in sawdust so they would not break." She held the basket up so Benjamin could see the eggs.

"What else is in there?"

"What else would I have?"

"News."

"News of what?"

Benjamin could see from her perplexed look that he would get no intelligence from her. She was either innocent or exceptionally artful.

Seth stood up and slung his rifle across his back. The lock was still warm and the muzzle still smoking. He tried to look casual, but his eyes gleamed. Benjamin had seen that look before.

"So you've sniffed gunpowder at last, Darby."

"Yes sir, I guess I have." Then Seth saw Kate. "Sister, where's Joseph?"

"Father sent him on a charge to Lancaster," said Kate. "He took Samuel and so I came on foot."

"Don't ever come alone again, Katie."

"I brought eggs."

"A few eggs are not worth thy life."

"These are more than a few eggs, Seth, and hard to come by."

"No matter if there were a hundred."

"For shame, Seth, to shoot at another human being."

"He was pleased enough to shoot at me."

Benjamin sent the foraging party back to retrieve the two wagons left on the other side of the ridge, but he turned his horse toward the crossroads. British regulars or no, he was going to look for that goose. He wasn't in a hurry to return to Valley Forge and the grumblings of his fellow officers. Many of them were resigning their commissions, and they weren't the only ones leaving. The army's strength has shrunk from twelve thousand to barely half that.

Benjamin searched the area, but he found only a few gray feathers. Most likely one of the Redcoats was riding home with the goose tied to his saddle.

Benjamin was about to go after them when he saw a group approaching. It was a parade, really, of five men and three times that many horses plodding along under swaying foothills of wooden trunks, wicker hampers, and pudgy traveling bags made of turkey carpeting. The wooden legs of folding cots protruded as though trying to wriggle free of the ropes.

The procession came from the direction of Lancaster. Lancaster was the temporary seat of the American government, so Ben figured they were not hostile. Four of them wore clothes of a European cut, and narrow-brimmed black silk hats with tall crowns. The fifth one carried a large, closed umbrella tied horizontally behind his saddle.

He was short and pear shaped. Circling his equator was a wide red sash tied in a loaf-sized knot with fringes hanging to his knees. His trousers, leggings, and gaiters were so white they gave off a glare. Horizontal rows of tassels, brass buttons, and gold braid crusted the front of his peacock blue jacket, which had a crimson collar, cuffs, and coattail turnbacks. Around his neck hung a jewel-studded gold medal as big as a saucer. A black tricorn trimmed with heavy gold lace perched buzzardlike atop his powdered hair.

The greyhound pacing alongside his horse looked like a bundle of willow sticks with a dogskin thrown over and shrunk to fit. Benjamin assumed they were a troupe of actors or a traveling menagerie. Maybe they intended to juggle or eat fire or walk on their hands.

With a vast smile on his lumpy face, the blue coat spurred his horse forward and extended his hand. *"Guten morgen, mein Herr,"* he boomed.

Ben spoke no German, but he observed the amenities. "Good day to you, sir."

The man waved his hand and one of the party rode up next to him. He looked no older than seventeen, and if the greyhound had been wearing spectacles on the end of his long, tapered nose, he would have resembled the young man to a remarkable extent. He spoke English with a dense French accent, and he sounded as though he were reciting a speech he had learned by rote.

"I am Pierre Duponceau, secretary to"—he doffed his hat and indicated the blue coat with a flourish—"His Excellency Baron Friedrich Wilhelm Ludolf Gerhard Augustin von Steuben."

Benjamin decided that Baron von Steuben resembled two hundred pounds of potatoes in a hundred-weight sack. His nose looked like candle-wax melting off his face. Its bulbous tip was red and bright enough, Benjamin supposed, to provide the baron a light to find his way to the necessary over rough ground.

"Baron von Steuben is a lieutenant general with twenty-two years in the service of Friedrich, King of Prussia," said Monsieur Duponceau. From a cylindrical tin dispatch case he shook out a roll of vellum sealed with a scab of red wax. He held it aloft like a lantern. "He carries a letter of commendation from your own Dr. Franklin in Paris. He wishes to present the letter to the commander in chief of the American forces, and to offer his services."

Dear God, Ben thought. Another foreigner come to lord it over us.

In the past year General Washington had seen a parade of European liars, fakes, gawkers, and adventurers. Benjamin sized the baron up as all of those, and a fool besides. He tried to imagine this merry band mingling with the crowd in the small house that served as General Washington's headquarters. The general's twenty staff officers and aides, and Mrs. Washington and her servants were already living cheek by jowl there. Not to mention the constant traffic of couriers, contractors, delegations, civilians seeking passes, and the merely curious. If the house hadn't been stoutly built of local fieldstone it would have burst at the seams by now.

Ben tried to imagine the baron navigating the narrow, winding stairway to the commander in chief's office on the second floor. Portly General Knox and the more than portly General Putnam had both gotten wedged there. They would have to pry the baron out of the stairwell with crowbars.

"Tell the baron that he missed the turn to the American encampment," Ben said. "Tell him I'll take him to General Washington."

Baron von Steuben beamed. *"Wunderbar."*

Definitely a fool, Ben thought. Washington will know how to get rid of him.

"GOTT IM HIMMEL! ACH DU LIEBER! SACRE BLEU!"

Benjamin could hear Baron von Stueben long before he reached the parade ground.

"Diese Hannebambel! Ein Dorn im Auge!" Stupid people! A thorn in one's side!

When Ben arrived he could see why von Steuben was miffed.

A hundred men milled to the beat of a drum. Some turned left and others right. They bumped into one another and waved their bayonets. If no one lost an eye before sundown it wouldn't be for want of trying.

Von Steuben had hand-picked these soldiers. He expected them to form the cadre that would teach the rest to march and handle their arms with precision. A few thousand of the rest lounged around the perimeter and watched the best show outside of Philadelphia.

Von Steuben did not walk. He bounced. He did not talk. He bellowed. He did not chide. He stamped his small feet, waved his arms, threw his hat down, and tore at his hair. Since before sunup he had bullied and jollied the men in turn. Because he could not speak English the enterprise was not going well. As afternoon shadows lengthened the baron showed no signs of slowing down or giving up.

Ben walked over to stand next to Captain Alex Hamilton. Hamilton was as overcast as the late February sky. He looked like he'd had to swallow so much pride it had lodged in his throat. Bad enough that Washington had appointed Baron von Steuben inspector general and put him in charge of training the troops in the manual of arms. Worse, he had assigned Hamilton as von Steuben's guide.

"The baron seems to have discovered the secret of perpetual motion," said Ben.

Hamilton grunted and continued to glower.

"I must say he's a good sport to lower himself to drill the men when our own officers won't do it."

Hamilton answered with another grunt. Then he moved closer so only Benjamin could hear him. "He's a fraud."

"How so?"

"His secretary shared a bottle of the local brew with me last night. It didn't take much to set his jaw to flapping."

"So von Steuben was not a lieutenant general in King Frederick's army?"

Hamilton laughed without enough humor to notice. "He was a captain for a brief time and has been without employment for years."

"Does General Washington know?"

Hamilton gave him a glance. "There's not much the general doesn't know, now is there, Ben?"

"*Blöde Bauernlümmel!* Steuben followed that with a volley of German, the words bouncing like cannonballs. "Duponceau!"

Pierre Duponceau peered through his spectacles at the men. "The general says you are stupid farmers."

"Bloody right! You tell 'em, Frenchie," shouted an onlooker.

"He says you are . . ." Duponceau searched for the correct words.

Someone tried to help out. "Balaam's ass in breeches."

"Jingle-brained nincumpoops," added another, and they all laughed.

"This is worse than herding Hissians." Alex Hamilton used the soldiers' slang for geese, but he didn't break a smile.

Benjamin agreed. In King Frederick's army, the one von Steuben had belonged to even if briefly, officers commanded and soldiers obeyed. Benjamin could have told the baron that was not the case here. Before these men followed an order they wanted to know the why and wherefore of it.

Benjamin had to admit that when Washington appointed von Steuben as inspector general he had made a mistake. This would never work.

Wherein Kate tries to buy a leg-o'-nothin';
Seth undergoes firewater and brimstone; Kate scratches her surface

MARY LUDWIG HAYES LOOKED AS IF SOMEONE HAD THROWN her clothes on her with a pitchfork. Her pinned-up skirts revealed a man's boots and stout ankles in wool stockings that she described as more holey than righteous. Her hair rioted around the ruffled bottom of her dirty linen mob cap. In Mary's case "mob" was an apt name for it.

She lived with the men of her husband's artillery crew, and she could have taught General von Steuben a thing or three about swearing. The stem of her clay pipe fit neatly into the gap left by a missing tooth. Her laugh carried the length of the encampment's makeshift marketplace. Kate waited for her to finish.

"Have I a brisket of beef for sale?" Mary waved a hand over the shriveled apples, dried peas, and sprouting onions in her baskets. "Why bless you, Kate, we've not heard a cowbell in a fortnight. I have here a leg-o'-nothin' and no turnips." She held thumb and forefinger an inch apart. "The boys are this close to mutiny for want of vittles."

Kate knew that. For two months she had gone on foraging expeditions of her own. What little she found she brought to Seth.

Kate and Mary looked up when General von Steuben started shouting on the parade ground.

"Ihr Esel! Zum Teufel mit euch!"

Mary had learned some of the baron's German. "He's calling them asses and telling them to go to hell."

Kate held out the bills she had received from the tavern keeper at Swede's Ford in exchange for her best silk dress. "How much for the onions and the sulfur?"

"That paper were better used as tinder than tender." Mary waved the money away. "It's counterfeit."

Kate didn't know much about money. She and her mother bought on credit, and her father settled the bills. She stared at the crisp notes.

"But they're well-made."

"That's what lets the cat out of the bag, don't it?" Mary winked. "The lines are sharper than on the ones Congress prints." She took a bill and snapped it. "The forgers use better paper too." She pointed to the words along the bottom. "D'ya see anything wrong here?"

"No."

"Exactly. On Congress's notes they spell Philadelphia with a *ƙ* instead of an *h*." Mary couldn't read anything except her name and the word *Philadelphia,* or *Pƙiladelpƙia,* depending on whose currency people were trying to give her.

"My brother has need of the brimstone, Mary. What will you accept in exchange?"

Mary balanced the bag of powdered sulfur in the palm of her hand. "If they discover I've pilfered this from the artillery stores they'll tickle me with the whip and cashier me hubby."

Kate untied the twill tape that held a pair of brocade pockets at her waist. "These contain a silver thimble, a spool of black silk thread, a case of fine steel needles, and a pair of tortoiseshell combs."

Mary took the pockets and handed over the sack of brimstone. "Tell no one where you got it."

"I promise." Kate bid her Godspeed and headed for Seth's hut.

The encampment had become the second largest town in Pennsylvania. It spread across the slopes with the hundreds of log huts laid out in neat rows by brigades. They commanded sweeping views of the hills around them. The British would have difficulty sneaking up on anyone here.

Smoke drifted from the mud-chinked chimneys. The huts looked cozy but Kate knew better. When she reached the tenth one, she pushed open the door on its leather hinges. The room was fourteen feet wide and sixteen feet deep. Two sets of berths, three beds high, stood along each side wall. The fireplace took up the back.

Kate noticed more clothing hanging from the wall pegs than on her last visit. The new quartermaster general's doggedness was having an effect. The soldiers' linen haversacks hung on the corners of the bedframes. Pewter plates and mugs made of cow's horn sat on a shelf.

Kate sat on a stump by the hearth and placed the onions in the embers to roast. She pulled a small pumpkin from the bottom of her basket and laid it next to them.

The door slammed open. Susannah Smythe edged a carrying yoke and dangling water buckets sideways through it. She waited for her two young children to come in, then kicked the door shut behind her. She set the buckets down and stood the yoke in the corner.

"God bless the owner of the ironworks at French Creek," she said. "He sent a thousand barrels of flour by barge down the Schuylkill."

Kate and Susannah patted out flat cakes of flour and water and set them on the rocks to bake. When the men came back from drilling, Kate was relieved to see that most of Seth's smallpox sores had healed. His face would have only a few small scars. The inoculations had pitted some of the others badly, but at least now they were immune to the scourge that had blazed through Philadelphia and almost every other city and hamlet.

Some of the men slid exhausted into their lower berths. Others perched on the top ones, but they all began exchanging footwear.

"We received shoes this morning before drill." Seth sat on the dirt hearth and eased his own shoes and stockings off. His heels were bloody. "We couldn't try them on but had to take what was handed to us."

"I brought Mandy's salve for blisters." Kate handed him a small jar.

"Bless thee, and bless Mandy."

"Who is the new man?" Kate murmured.

"He's a Hessian. His name is Hans, but we call him Spitz. It's short for Spitzklicker. He says it means trickster."

Spitz bowed. He had given up trying to tell his comrades that not all German soldiers came from Hesse. He himself was from the Duchy of Brunswick.

"He deserted the British army last summer and joined us." Seth chuckled. "Tell Kate what happened to you, Spitz."

"I vas drunk."

Seth elaborated. "Last fall the Americans ran out of shot while under siege at Fort Mifflin. The officers offered a gill of rum for every cannonball their men retrieved. Spitz says they raced to fetch the balls before they stopped rolling. Spitz earned so much rum he slept through the retreat. The British found him and thought he was one of theirs."

"*Die blöde Rotröck,* the stupid Redcoats, they take me to Philadelphia."

"He collected his bounty for enlisting again, drew a British uniform, bided his time, and escaped. He arrived here a week ago."

Spitz opened his arms to embrace the hut, the encampment, and the surrounding countryside. "Is goot here."

"I reckon this country looks mighty good if you come from a place where your king sells you like cattle and sends you across the ocean to be slaughtered." Seth stood up and paced and scratched.

"Thee will wear away thy skin, Seth."

"This itch has plagued us since the inoculations."

"I brought brimstone."

"Bless thee, Kate. Did thee bring tallow too?"

"Yes."

Kate mixed the sulfur and tallow, then covered her face with her apron when the men stripped naked. They crowded around and rubbed the sulfur and tallow into the almost-healed smallpox sores. One of them produced a flask of whiskey to dose their insides, and it put them into a good enough mood to joke about the effect the sulfur would have on their fleas and lice.

"Hold out your hand, Kate." Seth dipped a needle into one of his sores.

Kate didn't question the need for inoculation. She had seen smallpox victims in Philadelphia. But that was also a reason to dread this. "Will it make me very sick?"

"I don't think so. I did not suffer nearly so badly as most, and you'll be getting it from me."

He took Kate's hand and used the needle to scratch the matter under her fingernail. "Mandy has had the pox, so she can care for you. In about twelve days your head will start to ache. You'll suffer fever and vomiting. Four days after that the sores come."

Seth did not tell her what he had endured while she was away. General Washington had ordered all the men inoculated who had not already had smallpox. He couldn't incapacitate his entire army at once, so the men were treated in rotation. Secrecy was also a necessity, so Seth and a couple hundred others had spent two weeks in a barn several miles away.

Seth had helped to care for men with sores lining their mouths, throats, and nasal passages. Pustules covered their faces, forearms, the soles of their feet, and the palms of their hands. In the worst cases the sores converged into a single oozing mass and formed a crust that made movement excruciating. Seth had seen enough suffering in those two weeks to age him years.

After a feast of fire cakes, onions, and pumpkin, Kate helped Susannah bank the fire. The air chilled at once, and everyone climbed into their berths. Kate shared Seth's with him.

"Thee stinks of brimstone," Kate whipered.

"May that be as much as I ever know of hell." Seth paused. He wasn't used to speaking what was in his heart, especially to his older sister. "This winter would have been unbearable without thee, Kate."

"Thee is my brother, Seth, and I love thee."

Someone began playing a violin in a hut farther down the line, and everyone fell silent. The song was so plaintive it brought tears to Kate's eyes, but Seth's breathing grew deeper as he fell asleep.

Kate lay awake thinking about her young brother, the beloved stranger who had become her dearest friend. She asked herself the questions no one could answer to her satisfaction. Why did men endure this? Why did they march in lines, and lose their teeth to poor diet and their toes to the cold?

What did they hope to accomplish? They couldn't beat the British. And why did they want to? What was so bad about the world as it had been before all this started?

Come spring, Howe's well-fed, well-rested, well-supplied army would scatter George Washington's Continentals like sparrows. What would happen to Seth then? What would happen to all of them?

Joseph knocked on the door the next morning. He and Samuel stood with the morning mist swirling around their legs.

"How could you sneak away, Mistress Kate, and leave us to worry ourselves to death?"

"Because thee would have said me nay, Joseph."

"That I would. This place is full of sickness."

So much, Seth thought, for Washington's plan to keep the inoculations a secret. The whole valley must know of it.

Seth hugged Kate before he lifted her onto Samuel's back, behind Joseph. Neither of them said what they were thinking—that instead of protecting Kate, the inoculation might kill her.

Kate was putting her arms through her basket's shoulder straps when General Anthony Wayne rode up the beaten track between the lines of huts. Wayne made Kate uneasy. He had the fixed-bayonet stare of a man preoccupied with death and unconcerned about it at the same time.

Kate regretted that Anthony Wayne had taken a liking to Seth and worse that Seth had taken a liking to him.

"Private Darby, how is your itch this fine morning?"

"Cured, sir."

"Good. Then you're ready for duty."

"Yes, sir."

"Those damned fools in Congress don't realize we can't command starving men. I want you to join the foraging party I'm gathering.

"You're coming too, sir?"

"Hell yes. We're going after cattle."

"Sir, we've taken most of the cows for fifty miles around."

"That's why we're going to the Jerseys."

"Yes, sir." Seth seemed pleased at the prospect but Kate wasn't.

New Jersey was far away. Seth didn't know anyone there. If something happened to him how would she learn of it?

Kate thought that Seth going to New Jersey was as bad as could be. Then she and Joseph arrived home and saw her father's horse.

"We can tell him we went to Swede's Ford," said Joseph.

"No we can't."

Joseph sighed. The Quakers' refusal to lie was often inconvenient.

Kate's father was as angry as she expected him to be.

"I cannot trust thee in Philadelphia and I cannot trust thee here. Thee will return to the city with me today."

"Shall I tell thee how Seth fares?"

"No."

Philadelphia seemed distant and foolish to Kate now. She thought that someone else had lived her life there. She realized that she had come to think of herself as part of George Washington's pitiful army. She also realized that was an odd way for a Quaker to feel.

Eleven

Wherein Lizzie saves Seth's bacon; Kate has a night visitor; Philadelphia has an Arabian night; Peggy Shippen's knight prepares to decamp

IN THE WAGONBED ABOVE SETH'S HEAD THE FARMER'S SNORES rattled the loose boards of the sides. Seth lay wrapped in his blanket on the ground, curled up against the chill of early April. The soldier's life had given him the ability to fall asleep under worse conditions than these, but tonight he lay listening to the clatter of wooden pulleys against the masts of the ships at the docks. He smelled the familiar odors of Philadelphia's harbor, and he wondered what his old friends were doing. He debated whether he should try to sneak home and see Lizzie. It wasn't much of a debate, really. Pro won out handily over con.

He heard footsteps and saw a light dart along the ground among the parked farm carts waiting for the market to open in the morning. A pair of worn-down shoes and the dirty hem of a skirt stopped next to his wagon. A woman holding a small oil lamp peered under it. Her hair fell in greasy tangles around her face.

She called softly back over her shoulder. "I found a young one, Poll. A strapping lad, he is, with hair red as rust."

A second face, pitted with smallpox scars, joined the first. "And handsome as pie too. Mayhap ye'd fancy a go wi' the two of us."

"We're physickers," added Maggie. "We can inoculate ye against the plague of chastity."

Seth had gotten used to their type. In spite of General Washington's orders forbidding them, doxies were as plentiful at Valley Forge as lice and fleas. God only knew how many men they had laid low with disease and how much information they carried back to the British.

"It's the clap you'd inoculate me with."

"Not a bit of it, me bob cull. We're clean as two whistles, we are."

"By the looks of it, one of you already has a bun baking."

Maggie put her hands on the bulge of her skirt and laughed. "Then there's no danger ye shall have to answer for the by-blow, is there?"

"The Alms House baker heated more than one oven," said Poll. "And now the dough is rising."

"Comes the watch," muttered Maggie. "A pox on 'em."

The two women scurried off to avoid the night watchman. Seth fell asleep and dreamed of Lizzie.

The next morning he hoisted a basket of the farmer's bacon onto his back. British soldiers mingled with the crowd on Market Street, and this was the closest to lobsterbacks that Seth had been in a long while without them shooting at him. Seth had to remember not to grin at them. Inside his coat he carried a prime piece of trickery written in the commander in chief's own hand.

General Washington had created false reports of troops strength and movements. He wanted the British to receive them from disparate sources to make them more believeable. After Anthony Wayne and his men returned with almost two hundred head of New Jersey cattle, Wayne had recommended Seth for the assignment. He was to deliver the falsified reports to the patriot who would see that they reached General Howe.

Seth joined the throng flowing through the wide doorway of the markethouse that extended the length of the block. Along the east wall the country folk sold bread, beans, and dried fruit, pumpkins, apples, molasses, Indian corn, and grain. The shrill calls of the farm wives echoed in the cavernous building. The butchers in their bloody leather aprons occupied the west wall. The thud of their axes and cleavers provided bass for the women's high notes.

Seth stood amazed while people jostled past him. During the long, hard winter at Valley Forge he had assumed that everyone shared the army's privation. He had not expected to see hens, ducks, pigeons, and geese dangling in bunches like grapes. He and the foraging party had gone all the way to New Jersey for beef, and here were carcasses of it hanging alongside mutton and pork.

He left the bacon with the butcher and saw nearby the man he was supposed to meet. He was wearing the sleeveless jacket, black-and-white striped breeches, and high-crowned rabbit-skin hat that identified him. When Seth headed toward him, three soldiers moved to intercept him.

"Here's a likely looking recruit."

Seth smiled politely and tried to walk around them, but they shifted to block him. One brought his musket up to form a barrier.

"Why isn't a strapping lad like you wearing the king's colors?"

"I'm a Quaker." That wasn't the correct answer to the question, but it was the truth.

"Come with us, and we'll see if the recruiter's three guineas on the drumhead changes your religion."

They herded him toward the door. He was about to bolt, and the devil take the consequences, when Lizzie hurried toward him. He wanted to shout at her to go away, but then he noticed something strange about her. She walked spraddle-legged, with her back arched and her hands cupped under a huge bulge beneath her skirts. Her kinky black hair stood out in disarray, and her eyes had a look of panic.

She clutched at Seth's arm. "Husband, my water broke." She pointed to a puddle behind her. "The babe's on the way." She crowded close to the soldiers. "Any you gents birthed a baby?"

The soldiers turned red and remembered urgent business elsewhere. Seth took Lizzie's arm and steered her toward the door. On the way he bumped so hard into the man in the striped breeches that he knocked him over. As he helped him up he made fumbling attempts to brush the rotten lettuce leaves off him, apologizing all the while. Then he hustled Lizzie outside, around a corner, and into an alley.

Seth knew every back lane and byway in Philadelphia. When he and Lizzie reached safety, they stopped to catch their breath. Lizzie loosened her skirt strings and the gourd dropped to the ground between her feet. She and Seth collapsed, laughing, into each other's arms.

LIZZIE'S WARMTH IN THE BED AND THE GARRET'S FAMILIAR smells comforted Kate. The rebel army's encampment at Valley Forge seemed as far away as Africa. She had almost floated into sleep when she heard the window sash easing up in its frame.

" 'Tis only Master Seth," whispered Lizzie.

Kate and Lizzie sat up with the covers wrapped around them. Seth had climbed the vines from the shed roof. He felt his way to the bed and sat next to Kate. The odor of green wood smoke in his hair brought back the encampment as vividly as if Samuel the old plow horse had turned into a winged Pegasus and transported her there.

"God keep thee, Kate."

"Has thee returned home to stay, Seth?"

"I came to deliver something to someone here in Philadelphia." Seth stretched out on the mattress and sighed in contentment. "A real ticking with feathers. This is close enough to heaven for me."

"What did thee deliver?" asked Kate.

"Information."

"What kind of information?"

" 'Tis better for thee not to know."

Seth was pleased with himself. He had passed the papers to the man in the market when he helped him to his feet. They contained orders to attack New York. If all went well they would convince the British commander to keep his men in that city. General Washington's inflated figures of troop strength at Valley Forge would persuade Howe that the ragged little army was a threat to him in Philadelphia. Neither of the generals would come to the aid of the other. Without reinforcements it was doubtful either would attack what they thought was an overwhelming force. That would buy Washington time to recruit and equip his men.

All in all, it was a capital joke.

Lizzie pulled a roll of papers from behind the bed. "Whilst I was dusting I found these in a drawer in Major André's secretary. They look important."

"Lizzie!" Kate was horrified. "You must return them at once."

"All in good time, sister." Seth lit a candle from the embers and spread the papers out on the hearth.

Lizzie peered over his shoulder and even Kate couldn't resist looking. She had never seen troop movements, but she imagined this was how an officer would diagram them, with circles and arrows and lines indicating movement from one place to another. Seth took a pencil and a sheet of paper from his haversack and made a quick sketch of André's work.

"Seth, thee mustn't. What if they catch thee with that?"

"They won't." Seth rolled the diagrams back up. "Lizzie, can you creep downstairs as quiet as a mouse and put these back where you found them?"

"That I can." Lizzie took the papers and was gone.

"Seth, how could thee involve her?"

"It's a dance."

"What?"

"André must have designed a new dance. He even wrote the name of the tune to be played as accompaniment. 'General Howe's Victory.' Lizzie mistook it for troop movements."

"Then why did you copy it?"

"I think General Washington will like it." Seth grinned. "He's as able a dancer as he is a liar."

COOK ALWAYS SAID THAT MAJOR JOHN ANDRÉ WAS AS COOL AS a cucumber, bold as brass, and handsome as a new copper penny. Kate agreed that he was bold and handsome, but these days he hardly qualified as calm and collected. Maybe the warmth of May had affected him the way it did the squirrels that chased each other through the oaks shading the house.

Agitated and secretive he gathered a score of officers every night in his room on the second floor. Lizzie and Kate took turns replacing the candles and trimming the lantern wicks long after their usual bedtime. Kate's mother was certain that they were plotting the destruction of the rebel army and her son with it. She took to her bed with a tenacious headache. All day, every day, Lizzie and Kate laid wet cloths across her forehead for some small relief. With her mother ill Kate took over running the household.

One morning John André found Kate in the kitchen consulting with

Cook about what to feed so many men. He carried a dozen or more rolls of paper.

"Tell me what you think." He shoved aside the bread dough rising on the kitchen table. He unrolled several of the scrolls and used Cook's ladle and the bread paddle to hold down the sides.

Kate leaned over to look at the drawings. Instead of diagrams of troop movements and artillery positions, she saw sketches of women in low-cut dresses that clung to their bodies in a shameful way. The women looked like they belonged in an eastern pasha's harem, except that they wore towering turbans draped in bunting, with birds and tents and palm trees on them.

"You have considerable artistic skill, John."

"Yes, yes." André used Cook's toasting fork to point at the wigs. "What do you think of the hairdos and the hats? I have become a complete milliner, have I not?"

Kate was confused. What kind of military campaign was this?

"I don't know what is fashionable and what is not."

André unrolled more scrolls, drawings of men in baggy pantaloons, capes, boots with pointed toes, and hats like upside down toadstools.

"They look like Turks."

André clapped his hands. "That's exactly what they are. We shall have as our theme the Arabian Nights. Half of the officers will wear white satin pantaloons and capes and be called the White Knights of the Blended Rose. The Black Knights of the Burning Mountain will wear black and orange."

"Are you putting on a play?"

"No, no, dear girl. Sir William has announced his retirement."

"William Howe?"

"Himself." John André started rolling up the scrolls. "We will give him a farewell the likes of which these bumpkins have never seen."

A party? Kate thought. Was all this secretiveness about a party?

"We're calling it a Mischianza."

"Doesn't that mean 'medley' in Italian?"

"Yes, it does, you clever girl." He beamed his ivory and sapphire smile at her. He did have the most beautiful teeth and eyes. Kate felt the usual flutter in her chest whenever he was near.

"A fleet of barges will carry us upriver to the Wharton mansion. The entire army will line up so Sir William and a train of knights and ladies may parade between them. They will pass under a triumphal arch adorned with sword-wielding maidens standing on platforms its entire length. On top a figure of Fame will blow on her trumpet."

"You mean a real person?"

"Of course."

Kate wondered where in Philidelphia André expected to find a belle who could play the trumpet.

"There will be jousting followed by a banquet, then dancing until sunrise." He put his slender fingers under Kate's chin and tilted it up. "You will come, won't you, Kate? All the best sort will be there."

His touch sent a shiver through her.

"I see you as a maiden of the Blended Rose. The gown of white lawn will set off your copper hair and fair skin to perfection."

"You know I cannot."

"Your father isn't here. He would not know."

Kate gave him a look.

"No, of course you can't, dear Kate." André sighed. "What a tiresome religion that does not allow one to deceive, disobey, or disport."

Kate thought how fortunate it was that business had required Aaron Darby to travel to New York to see his old friend Thomas Buchanan. He had had a frank talk with John André when Kate returned home. André had assured him that he would not make any advances toward his daughter, nor would he allow anyone else to. If Aaron could have foreseen what André would do instead, he would have been outraged not so much by the British army's penchant for war and debauchery, as by its frivolity.

For the next two weeks shop clerks, servants, milliners, wig makers, seamstresses, tailors, shoemakers, and messengers trooped in and out of the house. As the day of the celebration approached, preparations became more frenetic. Women appeared with servants carrying trunks and bandboxes to take away the costumes André had designed for them.

André spent twelve thousand pounds sterling for silks and lawns, ribbons, tinsel, and gauze. The officers involved weren't necessarily the cleverest or the highest ranking, but they were certainly the richest. By the day of the Mischianza, Lizzie looked so harried that Kate offered to help her change the linens on General Grey's bed.

When she opened the cupboard to take out the sheets she heard Grey and André talking in the room beyond it. She didn't mean to eavesdrop, but curiosity overcame her. Grey was not in a good mood.

"Who would have thought that an army composed of the refuse of the earth and led by a damned negro driver could force us to retreat?"

"Ah, well, it's the French, now, isn't it?" said André. "They put the matter in a different light."

"The French don't give a damn about this benighted cesspit. They're after the Spice Islands."

"If a third of our army sails away to defend the islands, we can't hold Philadelphia, can we?"

"Who wants to. Burn the town and be done with it."

"I've become fond of the place. These colonials are an amiable lot."

"You relish being a large frog croaking in a small pond, André, as anyone can see from this ridiculous farce you're planning." Grey cleared his throat. "And what will you do about the Shippen trollope?"

"I'll deal with her when the time comes."

"She thinks she'll snag you for a husband."

"I can't help what she thinks, now can I?"

Poor Peggy. Kate remembered her saying that she would marry John André or know the reason why. Still, Kate was eager to tell Lizzie the news. The French had joined the fray on the rebel side. The British were leaving. Seth would come home. Life would return to normal. The only sad part about it was that John André would leave too. She would miss his laugh and his smile and the music of his flute drifting from his room.

A commotion started in the street below. Kate and Lizzie went to the window and saw a footman helping Peggy Shippen down from her father's carriage. Kate could tell from the way Peggy strode toward the front door that she was in one of her states.

"Dear God," Kate muttered. "Please, not now." She hurried down the stairs and a wail like a fiddle badly played came welling up to meet her.

"John. John, where are you?" When Peggy saw Kate she started screaming and stamping her feet. "I must go. I shall die if I don't."

"Calm yourself, Peggy." Kate led her into the parlor.

"What's all this?" John André sauntered in and Peggy rushed him.

"I am undone. Father has forbidden me to be a maiden of the Burning Mountain." She clutched the invitation between her breasts and looked as pathetical as one recently orphaned. "He says he will not have his daughter exposing herself so."

Kate was impressed that Edward Shippen had taken a stand on anything.

"I'll talk to him." John André patted Peggy's hand.

"It's no use. He says he will not bend. He says that not for the king himself will he have his daughter arrayed like a common strumpet."

Peggy started wailing again, and Kate handed her a handkerchief.

"Everyone will assume . . ." Peggy could not finish, but Kate knew what everyone would assume. Peggy was right about that.

British officers had gotten a large number of Philadelphia's fair elite with child. The young women could not hide their bellies under the clinging costumes André had designed. Gossip would declare any absent belle to be pregnant.

André put an arm around Peggy's waist, and she wilted against him like a begonia in a bread oven.

"I will speak with your father."

"It's no use."

"How would you like to meet the Marquis de Lafayette?"

Peggy's delft blue eyes flew wide open. "But he is a general in the Continental army. How . . .?"

"Howe indeed!" André winked. "Our spies have told us that within a few days Lafayette will leave the winter encampment and set up a forward position. Sir William is so confident of taking the marquis that he is issuing discreet invitations to dine with him after his capture. Need I say that the guest list will be a select one?"

"Shall I be invited?"

"I will see to it, pretty Peg, but you must not tell anyone."

Peggy promised but left not much mollified. Dinner with a marquis was not so fine as dressing like a Turk and dancing till dawn.

Kate waited for John André to admonish her to keep mum too, but he must have assumed that because she was a Quaker, she was worthy of his trust. She felt bad about that because she couldn't be trusted. Maybe Seth would be among the soldiers chosen to camp with Lafayette. She had to warn him. The Darraghs had gone to stay in the country, so she could not ask young John to deliver the message. She would have to go herself.

Twelve

Wherein Captain André turns milliner; General Lee allows no rest
for the wicket; a louse lays Kate low

THE TWO DOZEN YOUNG WOMEN IN THE DARBYS' TWO FRONT
parlors generated enough erotic energy to turn a millstone. The air fairly
shimmered with it. Kate moved cautiously through it, as though breathing
it could infect her with a galloping case of depravity.

The prospect of André's Arabian Night had the belles in a seethe, but
the man himself occupied their immediate attention. Kate had never seen
such tilting of chins, such fluttering of eyelashes, such giggling and sim-
pering and fawning. Incessant as cicadas they chirped for him to adjust
their sashes and periwigs. They brushed against him. They peered at him
over their lavender-scented handkerchiefs. They pretended not to see him
when they adjusted their silk stockings and garters.

White-clad nymphs of the Blended Rose milled in the Darbys' north
parlor. The huge orange turbans of the maidens of the Burning Mountain
made the south parlor look like a pumpkin patch. The preposterous head-
dresses reminded Kate of the afternoon she and André sat at the kitchen
table and drank noggins of Cook's thick barley beer. Pride was a sin, but
she had to smile at the thought that every belle in Philadelphia would have
given their dowries to be in her place then.

"Why do the girls wear all that frummery anyway?" Kate asked. "I should think it would give them sore necks."

"It's part of a game that's as old as the earth, Katie," he had said. "It's harmless, it gives them pleasure, and it provides employment for a multitude of tradesmen whose children would otherwise starve."

"I cannot think that God approves."

"Ah, my girl, you take life too seriously." André had dipped his fingers into his beer and flicked them at her. She had laughed and tossed a handful of flour at him.

" 'Give Chloe a bushel of horse hair and wool,' " he recited.

Of paste and pomatum a pound,
Ten yards of gay ribbon to deck her sweet skull,
And gauze to compass it 'round.

Thus finish'd in taste, while on Chloe you gaze,
You may take the dear charmer for life;
But never undress her—for, out of her stays,
You'll find you have lost half your wife.

Kate laughed again. In fact, she laughed more that afternoon than she had since this war began.

Today John put her in charge of tasks that required needle and thread. She took tucks and sewed on plumes and spangles. While one young woman after another stood on a stool, she sat on the floor and raised their hems or lowered them.

She wanted to warn Seth about Howe's attack but leaving now would cause suspicion. Besides the British army certainly wasn't going to march on Lafayette's camp with its officers dressed as Turkish pashas. With all the brandy André had ordered, Kate suspected that they wouldn't be eager for a battle the next day either.

First thing tomorrow Kate would go to her mother's room and kiss her as she did every morning. Then she would inspect the kitchen and discuss the next few days' meals with Cook. She would tell Lizzie and Cook that she would be back in two days, certainly before her father returned.

"LEG BEFORE WICKET! ILLEGAL INTERFERENCE!" GENERAL Charles Lee waved a knobbly finger at Benjamin Talmadge. "He's dismissed, I say!"

Lee was as bad at cricket as he was at dancing, but that didn't stop him from criticizing all the players except the commander in chief, and he barely braked short of that. During his year as a prisoner of the British, Lee had learned the new rules laid down by the Hambledon Club. He had insisted on installing proper wickets in place of the tree stumps that had always served them before, and now he was determined to turn the game into a complicated ordeal. He was a poor loser and a worse winner.

Benjamin stalked off the field, fighting to keep his temper in check. He could understand why the British had been eager to get Lee off their hands. They had exchanged him recently for their own general, who had been captured in bed with doxies. At least the two officers had provided everyone with opportunities for sly jokes about tits for tat.

Lee proved that if a man was peculiar enough, people would believe him a genius. When the British discharged him Washington had ordered the entire army to form two lines along the road to welcome him. Washington had thrown his arms around Lee and greeted him like a brother. That night the commander in chief and Mrs. Washington had entertained Lee with an elegant dinner and had a room prepared upstairs for him. Lee had repaid them by coming down the next morning dirty and disheveled. He had spent the night with a sergeant's wife he had sneaked up the back stairs. Lee might fool everyone else, but he could not pull the wool over Martha Washington's eyes. She refused to let him spend another night under her roof.

Now Lee was spoiling what could have been a perfect May day, but General Washington didn't seem to mind. And who could blame him for being in good spirits? Spring recruitment had increased the army's strength to almost twenty thousand. The rank and file were clean, clothed, shod, and eating almost regularly. They had flour to squander in powdering their hair.

General von Steuben had performed a miracle equal to hocusing brandy from branch water. He had turned a disorderly mob into a disciplined force. And now the French had thrown in with them, and the Spanish were rattling their sabers too, forcing the British to face the prospect of a war on three fronts. The air of a Sunday lawn party had replaced the winter's misery.

With his jacket unbuttoned and his hair escaping from the ribbon that tied it into a queue, General Washington ran and bowled and batted. Martha and the other wives sat in camp chairs under a striped awning. They sipped tea laced with brandy and discussed last evening's theatrical performance of "The Fair Penitent."

As Ben walked toward the marquee where von Steuben's secretary was dispensing pear brandy on the baron's orders, Mary Hayes angled out to intercept him. She reminded Benjamin of a farm cart draped with laundry. A worried look had replaced her gap-toothed grin.

"A word with you, Major."

"Yes, Mrs. Hayes."

"A few of the women has took sick. One of them is the Darby girl what you brought in a week ago, all footsore and wore to a nubbin walking from Philadelphia. I tied a bag with their nail parings to an eel and loosed it back in the river, but for all the good it done I should've stewed the critter and et it."

"Nail parings and an eel?"

"To take their fever away."

"They have fever?"

"Their skin is hot enough to boil tea. Pains in the head. Aches in the joints. And now red bumps all over 'em, blessed poor things."

"Did you fetch Dr. Waldo?"

"Yes, sir. He says they must be carted to the hospital in Lancaster, but the Darby girl's brother is off foraging. She was waiting to see him before she headed home, and then she got the fever and ague with the rest."

"When Corporal Darby returns I'll see that he's told where she is."

"Thank you kindly, sir."

Mary Hayes strode away and Benjamin cast a longing eye toward the awning where the officers lounged in folding canvas stools in the shade. It also sheltered a keg of brandy. No Bedouin in the desert could have desired a drink more than Benjamin did.

He sighed and followed Mary. He couldn't say why he felt responsible for Kate Darby, but he did. She had set out through a lawless countryside to bring word of General Howe's plan to attack Lafayette's men. She had no way of knowing that Washington's informants had already delivered the news.

Now she was sick and alone. Benjamin figured the least he could do was give her some little comfort. If she had ship fever he knew what the next stage would be. She would become delirious, and possibly comatose, but maybe that was just as well. At least she would not know that she was far from home and family, and not likely to live to see them again.

THE SUN OF MID-JUNE PRODUCED ENOUGH HEAT TO SOFTEN lead. Kate's bones felt as though they had turned to pudding, and every jolt of the cart sent blades into the backs of her eyes. She sat in a far corner of the farm wagon crammed with women and children. Some suffered the flux, others were sick to their stomachs. Kate dampened her handkerchief when the bucket of water was passed around and held it over her nose and mouth to keep out the worst of the smells.

She was happy anyway. She had survived the blistering and emetics, the cold-water baths and the bleeding that served as treatment at the hospital. She hadn't died, although she had wanted to, and everybody had assumed she would. Someone told her that Seth had come to see her and to leave money for her burial, but she had been too deranged to recognize him or remember.

Now she was going home. Better yet, Seth was already there. The British had left Philadelphia and the American army had re-taken it.

As they entered the city's outskirts Kate peered through the side slats. Soldiers had cut down the ancient elms and oaks that had lined the streets, and they'd used the logs to build fortifications. They had leveled houses and destroyed fields, but when the cart approached the center of town the streets began to look as they always had.

The procession of wagons stopped at the State House where men were shoveling horse manure from the rooms the British had used as stables. A soldier helped Kate climb down. The other women scattered, and Kate headed for home. Her legs wobbled her up the broad steps. She rang the bell and when no one answered she put both hands on the iron-banded oak door and leaned her weight forward. The door swung open with a shriek of rusty hinges. She stepped into the dim light of the front hall.

"Mother?" Her voice echoed. "Father?"

She wandered from room to room, all of them stripped of furniture and curtains. She found heaps of chicken manure in one parlor, lumber in the other, and dirt everywhere. Books littered the floor of the library. The plaster on the ceilings was falling away in great patches. Rain had come through the broken windows and left mildewed stains on the walls.

Kate wandered in a daze to the kitchen. She screamed when someone moved there. Someone screamed back.

"Oh, Miss Darby, you gave me such a fright." The woman rose from the pile of straw in the corner. Her four small children peered from behind her skirts. "I thought you was a ghost come to haunt us."

"Sarah?" Kate recognized her from visits to the Bettering House.

"Rebel soldiers quartered in the Poor House, ma'am, and threw us into the street. The folk round-abouts helped themselves to everything after your family left, so we didn't see no harm in sheltering here."

Kate surveyed the shambles that had been Cook's orderly kingdom. "Is there anything to eat?"

Sarah gave her a corn cake that tasted like dust, but Kate was grateful for it. She scooped up water from the barrel and washed the cake down.

"Flour is selling for ten guineas a sack," Sarah said, "and bacon is not to be had. The rebel soldiers devour vittles like starved wolves."

"Why did you think I was a ghost?"

"We heard you was dead, mistress."

Kate swayed. The air felt like a blanket soaked in steaming water and wrapped around her head. "Do you know where my family went?"

"They thought you was dead too, miss. Your mum cried buckets, she did. They left with the Tories, bound for New York."

"They left?"

"Aye. And quite a scene it were too. Thousands of them scrambling to carry off their goods. Such weeping and wailing." Sarah couldn't resist satisfaction at seeing the better sort brought low. "Just before the British left, your mum brought us bread and beef, the last beef I've had. She said she and your father would stay here and ask the Americans where you was buried. But when the lower sort heard the rebels was coming back they muttered about fitting your father in a suit of tar and feathers."

"But he's not a Tory."

"You know how rumors run."

"What rumors?"

"That your father was selling goods to the British."

"Everyone sold to them."

"They say he was speculating, buying up food and supplies and hoarding them so's he could sell them dear."

My father would not do that."

"Well, mistress, you know how people is. I think it were envy and greed that caused them to say such things." The woman began gathering up her few belongings. "Come along children, we must leave the gentle lady to her house."

"No, stay. I'll sleep upstairs."

Kate walked through the devastated rooms, a blur now on the other side of her curtain of tears. In the third-story room she had shared with Lizzie the linens had been stripped from the bed, but otherwise everything looked as it had when she had left it, more than a month ago.

She spread her cloak on her mother's bed, lay down, and inhaled her mother's aroma in the ticking. Tomorrow she would search for Seth. She laid her head on her satchel of clothes and the spare pair of shoes that miraculously had not been stolen in the hospital. She wanted to cry, but she was too tired. She didn't drift into asleep. She plummeted into it as though down a very deep well.

Thirteen

Wherein Kate doesn't ask a favor of General Benedict Arnold;
her world goes up in smoke

KATE STOOD AT THE DOOR OF THE AMERICANS' HEADQUAR-
ters. Keeping her chin high took effort. Her family had always employed
laundresses, but Kate had no money for that now. She had washed her
clothes as best she could, but she couldn't rid them of the stains from the
hospital in Lancaster. She was good with needle and thread, but her skirts
and bodice, waistcoat and shawl still looked tattered. Her best black leather
shoes were scuffed and down at heel.

Neighbors muttered when they saw her and refused to speak to her.
The members of the monthly Quaker Meeting had read her brother and
her father out, and Kate did not feel welcome there. Spies and counterspies
lurked everywhere. Kate could not trust anyone.

She knew where her mother hid a few shillings of egg money under a
loose floorboard so her father wouldn't find it. Her mother felt guilty
hoarding it and Kate felt guilty taking it, but it didn't buy much anyway.
For the past week Kate had gone to the market as it was about to close. She
was less likely to meet anyone she knew then, and she could buy the en-
trails, wilted cabbage, and wormy flour that the merchants sold for pennies. She lived on those and the apples and potatoes from the root cellar,
and the eggs from the few hens that the looters had overlooked.

She spent her mornings cleaning the rooms and her afternoons going to the buildings and encampments where the American soldiers were quartered. Someone told her that Seth had been sent into New Jersey on a scout, so at last she went to the army's headquarters to ask the new military governor for help.

She was about to knock when the Shippens' carriage pulled up and Peggy swept out in a rustle of silk taffeta.

"Katie, my dear friend! You are alive! And in Philadelphia."

"God keep thee, Peggy." Kate was surprised to see her. She had assumed that the Shippens had fled with the other British sympathizers.

Peggy rapped vigorously on the door with the butt of her green silk parasol, then edged farther away from Kate. Kate couldn't blame her. She had scrubbed herself with soap and creek water, and poured vinegar and larkspur over her head to rid herself of lice, but Peggy couldn't know that.

"So sorry to hear about your family and your house, Katie. The lower sort are dreadful, aren't they?" Peggy looked her up and down. "I shall send Dolly by with clothes. They've gone completely out of fashion, but that doesn't matter to you, does it?"

"I thank you, but I do not need anything."

The door opened and a private led them into a side parlor. The family's furniture, keepsakes, and portraits looked so normal that for an instance Kate thought she might have dreamed the past week.

"Papa wants to ask General Arnold to dinner. She held up the invitation, a folded piece of vellum with a red wax seal. "I simply must meet him. He's a hero, you know."

"Benedict Arnold?" Kate had only seen him from a distance at Valley Forge. He was short, with a mastiff's head, a limp, and, Seth said, a chip on his shoulder as big as a yule log. Congress had given credit for the victory at Saratoga to General Gates, but Arnold had won the day. The slight didn't sit well with him.

"Yes. He led an assault on the British redoubt at Saratoga, riding into the storm of their bullets." She pointed an imaginary sword. "He cried 'Follow me, boys.' It must have been thrilling. His wound mortified and the surgeons wanted to cut his leg off, but he forbade them. Don't you think a limp makes a man more romantic?"

A lieutenant appeared. "The general will see you, Miss Shippen."

Peggy waved the invitation at Kate. "Shall I ask Papa to invite you to the dinner? All the belles will be there."

All the belles? Were the same young women who had danced with the British now dining with the Americans?

"No, thank you kindly."

Now that Kate was about to see General Arnold she couldn't think what to say to him. She had come here with a vague notion of petitioning him to assign a guard to the house, or issue a statement saying that her parents were not traitors. She wanted to ask the Americans to pay for the damage done. She wanted Seth to come home. She wanted her parents to return. She wanted life to be what it had been before. But now that she was here she knew, instinctively, that whatever she asked of General Arnold, he would not grant.

Peggy swung her hooped skirts sideways to maneuver them through the door, but Kate backed away. As she left she passed Seth's old friend, Stork Whithers, coming in. He greeted her awkwardly and made some comment about seeking employment. Kate bid him Godspeed and hurried down the street, avoiding the eyes of passersby. She had heard the whispers in the marketplace. "Tory whore." The sight of all those young women coming in and out before the Mischianza had started the rumor that Kate and her mother were operating a disorderly house. Kate had become a stranger in the town where she was born.

She came home to find the place empty. Sarah and her children had found other quarters. Kate missed the company, but at least the house was as clean as Kate could make it. She went to sleep that night in her old room on the second floor.

The noise of a crowd awakened her. She went to the window and saw a mob with torches. She wanted to call down to them, to reason with them, but she was so terrified the words stuck in her throat.

"Traitors!" They spotted her. "Collaborators. Speculators. Burn them out."

They threw torches through the downstairs windows, and Kate heard the crackling of the flames. She felt her way through the smoke on the stairwell, and ran to the barrel in the kitchen. She fetched water in an old pot and tried to douse the flames in the front parlor, but the effort was useless. She heard more shouts at the back door and torches came through the window there.

She grabbed the market basket and stuffed what she could into it. She pelted up the servants' stairs, which were dimly lit by the flames below. From the third-floor window she climbed down the vines and onto the shed roof. From there she could see the neighbors gathered in the street to watch the fire. No one tried to put it out.

Kate found some apples and potatoes in the root cellar, then she hid in the hen house near the creek. She could hear the roar of the fire and feel the heat. A little before dawn she felt under the hens and collected four eggs. She turned the chickens loose and ventured outside. The shed had collapsed on the entance to the root cellar and it was still smoldering. Kate put two potatoes on the hot coals. She found a rusty tin and scooped sooty water from the rain barrel. She put the eggs in it, set it over the coals, and waited for the water to boil.

The sky was growing light by the time she finished eating one of them. She wrapped the other cooked potato in her kerchief and put it in the basket with the three eggs. The house was a roofless brick shell, outlined black and ragged against the pale gray sky. Kate's mother always said that hating was like taking poison and wishing that one's enemy died. Kate hated the Americans anyway.

She peered into the street. It was empty. She had heard that the British were heading for New Jersey and a spit of land called Sandy Hook. From there they would probably take ship across the Narrows for New York.

Kate stood irresolute in the road. She had no maps, no money, and no idea where Sandy Hook was, nor how far away. She did know which direction was north. She took a deep breath and started walking.

Fourteen

Wherein Seth burns bridges; Kate becomes baggage;
Seth converses with a corpse

BURNING A BRIDGE WAS HARDER THAN SETH HAD IMAGINED. General Wayne couldn't do it, and Seth believed Mad Anthony Wayne could do anything. The bridge was still sodden from the rain that had turned the fields to bogs.

Seth had lain in a soggy hayrick all night. He had held his musket in his arms with the lock between his thighs to try to keep it dry. Now he looked up at the cloudless sky, thrumming with heat, and wished the rain would start again. The men in Seth's detail asked to see General Wayne's thermometer so often that Wayne lost his temper and ground it under his boot, but not before it marked a hundred degrees.

Now Wayne was losing his temper again. "We'll have to chop the bastard down."

The twelve men waded into the river under the bridge and started hacking at the king posts. General Wayne attacked the trusses. Seth was used to Wayne's odd ways by now, but the man still surprised him. No other officer would roll up his sleeves when work needed to be done.

When they heard two loud cracks Wayne shouted, "Stand off, lads." He put the sole of his boot against one of the posts and shoved.

The bridge shuddered and swayed. Seth and the others cheered when it

buckled in on itself, the planks of the bed flying up in succession and landing with a clatter.

Wayne held up his empty food sack. "We've consumed our belly timber,
lads. Time to face about."

"Turn around because we're out of vittles?" the sergeant grumbled.
"What's the army coming to?"

Seth knew they would hear about the sergeant's flight from Fort Ticonderoga through a Canadian winter.

"You cannot say you're hungry until you've eaten pomatum and shaving
soap."

"You had pomatum to eat?" Seth couldn't resist needling him. "We had
no delicacies like pomatum and shaving soap at Valley Forge."

The men chuckled but the sergeant bristled. "A soup of boiled shoes and
cartridge box tastes right savory when your stomach is rubbing up against
your backbone like a tom cat in rut."

If only we had had shoes at Valley Forge, Seth thought. We could have
dined on them.

The sergeant had stories about the Ticonderoga climate too, cold that
would snap toes like pea pods. But those tales didn't seem appropriate with
the mercury rubbing against a hundred degrees like the sergeant's amorous
tom cat.

For all that, Seth didn't want to go back to camp either. Marching with
the main body of the army was tedious. Raiding with General Wayne's
men was not. Even on foot Seth and his company of Pennsylvania Rifles
had easily outpaced the British. Mad Antony Wayne traveled light. The
British general, Clinton, did not.

Wayne's job was to slow Clinton down even more. This was the first
bridge the company had destroyed, but they had felled trees across roads
and shoveled sand into wells. Seth felt bad about the wells, but Wayne
quoted Cicero on the subject: *Silent enim leges inter arma.* "Laws keep mum
in war."

They hadn't gone far when seventeen soldiers, their hands on top of
their heads, emerged from the woods.

"More Fritzes," Seth called back.

The Germans had dropped their muskets and their eighty-pound packs.
They had unbuttoned their green wool tunics, but their faces were as red as

boiled beets and they staggered in the heat. They raised their hands and lined up. Their sergeant shouted in German.

"Spitz," Wayne shouted. "What're they saying?"

Everyone knew what they wanted. The Americans had found squads of Germans passed out by the side of the road, felled by the sun.

Spitz conferred with the newest arrivals. "They say 'Blöde Rotröcke, stupid Redcoats.' They say, 'Blöder Krieg, stupid war. Blöde Hitze, stupid heat.'"

"Bloody right," muttered Seth.

Wayne's detachment circled wide to avoid British flankers. On a high hill they looked down at the fifteen hundred wagons in General Clinton's baggage train. Four thousand loyalist refugees from Philadelphia had doubled the usual army of camp followers. The column wound for twelve miles among the hills. More Tories joined the march each day.

General Wayne crooked his leg around the pommel of his saddle, rested his elbow on his thigh, and chuckled. "When Clinton enters Monmouth his strumpets will be stinking up the streets of English Town."

The British artillery caissons, horses, wagons, and yesterday's rain had churned the road below into a quagmire. So many people had tried to avoid it that the fields bordering it had become as bad. Clinton's army was covering barely five miles a day. The refugees were struggling to carry their children and push their overloaded carts through the mud and the heat. Seth didn't feel sorry for them. If they stood with their country instead of betraying it they would have been taking their ease at home now.

He wished he could see Lizzie, but at least she and Cook and his parents were safe in Philadelphia. And Kate? Grief knocked the breath out of him, like the butt of a pike between his shoulder blades. Kate was dead, and he was to blame.

THE STRUMPETS WERE THE MERRY ONES. THE OPEN ROAD meant the chance to plunder the luckless locals. Some of the women had already bored a hole in a cask of Barbados rum in one of the wagons. They had drained it off into tankards, flasks, and canteens, hats, boots, and at least one chamber pot.

Primed with spirits they laughed and chattered and gave off a polecat aroma too powerful for the cloud of smoke from their corncob pipes to mask. With their hair unpinned and the rags of their skirts hitched up, they bared their breasts, spit snuff, and shouted obscenities at the local citizens. They carried their worldly goods slung in sacks on their shoulders. This march hardly differed from others they had taken, and they had little to start with, so they had little to lose.

The loyalists had lost everything except what they could carry. As their carriages and carts broke down, they were losing even that. They tried to barter for food, but the local folk had acquired all the wing chairs, lowboys, highboys, sideboards, china, and harpsichords they needed.

The soldiers' wives were too burdened to be merry. Some nursed infants and others bulged with progeny that would require nursing soon. Most were bent under wicker baskets loaded with pots and pans, griddles, gristmills, and sad-eyed waifs. No one, however, expected the strumpets to produce waifs or prepare meals. They were free to smear mud on their faces and arms to keep the sun from burning them. Shrieking with laughter they threw more mud at each other than they plastered on themselves.

The mud was as thick as mortar and it weighted the hems of Kate's skirts. It sucked at her bare feet until she needed all her strength to swing each one forward. Her stomach cramped with hunger, but the fields had been stripped of corn. Rebel marauders had filled the wells with dirt, and people cursed them for it. Kate had drunk at the last stream, but that was hours ago. Her perspiration-soaked clothes clung to her.

She looked longingly at the wagon rumbling ahead of her. Red-coated soldiers had used their bayonets to chase the women out of it amid a hurricane of imprecations and pleas. As soon as the men marched off, the strumpets clambered back aboard. They reached over the sides for the children that the wives handed to them, and they helped up the bolder of the wives themselves.

Kate wouldn't have ridden in a wagon even if General Clinton had allowed it. She had to keep moving toward the head of the column. Her parents must be up there somewhere. Dizzy with hunger, thirst, and heat she moved through the dejected crowd. Most of the loyalists wore clothes and shoes made for city streets. Kate's own thin-soled shoes had fallen apart. She circled the mired carts and their owners who pleaded with passersby to help push them out. She avoided the frightened eyes of the women and children, as though their fear were contagious.

They had reason to be afraid. They were surrounded by hills and ravines that could hide several armies. The Provincials, as they called the Americans, were so close behind them that Kate could see their camp fires at night. If a battle started, the refugees would be caught between the two armies.

The wagons stopped, the halt spreading back along the line. Maybe the soldiers were clearing more felled logs somewhere miles ahead. People squatted in the shade of their carts or dispersed under the trees or looked for a well or asked for food in the village of Monmouth. Several of the strumpets headed for a nearby farmhouse. The boards nailed across its door and the large black Q painted on it indicated that it was quarantined for smallpox, but they didn't care. They'd broken into sealed houses before looking for anything of value.

The wagons didn't move again that day, but Kate kept putting one foot doggedly in front of the other. By nightfall she was only a mile or so from the beginning of the line, but she doubted she could find her parents in the dark. She curled up in her cloak among the roots of a maple tree. The sound of children crying, people coughing, mothers calling for strayed little ones, and the laughter of the strumpets made Kate feel lonelier. She wondered if Seth was out there in the darkness. And if so, was he as lonely and frightened as she was?

GENERAL WASHINGTON SAT ON HIS OLD WHITE CHARGER ON the crest of a hill so far forward that cannonballs began to land around him. Seth wanted to shout at him to drop back out of harm's way, but one did not give orders to the commander in chief. Seth let his breath out in a gust of relief when Major Tallmadge coaxed the general back to safety.

Seth lay on his stomach with his comrades behind the rail fence and watched the British Grenadiers form ranks on the other side of the wide ravine. The sun glinted on their brass buttons, which Seth figured must be hot enough to singe the hair off a possum by now. The men around him were drenched in sweat. They were hungry and thirsty and as ill-humored as tanyard curs. The approaching troops were the source of their ills, and they were eager to make them pay for it.

If General Charles Lee had had his way they would not have fought at all. He had dithered and vacillated and finally ordered a retreat of the troops under his command. Anthony Wayne had been beside himself with fury, and the men muttered that this was a fight, not a footrace. General Washington had arrived and demanded to know why the troops were withdrawing. "Sir," Lee replied, "these troops are not able to meet British Grenadiers." "Sir!," Washington had shouted, "they are able, and by God, they shall do it!"

He had some uncomplimentary things to add about Lee himself, and when he ordered the men to turn and take their positions again they cheered until they were hoarse. Now they were waiting, something soldiers did a lot.

"Steady, lads," Anthony Wayne shouted. "Do not fire until I give the signal."

"When will that be, sir?" Seth called out.

"When you see your freckles reflected in their buttons, Corporal."

The Americans' cannons on the hill behind Seth opened fire with a roar that vibrated his teeth. The Grenadiers marched into the ravine with heads bowed and shoulders hunched, as though leaning into a heavy rain. Artillery shot opened gaps in their lines, but they moved to fill them, and they kept coming. Like wheat mowed down, Seth thought.

He watched them from somewhere outside his body. He did not think of them as men like himself, with aspirations in their hearts and portraits of loved ones in their pockets. He concentrated not on the right or wrong of killing but on the mechanics of it. The Pennsylvanians' rifles had better range, but the British could load their muskets twice as fast. That meant they could keep more lead in the air. Seth and the others had to time their volleys well.

Seth selected his mark, a brawny fellow running directly at him. As though sighting on a buck, he aimed for the spot above and to the left of where his white straps crossed at his chest. He waited. And waited.

The Grenadiers looked about to overrun their position before General Wayne lowered his sword. Seth steadied his barrel on a rock and squeezed the trigger, but the smoke from the weapons and the cannons rolled out like a fog and he could not see if his man fell or not. The Grenadiers retreated from the scathing fire, but they regrouped. They charged and withdrew again, with scores of their number falling.

All day, through the heat and the suffocating fumes, slipping in blood, Seth and his comrades moved from position to position. They did it with at least some of the precision and discipline that Baron von Steuben had taught them, but the world seemed to come apart around them. Seth's rifle became too hot to touch, and he could not coax even a drop of water from his canteen. His eyes stung. His throat burned.

When Mrs. Hayes appeared toting a pail of water Seth thought she was the prettiest sight he had ever seen. She moved among the men, oblivious to the bullets and the shells. As the afternoon lengthened the men started calling her Molly Pitcher. They did not notice that the water had a pink tinge from the dead fallen in the creek.

Waves of red coats and blue ones swept across the rolling countryside, fragmenting, scattering, coalescing again. As the American troops advanced more and more bodies littered the fields, ravines, and hillsides. Over the shouting and the musket fire the artillery thundered without ceasing. Seth had not imagined that war would be so loud and so disorderly.

He slipped into the pattern of survival: take cover, prime, load, aim, fire. He did not contemplate the ability of the mind to transform carnage into commonplace. As the day's light began to dim he used a pile of enemy dead as a shield. He rested his rifle barrel across the blood-soaked thigh of the corpse on top, avoiding the wound in the man's abdomen.

He was about to fire when the corpse turned its head and said, "How fare you, Seth?"

Seth jumped, sending the bullet into the tree canopy at the field's edge. "Is that you, James?"

"For the time being." The young ensign who had served as Major André's aide in Philadelphia coughed, then moaned at the pain it caused him. He had the sort of wound that could take an eternity to kill a man.

"It will be dark soon." Seth remembered that the lad had been sweet on Kate. He wished he had water to give him. "When the fighting stops the littermen will come for you."

"The butcher's bill will be dear this day." The ensign tried to smile. He had been the one to settle accounts with Seth's mother each month for the food that her British lodgers ate, but pork chops and rump roasts weren't the sort of butchery he meant.

"Ay, that it will."

"We wondered where you'd gone. Captain André thought you might have turned rebel."

"A man must fight for his country."

"England is your country."

Seth realized there was no sense in arguing with a man who was as good as dead, or as bad as dead. "I'll send the littermen for thee, friend." He laid a hand on James's forehead. "May God protect thee."

Darkness caught the two armies on opposite sides of a wide gorge. The cannons stilled, leaving a ringing in Seth's head that was almost as loud. He found five or six of his comrades squatting around a small fire. He knew them only because he heard Spitz's unmistakeable accent. Their faces were black with powder. Their clothes were filthy and torn and blood soaked.

"Gather grass, Seth," Spitz said. He was within arm's reach, but his voice sounded far away and hollow.

"Why?" Seth wondered if that was his own voice.

"Make a bed for yourself, else the human vultures mistake you for wounded and plunder your pockets while you sleep."

Seth hadn't the energy to answer, much less gather the makings of a bed. He dropped to his knees, then fell flat out in a clump of grass that had survived the artillery's harrowing fire.

The moon's light illuminated the heaps of dead around him. He fell asleep with the groans and screams of the wounded men and horses competing with the ringing in his ears. He did not see the furtive shapes of men and women skuttling from body to body, yanking off shoes and stockings, rifling clothing, taking watches and buttons.

He did not see General Washington wrap himself in his cloak and, surrounded by his aides and his life guard, lie down to sleep on the same blood-soaked field. Seth whispered thanks to God for keeping him alive, and then he floated into sleep's abyss like a hawk on a warm current of air.

He did not hear the screams of the wounded. He did not see his comrades roast three rats in the brass curaise of a dead British Grenadier. He did not hear the sizzle of grease or smell the tantalizing aroma.

Fifteen

Wherein Old Put patters; George Washington gets the finger;
Benjamin Tallmadge takes on Mad Anthony

A BLACKSMITH HAD REINFORCED THE OAK FRAME OF GENERAL
Israel Putnam's canvas chair with iron bands, but under Old Put's bulk it
sagged like a basket full of cannonballs. It protested if he even winked, and
Old Put was as fond of winking as he was of pickled pigs' feet and tipsy
parson—layers of brandy-soaked sponge cake topped with almonds, cus-
tard, and whipped cream. He wore his usual summer uniform, a pair of
worn leather riding knee-breeches and a soiled linen shirt under a sleeveless waistcoat with long tails that parted company around the plateau of his
thighs.

"So there I was, tied to a stake with the painted savages heaping kindling at my feet. I'll tell you, boys, my future looked mighty bright . . ." He
winked at the officers lounging in the shade of his faded canvas awning.
". . . for there's nothing brighter than a bonfire."

The savages must have had a powerful long rope, Benjamin thought, to
encompass Old Put.

He knew General Putnam would chase his almost-burned-at-the-stake
story with his tale of being shipwrecked off the coast of Cuba. After that
he would tell of the Tory spy who had tried to assassinate him, and he
would recite his reply to General Howe's plea to spare the man's life. Old

Put knew that Lieutenant Nathan Hale had been Benjamin's friend. He told Benjamin that when he composed his answer to Howe he wrote Nathaniel instead of the aspiring assassin's real name. He did it to remind General Howe of his summary execution of Hale to fifes playing "The Rogue's March." He did it to protest Howe's letting the lad dangle from the apple tree for three days.

> Sir;
> Nathaniel Palmer, a lieutenant in your king's service, was taken in my camp as a spy. He was tried as a spy. He was condemned as a spy, and you may rest assured, Sir, he shall be hanged as a spy.
>
> I have the honor to be Israel Putnam.

Putnam said he took particular satisfaction in adding the postscript. "Afternoon. He is hanged."

Nathan. The name meant "Gift of God."

The Lord giveth, Benjamin thought, and the Lord taketh away.

Hardly a day went by that Benjamin didn't think about Nathan. In their letters they had referred to each other as Damon and Phintias, faithful friends two thousand years old. On the rare occasions that Benjamin received mail he still looked for his friend's familiar hand. In countless dreams he saw Nathan standing at the gallows with no one to comfort him.

Benjamin wished he could have thundered in with a regiment of dragoons, cut the rope around his friend's neck, pulled him up onto his horse, and ridden away. He wished he could at least have stood there with him, one caring heart in that hostile crowd, but *"Dis aliter visum"* as Nathan would say. "The gods saw otherwise."

Benjamin also wished he could find Nathan's executioner, Provost Marshal William Cunningham, the man who had taunted Hale on the gallows. Benjamin wanted to throttle the life out of him, but he had learned that though vengeance may be sweet, it was not effective. General Putnam's execution of the Tory assassin should have eased Benjamin's grief, but it didn't. In the first place the condemned man's wife had come with their young children to plead for his life. Putnam refused to commute the sentence, but

Benjamin had donated his pay and collected money for her from some of the other officers. He had found a farmer who would carry her husband's body home in the cart that hauled cabbages to market.

Besides, the man's death could not bring Benjamin's friend back, nor even change the manner of his execution. The British had treated Nathan worse than a stray dog. They would have dignified a dog's death by shooting him, not by dangling him from a tree. Benjamin only knew of Nathan's fate because a gallant British officer had come under a flag of truce to tell the Americans that the young lieutenant had met death valiantly. He had relayed Nathan's last words. "I only regret that I have but one life to lose for my country." Nathan was twenty-one years old.

Old Put was an antidote for sadness, though. When Putnam got himself outside of enough brandy to founder a dinghy he would lead the officers in a rendition of "Maggie Lauder." He particularly liked to bellow out the lines, "Jog on your gate, ye blatherskate, my name is Maggie Lauder." Old Put sang it with a Scottish brogue that would fool anyone who couldn't trace his lineage to one of William Wallace's spearmen presenting his bare backside to the Earl of Surrey on a misty September morn in 1297 Anno Domini.

While Ben waited for the musical interlude of Old Put's show he tried to imagine Israel Putnam thin. He couldn't do it. He tried to imagine Israel Putnam young. He couldn't do that either. Benjamin was twenty-four, born in 1754. That was the year Putnam, along with the young lieutenant George Washington, joined the British army to fight the French and their Indian allies. Putnam had been at least forty then.

Benjamin was relieved when a corporal came to fetch him. He went out into the heat of a sun determined to stew his brains inside his own brass dragoon's helmet. He walked through a camp that had the good-humored air of victory, even though the Americans had not really won this fight.

Their opponents had sneaked away in the night. According to local farmers, they had headed for Sandy Hook to board the ships that Black Dick Howe had waiting there. The American soldiers were already reciting a couplet in honor of the British army's loyalist followers.

The Tories with their brats and wives
Have fled to save their wretched lives.

Ben knew that the British high command would soon board ship. They would pull their chairs up to a table sagging with roasts and meat pies. They would drink to each other's health and the king's.

The American ranks didn't care though. Soldiers splashed naked in the river while they washed their clothes. Others cleaned their weapons, or read the letters and newspapers they had found in the British packs left behind in their owners' flight. Some cooked the rations of salted beef and dried peas that Washington had ordered cached along the route two weeks before. The local farmers had freshly butchered pork to sell, but the soldiers weren't buying any. They could not be sure that their fallen comrades had not provided the pigs with their last meal.

Benjamin noticed more than the usual number of trollops. Black Dick must not have had enough room on his transports for them, and they were drifting back to the only other plentiful supply of customers. As Anthony Wayne angled over to walk alongside Benjamin he nodded toward them.

"To the victors go the soiled."

"I would wager that full half are informants in the pay of the King."

Wayne shrugged his meaty shoulders. "The Devil himself can't manage doxies." He spoke with some authority on that subject. His imposing proportions and rogue's eyes attracted doxies and decent women alike. He always made Benjamin feel tongue-tied and pocket-sized.

Wayne was in a jovial mood. Many more British had been killed, wounded, and captured than Americans, not to mention the six hundred or more Germans who had deserted. "Ah, Tallmadge, we can tell the Philadelphia ladies that the pretty Redcoats, the knights of the Burning Mountain and the Blended Rose, have humbled themselves on the plains of Monmouth."

"The knights of the Burning Mountain and the Blended Rose are tom fools and damned fools, and that's the only difference between them."

Benjamin couldn't imagine Old Put and the other American officers spending a king's ransom to dress like Ali Baba, devour bushel baskets of roasted pigeon tongues, and challenge each other to jousts. He had long since stopped thinking of himself as British, but the silliness of André's *Mischianza* proved that the gulf between the mother country and America had become much wider than that cod pond called the Atlantic Ocean.

Corporal Seth Darby approached and saluted. "Colonel Wayne, sir, I have set up the quoits pitch. I used tent pegs for the hobs. I couldn't find the box of quoits in the baggage wagon, but we have horseshoes."

"So, my boy, are you prepared to lose that shilling I let you win last week?"

"Yes, sir."

"Then let's have a go." Wayne put one arm around Seth's shoulder and gestured with the other as the two of them walked away. They were both built along the same lines, and if Benjamin hadn't known better, he would have assumed they were father and son.

Benjamin continued on to field headquarters. Washington's marquee tent always reassured him. It signified order, dignity, and the attention to detail that in war meant life instead of death. Its scalloped awning was as wide and deep as the tent itself. Washington's big oak table and chair sat on the planks laid out as a floor under it. The inkpots, quills, quires of paper, and jars of sand for blotting the wet ink were all precisely placed on the table, along with tins of tobacco, smoking tools, and slender ember tongs for pipe lighting. The travel trunks of documents and the canvas folding stools for his aides were always set in the same positions.

Washington's canvas headquarters reminded Benjamin of the Presbyterian church on Setauket's main square. Like the church, and like Washington himself, it was bigger than everything around it. It was predictable, reliable, and connected to a higher authority. The tent reassured Benjamin that the man who occupied it was more competent than most.

Washington sat like the calm eye in the storm's center as officers, petitioners, and couriers milled around him. Benjamin saluted. The general led Benjamin inside and dropped the canvas door closed behind them. Ben labored to draw breath in the musty heat, but Washington didn't seem to notice it. He gestured to one of the stools and Benjamin perched errect on it, at attention even while sitting.

The general held out an ornately carved snuff box. "A present from our French allies." The portrait on the lid was of Benjamin Franklin with his unpowdered gray hair, red button of a nose, and mangy fur hat. Franklin's image adorned just about everything French, but Washington probably didn't mind. Mon Papa, as the Parisian women call Doctor Franklin, had cajoled their reluctant government into supporting the American cause.

Washington settled into an oversized morris chair and let his long legs sprawl with the polished toes of his black, knee-high boots pointed outward. He was a man born to wear a soldier's uniform. He wasn't just taller than everyone else, he was well proportioned and solidly built. His white leather breeches and long-tailed blue coat with its gilt braid and scarlet turnbacks fit him perfectly. He had weathered the calumny and plots of ambitious men like General Charles Lee, and his refusal to admit defeat in the face of the most overwhelming odds awed Benjamin.

Washington picked up a pair of wooden disks from the table. A length of string was wound on the short dowel that connected them. He put the loop at the end of the string around his middle finger and dropped the disks over the side of the chair. They plummeted toward the floor, but with a flick of his wrist he coaxed them back up the string to nestle in the palm of his hand.

"It's very calming." When Washington smiled, his false teeth made his cheeks bulge and rumple. "Lafayette gave it to me. The French call it *l'incroyable*."

"The incredible," said Benjamin.

"Yes."

Washington had had leisure time this morning for more than the *incroyable*. He had had time to sit with a conical metal mask over his face while his hair dresser powdered his sorrel-colored mane. He had tied it into a queue and put a black velvet bag over it so the powder wouldn't soil the general's collar.

Old smallpox scars pitted Washington's long, full face. His small, pale blue eyes were set deep under his high forehead, and curved folds of bruised-colored skin hung under them like the canvas satchels the soldiers carried. Ben imagined the commander in chief carrying his woes and tribulations in those bags under his eyes.

God knows, Benjamin thought, he has had woes and tribulations a-plenty.

While Benjamin waited for Washington to speak he studied his face. He was looking for clues to his ability to prevail under conditions that would defeat other men. Ben remembered the scrap of paper he had seen on the floor of the general's tent in the darkest days at Valley Forge. He had written three words: "Victory or death." Benjamin knew that while he and the other company-grade officers would likely be pardoned if they lost the war, Washington, the arch-rebel, would most certainly hang.

Washington poured them each a glass of hard cider laced with the gentle euphoria of fermented apples. "Mrs. Washington asks me to inquire after your family." His voice was mellow for such a big man and softened further by that genteel Virginia drawl, a gift from his African slaves.

"My father's last letter from Setauket spoke of the family's good health," Benjamin said, "But they continue to suffer the inconveniences and indignities of the British regulars quartered among them." Ben nodded to the small portrait of Martha Washington on the table. "Please extend to your good lady my gratitude for her kind concern, and my fervent wish that she remain in perfect health."

Benjamin wanted to add "and safety," but didn't. No sense reminding the general about the rumors of plots to kidnap Martha. Benjamin didn't believe them anyway. William Howe's replacement, Sir Henry Clinton, was a harder man than his predecessor, but surely he would not condone hostile action against a woman.

Benjamin remembered a talk Martha had had with the officers before this battle. "I hope you will all stand firm," she had said. "I know that George will." Benjamin tried to imagine calling the commander in chief "George."

"I will convey your sentiments." Washington paused, and Benjamin thought he could guess what was on his mind.

"Have they found it, sir?"

"No." Washington uncorked a wide-mouthed jar. "A courier brought this from Philadelphia. We're looking for the man who left it behind."

Ben caught a whiff of the contents. "Rum?"

Washington used a pair of ember tongs to lift out something cylindrical. It ended in a fingernail with a half moon of black dirt underneath it.

"Is that the first joint of a finger?"

"It is." Washington replaced the finger and rotated the jar so the joint swirled with the rum. "The box that held the document was nailed to a large table. It had a second lid with holes that resembled finger grips. It was designed so that when the thief picked the lock he inserted his fingers into the holes to raise the lid. That triggered a spring that released a pair of steel jaws. They cut through one finger, and I would wager they mangled the others."

"But he obtained what he was after anyway."

"He did. There was so much confusion when Congress moved every-thing from Lancaster back to Philadelphia, they don't even know where or when it was stolen." Washington sighed. "No doubt General Clinton will use it for propaganda on the fourth of July."

"That's five days from now."

Washington nodded.

"But there are other copies."

"This one is special."

Washington took the set of hippo teeth and elephant ivory from his mouth and set it on the desk. He put a hickory nut between the teeth, and pounded it sharply with his fist to crack it. It was the only sign Ben had ever been able to detect that he was agitated.

"We have a man among them who might know what happened to it. He'll be waiting at the Cock and Bull tavern near Sandy Hook. We need someone to communicate with him. It is not a dangerous enterprise. The territory is ours, so he must only fool the local Tories who think our man is one of them."

"I recommend Corporal Darby."

"The Quaker lad? Capital. Recruit him and report to me."

"Yes, sir."

"And tell the boy not to confide in anyone. Someone in camp is passing intelligence to the British command."

"Do you have any suspicions as to who it is?"

"From the quality of the intelligence we think he's an officer, and a high-ranking one." Washington leaned closer and lowered his voice. "I have something else to ask you, Benjamin."

"Yes, sir."

"Think of those you know who could be of use to us when we reach White Plains. They should be persons who have never taken an active part in this conflict and would be least liable to suspicion."

"You mean to act as intelligencers, sir?"

"Yes. It is best that they have lived among the Tories and so won't be suspected by them. I will not countenance another tragedy like the one that befell Lieutenant Hale."

"We shall need hard money to pay them, sir."

"You shall have it."

Benjamin went to look for the quoits pitch and General Wayne. He anticipated an argument about sending the Darby boy out as a spy again, and Wayne could turn into a stone wall when he wanted to. It was one thing to send Seth into Philadelphia, the town where he had grown up. It was quite another to dispatch him to New Jersey.

Ben knew that Seth would be willing. He remembered what the boy once had told him. "I would gladly give up everything for the sake of my country."

The boy had the elements of a fine agent. Benjamin would do everything he could to protect him. He liked Seth almost as much as Anthony Wayne did. He had liked Seth's sister too. He suspected that her red hair made being one of the blessed meek a difficult task for her. He would have wagered a month's pay that in spite of those ingenuous blue-green eyes, she had had mettle. What a pity typhus had taken her.

Sixteen

Wherein Kate looks for Seth among the fallen and loses something
that does not belong to her; a friend is not what she seems

KATE POKED HER NOSE OUT OF HER CLOAK AND SNEEZED. IN spite of the heat, she had curled up inside the cloak and wrapped it around her head to keep the rats from eating her ears while she slept. The rats had reason to be ravenous. Foragers had left nothing in the root cellar except the old turnip she had eaten the night before. But it had sheltered her from the ghoulies and ghosties, long leggitie beasties, and the things that go bump in the night that Cook had always warned about.

Kate pushed open the wooden trapdoor set into the hillside. In the pale dawn light she could see that the British army had moved out. They had left the usual litter of blackened cookfires, white clay tobacco pipes, beer bottles, beef bones, vegetable parings, and rags.

Kate hadn't found her parents or Cook, but she had met family friends who said the British had ships waiting off Sandy Hook to take them to New York. She decided to stay behind and look for Seth. He might still be lying hurt where the big guns had roared incessantly the day before. If she didn't find him there she would look for him at the American camp.

Kate drank at the creek, washed her face, and scrubbed her teeth with her finger. She rinsed out a bottle, filled it with water, and used a rag as a stopper. She stuffed it into the basket pack that she still carried.

Hundreds of crows circled beyond a nearby hill. She headed for it, trying on discarded shoes as she went. She found two that were serviceable. One was black and one was brown, but she put them on.

She reached the crest and gasped. The countryside below was strewn with broken equipment and the bodies of men and horses. Cries for water mixed with the cawing of the crows. Kate walked downhill into the lingering odor of gunpowder and headed for the nearest blue-coated body. When she tripped over a severed arm she screamed and ran, but as the morning lengthened she passed so many mangled bodies and their disconnected parts that they became part of the landscape. What she could not get used to was the sight of the crows, dogs, and pigs eating them.

She saw a familiar figure going through the dead soldiers' pockets. He was the resurrectionist who had come looking for John André in Philadelphia in what seemed another lifetime. His lopsided face made him unmistakeable, but now part of a finger on his right hand was missing. The first joints of the two fingers next to it bent at ninety degree angles.

"Excuse me."

He jumped and scowled. Kate realized that he didn't recognize her.

"I'm looking for my brother."

"God go with you then."

"Have you seen a red-haired boy?"

"I don't remark their faces." He went back to work, moving efficiently from one body to another.

Kate continued her search. Whenever she saw litter bearers carrying wounded on the doors they used as stretchers, she asked about Seth, but no one had seen him. She found abandoned canteens and used them to carry water to those still alive. She closed the eyes of the men who had died staring at eternity. She prayed for all of them.

An old man pushing a barrow said he was looking for his son, but he found a neighbor's boy instead. He knelt beside him.

"He was a good lad." He looked up at Kate. "As agile as an otter."

Kate helped him lift the soldier's body into the barrow. The old man shared his bread and cheese with her, then he called God's blessings on her and trundled the barrow away.

By mid-afternoon Kate had wandered to the far edge of the battlefield and she heard one of the bodies call for his mother. The soldier had been stripped of everything but his shirt and trousers, and a wound just above his belt had turned them crimson. He was the ensign who had lived in her house. Kate crouched to offer him water.

"James, it's me. Kate Darby."

"Miss Kate." He tried to smile. "Fancy meeting you here."

"I shall find help for thee." She shouted at a pair of soldiers carrying a door that served as a makeshift stretcher.

"I saw your brother, Miss Kate," James murmured.

"When?"

"A very long time ago. Yesterday, I think."

The two litter bearers gave the ensign a glance and started off again.

Kate ran after them. "You cannot leave him here."

"Can you cipher, miss? Do you know your numbers?"

"Yes."

"Then cipher this. There are thirty-two of us, which means we can carry sixteen wounded men at a time. To go to the village and return requires most of an hour. We must save the ones who might live. Besides he looks like a bloodyback to me."

James shivered. "Do not leave me, Kate."

"I won't." Kate found a blanket and draped it over him.

He tapped his chest, and from under his shirt she retrieved a bloody bible and a packet wrapped in leather and tied with a scarlet cord.

"Twenty-third psalm please, Kate."

The book was too ruined to read, but Kate knew the psalm. She held his cold hand while she recited it. He moved his lips, repeating it silently.

The Lord is my shepherd, I shall not want.
He maketh me to lie down in green pastures,
He leadeth me beside the still waters.
He restoreth my soul.

She had reached "Thou preparest a table before me in the presence of mine enemies," when life's last ember died in his eyes. She closed his eyelids with the palm of her hand while she finished the psalm.

" 'Surely goodness and mercy shall follow me all the days of my life: and I shall dwell in the house of the Lord forever.' "

When she stood up the packet fell from her lap. It probably contained letters to his family. Seth said that officers were preferred targets and they went into battle expecting to die. Many of them wrote letters to loved ones and left their valuables with friends at the rear so they wouldn't be stolen from their bodies. Kate put the packet into her basket. She would do her best to see that it reached his people.

When night fell she followed the litter bearers to the village of Monmouth. The doors had been pulled off the abandoned cottages to serve as stretchers and through the openings came the moans and cries of the wounded. They were mostly British soldiers left behind, but Kate went from house to house searching for Seth. One cottage had the door left on with a bar across it and a soldier guarding it. A small lantern threw light along the ridgeline of his remarkably large, sharp nose.

"I'm looking for my brother, Seth Darby," Kate said. "He's with the Second Pennsylvania."

"I don't know him, miss, but I can tell you he ain't in there." He rapped on the door with his musket butt and women's cries started up inside.

"Who is that?"

"Whores with the smallpox. The bloodybacks sent them here to infect us." He pointed his chin toward a building on a rise near the village square. "Look for your kin in the meeting house over yonder. The surgeon's at work there."

"God keep you." Kate was so weary that she wanted to go to sleep in the dust of the lane, but she knew the sentry would order her to move on.

Move on. She had been moving on for months. She wondered if she would ever be able to stop moving on.

She wanted to weep for the dead and the maimed and for the old man searching for his son, but she was too tired. She wanted to weep for Seth and for her parents, wherever they might be, and for Cook and Lizzie. She wanted to weep for her home burned to rubble and the good life that was gone. As for the women locked inside this house, Kate was immune to the pox, so she could at least bring them food and water in the morning.

The meeting house's open doorway glowed a golden welcome of lantern light. At first glance it looked like a normal church, filled with rows of pews flanking a center aisle. Each pew was partitioned off into a chest-high, white-washed booth with a gate to allow entrance. At the front of the room a pulpit large enough to hold half a dozen preachers soared above the congregation. Today the congregation consisted of the wounded and the dying, and they were not suffering in silence. The pews were covered with blood. The floor was awash in filth and heaped with severed arms and legs.

The surgeon had placed a window shutter across the tops of the narrow stalls to serve as an operating table. Glistening with sweat he stood in the aisle next to it while his assistant helped him strap down a screaming patient. Kate stood in the doorway, stunned by the church's resemblance to the butchers' shambles in the markethouse in Philadelphia. She wanted to leave, but what if Seth were here?

"We've no more rum. Bite down on this." The assistant put a cloth-covered peg into the man's mouth and at least the screaming stopped. He muttered, "No more thongs for the arteries."

"No time to tie them off anyway."

The assistant rotated the stick that tightened the leather tourniquet around the man's thigh, then leaned across the leg to hold it steady. The surgeon honed a knife like the one Cook used to separate the rump roast from the sirloin. With the knife poised above the leg he glanced at Kate.

"You there, turn that sandglass over." He nodded at a small hourglass sitting on a shelf.

Kate upended it. The surgeon sliced into the leg as the grains of sand jostled through the narrow opening of the glass. The soldier was young and his heart was strong. In spite of the tourniquet it kept pumping blood out to his hinterlands. The heart's proprietor, mercifully, fainted.

The surgeon beckoned. "Come here, miss, and hold the muscles out of the way. And pinch off the arteries while you're about it."

"But . . ."

"Hurry!"

Kate stared at the neatly bundled muscles and the red and blue cording of artery and veins. The blood was the deepest crimson she had ever seen, and so beautiful that it calmed her. Peggy Shippen, she thought, would covet a dress this color.

She shoved her fingers into the cut and with her palm pushed the flesh like sausage meat back into its casing of skin. With her other hand she pinched the vein and artery between her thumb and fingers. When the surgeon reached the femur, he held the knife in his teeth, and started sawing. Kate recited the Lord's Prayer to cover the rasp and scrape of metal on bone.

The surgeon cut through the femur and tossed the saw onto the blood-soaked pew. He glanced at the hourglass.

"Less than three minutes!" He threw the leg over his shoulder and wiped the knife and his hands on his bloody apron.

The assistant took the glowing bayonet from the coals and pressed it against the wound. The smell of seared flesh filled the church. Kate tore a strip from her filthy petticoat to use as a bandage.

After Kate had helped with the last screaming soldier she climbed the steps to the high pulpit. She wrapped herself in her cloak and slept with her head pillowed on her arm. For two days she brought water, changed dressings, and sewed up wounds as though mending torn shirts. She carried food and water to the women locked in quarantine, but it took all her courage to open the door. She had gone with her mother to the poorhouses and hospitals in Philadelphia, but she had never seen so many sores squirming with maggots.

When soldiers delivered rations to the church Kate asked if they had seen Seth. No one had. On the third day she went looking for the Pennsylvania Line. She found them packing their rucksacks.

"Where are you going?" she asked Spitz.

"To chase the bloodybacks to New York."

"Where is my brother?"

The men looked at each other. If Kate had been more familiar with duplicity she would have recognized it in their eyes.

"Foraging."

"Yah," Spitz agreed. "He brings cows."

"When will he come back?"

No one knew.

"We thought you died," one said.

"Not yet. Where is the commissary officer?"

"T'other side of that gully."

The commissary officer was a harried man with a face like a pine board, rough cut and left to weather. He was in no mood for shabby, skinny, red-headed girls with questions.

"I sent out no foraging party."

"Are you certain?"

Instead of an answer he brushed past her, shouting as he went. "Hell and confusion! Have a care with that flour, you loggerheads."

Kate had run out of ideas. She stood like a signpost pointing nowhere in the middle of a busy crossroads until a runaway barrel of salted beef forced her into motion. She dodged it and walked to the shade of a nearby apple orchard.

The orchard was occupied by two men smoking their clay pipes and eluding the attention of anyone who might require work of them. One of them was tall and stooped and the other short.

"God keep thee." Kate started to walk around them, but they got to their feet and stood in her path.

"Here's a bit of laced mutton."

The stocky one tugged on her skirt. "Show us your commodity, miss."

"Leave off." Kate tried to pull away from him.

"Give us a kiss."

Fear paralyzed Kate. No one had ever laid hands on her before. She almost cried with relief when a women approached.

"Shame on you, Jedekiah."

Kate had seen her often at the encampment at Valley Forge. She had wandered among the huts selling sewing notions to the soldiers.

"Don't meddle in someone else's business, Nan."

"I shall tell General Putnam you stole that pair of shoes. You know they hang thieves."

"I'll forswear it."

Nan set her basket down. She took a razor from among the goods in it and opened the blade out from the handle, as though intending to demonstrate it to a prospective buyer. Instead she grabbed the short one's left ear and yanked it taut. She held the blade above the crevice where it connected to his scalp. He tried to jerk away, but the harder he pulled the more his ear pained him. He wasn't the brightest wick, but he could see that if he tried to grab the razor from her, he would slice his hand open.

"We was only having a bit of sport."

"Well, you've had your sport. Now get you gone."

When they had slunk off, Nan returned the blade to her basket. "Are you alright?"

"Yes." Kate put her skirts back in order. "Would you have cut his ear off?"

"Of course."

Nan had been a beekeeper and a schoolmistress before she began selling buttons and thread to the soldiers. She was what Cook would call a cool customer. Kate had never heard her raise her voice in anger, not even today. The crown of her straw bonnet reached as high as Kate's nose. Her clothes were old, but clean and neatly mended. As far as Kate could tell, nothing ruffled her. Even her hair stayed tucked into its knot at the nape of her neck.

"I'm looking for my brother, Seth. Have you seen him?"

"No, but I am sure God has kept him safe."

Nan took Kate to the inn called the Bag O' Nails. Her small room under the eaves was hot as a bread oven. Nan rummaged in a battered wicker trunk and pulled out a skirt, apron, bodice, petticoat, and sleeveless waistcoat. They were threadbare but clean.

"These should fit, though you're taller than I and too thin by half."

"I cannot take your clothes."

"Don't be a goose." Nan waved a hand at her, as though to shoo her into them. While Kate put them on, Nan rolled her filthy clothes into the bodice and tied the sleeves. "The tavern's laundress can wash these."

"But I have no money."

"Don't fret yourself. I shall give her six pence."

When Kate had dressed, Nan took her downstairs to the taproom and called for turkey hash, beaten biscuits, cheese, Indian pudding, and a tumbler of table beer. Kate ate like a starved bear. She mopped up the last of the hash with a bit of bread.

"You may share my bed tonight," Nan said. "In the morning you can decide what you want to do."

A full stomach, a roof, a bed, kindness, and the hum of taproom conversation—they were all too much for Kate. She started to shake, and then to cry. Nan put an arm around her. Kate sobbed as if tears could sluice away loneliness and despair.

"There, there." Nan stroked her hair. "I'll help you look for your brother."

"No one knows where he's gone. Better that I search for my parents in New York."

"You plan to go among the British then?"

"I do not hold with one side or the other. I want only to be with my family again."

Kate reached into her pack and pulled out the papers tied in their leather wrapping. "I must deliver these letters to the family of a British soldier killed in battle."

"Did you read them?"

Kate was mortified at the thought. "Of course not. I shall deliver them to an officer."

"Did you know him?"

"James Stuart. He was quartered at our house." Kate put the packet away again. "He served as aide to John André."

When Kate went upstairs again she fell onto the bed and slept until Nan woke her. After a breakfast of porridge and warm milk Nan put Kate's clean clothes in the pack, along with a loaf of bread and some boiled eggs and dried beef. Then she walked with Kate to the crossroad to make sure she took the right path to Sandy Hook.

"You should reach Colt's Neck by afternoon. And who will you ask for there?"

"Amos Garrett, the carpenter."

"Hold out your hand."

Nan laid a hand-wrought, rose-head nail in her palm and closed her fingers around it. "Give Amos this token and say Nan Baker sent you. His goodwife will feed you and tell you who will shelter you in the next village.

"Then you do not hate me for going to the British?"

"Who could hate you, dear child?" Nan kissed her on the cheek. "God go with you, Kate."

Kate adjusted her pack and set out for the spit of land called Sandy Hook thirty miles away. The day was hot. Thick red dust swirled and rose under her feet, but the birds were singing. The sky pulsed a dazzling blue, and no dead bodies lay about. When Kate reached the first curve she turned and waved to Nan. Nan waved back.

As for getting to New York from Sandy Hook, Kate decided not to worry about how she would cross the water until she came to it.

NAN JUMPED DOWN FROM THE CART FULL OF CORN FOR THE
American army bivouacked at Brunswick, New Jersey. She shook the dust
from her skirts and went in search of Colonel Carlisle of the Seventh Pennsylvania Foot. She found him shouting at his young servant.

Nan waited until Carlisle stopped for breath and then scratched on the
canvas. "Colonel, I hear you are in need of buttons."

Carlisle planted a boot on the boy's backside and sent him flying past
Nan. He turned to scowl at her, but Nan was not intimidated. She untied a
calico kerchief to reveal the half dozen brass buttons inside. Carlisle pulled
a similar cloth from his coat and laid it next to hers. Both had been torn in
half, and the flowered pattern of the two matched.

Carlisle leaned out of the tent's door and looked around. He lowered his
voice. "What have you for me?"

"An item worth at least ten guineas." Nan produced the packet, untied
the cord, unfolded the sheepskin and then a wrapping of oiled cloth to reveal the papers inside.

"It's of no use militarily." Colonel Carlisle's smile lacked both warmth
and humor. "But I would say for propaganda value alone it is worth ten
guineas."

Seventeen

Wherein Kate finds Amos Garrett at the end of a rope;
Cook spoils the wroth; Benjamin Tallmadge parts the waters

LOCATING AMOS GARRETT IN COLT'S NECK WOULD HAVE BEEN easy had this not been both market day and the fourth of July. The village square teemed with farm folk and the livestock and poultry they'd been able to hide from the British when the army marched through almost a week earlier. Women hawked homemade sweets, small flags, and cockades of red, white, and blue ribbon.

A boy kept up an incessant banging on a drum, and dogs howled accompaniment for a fifer. The drum, fife, and dog drew attention to a sergeant who had erected a sign, written on a board with charcoal. It invited all patriots to volunteer for the Continental Army.

He was doing a brisk business. The retreating British soldiers had turned plundering into a form of entertainment. They had burned houses and broken furniture and windows. They had destroyed crops and ravaged more than a few women. People were eager for a chance to shoot at them.

A dozen men were raising a forty-foot-long Liberty Pole on the dusty green, while a hundred more shouted advice. The task required a lot of shouting and swearing, because the pole swayed one way and then another and the guy ropes tangled with the banners, ribbons, and bunting tied to it.

Amos Garrett was a carpenter and strong enough to handle a line without help from anyone. He wore hobnailed shoes, faded blue worsted stockings, patched leather breeches, and a battered felt hat. His sweat-soaked shirt was woven of linen and milkweed floss spun together. He had rolled the sleeves up over the bulge of his biceps.

When the men got the pole planted they headed for the barrel of corn liquor to celebrate. Kate knew better than to get between them and the barrel, so she waited for a chance to speak to Garrett. He unrolled a large piece of parchment and held it up for the others to see. It was a caricature of a man with a huge nose and ears sticking out like tree fungi. Garrett read it aloud, his voiced sharp with disapproval.

" 'Two hundred guineas reward offered for a certain William Livingston, a lawless usurper and incorrigible rebel.' "

The men roared in protest. William Livingston may not have been handsome, but he was the governor of New Jersey and a patriot. The locals might ridicule him, but a Tory did not have that privilege.

" 'If his whole person cannot be brought in, half the sum above specified will be paid as bounty for his ears and nose, which are too remarkable to be mistaken.' "

Everyone laughed. The noses and ears of vermin like wolves and foxes earned a bounty.

"This is the doing of that miscreant James Moody, may God damn him." In a rage Garrett crumpled the paper.

Kate tugged at Garrett's sleeve. "Amos Garrett?"

"Yes?"

Kate held out the nail. "Nan Baker bade me show you this."

Garrett went pale along the rocky coastline of his jaw, and Kate thought it odd that a nail could so afright a carpenter.

"Put that away." He grabbed Kate's arm in a vise grip and hustled her through the merriment to a cottage on the outskirts of the village. White oak timbers were stacked and drying in the shade of an elm tree. A broken lathe stood like a crippled sentry nearby. Wood shavings carpeted the dooryard.

When Kate walked into the kitchen Goodwife Garrett was testing the temperature of the brick oven built into the hearth by holding her hand inside and counting to ten. Kate took off her basket and set it on the floor. She rubbed her shoulders where the straps had cut into them.

Garrett whirled his wife around, then danced a jig step as he smoothed the crumpled paper out on the table.

"The lad is at it again."

"James Moody?" Goodwife Garrett wiped her hands on her apron. When she saw the caricature she threw her head back and laughed. "May God bless him."

"And here is a loyal friend to the king, sent by Nan Baker."

Goodwife Garrett threw her plump arms around Kate and smothered her in a floury embrace. Kate sneezed and stood dazed while they peppered her with questions. How fared their dear friend Nan? When would the British return and wrest the Jerseys from the wretches who had turned on their sovereign like tanyard curs? Did Kate have any intelligence for them to pass along to General Clinton? Did she know of any able-bodied men who wanted to join the secret loyalist militia that Amos was forming?

When Kate told them that she only wanted to find her family in New York, they clucked in sympathy. They piled food in front of her. They drank toasts to the health of King George and General Clinton, and confusion to Congress and George Washington. They gave her the name of a family that might be able to find a boat to take her to New York. With tears and earnest wishes that the King's men prevail and order be restored soon, they bid her farewell.

As Kate set out she wondered if anyone was whom he seemed.

FROM THIS POINT, ALMOST THREE HUNDRED FEET ABOVE THE long spit of land called Sandy Hook, Benjamin Tallmadge could see the heights of Brooklyn across the water, but he focused instead on the two-story clapboard house in front of him. Rumor was that a loyalist occupied the house, and he might know which officer in Washington's army was betraying his country.

Benjamin wore the linen breeches, black domestic waistcoat and jacket, pointy-toed shoes, and round-crowned hat of an itinerant schoolmaster. He had intended to pass himself off as a Tory and lure information from the house's inhabitants, but a band of plunderers mascarading as patriots had beaten him to the door. He stood with a hand on the sweaty neck of the sway-backed roan he had borrowed. A school teacher would not be riding a horse like Benjamin's black.

He could turn this to his advantage. He could win the family's confidence by chasing their tormenters away. He primed, loaded, and cocked the pistol he kept in his canvas satchel. He flung open the front door and found himself in company with the four thieves who were facing the muzzle of a musket. These loyalists didn't need rescuing.

A raw-boned, broad-beamed woman stood at the far side of the room with the other members of the household huddled behind her. She rested the long barrel of the musket on the corner of the mantle so she could hold it steady.

"Move and I shall shoot you too, you Whig weasel!" She waggled the barrel at Benjamin.

Benjamin could see why the thieves had stopped in their tracks, even though they had four guns and she only one. Each of her eyes had a mind of its own. Her stare was so wild that she looked quite capable of murder. Her line of sight was so unpredictable that the intruders couldn't tell which of them she had in mind for the shortest route to dust and damnation.

Benjamin was more embarrassed than alarmed. He lowered his pistol and tried reason. "I am a friend."

"And I am Mab, queen of the fairies."

"He tells the truth, Cook."

Benjamin was astonished to see Kate Darby step out from behind the woman.

"God keep you, Benjamin." She smiled with such joy at seeing him that Ben could only imagine how hard had been the road that led her here.

"You had best get out of Cook's way." Kate laughed at the look on his face. "And no, I am not a ghost."

Seeing Kate Darby alive wasn't the only surprise for Benjamin. He realized that she had changed in the months since he had lifted her, raving and fever-plagued, onto the wagon bound for the hospital in Lancaster. Her hair formed a cloud of dark spun copper around her slender face. The strength of will that he had seen in flashes before was now etched into the curves of her jaw and mouth, her cheeks and brow. The color of her eyes still shifted from pale green to gray blue depending on the light, but they had a depth and complexity and sadness to them now. Whatever she had endured had not hardened her. She had aged years in a few months, and had become lovely in spite of it.

With his pistol leveled at the thieves Benjamin moved to stand next to Kate, and he rummaged his brain for a new story. Now that he'd been recognized, the old one wouldn't do.

"Lay your weapons on the ground." The four men posed the most immediate problem. "Miscreants such as you bring shame on the fair cause of liberty."

The biggest of them pointed his chin at Cook and the family behind her. "They're filthy traitors. They deserve whatever ill befalls them." He spat. "I had as good will to kill them as a dog."

"I'm an officer in the Continental Army," said Ben. That much was true. The next part wasn't. "My foraging party is nearby. If we see you anywhere in this vicinity we shall arrest you and sentence you to death by the cord." He waved his pistol at them. "Now put a large amount of daylight between yourselves and this house."

When they had skulked out the family crowded around Benjamin, except for the one Kate called Cook. She looked as though she would as soon shoot him as the newly departed. The others thanked Benjamin and God and protested their unswerving loyalty to the American cause. Ben knew he would get no useful information from them. And besides, if Kate Darby was among them, maybe they weren't Tories after all. It wouldn't be the first time a vindictive neighbor had started rumors.

Kate caught Ben's coat sleeve and asked him the question he had been expecting, and for which he had been trying to invent an answer.

"Do you know where my brother is?"

"He is well." Ben wondered why he found it so difficult to lie to her. "He is marching with the army."

He certainly couldn't tell her that at midnight the night before, within sight of this house, he had put Seth into a fishing smack with a man who would row him to Brooklyn. From there Seth would have to travel seventy-five miles or more to deliver a message to Setauket. He carried a letter that Benjamin had written in tiny script, folded, and hidden in a few hollow lead bullets that blended in with the rest of the balls in the boy's pouch.

Sending the boy off alone reminded Benjamin of Nathan setting out into enemy territory. But Nathan's assignment was to go among the British and observe them. Seth's was to avoid them. Even so it was a dangerous mission, and Benjamin had already been wracking his brain for a lie that would satisfy Anthony Wayne. The fewer people who knew what Seth was about the better.

To distract Kate he asked, "Why are you here?"

She sat wearily on a stool. A handsome young woman moved to stand behind her. She put her hands on Kate's shoulders as though to protect and comfort her. The woman was African and probably a servant, but she looked directly at Ben. He saw himself reflected in her brown eyes, and he had the feeling that she suspected he was lying about Seth.

Kate covered the girl's hand with her own. "I came in search of a vessel to carry me across the water. I found Lizzie and Cook already here."

"You know them?"

"They're part of my family. There was no room for them on the transports so my parents had to leave them behind. They've been waiting for someone to carry them to New York."

"I'll arrange for a boat to take you to Admiral Howe's flagship." Ben smiled. Commandeering things was what he excelled at. "The officers there will help you find your parents."

Ben considered the advantages of an agent living in New York City, the daughter of a well-placed Quaker family perceived as loyal to the king. He glanced at Lizzie who stared steadily back at him, her eyes pleading for information about Seth that Ben couldn't give her. Make that two agents.

THUNDER CRASHED AND TONGUES OF LIGHTNING LICKED AT the horizon. The gale snapped the large white flag overhead. The water of Amboy Bay washed over the sides of the tubby little fishing shallop. Benjamin sat stolidly in the bow as rain pelted him. Kate, Lizzie, and Cook clung to each other in the middle of the boat. Lizzie started to retch and Kate held on to her skirt so she could lean over the side.

Benjamin's crew kept rowing even when the waves lifted the boat out of the water and the oars flailed the air. Through the rain and fog the hull of the man-of-war grew larger. The ship's cannons looked like they were aimed directly at Kate.

The sun broke through the clouds and Kate saw red-coated soldiers lined up on the deck, their muskets pointed toward her boat bobbing about like a cork.

Benjamin stood up and shouted through his cupped hands. "Requesting permission to board."

"Denied."

But a ship's tender dangled over the side, and sailors spidered down the nets and took their places at the oars. Kate could not believe her good fortune when she saw John André, his uniform starched and gleaming, seated in the bow of the boat.

After a brief consultation between John and Benjamin, the British sailors helped Kate, Lizzie, and Cook aboard. On the trip to the man-of-war John André lounged with his back against the bow's freeboard as though the tender wasn't bucketing through the whitecaps like a mule with a burr under its saddle. He graced Kate with the smile that could charm cobras.

"Miss Darby, we shall have to find you a more suitable ensemble in New York." John André waved a slender, languid hand at her clothes.

Kate looked down at the filthy hem of her patched, homespun skirt. She thought of the gorgeous silk costumes worn at the Mischianza. As foolish as she had once judged that Arabian night, it brought back a rush of memories of happier times.

"And dear Cook . . ." André said, "I have longed for your Yorkshire puddings, and your spider-and-brandy cordials to chase away the effects of overindulgence."

As always he reduced Cook to a girlish titter and a curtsy even while sitting on the wooden seat with her knees almost to her chin.

"And what of your brother, Miss Darby?"

Lizzie answered before Kate could. "He is killed, your lordship." Lizzie wiped a tear from her eyes, or maybe salt spray.

Kate started to correct her, then stopped. Maybe it was best if the British thought Seth dead. Still, not correcting the lie wracked Kate's conscience as much as telling it herself.

"John, I was with James Stuart when he expired," Kate said. "I have a packet of correspondence to deliver to his family."

André jerked to attention. "May God keep his soul." He crossed himself from left to right like a good Anglican. "Have you opened the packet?"

Kate tilted her chin up in indignation. "I would not read someone else's letters." She rifled through her pack and looked up in consternation when she couldn't find them. For the first time ever, Kate saw André frown.

"Could they have fallen overboard?"

"The things on top of them are still in place." Kate furrowed her own brows, trying to remember details of the past few days.

"When did you see them last?" His tone was casual, as though trying to help a friend recover a lost handkerchief.

"In the village after the battle." Kate realized with a start that Nan Baker was the only one she had told about the letters. But why would Nan steal them?

She didn't mention her suspicions. She could not accuse Nan of theft and brand her a criminal. Kate owed Nan her virtue, a pair of shoes, the reunion with Cook and Lizzie, and maybe her life.

When they reached the ship the crew lowered a net sling for Kate. As she was lifted thirty feet alongside the weathered oak of the hull she held on to the supporting ropes so tightly her knuckles paled. She banged her knees against the taffrail and the sailors helped her out of the net. She waited at the rail until Cook and Lizzie were safely aboard, then John André offered her his arm and led her to Admiral Howe's cabin.

The officers rose and bowed when she entered, and General Clinton held out his hand and insisted she sit next to him. She tried to answer their questions graciously, but she could not take her eyes off the roasts and puddings on the long table.

They all fell to while a fiddler played in a corner. Claret sparkled in crystal glasses. Laughter and good-natured banter volleyed back and forth across the table. Elegant manners, refined accents, learned conversation. Kate imagined heaven as something like this. And best of all she did not have to wonder where lay the loyalties of anyone in this room.

Eighteen

Wherein Seth finds himself in a bind;
field mice get a taste of Independence

LIGHTNING ILLUMINATED THE SHADOWS AROUND THE DARK,
hulking furniture in the farmhouse parlor. Seth perched on the edge of
a bench by the fireplace and tried to assess the politics of Mr. and Mrs.
Fothergill, their two teenaged daughters, and their sullen stripling of a
nephew. All of the Fothergills, and the nephew, were assessing him in return with a discomfitting intensity.

When Seth accepted the glass of wine from Usual Fothergill he intended only to pretend to be tipsy. He figured that a man in his cups would
not be thought much of a threat. Caution was the prudent course because
he was not sure where lay the loyalties at the prosperous-looking farm
called Fothergill's Folly near the village of Flatbush.

When Usual's wife began shaving tea off a small black brick of it Seth
suspected that he had sought shelter in a nest of Tories. Patriotic Americans did not drink English tea. In patriot households women used dried
loosestrife leaves and called it Liberty Tea.

Still the satiny aroma of the steeping leaves made him think of his
mother, the fragrant steam wreathing her head as she poured. It reminded
him of Kate too. When he was a child she had pretended to read his fortune in the leaves in the bottom of the cup.

He realized now that she had always predicted a fine future for him. He would be prosperous, she said, with a loving wife and a swarm of children. He knew he would see his mother again, somehow, somewhere, but his eyes stung at the memory of Kate and the tea leaves, a paisley scarf tied around her head gypsy fashion, her blue-green eyes wide with portent.

Seth might not have gotten into trouble if he had drunk only the tea, but Usual Fothergill made his own wine. Depending on the season he coaxed intoxication from gooseberries, currants, raspberries, elderberries, strawberries, dandelions, and just about everything else not quick enough to avoid being picked. Or maybe Seth would have gotten into trouble anyway. This war had taught him that trouble came to the drunk and the sober alike.

Usual Fothergill poured Seth more of his cowslip wine and asked him to propose a toast. Seth thought carefully as he raised his glass.

"To the return of peace."

Usual followed that with, "And to the establishment of proper authority."

The toasts became more amicable to the crown as the rainy afternoon wore on, and Seth became more certain he had fallen in with Tories. The nephew kept glowering though. Seth worried that he was not convinced of his politics, so he hinted that he was recruiting men for a loyalist militia. Usual Fothergill thought that was a topping idea, worthy of another round of drinks.

By dusk the nephew was still glowering, but the daughters were finding excuses to brush Seth with their hips and bosoms as they poured more wine. By nightfall Seth and Usual were the best of friends. They were such good friends, in fact, that Usual insisted Seth take possession of the four-poster bed in the corner of the parlor. He would not even have to share it with the nephew.

Mrs. Fothergill and the daughters threw back the feather ticking and took forever tightening the rope mesh that kept it from sagging, but at last the family retired to the second-story rooms. Seth fell back onto the covers, trying to marshal rational thoughts from the jolly mob tossing cowslip flowers around inside his skull. He knew he had best sneak away, but he couldn't get his legs to cooperate. And then the two Fothergill daughters, dressed in white linen nightshades and old enough to know better, slipped into the room.

They bounced onto the bed and started a game of Tom-come-tickle-me.

They were strong and their fingers felt like tent pegs being driven into his sides. As he tried to fight them off they pestered him with questions. Did he think them comely? Which one did he judge the prettier? Did he have a sweetheart? Where was he going? What brought such a big, handsome stranger to Flatbush? Was he really on the king's business?

Seth protested that they were both beautiful, but he was bespoken. Then a surge from the depths of his stomach brought up the taste of that last pint of fermented cowslip flowers. He scrambled on his hands and knees across the tangle of sheets and counterpane. His queue had come untied in the horseplay, and his hair fell around his face when he hung over the edge.

He retched into the family's prized possession, a queen's ware chamber pot of cream-colored porcelain. Glazed in black letters on the inside bottom were the words, "Treat me nice and keep me clean, and I'll not tell what I have seen." Those words were the last ones he remembered before he passed out.

When he woke up, the room was still dark. A sharp pain caromed behind his eyes. He lay stretched out on his stomach on the bed, and when he tried to sit up he discovered that someone had tied his hands behind his back. His feet also refused to separate. Whoever had tied his hands had not forgotten his ankles. While they were about it they had thoughtfully gathered his hair back into its queue.

"Samuel." The girl's soft voice roared into his ear and clanged around in his skull like a crowbar beating on an iron pot. "Are you awake?"

Seth wondered to whom she was talking, then remembered that he'd told the family his name was Samuel. He was fairly certain that if he spoke he would spit lint, but he gave it a try.

"Why have they trussed me like a calf?"

She giggled. "You are trussed because you are not trusted."

"But I'm a loyal subject in service to the king."

"The king is an odious tyrant who would make slaves of us all. We feigned to care a fig for him to see what mischief you were up to. We had heard that a spy was engaged in the Devil's work hereabouts. To fool you we even trotted out that old lump of tea." She beamed in the candle's light. "That was my idea." With thumb and middle finger she gave him an affectionate thump on the side of his head that he thought would shatter it like a quail's egg. "We are all patriots in this house."

Seth groaned. He had badly miscalculated. "So am I."

"Of course you would say that."

But Seth felt her untying the ropes around his ankles.

He wasn't too worried. He knew that if he were arrested here and turned over to the American army, Washington would arrange his release or at least his escape. The general had done that before for agents posing as British spies and caught by their own side. The worst he might suffer would be humiliation, and maybe a bullet or two escaping from an American guard who couldn't be let in on the scheme.

"Will your father turn me over to the Continentals?"

"My father would, but my cousin has gone to fetch the men of the district. He intends to hang you, and no one the wiser." She was untying his wrists now. "The blood is up among the rustics. I doubt Father could dissuade them."

He sat up and rubbed circulation back into his wrists. "Why are you helping me?"

He felt her feather-light lips brush his cheek. A wisp of her hair tickled his eyebrow.

"T'would be a pity to see the crows pecking out those pretty green eyes of yours whilst you dangle from a limb at the crossroad."

Seth couldn't have agreed more.

"They're coming." She hurried to finish untying him.

Seth heard the voices too. He heard a lot of them.

"Help me pull the bed away from the wall," she said.

She handed him his hat, his rifle, his powder horn, and bullet pouch. Then she removed a section of wainscoting from behind the bed and pushed him through the opening. Seth felt the bag of bullets, hoping that the three hollow balls still lay among the others.

She held up her candle so he could get his bearings. "Follow the passage to the end," she whispered. "You'll find steps that will bring you to the root cellar. From there you can make your escape."

"What will become of you?"

"Oh la." She gave a wave of her hand. "I am the apple of my father's eye and my cousin is besotted with me. Besides I shall deny everything."

"What is your name?"

"Chastity."

"I won't forget your kindness."

The voices were converging on the front door now. Chastity replaced the wainscoting, and Seth heard the scrape of the big oak bed sliding back into place. Chastity was much stronger than she looked. Seth suspected she had spent time behind a plow.

Seth carried his rifle in one hand and with the other felt his way along the damp stones of the passage. The rain had stopped, but clouds still covered the moon. When he emerged from the cellar he found the night almost as dark as the tunnel.

Lanterns and torches milled around the dooryard like overweight fireflies, silhouetting the hundred or more men there. The light also threw into sharp relief a forest of musket barrels, pikes, and pitchforks. Fothergill's nephew emerged from the house and announced that the treacherous wretch had escaped. The mob wasn't happy about it. Nephew began dividing them into parties to quarter the township to hunt for the fugitive.

With no stars visible Seth was not sure in which direction Setauket lay. He certainly could not ask the route as he went. By now everyone for miles around would be on the lookout for him.

He unpinned the brim of his tricorn so that it drooped low, shielding his face, but he knew the locals would more likely notice his graceful rifle than they would him. He draped his waistcoat around it as though to protect the works from the dampness. Then he sauntered over to join the two dozen men the nephew had assigned to search the roads leading north. As Seth slipped in among them he hoped they would not hear the rat-a-tat-tat of his heart.

A LITTLE BEFORE DAWN, AS SETH WAS ABOUT TO FADE INTO the woods before the sun exposed him, the posse cornered a peddler trying to hide behind a stone wall. In his shoes they found reports of the number of able-bodied soldiers in the Continental Army and orders for their deployment.

Seth didn't doubt that Washington had falsified the reports and arranged for this fellow to sneak a look at them. It was one more instance of the commander in chief's trickery.

So this man might be a Tory about to hang for doing the commander in chief an unwitting favor. But what if he were one of Washington's own mascarading as a loyalist spy? In that case he mustn't hang. The complications made Seth's head ache more than the effects of the cowslip wine.

The leader of the pack had brought his rope with him. He looked to Seth like one of those angry individuals perpetually in search of offenses. He called for meting out justice here and now. He was selecting a tree with a serviceable limb when Seth muttered just loud enough for the men standing near him to hear.

"Seems like General Washington'll want to talk to the rascal. Find out what he knows."

"That's right!" The men who heard him repeated it to those who hadn't.

Seth was pleased with himself. If the man was an American spy, Washington would see that he escaped. If he was a Tory spy, Washington would see that he didn't escape.

The sky was beginning to glow along the horizon, throwing a tea-colored light across the tops of the trees. The lynching that had seemed a good plan last night didn't look so appealing in the glare of sunlight. Seth left them to argue about it and slipped into the grove of apple trees bordering a field. He passed an outcrop of rocks without glancing at it.

In a "post office," a sheltered hollow among the rocks, lay the packet that the British agent had intended to retrieve. His assignment was to pass it and the troop reports to his contact in Brooklyn. He in turn would have seen that it reached General Clinton.

In the coming weeks summer would turn to fall. Rain would pelt the rocks. Field mice would dine on the leather protecting the first official copy of the Declaration of Independence, so carefully transcribed by Thomas Jefferson in his second-story apartment in Philadelphia two years before.

Nineteen

Wherein Kate and Lizzie are mistaken for tarts;
Robert Townsend is mesmerized; Seth wrestles with poultry in motion

DOZENS OF MILITARY AND MERCHANT SHIPS STOOD AT anchor in New York's East River. Their masts, rigging, and furled sails formed a thicket that filled the harbor. Goods arrived in New York from all over the world, but never a cargo like this one.

"Kiss my commodity, you hen-hearted whoreson." The woman hurled a handful of dockside offal with unerring aim. It knocked the portly merchant's wig awry and sent his high-crowned hat flying into a pool of sewage as gracefully as a seagull gliding in for a landing.

He had called her a three-penny upright and an ill-favored one at that. He was lucky her associates weren't so easily insulted. He never would have gotten his peacock blue velvet breeches and waistcoat clean.

New York's waterfront swarmed with women, thousands of them— short, tall, white, brown, young, and vintage. The rows of warehouses amplified their voices, shrill with complaint, bravado, and come-hither. They out-oathed the stevedores, the sailors, and the bargemen. Their clamor muffled the squeal of winches, the clatter of crates, and the rumble of casks rolling along the loose planks of the docks.

New York always stank, but the women had spent six summer weeks crowded into the 'tweendecks of twenty ships without fresh air or privies.

They exuded a pungency all their own. It was so strong that Hercules Mulligan smelled it at his shop three blocks away and came to investigate.

He was not a delicate man, but he took a resin-and-sulphur-coated sliver of wood from the box of them, and ignited it in the embers in a barrel of sand outside the Merchants' Coffee House. He used the match to light his pipe and stood in the aromatic fog of smoke. He also hoped the tobacco fumes would discourage the women's lice and fleas from emigrating in his direction, but he didn't retreat. Even in New York where anything was possible, he knew he would not likely see a scene like this again.

Barges and whaleboats were awash with the weight of more feminine cargo. The latest arrivals scrambled onto the piers, and the contractor's hirelings used belaying pins and cat-o'-nine-tails to keep them from straying. And stray they would. Why should a lass serve many men if she could serve only one? They set about accosting passersby, no doubt with unauthorized matrimony in mind. They had larcenous motives as well. Hercules put his watch and chain inside his shirt front and kept a hand on his wallet.

Robert Townsend was headed for a warehouse and the shipment of calicoes stacked there, but he stopped next to Hercules. He had recently bought half ownership in a dry goods store, and now he was the clerk he had always resembled. He was a tall, dark-eyed, craggily handsome man but not the best advertisement for his own wares.

Townsend and Oakman, Ltd., carried brightly dyed eelskins as hair ties, but Rob used a length of twine to hold his chestnut-colored hair in a long tail at the nape of his neck. The shop sold and rented stiff new hats of silk and of rabbit fur, but Rob didn't notice that moths had feasted on his beaver-felt tricorn. He had knotted the broken strings tieing his scuffed leather shoes. His rumpled brown corduroy breeches fastened at the knees with tarnished pewter buttons. He wore a tow linen shirt and a tobacco-colored waistcoat with broad tails frayed at the hem. Hercules Mulligan said that Rob looked like a plowed-under corn field.

Mulligan was a different matter. He had prospered from the arrival of several thousand wealthy gentlemen officers for whom death was preferable to ill-fitting clothes. He dressed accordingly in a pair of spanking-new canary-yellow linen trousers, blue-and-white–striped kashmir stockings, and a high-crowned black hat bound with red silk tape. He wore a checked silk handkerchief knotted around his neck, a green linen shirt, and a blue surtout coat.

He held his hands out, palms up, and tilted his head back to look at the bright blue September sky. He had to speak loudly to be heard over the women's repartee.

"It's raining trollops and me without a waterproof for the little lord."

"Waterproof?"

Hercules patted the front of his trousers. "A condom, lad, a bit of the sheep's gut to avert the French welcome."

Rob still looked perplexed.

Hercules shouted louder, in case Rob couldn't hear over the noise. "The French welcome, Townsend, the Spanish pox, Venus's curse. The clap, sir, the nip of the gonorrhea goose." Hercules shook his shaggy head. "You might know the town's gossip, Robert, but for a man twenty-four years of age, you are astonishingly unacquainted with the joys of folly with women. How do you of the Quaking persuasion multiply and replenish the earth?"

"We place our reliance in the stork."

Hercules laughed out loud. Rob might not know much about fornication, but he always knew the latest gossip, maybe because women made up most of his clientele at the dry goods shop.

"The walls of Bridewell prison must ring hollow, what with all the inmates transported here." Hercules glanced at Rob. "How many crack reinforcements do you reckon the Redcoats have recruited?"

Robert knew the word *crack*. It could mean "excellent" or it could mean "whore."

"Three thousand, five hundred," he said. "They're listed as the intimate property of the British army. The quartermaster will pay the contractor two guineas a head for them."

"More than seven thousand quid for a bit of laced mutton? Tis more lucrative to undress chaps than put clothes on them. I wonder how reads the bill of lading."

"Officially there is none. This is all under the rose."

"No one has the backbone to sign for a brigade of bawds, eh?"

Robert Townsend sighed. "As if the city hadn't more than enough of the poor creatures already."

" 'Fucking's the end and cause of human state,' " Hercules recited. " 'A man must fuck or God will not create.' "

Robert couldn't argue with that, but he thought of the woman who had solicited him on his way here. He could tell from her clothes, once stylish but now shabby, that this was not her usual line of work. He had given her a few shillings and directed her to the poorhouse run by the Quakers.

The fire of 1776 had left even members of the middle class homeless. The British had commandeered the scant supplies of construction materials to erect barracks. They had taken over the public buildings for hospitals, prisons, and storage.

No one had tried to rebuild the large part of the city that the flames had destroyed, but New York teemed with humanity anyway. Thirty thousand souls lived here now, many of them homeless loyalist refugees.

There were plenty of accommodating women in the city but still not enough. Soldiers had taken to accosting the daughters and wives of the decent sort. Hence this shipment of intimate property, or wet goods as one officer put it.

"I see Ireland is well represented." Hercules nodded toward a group of women lifting their skirts to shake the bilge mud from them. "Irish lasses have obtained permission from the pope, don't you know, to wear the thick ends of their legs downward."

"The rumor must be true." Rob watched a barge-load of women join the others. Most of them were as black as coffee boiled three times. "They say one ship sank in a storm, and the contractor replaced the lost cargo in Barbados."

Hercules wanted to ask him who "they" were, but he didn't bother. Rob was as tight-lipped about his sources of information as he was about his love life. Hercules knew Rob had information. He doubted that he had a love life, which he thought a pity, for the lad was tolerably handsome in a gangly, awkward sort of way. Hercules had seen the effect of Rob's shy smile on the lasses, but Rob himself seemed unaware of it.

"Those two don't appear to be as light-heeled as the rest." Hercules pointed his wedge of a chin toward a pair of young women, one tall, slender, and pale as porcelain. The other stood half a head shorter, dark as chocolate, and she looked far more able to withstand a high wind. They each wore dark green hooded cloaks with slits for their arms. They carried market baskets in their right hands and with their left they lifted the hems of their skirts to avoid the dockside garbage.

"I would say that tall lass was Irish," said Hercules, "except she has ankles a gazelle would covet."

"They should not come here unescorted." Rob tried not to stare, but he agreed with Hercules. Such lovely, tapering ankles caressed by the swaying hems of her skirts. Robert had a sudden desire to cradle her delicate foot in his hands and kiss the hollow next to the ridge of her Achilles tendon. His cheeks grew so hot that he took out his handkerchief and pretended to blow his nose.

The two women looked up in surprise when the flood of transportees surged around them. Rob started toward them to try to avert the mistake that was about to happen. The two women sidestepped to the fringe of the crowd and found their path blocked by a burly odd-job man armed with a barrel stave.

"And where do ya' think you're going, miss?"

"That's no concern of yours." The tall one took the other by the hand and tried to walk past him, but the hireling moved in front of them.

"There'll be no sneaking off. You was bought and paid for, and you'll go where you're sent." He raised the stave to menace them.

They didn't seem menaced.

"Beef-witted mutton monger," muttered the dark one.

"You're mistaken," said the pale one. "No one has bought us."

That should have been obvious, given the cleanliness of their clothes, but he was not going to be gulled by a pair of trollops sly enough to appear neat after six seasick weeks in a ship's festering hold. He raised his stave to drive them back into line. The tall one stepped in front of her companion, put her arms back to form a protective palisade around her, and stared calmly up at him. Her hood fell away from her face and Rob saw the nimbus of red-gold hair that framed it.

Rob intended to try reason on the brute, but Hercules moved faster. Whoever first observed that it took nine tailors to make a man had never met Mulligan. The ruffian jerked around when he felt a yank on the stave. He refused to let go, so Mulligan lifted him onto his toes and shook him like a puppy until he relinquished his grip.

"These morts be not on the bill of lading." Hercules took the onguard stance with the stave, left hand raised behind him like a fencer. "So be off, you whiffling cur."

"You are stealing the king's goods." The man backed away to avoid the stave's jabs. "Me master'll send the provost's guard 'round for you."

Hercules slapped the taut rear end of his breeches where the yellow kidskin fit as snugly as a glove. "Cunningham and his guard may kiss this."

Muttering oaths the bully retreated while the wet-goods jeered and pelted him with garbage, feces, and old fish.

Several of them surrounded Hercules and proposed marriage, or something like it. He blew them kisses, checked the security of his wallet, and waved them off. With the stave shouldered like a musket he led the two women away from the uproar. Rob followed.

Rob knew about animal magnetism, the new theory proposed by the Austrian physician, Franz Mesmer. Mesmer said that people had a power within them like that of a magnet's influence on iron filings. Mesmer claimed it could cure the sick, but most people scoffed at the idea. Rob had too when he read the article in the *Royal Gazette*. Now he believed. The sparks of sunlight in the young woman's ember-colored hair and the sway of her skirts drew him with a force that was as irresistible as it was perplexing.

He wanted to ask her name. He wanted to ask where she lived. He wanted to ask if he could call on her. He froze when she turned and looked directly at him. Her green velvet hood lay in graceful folds on her shoulders. Her voice was the music that his Quaker religion forbade him.

"I thank thee both for thy kindness."

She was a Quaker too, and she had used the form of speech usually reserved for close friends and family. Rob couldn't believe his good fortune.

She was almost as tall as he was. She smiled at him with eyes whose colors shifted like the ocean with changes in the light. Robert felt his wits set adrift by them. He wanted to call to her as she and her companion walked away, but he feared his tongue would make a fool of him.

Rob had never cared about appearances. A concern for looks had always seemed vain and foolish, but her laughter as she walked away made him conscious of his shabby clothes. She was probably making fun of him.

LIZZIE AND KATE COULDN'T STOP GIGGLING. THEY HAD MET so many villains and escaped so many hard scrapes in the past months that a bully with a barrel stave hardly bothered them. The more they thought about it, the funnier it became. Kate would never tell her parents that she had been mistaken for a trollop, but she would amuse John André with it the next time he called.

Lizzie put a hand on her hip and strutted toward the fish market. "Is not bawdry the most worshipful of trades?" She looked coquetishly over her shoulder at Kate.

"How says thee so?"

"The lawyer thrives on the woes of his client, does he not? And the physician on his patient's maladies. But the bawd's fortunes grow only with the rise of her customers." She made a rude gesture in the vicinity of her crotch.

Kate laughed. "Thee has a wicked tongue, friend."

Lizzie glanced back in time to catch Rob Townsend watching them. "You've made a conquest, Kate."

"Of whom?" Kate turned and saw the tails of Rob's long brown surtout disappearing into a warehouse.

"The handsomer of our two gallant knights. That winsome, tongue-tied cove."

Kate started to protest that she hadn't noticed him but that would have been a lie. She shrugged instead. "He appears a shy fellow."

Lizzie led her through the fish market toward the docks at the foot of Broad Street. Dozens of sloops and wherries nosed into the piers there. The broad-beamed Dutch fly boats were loaded with cornmeal, meat, butter, and poultry, much of it smuggled out of American-held territory. A fleet of grocers' wagons waited to carry the goods to the city's markets. The farmers came from Long Island and the upper reaches of Manhattan. English had replaced Dutch in most parts of the city but not here.

"Thee shopped at the market this morning, Lizzie. Why comes thee here now?"

"I saw Phoebe, the barmaid from Fraunces' tavern. She told me we might meet someone." Lizzie didn't mention that Phoebe Fraunces had come looking for her to deliver the message.

"Who?"

Then Kate saw Seth. She wanted to cry out with joy, but she dared not. Seth was selling chickens to an ensign whose crimson coat flashed like a beacon flare among the farmers' brown and gray homespun. She wondered if he had taken leave of his senses.

Kate started toward him, and Lizzie caught her cloak to hold her back.

Kate tried to pull away. "We must warn him. If they discover he is a rebel they will arrest him. If they judge him a spy they will hang him."

"That's why we must not let on we know him."

They waited until the soldier left carrying Seth's wicker cage with two chickens in it.

"Why chickens? Seth never liked our chickens at home."

"And they never liked him either," added Lizzie. "Remember how he used to chase them when he was young?"

Kate wanted to run to him and throw her arms around him. She could imagine how badly Lizzie wanted to the same, but neither of them dared so much as smile at him.

Seth pretended not to notice them either, but that wasn't difficult. His rooster and three remaining hens kept him busy. He had scratches on his cheek that looked as if they'd been left by a rooster's talons. He had tethered the hens to each other with cords tied around their ankles, but they were trying to run in three directions. The rooster, intent on servicing the hens, chased them in circles until his string and theirs had wound around Seth's legs.

Laughing, Kate caught one chicken and Lizzie two. Seth grabbed the rooster and received more pecks to add to the bloody ones on his hands. While the three of them leaned down to sort out the tangle, Seth whispered, "Thanks be to God, sister. I never thought to see thee in this life. They told me the fever had taken thee."

Kate smiled sideways at him. "They exaggerated."

"Where is the family staying?"

"With Thomas Buchanan on Broad Way. Cook is with us too."

"Thomas Buchanan the Tory?"

"He has kindly offered us shelter, Seth, when we had none."

"How fares mother?"

"Mother and Father are well enough, though they grieve the loss of thee."

"I doubt that Father cares a fig."

"Shame on thee, Seth. Of course he does."

Kate helped Seth tie the hens' ankles more closely together so he could carry them upside down by the cord. She wanted to ask him why he was peddling chickens in New York, and a hundred other questions besides, but she watched him walk away. The rooster was still trying to inflict damage on whatever part of him he could reach.

Lizzie held up a folded piece of paper. "Seth slipped this to me while we were sorting out the chickens."

Kate felt a stab of resentment. She knew why he had given the letter to Lizzie instead of her. For one thing he had thought she was dead when he wrote it. And for another he had probably written something for Lizzie's eyes only. Kate understood that he wouldn't stop loving her just because he loved Lizzie, but she asked God to forgive her for her envy.

"Is he still with the army? What does he say?"

"He's still with the Pennsylvania Rifles." Lizzie scanned the letter. "He says to please tell his mother he is well." Lizzie looked up at her. "It's too dangerous for him to come to the Buchanan house, Kate. You know how Mister Buchanan feels about the patriots' cause."

"Yes, I know."

Kate wondered why Seth put his life in peril by coming to New York if he could not see his family. Then she looked at Lizzie's lovely face and knew the answer. Seth and Lizzie had probably agreed to meet in some secret place. Kate shook her head at the surprise of it. She could not have imagined that a scapegrace like Seth would risk all for love. Maybe the poets were right. Love could make even a dog howl in pentameter.

Twenty

Wherein Abraham Woodhull braves Hades; Rob Townsend shares a dish of essence-of-old-shoes in the alligator's nest; the game is set afoot

THE STENCH OF DEATH REACHED ACROSS THE EAST RIVER TO grip Brooklyn. The inhabitants of New York probably didn't notice it as much as Abraham Woodhull did. He held a bandana soaked in orange water and cloves to his nose, but he could feel death soaking into his clothes and skin. He stood at the rear of the flat-bottomed ferry to postpone his arrival for as long as possible.

Always at this point in his fifty-five-mile journey from Setauket he regretted leaving his farm on Conscience Bay. The worst stink there was of dung and dead oysters. The loudest noise was the lowing of the cows who produced the dung. The oysters had blessedly little to say.

Abraham looked ten years older than twenty-six. Worry lines furrowed his forehead and bracketed the narrow ruche of his lips. His dusty hair had already ceded much of the territory north of his swampy brown eyes. He was pale and nervous and so small that the saddlebags he carried over his bony shoulder hid half of him.

He had left his horse with the hostler in Brooklyn. A horse would mark him as prosperous, and prosperous was a temptation to thieves. Felons, filth, and New York's fetid bouquet were the reasons he wore his oldest clothes whenever he came here. When he returned home his wife would soak them in ashes and hot water in her bucking tub. She would spread them over bushes so the sun's healing rays would rid them of contamination from small pox, bloody flux, and whatever other diseases were all the rage in New York.

Two British sentries had questioned every ferry passenger except the dozen red-coated officers returning from holiday in Oyster Bay. Abraham had never paid much attention to the soldiers, but now they terrified him. He knew the fear wasn't reasonable, yet he imagined that these fellows lounging with their boots propped up on the rail and their red jackets unbuttoned could read his thoughts. Today discovering his thoughts would be dangerous.

Once ashore the most horrifying obstacle for Abraham was the defensive trench dug by the American troops and abandoned two years ago. For him New York was Hades, and this trench the River Styx. Stagnant water filled it, black as pitch and lumpy with garbage and feces. Dead dogs, cats, and rats always bobbed about, but today a naked corpse floated with them. Crows perched on his back as though out for a sunset cruise.

Abraham waited while the soldiers sauntered over the wide plank laid across the trench. He pressed the handkerchief against his nose, took a firmer grip on his saddlebags, and inched out onto it. He had a horror of falling, or worse, being thrown in after thieves knocked him unconscious and stole everything, including his small clothes. That was probably what had happened to the poor chap floating there now. In his own bed Abraham dreamed of waking up covered with dead rats and rotten sauerkraut in this ditch.

The smoke from the cook fires in the charred ruins called Canvas Town hung like a shroud over Lower Manhattan. Abraham wiped his stinging eyes with his bandana. He turned left onto Water Street and the tall brick buildings closed in around him.

Tenements hung out over the tangle of narrow alleyways. Blood from a slaughtered hog ran in the gutter. Sounders of swine rooted through the garbage and the chamber pot contents that the lower sort threw out their windows. Whenever Abraham entered New York he felt as though a beast with very bad breath were swallowing him.

Wagons, sledges, barrows, and carriages filled the roadways. The racket of wheels, carters' oaths, and horses' hooves echoed between the brick walls. Fops minced past followed closely by their footboys who were referred to as "catchfarts." The gents' tricorn hats perched so high on their upswept wigs that they saluted each other by touching the brims with their walking sticks. Merchants, servants, mechanics, apprentices, and shopboys jostled Abraham as they hurried by. They all made way for the packs of Royal Grenadiers.

Abraham tried to avoid importuning women and keep away from the open sewer in the center of the street. He managed to fend off the women, but a galloping horse spattered him with filthy water from the gutter. In swearing at the rider he made the mistake of shifting his attention from the cobblestones. One of them rolled, twisting his ankle. He swore again and hobbled half a block to the three-story brick house where his sister and her husband took in lodgers. Bars enclosed the windows at the street level. Abraham shook his head at the sight of them. Until this war started he had never even slid the bolt home on his door in Setauket.

He limped up the brownstone steps and rapped the lion's head knocker against the oak door. He was wiping at the stains on his coat when his sister slid open the triple bolts. He limped into the smell of cabbage and fried lard. He lowered the saddlebags to the floor and rubbed the aching indentation the strap had gouged in his shoulder.

Mary Woodhull Underhill resembled her brother, except she had a rick of wild, faded brown hair that looked like one of Dr. Franklin's electrical experiments gone awry.

"How did you find the journey, Abraham?" She helped him off with his coat. "Any sign of those dreadful banditti?"

"Is there any other sort of banditti but dreadful?" He kissed her on the cheek. "From Oyster Bay I rode behind a group of soldiers, so no one molested me." Abraham paused. He didn't usually truck in gossip, but this was significant. "A British colonel has taken a fancy to Sally Townsend."

"Robert's sister?"

"Yes. You know the British have taken up quarters at the Townsend house."

"And does she fancy him?"

Abraham shrugged. "I don't know." Women, including his own wife, were a mystery to him, but the colonel's infatuation could prove useful. He handed his sister a letter from their mother.

"The seal is broken, Abraham."

"The sergeant at the guard station insisted on reading it."

He didn't tell her that he had almost soiled his breeches when the sergeant took it from him. His mother had written nothing more incriminating than a report of the family ailments and the village gossip, but in future he might carry letters that could hang him.

"Mother sent scones and a round of cheese."

Mary's thin face lit up. "We can have them with the pekoe that Robert bought yesterday. He found the real goods instead of the sawdust and loosestrife they try to pass off as tea. The commissary sergeants pick the stalls cleaner than a plague of locusts, but Robert is resourceful. He knows everyone at the docks and markets."

That, Abraham thought, is what I'm counting on.

He glanced toward the steep stairs leading to the second and third floors. "Is Rob in?"

"He went to the coffee house a short while ago." Mary saw Abraham favor his left foot as he headed down the hall toward his room. "What happened?"

"A loose cobblestone. If they can't be bothered to rebuild the city they could at least repair the roads."

"The stones only come loose again, or the lower sort take them to build their hearths."

"Or to throw at each other, or heave through the window panes of honest folk," Abraham grumbled. "I can't understand how you abide this place, Mary."

"It's not so bad when you get used to it." Mary laughed. Abraham said the same thing every time he visited. "Setauket seems dull as dishwater to me now. There's always some raree-show to amuse us, and such extraordinary fashions to be seen along the Broad Way." She called after him. "You'll find clean clothes in the trunk."

Abraham wiped his face with his bandana and held it up so she could see the soot stains on it. "I've only been in the city a short while and already I look like the bowels of a chimney."

Mary laughed. "Leave those clothes outside the door and Sukie will wash them. I'll make a horseradish poultice for your ankle."

"No time for your restoratives, Mary dear. I'll change, then go look for Rob."

"You know where to find him." Mary laughed again. She had always done the laughing for both of them. "He'll be at the coffee house, curing his outside like jerk beef in tobacco smoke and preserving his insides with that vile essence of old shoes."

ABRAHAM DIDN'T MUCH CARE FOR COFFEE, THE ESSENCE OF old shoes, as Mary called it, but usually an evening in the Merchants' Coffee House delighted him as much as anything could. The building gave off a raffish air, left over from the time when pirates roosted here between plunderings. It was built on the dock itself, with rear doors for quick piratical exits to waiting ships. Four years ago in this same room John Jay drafted the proposal to establish the Continental Congress, the seed of the current rebellion. The loyalists who patronized the place nowadays reckoned that the pirates and John Jay had a great deal in common.

The place exuded an atmosphere of profits only slightly less ill-gotten than the pirates'. The dark oak paneling made Abraham feel part of something more cosmopolitan than Austin Roe's tavern in Setauket. Even though the clientele was Tory, the conversations were a cut above the coffee houses where the lower sort congregated.

Usually Abraham would exchange tuppence for a fistful of tobacco and the lease of a long-stemmed clay pipe. When he finished with the pipe the proprietor would snap off the wet end, and it would be ready for the next renter.

For another penny Abraham could rent a copy of the *Royal Gazette* and a candle to shed light on it. He would fire up the pipe, spread the newspaper on a table, and see what loyalist calumnies that unctuous son-of-a-bitch, James Rivington, had printed. His curbed outrage would keep him alert well past seven o'clock, his usual winter bedtime in Setauket.

He had always felt safe from New York's evils in the coffee house. The fog of tobacco smoke purified the unhealthy air. Beggars were denied admittance, pickpockets were ejected, and women were not tolerated. The soldiers who gathered to play at backgammon carried sabers that discouraged the sort of mayhem perpetrated in the alleyways outside.

Today the sight of all those crimson coats, gold braid, and shiny black boots no longer reassured Abraham. He imagined the working ends of the swords pressing into his bony brisket. He took a deep breath and scanned the room in search of his friend.

Rob Townsend was easy to spot, even through the smoke. His clothes were the drabbest in a roomful of spotted, checked, and striped knee breeches so tight their occupants did not bend to pick up anything they dropped.

James Rivington sat across from Rob, but Abraham knew he didn't stay long in one place. Soon he would circulate around the room, bowing and scraping and collecting gossip and scandal. His thin little mouth would draw up in a smile while his eyes calculated the advantages to be gained by an outlay of congeniality.

Abraham took his time navigating around the soldiers with their chairs tilted onto the rear legs and swords and helmets hanging from the high backs. He avoided the bustling attendants, the lounging dogs, boots, tasseled walking sticks, and pot-bellied spittoons. When he reached the far corner Rivington had moved on, but his voice could be heard over the general hubbub. He was telling his favorite story about what happened when the American general, Ethan Allen, received parole from a New York prison.

Rumor had it that they let Allen out because he caused too much trouble for a prison to contain. Even in manacles he attacked the guards, chewed nails, and berated his keepers with a highly seasoned mix of obscenities and scripture. Once free, his first order of business had been to find Rivington and exact retribution for the libelous stories he had printed about him. Abraham had heard the story before, but Rivington told it so well.

"I heard him on the stairs," Rivington said, "His long sword clanking at every step, and the urchins in the street below cheering him on with huzzahs. I looked at the bottle of Madeira before me. "If such Madeira cannot mollify him," I said, "he must be harder than adamant. A fearful moment of suspense and in he stalked."

Abraham reached Rob's table, but he stood to hear the end of the story.

"'Is your name James Rivington?' he demanded. 'It is, sir, and no man could be more happy to see General Ethan Allen.'"

Rivington paused for effect. "'Sir, I have come . . . ,' Allen says. 'Not another word, my dear Colonel,' says I, 'until you have taken a seat and a glass of old Madeira.' 'But, sir, I don't think it proper . . .' 'Not another word, Colonel. Taste this wine. I found it in a far corner of the cellar, snug in the bottle for ten years.' Allen took the glass, swallowed the wine, smacked his lips, and shook his head approvingly. I insisted he take another glass, and in short, we finished two bottles of Madeira, and parted good friends."

Abraham chuckled and sat down across from Rob Townsend. "I take it you received my message?" He was never one for amenities.

"Yes. A red-haired lad with a bellicose rooster delivered it."

"A trustworthy boy, that one."

"He seemed so."

"Then you know why I'm here?"

"You want me to gather useful information. You will come to New York once a week, transcribe it into a report, and return to Setauket with it."

Abraham leaned across the table and hissed, "For goodness sakes, man, be discreet." He directed his chin at the roomful of loyalists and officers, and at Rivington, the most strident Tory in New York. "Shouldn't we discuss this in the privacy of your lodgings?"

"With due respect to your sister, Abraham, the walls of her goodly house are thin as starched linen. Mr. Blodgett in the room adjoining mine finds entertainment in peeping at me through a knothole."

Abraham regarded him suspiciously. Rob's somber expression did not always mean he was serious. "How do you know?"

"Sorely wanting in entertainment myself one night I peeked through the knothole and came eyeball to eyeball with him."

Abraham sighed. He had known Rob for years, and he still found it difficult to detect when he was tweaking him. But when Private Seth Darby delivered Major Ben Tallmadge's letter to Abraham in Setauket he immediately thought of asking Rob for help. Rob was smart, educated, and honest, and he harbored strong views for a Quaker.

"They've diluted the brew." Rob signaled for a second dish so Abraham could share his pot of coffee. "It's not quite strong enough to cause palsey."

The attendant was a lop-faced fellow with one severed knuckle and the ends of two fingers permanently bent. Abraham didn't speak until the man had set down the dish, made a perfunctory bow, and left. He glanced around. "I worry about Rivington. He would sell his grandmother for a price."

"And a modest price at that." Rob smiled. "Still we're safer here in the alligator's nest." He poured coffee into Abraham's china dish then took a sip from his own.

"Alligator's nest?"

"I was talking yesterday with a merchant newly arrived from Charleston."

"Does he deal in alligators?"

Rob smiled. "No. Rice and sorghum. But he told me that a turtle will deposit her eggs alongside the alligator's. The alligator defends her nest and the turtle's eggs with her own."

"What happens when the baby turtles hatch?"

"If they're lucky they escape to the water unharmed."

"And if they're not lucky?"

Rob put his elbows together and clapped his long hands like powerful jaws snapping shut. The sharp report startled Abraham so badly he almost overturned his chair. Men glanced in their direction then went back to their discussions.

Rob smiled at Abraham. "We are smarter than turtles."

"Then you have decided to help me collect information?" Abraham felt a flutter of fear in the small dark part of him that had hoped Rob would refuse and give him an excuse to do the same.

Rob rested his forearms on the table and leaned across it. His smile was so guileless that anyone glancing his way would think he was discussing the price of molasses. "I must do whatever I can to help my distressed country."

"To tell you the truth, Robert, I had hoped you would say me 'nay.'"

"We have no choice but to accept. We could not share our carcasses with our consciences if we allowed tyrants to usurp our liberty."

"But the risk . . ."

"Life is a risk, my friend."

Twenty-one

Wherein Kate lives in a house that dances; Stork pays a visit;
Robert has a chancy encounter in Canvas Town

THE GARRET'S SMALL WINDOW DANCED IN ITS FRAME WITH A
sprightly four/four beat, and Kate knew the Buchanan family's Christmas
festivities had begun downstairs. The evening was too young for the jigs
and reels. Kate guessed this was a gavotte and not a minuet or allemande.
She shouldn't know a gavotte from an allemande, but in recent weeks she
had joined the Buchanan's household staff on the stairs to watch other
balls. The servants named each tune and dance, trying to make up for her
ignorance.

Kate's mother rarely left her room, her books, and her needlework. She
was frail with an illness that doctors could not diagnose, but Kate, Lizzie,
and Cook could. Her wounded heart mourned Seth's absence.

Kate sat with her every morning. To make her mother laugh she told her
stories of the antics of Seth and his comrades at Valley Forge. Kate could
even do a passable imitation of Baron von Steuben. She did not mention
that Seth had come to New York. She did not talk of the possibility that he
might not live through the conflict.

This war had even unsettled commerce in the southern latitudes, and
Kate's father had sailed for Jamaica to try to reverse the downward slide of
his fortunes. Now that his family was safely housed Aaron Darby planned

to spend a year or more tending to his business there, and Thomas Buchanan's too. With no one to forbid it Kate could perch with Lizzie on the stairs. She could lean her head against the ballusters, her foot pitapatting to the music and guilt sulking in a dimly lit corner of her soul.

Tonight Kate's mother gave her a gentle lecture on avoiding the temptations of the world and on improving her spiritual state. She had looked down at the floor and the ballroom below. "Hell," she said with her wan, sweet smile, "is thick with fiddlers."

Kate took the chiding to heart. She intended to spend the evening reading *The Morals of Confucius* instead of watching the dancers. But she was discovering that the road to hell was paved with as many good intentions as fiddlers. Thomas Buchanan had instructed the carpenters to install springs beneath the floor of the ballroom on the second floor. When a hundred feet stepped in time, the floor set up a vibration that pulsed like a heartbeat throughout the house. The music itself seeped through the boards underfoot, and Kate realized why her people frowned on it. The Devil must have a hand in something this seductive.

As the winter daylight faded, Kate lit a candle. She pulled the old blanket around her and hitched her stool closer to the heat radiating from the chimney. Thomas Buchanan had furnished the first three stories of his house extravagantly, but his extravagance stopped short of fireplaces in the servants' quarters on the fourth floor.

Two colonels and their aides had commandeered the ground floor. This weekend they were joined by Colonel Simcoe and his staff, who usually quartered on Long Island. The lower quarter of the house smelled like tobacco and shoe polish. It resembled a barracks, with red jackets, boots, helmets, sabers, men's corsets, and shaving kits strewn about.

The ballroom took up most of the second floor. The Buchanans occupied the third floor along with their refugee cousins-in-law, New Jersey loyalists whom Cook called "elbow relations." Cook sniffed that the elbow relations left little elbow room, but what to do?

Thousands of Tory refugees had flooded into the city to escape the wrath of their rebel neighbors and the depredations of the gangs roaming the Neutral Zone, the territory between the armies. A fourth of New York was still charred rubble. The British army had taken over the public buildings, and the officers had moved themselves and their doxies into homes abandoned by fleeing rebels. The only lodgings available were, as Cook put it, little better than a Dutch tavern in fly time.

The Buchanans had made room for their old friends the Darbys up here under the eaves. With so many extra people in the house Thomas Buchanan's wife, Almy, was happy to acquire the services of Cook and Lizzie. Cook immediately set about terrorizing the Buchanans' servants and the British ensigns and lieutenants too.

"Beef-witted codshead!" Lizzie strode into the room with her bodice laces untied and her hair more disheveled than usual. "That satchel-arsed ensign tried to take a flourish with me on the back stairs again."

"Colonel Simcoe's aide?"

"Yes. I did as Major André instructed and struck him with my fist on his cucumber of a nose." She giggled. "It bled like sixty. He scoured off mumbling, 'I say, you saucy brown baggage, I say.'"

She imitated him so perfectly that Kate laughed until Confucius fell off her lap. "Cook says that every day is Leap Year here." When Kate leaned down to retrieve the book she laid her palm on the boards to feel the carefree pulse of the dance.

"Ay. The officers have but to ask of New York lasses and they shall receive." Lizzie put her hands on her hips and looked stern. "Speaking of officers, Captain André says if you do not join the party he will march up here and take you prisoner."

"Tell him my frock is fit only for marketing. I would not embarrass our hosts by appearing like a draggletail in such distinguished company."

Lizzie pulled one kidskin dancing slipper from each pocket and shook them at Kate. "He said to tell you that these do not have high heels, which he knows you Quakers consider instruments of the Devil." She held up the velvet dress draped over her arm. It had no lace or ruching, but it gleamed the deep blue of the sky around a full moon at midnight.

Kate stroked the cloth. "It's beautiful, but I can't accept it."

"He said you would say it's beautiful, but you can't accept it. He said to tell you to stop dithering, pitch the gown over your head, corral your mane with a ribbon, and come downstairs. He says a friend of yours has recently arrived from Philadelphia and asks to see you."

"Who?"

"He would not tell me, though I pleaded."

Kate laughed. "He knows we women are as curious as cats."

"He knows that about women, and a lot more." Lizzie rolled her eyes. "Captain André could charm the warts off a toad."

Kate laughed again. That he could.

KATE AND LIZZIE PEEKED AROUND THE DOOR AT THE LOFTY young slat in the side parlor. He had struck a pose for the mirror over the mantlepiece. He stood bent slightly at the waist with one foot extended and his rounded posterior projecting far enough out to set a tea cup on. He wore glove-snug breeches of lime green silk and a cut-away coat of flowered taffeta. He was trying to take snuff off the top of his hand without inhaling the six-inch lace ruffle at his cuff, and keep his foot-high wig from toppling forward onto his nose.

Lizzie ducked back into the hall. "Dear God in heaven, it's Stork."

"Thee shouldn't use the Lord's name in vain, Lizzie."

"He's no lord. He's Ned Withers. Seth's old friend. Skinny-legged Stork Withers." Lizzie peeked around the corner. "Doesn't he cut a dash, though. He's gone for a macaroni."

Kate knew about macaronis. They were young men who took on Italian airs and fashions. John André said they talked without meaning, smiled without pleasantry, ate without appetite, and wenched without passion. Lizzie said she didn't see how they could do any proper wenching in those enormous wigs. And by the time they struggled out of their skin-tight breeches, passion would have died of boredom.

Kate peered over Lizzie's head. "What happened to his legs?"

"I reckon he stuffed those wool forms into his stockings like the other swells. And he's padded his posterior too, I trow." Lizzie glanced over her shoulder at Kate and winked. "He always was a little behind."

Kate laughed out loud as she walked into the room. Stork smiled as best he could without cracking the crust of face powder, or dislodging the black beauty mark pasted at the corner of his mouth. He minced forward, impelled by his wig and its stuffing of yarn, tow fibers, tufts of wool, hay, horse hair, and two pounds of flour scented like lilacs and colored periwinkle blue for evening wear.

"Miss Darby, so dashed swell to lay peeps on your viz. And you too, Lizzie, my bob dell."

Lizzie murmured a translation. "The cull's glad to see us."

Stork's scalp must have sprung an itch. He poked into the wig with an ivory scratcher in the shape of a monkey's claw. He disturbed a mouse who emerged, whiskers quivering. Lizzie coughed to cover her laughter.

The mouse surveyed the room, then disappeared back into the curls. Ned probably wore the wig, waking and sleeping, for months. Except for the scratching stick and Stork's sneezing, the mouse could live unmolested, feasting on flour. Kate wondered if it was raising a family in there.

"What brings you to New York, Ned?" she asked.

"A cart wheel. But while here I purchased these rum duds for myself. A fellow named Mulligan on Dock Street is a bang-up botch."

"Botch means tailor," Lizzie said between giggles.

Stork turned slowly to give them the full view. "A varment coat, what?"

"Varment means dashing," Lizzie whispered.

Kate needed further translation. "A cart wheel?"

"A hat," Stork said. "To be precise, the flat-crowned straw hats that French peasants wear and their queen affects. The sort with the brim out to there." He swirled his lace cuffs at arm's length in front of his forehead to indicate the far limits of the brim.

"Is it now the fashion among gentlemen of Philadelphia to dress as Marie Antoinette?"

"You are such the go, Mademoiselle Darby." Stork guffawed through his nose, scattering a shower of snuff. "The topper is for a mort. A lady of your acquaintance. The evanescent Miss Shippen."

"Are you in love with Peggy Shippen, Ned?"

"Nay!" He brayed a laugh. "Cupid has fired his dart into my employer's arse, not mine."

"An arrow's point could never reach Stork's arse under all that padding," Lizzie murmured.

"He is besotted with her." Ned didn't hear her through the horse hair and wool batting over his ears. "And since I am General Arnold's *bonne à tout faire,* his do-everything, he sent me to satisfy her latest whim."

"Benedict Arnold, the military governor of Philadelphia?"

"Poor fellow," blurted Lizzie.

"*Poor* fellow indeed," said Ned. "Miss Shippen has driven her father to the very gates of the almshouse, and now she has taken the whip to General Arnold's fortunes." He leaned closer. "Here's a secret. General Arnold trotted out the same impassioned *billets doux* he penned for his late wife and his last paramour, changing the salutation from Betsy to Peggy."

It was Kate's turn to translate for Lizzie. "*Billets doux* means love letters."

Stork struck a rhetorical pose to quote Arnold. " 'Suffer that heavenly bosom, which cannot know itself the cause of pain without a sympathetic pang, to expand with a sensation more soft, more tender than friendship.' "

"That old apocathery?" Lizzie had heard about Arnold. "He's twice Miss Shippen's age."

"He's the hero of Quebec and Saratoga, Lizzie. I'm sure Peggy admires him for his valor."

"She admires his chink," said Lizzie, "and his office and fame."

"His office and fame perhaps," said Ned, "But at the rate he's striving to satisfy her fancies, the hero of Saratoga soon will not have enough chink to keep her in hat pins and lappets."

He jackknifed into a bow and invited Kate to sit. Lizzie stood behind her, alert for a reappearance of the mouse. Ned perched on the edge of the settee, one stork's leg straight, the other angled. He draped a languid hand over the carved whippet's head on the butt of his mahogany walking stick, and lost himself in contemplation of the jeweled buckles on his shiny, square-toed shoes.

Kate interrupted his revery. "Does it not give you pause to come here?"

"You mean do I fear mingling as a hare with the hounds?" He snorted his laugh again. "We are all gentlemen, His Majesty's officers and I, and they treat me courteously. Captain André has been most cordial."

John André, Kate thought, would be cordial to the Devil himself.

"How fares our dear Philadelphia, Ned?"

Stork reverted to the old self that Kate had always known.

"Everything is in short supply there, dear Kate. Forestallers and speculators have bought up food and now sell it high. A broken-down jade of a horse costs two thousand continentals. American money is more valuable in the privies than in the marketplace."

"Can't General Arnold stop the speculating?"

"He's as busy as a devil in a high wind, yet the practice flourishes." Ned didn't mention the gossip that Arnold was speculating himself. "But what I really want to know, dear Kate . . ." He levered forward until he was almost beak to nose with her, and she saw the old Ned in his pale blue eyes. "What I really want to know is how fares my dear chum Seth."

"He is not with us." Kate meant that he was not living in this house, but Ned understood differently.

"I'm so sorry, my dear girl." He dabbed at his eyes with his handkerchief, and Kate was surprised to see real tears. "Please extend my condolences to your esteemed parents."

Kate started to correct his error, but Lizzie poked her between the shoulderblades. So she said, "I thank you for your kindness, Ned." And wondered if she had lied, or only neglected to tell the truth.

THE CHILDREN SQUATTED AROUND THE SAILOR'S BODY AND worked with business-like efficiency. Some rifled the pockets. Others pulled off his shoes and stockings and tugged the stiffened arms out of the shirt sleeves. When they saw Rob approaching they scoured off, disappearing down holes and into the vast underground warren of burned-out cellars that honeycombed Canvas Town.

Rob Townsend knew the thought was uncharitable, but with their soot-stained faces and clothes the children reminded him of rats. They swarmed in packs among the charred beams and tottering brick walls. They foraged, scavenged, begged, stole, fought, blasphemed, and even, on occasion, laughed and played. Often Rob distributed pennies to them and delivered food to their families, but today he had business to transact, and he held the muslin-wrapped package close to his chest. He also wore his wallet under his shirt. The children's deft fingers had a way of getting into places they didn't belong.

Canvas Town was a quarter of a mile and a world away from the brick mansions and fashionable shops of upper Broad Way. Here the blackened chimneys still rose above the rubble of Lower Manhattan. Beneath the layer of smoke from the cooking fires stretched gray acres of stolen sails, wagon covers, shop awnings, and army tents. In the dirt-floored cellars under them, heaps of garbage separated one family's space from another's.

Rob stopped at the only spot of color in the landscape, a dingy blue-and-white-striped tent with scalloping around the roof. Like a hocus-pocus artist, a British major had made it vanish from the quartermaster's inventory and then reappear here in payment for services rendered. When Rob approached it, a dog started barking inside. His voice was so resonant he sounded as though he were serving notice from the bottom of a well.

"Gwendolyn, I have the cambric you ordered."

"Come in, dearie. Brutus is leashed."

Rob entered warily. The mastiff strained at the end of his short chain and growled until Rob gave him the bit of beef he'd brought for the purpose. A small iron stove of Dr. Franklin's invention cajoled the chill from the air.

Gwendolyn wore a lace chemise as he prepared for an evening with the major. He hadn't put his elaborate wig on over his skullcap, but he had powdered his face and painted his cheeks and lips with rouge. He had plucked his eyebrows and penciled in high, dark arches.

He held out a pale hand with dirt half-mooned under the long fingernails. "Let us see what you've brought us, darling." He took the sack of shillings tucked between the folds of the cambric cloth and slipped it between the peaks of his padded bosom.

When he had passed along everything that the major had let slip about the goings and comings of the English transport ships, Rob started home in the gathering dusk. He turned a corner and was elated to see the figure in the long green cloak that had haunted his dreams.

She handed out something to the children who clustered around her, then she turned the basket upside down to show them it was empty. She started away with a wake of importuning urchins behind her. Rob followed her too, drawn by those mesmerizing forces.

A few mansions at the lower end of Broad Way escaped the destruction of the fire in 1776. General Henry Clinton had selected as his quarters the most opulent of them, the home of the loyalist Kennedy family. Late each morning he and his entourage left Number One Broad Way to gallop up the avenue to a gaming house north of St. Paul's Chapel. They spent most of the day indulging in brandy, faro, billiards, bowling, and bawds.

Now, at the end of the afternoon, fifteen or twenty officers raced their horses back. They slowed for no one. Carters ran up over the curb to escape them, and people fled helter-skelter. Rob started to run as they headed for the young woman and the urchins crossing the street.

The children scattered, but one of them fell. Rob scooped him up and kept going. The horses passed so close that a hoof ripped his breeches and bruised his leg. When they had galloped away without looking back, Rob set the wriggling boy down and watched him scurry after the others.

"That was brave of thee." The young woman glanced up at him and then away.

She had used the Quakers' familiar form again, which gave Rob courage to ask, "What is thy name?"

"I am called Kate.

"The streets are dangerous, especially Canvas Town." Fool, he thought. Of course she knows that.

"I'm going home now." She looked off to one side, and down, and he wondered if she was shy too, or more likely, uninterested.

"May God keep thee." He wanted to ask if he could accompany her, but didn't trust his voice not to stammer.

"Thee is a Friend?"

"Yes. My name is Robert."

"May He hold thee in his care also." She started away.

"May I call on thee some time, Kate?"

"Yes."

"Where does thee live?"

My family is staying with Thomas Buchanan."

Robert felt as though he had grown taproots that made his feet fast to the cobblestones. As he watched her walk away he berated himself for a fool, a boor, and a coward. He had not thought to mention that Almy Buchanan was his cousin.

He put a hand in his pocket. His watch was gone. The urchin he had saved from being trampled must have filched it. Not one to waste opportunity, the little felon had pulled a loose brass button off his coat too.

Rob didn't care. He knew Green Cloak's name and where she lived. The question was, would he do anything about it?

Gathering intelligence under the enemy's nose, a hanging offense, did not worry him much, but he doubted he could summon the courage to knock on his cousin's door and ask to speak with the lovely Kate.

Twenty-two

Wherein Lizzie flirts with sedition; Kate sees stars;
Rob makes a delivery

JOHN ANDRÉ TURNED IN HIS SADDLE SO THE WOMEN COULD hear him. "I say, Jack, whatever happened to Smythe?"

"He died insolvent," said Colonel John Simcoe.

"He didn't die in Solvent." Almy Buchanan had heard this old joke before. "He died in Philadelphia. I'm sure I was at his burying."

Kate and Lizzie laughed so hard that Kate held on to the pommel and Lizzie wrapped her arms around her to keep from falling off the horse. The two of them would quiet down for a while, then burst into another squall of laughter. The joke wasn't funny, but the fresh air of Long Island made them giddy. Kate couldn't remember when she had felt this carefree.

The roan seemed as happy to leave New York as everyone else. He pranced and shook his head and flirted with Almy Buchanan's coquette of a mare. Almy wore a purple riding habit with the waistcoat unbuttoned to reveal the ruffles of a man's white linen shirt. Her three-corned hat perched at a jaunty angle on her powdered wig. A dark green silk handkerchief was knotted around her neck.

A trio of pack horses plodded along under a mountain of baggage, most of which belonged to Almy. She could not decide what to leave behind, so she brought it all—paste pots, beauty patches, paints, scent bottles, rouge, lotions, and creams. She packed lozenges to sweeten her breath, powdered antimony mixed with sheep's fat to darken her eyelids, and brushes to whitewash her face. She had wanted female companionship on this outing among soldiers, and Kate was elated that she had asked her to come along.

Lizzie rode pillion and she murmured in Kate's ear. "This is a bang-up way to travel, Mistress Kate. Not like that march through New Jersey with stiffs cluttering the countryside and men taking potshots at us. Plenty of vittles. Shoes on our feet and a horse under us."

Kate agreed. The day was mild for early March. Last night's inn had had beds that were almost free of vermin, and passably edible toad-in-the-hole, beef baked in a pie crust.

The escort of six handsome Queen's Rangers meant that neither brigands nor foragers nor the British guards at the sentry posts would bother them. The officers' pack of hounds kept the local curs at bay. John André and Jack Simcoe entertained Kate, Lizzie, Almy, and her maid, Betsy, with stories, ditties, and scenes from farces in which they had acted.

They played travelers' piquet, a game in which objects counted for points. The first to reach a hundred won. A person walking was only worth one point, but a skein of geese had a value of ten and a flock of sheep twenty. A cat looking out a window earned sixty points and a parson on a gray horse won the game. When something valuable appeared, they argued passionately over who had seen it first.

They were all as happy as if they'd been released from prison, which in a way they had. By March of 1779 the war had slouched into a stalemate with New York under a marginally effective seige. The French fleet had sailed away to see to their interests in the Caribbean. John André observed that once again the French had left their American allies in the lurch, a term that came, appropriately enough, from the old French dicing game called *lourche*.

British ships controlled the waters around New York, but the American army occupied Pennsylvania and New Jersey, limiting food and supplies coming in by land. North of the city General Washington's troops had settled into camps in an arc from Mamaroneck on Long Island Sound to Dobbs Ferry on the Hudson. The British controlled Long Island itself, and the officers had made it their hunting preserve and playground. The people of New York survived on the produce from the Long Island farms.

John André was entertaining them with Oliver Goldsmith's "Elegy on the Death of a Mad Dog . . ."

This dog and man at first were friends;
But when a pique began,
The dog, to gain his private ends,
Went mad, and bit the man.

The wound it seemed both sore and sad
To every Christian eye;
And, while they swore the dog was mad,
They swore the man would die.

André nodded to Kate to join him on the last stanza.

But soon a wonder came to light,
That showed the rogues they lied;
The man recovered of the bite,
The dog it was that died.

"If the Americans are the ungrateful cur who dies," said Lizzie, "Does that mean they will lose the war? Or does it mean that England, the man, is the rabid one after all?"

"It means the ungrateful curs shall lose the war, dear girl." Colonel Simcoe's aide had flanked Lizzie the entire trip. He was still trying to woo her, but he kept his nose out of range of her fists.

"Dr. Johnson is right," said Simcoe. "'Americans are a race of convicts, and ought to be thankful for anything we allow them short of hanging.'"

"If Americans are snafflers," muttered Lizzie, "It's because England nabs its footpads, foists, cutpurses, and nip-cheeses and lags them here."

"What did you say, dear girl?" The ensign veered closer.

Kate translated. "If there are thieves in America it is because England transports them here."

"The transportees are sent here for the improvement and well-peopling of the colonies," said Jack Simcoe.

"That policy is a good horse in the barn," Kate said, "But an arrant jade on a journey."

André chuckled. "Touché, Kate."

"I agree with Doctor Franklin's proposal." Kate figured she might as well be hung for a sheep as a lamb.

"What proposal is that?" asked John André.

"He suggests we round up all the rattlesnakes in America and send them to England in exchange for the human serpents she ships here."

Simcoe was not amused. "Benjamin Franklin shall be second in line for hanging, right after that misbegotten scourge, Mr. Washington."

"There is no arguing with Jack," said André. "When his pistol misses fire he clubs you with the butt of it."

"Colonel Simcoe," Lizzie whispered to Kate, "is a horse's butt."

Kate turned around and put her finger to her lips before Lizzie could become third in line for hanging.

Jack Simcoe was returning to Oyster Bay and his pursuit of Sally Townsend. He was in a good mood because he had taken up lodgings in the Townsend house, and so had the inside track. He wore the uniform of the loyalists' Forty-first Infantry Regiment of Queen's Rangers, a dark green coat with deep blue lapels and facings. A plume fluttered from the crest of his helmet. His touseled chestnut curls were unpowdered. He thought himself unbearably handsome, but his eyes were too close and his mouth too thin. Lizzie said when he smiled his lips reminded her of snakes wooing.

They had almost reached Oyster Bay when they met a woman riding toward them. When she passed them Almy turned to watch her go.

"Do you know her?" asked Kate.

"Aye." Almy reined her mare close to Kate's grey and lowered her voice. "That's Anna Strong of Setauket. The British arrested her husband for corresponding with the rebels. They imprisoned him on the *Jersey*."

"The *Jersey?*"

"That hulk we saw anchored in Wallabout Bay near the ferry landing." said Lizzie. "They keep rebel soldiers there."

Kate remembered the ship. She had thought it was abandoned. The idea that people lived aboard it surprised her.

"Folks say conditions are so bad that men die like flies," said Almy. "Anna Strong takes food to her husband."

"Why doesn't she appeal to General Clinton for his release?"

Almy rolled her eyes. "Had you met the man, you would not ask."

Kate called to André. "John, ask Henry Clinton to release Anna Strong's husband on parole."

"I did, fair lady." John André shrugged. "He will not. Strong acted as a spy. It is only through the good offices of his Tory relatives that he has not yet swung from a gibbet."

The party cantered down the main street of Oyster Bay, past neat cottages and kitchen gardens. The houses were intact, but only the frames of barns and outbuildings remained. Simcoe's Rangers had pried off the boards to construct barracks.

On a hill overlooking the village stood a redoubt surrounded by an abatis of felled trees with their sharpened limbs pointing outward. With the war on a low simmer Simcoe kept his men busy expanding the defensive works. Only stumps remained of the apple orchard that had surrounded them.

Across from the fort stood a white clapboard house. The party dismounted and handed the reins to the servants. A man and a young woman hurried across the yard. Colonel Simcoe bowed to kiss the woman's hand. Kate guessed she was Sally Townsend. She could see why Simcoe was smitten with her. She was tall with dark hair, a tiny waist, and strong, handsome features. She wore a simple wool frock and linen mob cap.

Then Kate realized that Sally Townsend's companion was the man she'd met first at the docks and then several weeks ago in Canvas Town. Why had he come here? Was he in love with Sally too?

He grinned, clapped John André on the back, and shook hands all around. He said something that made André and the ensigns throw their heads back and roar in laughter. Kate thought she might be mistaken in thinking she knew him, but if he wasn't the somber churl she had met, he resembled him to a remarkable degree.

"Almy," Kate whispered. "Who is that?"

"My cousin, Rob Townsend. I told you he lived in the city and that he would be visiting his family here."

Kate wanted to say, *You did not tell me that your cousin is Robert, a man who says he will call, and then does not.* "But he is a Quaker . . ."

"And I am not." Almy shrugged. "My family is of the world, as your people say." She waved her hat at Rob. "Come here at once, you animated bean pole, and meet a dear friend." Almy caught the look on his face. "Or have you met already?"

"Yes," Kate murmured. "We have."

She inclined her head in greeting, then with her heart skittering like a cat on ice, she went to find Lizzie.

LOGS CRACKLED IN THE FIREPLACE OF THE MAIN ROOM OFF the downstairs hall. Everyone's cheeks glowed red from their afternoon ride along the sound, while Jack Simcoe and his staff potted at the ducks and quail their dogs flushed from the reeds. Laughter circulated around a table loaded with tea and coffee, cakes and syllabub, beer, punch, wine, and smoked oysters. The banter was so light-hearted that Kate could almost imagine she was in her family's house in Philadephia and that the war had never happened.

"A Frenchman and a Swiss were drinking together one night," said Rob. "'Why is it,' the Frenchman asked, 'that you Swiss always fight for money while we French fight only for honor?' 'I suppose,' said the Swiss, 'That we each fight for what we most lack.'"

John André stood up amid the laughter and raised his glass in the old Royal Navy toast. "Confusion to the French."

"Huzzah!" the company shouted.

Sally Townsend had seated Kate across from her brother, Rob. Kate sipped her mulled wine and tried not to stare at him. She had thought him bashful and awkward. Now she discovered that he could match wits with John André, and he easily outpaced Jack Simcoe. His dark eyes lit up, his black eyebrows danced. His smile transformed him into someone more handsome than Kate would have guessed. Whenever she looked at him she felt a pressure around her heart.

Rob was enthused about the scientist William Herschel. With his improved telescopes, Rob said, Herschel had discovered nebulae and galaxies strewn across the heavens as a farmer could scatter flaxseed.

"Oh la." Sally sent a radiant smile around the table. "On his last visit Rob was all agog about electricity. He says it will cure bunions."

"Rheumatism, dear sister, not bunions. And as for the heavens, according to Herschel, our earth and sun are but specks in a cosmos of light that's unimaginably vast. Two grains of sand on an infinite shore."

"Prying into the workings of God's universe smacks of heresy," said Sally.

"Maybe Edmund Spenser was right," said Almy. " 'He that strives to touch the stars, oft stumbles at a straw.' "

"I see no conflict between science and religion," said Kate. "Such study makes His creation more awe-inspiring."

"Exactly." Rob smiled at her.

"Well, I must see these nebulae that God the Farmer has sown in the back forty of his heaven." When it came to heresy, Almy was no slouch.

With beer in hand she rose and, trailing everyone in her wake, headed for the door. The night had grown cold, and they blew on their fingers and stamped their feet as they stared up at the spangle of stars. The arm of Rob's coat brushed Kate's cape and she saw tiny sparks dance in the wool.

She remembered a lecture she had seen in Philadelphia. It had been billed as a demonstration of electricity, but in fact it had featured Dr. Franklin's kissing machine. An assistant turned a crank on a box of copper coils. Whenever a woman put a hand on it and kissed the lecturer on the lips she received a tingle. The thought of kissing Rob set Kate's heart to thumping like the dasher in a butter churn.

Rob swept his arm along the course of the Milky Way. "The Greeks called this *Galaxias kyklos,* Circle of Milk," he said. "Our sun and earth are part of it, glowing orbs hovering at the outer edge of a mass of stars beyond counting."

"Rob, you are an imbecile." Almy stamped her thin-soled pumps on the frozen ground. "Does this dirt glow like a star? Are stars made up of horse manure and pig dung and the castings of worms? I think not."

Sally headed off an argument by pointing out the Big Bear and the Dipper. The others chimed in, each star creature more ridiculous than the last, until finally John André claimed to see George Washington in chains. Simcoe identified King George on his throne surrounded by cherubim.

Maybe the wine affected Kate, or the glory of God's creation, or the puzzling man standing next to her.

"I feel I could wrap the stars around me like a cloak." She had the urge to lean back against him and feel his arms around her. The audacity of it heated up her cheeks.

" 'You never enjoy the world aright,' " Rob recited, " 'Till the sea itself floweth in your veins, till you are clothed with the heavens, and crowned with the stars: and perceive yourself to be the sole heir of the whole world.' "

"Thee has read Thomas Traherne then?"

"Yes."

Kate finished. " 'Till you can sing and rejoice and delight in God, as misers do in gold and kings in sceptres, you never enjoy the world.' "

Almy grew bored with poetry, infinity, and the frigid wind, and led the retreat back to the house. Rob held Kate's elbow to guide her across the dark ground. In the entryway she took the candle Sally Townsend gave her and followed her and Almy up the narrow stairs. When she reached the top she could still feel his phantom touch on her arm.

"May God keep thee safe through the night." Rob said it too softly for Kate to hear.

And would that our abilities could keep wing with our desires, he thought. He realized that the convolutions of the heart were more confounding than the infinite expanse of the cosmos.

He joined John André and Jack Simcoe at the fire in the room off the entryway, which served as Rob's father's mercantile and Simcoe's headquarters. The place smelled of spices, fresh-made paper, and the sizing in the calicos and ginghams. Rob had procured the goods at the docks in New York and sent them here, but his father had not thanked him.

Samuel Townsend had gone upstairs early. If Jack Simcoe knew how much the elder Townsend disliked him and his occupying force, he gave no indication. Rob knew about it though. He knew his father's disdain extended to those who fraternized with the British. He knew it included him.

As Rob talked and joked with Simcoe and André and shared their pear brandy, he prayed they would retire soon. He had miles to travel before first light.

Twenty-three

Wherein Seth and Lizzie have loft ideas; a cow saves Rob from prevarication; frost heaves up more than fieldstones

BITS OF HAY, SMOTHERED LAUGHTER, AND GASPS OF PASSION filtered between the planks of the loft and rained too gently onto the sleeping horses to wake them. Seth and Lizzie possessed the exuberence of youth, and neither cold nor consequences could distract them. As trysting places went, this one excelled. The Queen's Rangers had not stripped the barn of its shingles, beams, and joists only because Colonel Simcoe required shelter for his hounds and horses. The building's stone walls blocked the January wind, and hay mounded soft and fragrant under them.

In the past three years they had met under hedges, in wagons, spring houses, woodsheds, a beached whaleboat, and a closet. Lizzie joked that if needs be they could take a flourish in an apple crate. She and Seth rolled together in the hay until they wrapped themselves up in her cloak. In the dark he traced her full mouth, her nose, and the ridges above her eyes with the tips of his fingers. Then he kissed them all.

"Where have you scoured off to these long weeks?" she asked.

"I landed in a nest of king's men and told them I wanted to join the loyalist company they were raising. I even peeped the muster list."

"I fear for you, Seth, to dissemble among the enemy."

"I've had some narrow squeaks, but it's the Americans I fear. They mistake me for an enemy spy now and then and collar me. Once I had to make a frog's leap into a ditch and stem off smartly to keep them from turning my carcass into a flour sieve."

"Surely your own officers would not turn you off."

"They wouldn't hang me, but if they reveal who I am, the jig is up."

"If ill were to befall you I could not bear it."

"I have been nabbed and legged it too often. If it happens again the loyalists will be fly to the lay, they'll suspect the scheme." He spoke in a murmur with his mouth against the hollow of her shoulder. "Major Tallmadge says I must rejoin my company. The major says General Wayne has threatened to come looking for me."

The barn door creaked and the two of them strained to hear in the darkness. Seth felt Lizzie's heart pounding against his chest. Footfalls crossed the barn and stopped at the foot of the ladder to the loft.

"Are you there?"

Seth untangled himself and lay on his stomach so he could look over the edge. "Yes," he called softly.

Lizzie straightened her skirts, and Seth tied the strings on his breeches while Rob climbed up. Rob shrouded his lantern so that only a firefly glimmer illuminated the loft. The sight of Lizzie startled him then made him angry. Abraham Woodhull had asked him to help the boy escape, and this was the thanks he got. Maybe Cousin Almy was right when she said that no good deed goes unpunished.

He was about to say, "You would risk exposing my family and your duty for a frolic in the hay?" But Seth spoke first.

"This is Lizzie, my betrothed."

Betrothed. Rob looked at their faces, so young and earnest, so suffused with a glow that had nothing to do with the lantern. Because of Kate Darby, for the first time in his life he understood that glow.

"She will not betray us." Seth put his arm around Lizzie's shoulders.

"How do you know her?"

"She is my sister's maid."

Rob was confused and suspicious. The universe must be playing a prank on him. Lizzie was Kate Darby's maid, and Kate was a Quaker. And Seth? Well, Seth was a different person each time Rob saw him but never a Quaker.

"You are Kate Darby's brother?"

"I am the only son of her father."

This was an unlooked-for complication. Rob had planned to make sure the boy arrived safely at the rendezvous, but now he felt an overwhelming responsibility. He could not be the cause of anyone's death, much less the brother of the woman he realized, finally, that he loved.

"We've little time," he said. "I must return before Simcoe and André arise."

"I can go alone."

Rob shook his head. "It's a long, dark, boggy, dirty way. I know the lanes and cowpaths. You would have to stay on the roads where the patrols would make short work of you."

Seth picked up his satchel of belongings, his musket, powder horn, and bullet pouch. He leaned down to kiss Lizzie lightly on the lips. She put her arms around his neck and whispered, "May God keep you."

"God and General Wayne will see that no harm comes to any of the Second Pennsylvania." Seth stroked her hair, as if to imprint the wiry softness of it on his hand and in his memory. "You mustn't tell Kate that you saw me. We cannot risk anyone knowing Rob is involved in this."

"Yes, Seth."

"When I am with the Rifles again I will send her and mother a letter. And I will write to you every day." He brushed back her hair and kissed her forehead. Then he started down the ladder after Rob.

"When will I see you again?" Lizzie called softly.

Seth reached out a hand and she took it. She lay on her stomach and hitched out over the edge of the loft so she could hold onto it as long as possible. When the tips of her fingers lost contact with his she looked as though she were watching him sink for the third time into a deep pool of murky water.

"I love you." Seth crossed the barn floor and slid out the door that Rob had left ajar.

ROB FIGURED THIS WAS ONE OF THOSE TIMES WHEN REFUSING to take up arms had a distinct advantage. Seth's Pennsylvania rifle would have labeled him as an outsider here, so he carried a British Brown Bess musket. Rob figured it must seem to weigh a hundred pounds by now. Seth shifted it from one shoulder to the other as he walked.

When Rob told Seth that the route along the coastline of Long Island Sound was long, dark, boggy, and dirty, he understated the case. He dared not take horses from the barn, so he and Seth went on foot. The night had turned cold, and they wore their wide-brimmed hats pulled low and their coat collars up. They used the stars and the full moon for light.

Rob looked up at the brilliance of the heavens. Had he really stood next to Kate Darby under this same sky this very night? Had he seen the stars reflected in her eyes or dreamed them? He tried to walk and stargaze and think about Kate Darby's blue-green eyes and red-gold hair, but love and astronomy tripped him up. His foot went through the crust of ice and into a hole. Icy mud and water filled his high boots. Seth pulled him out and soon both were soaked to the skin, and shivering.

Nothing dismayed Seth and he never complained. He never asked how far they had to go. Someone with less sense would want to know why Rob hadn't arranged to meet the boat at the shore behind the Townsends' fields instead of slogging across creation in the dead of a late winter's night. Someone with less sense would not think about implicating the Townsend family if caught on their beach. Rob wondered if Seth's sister was made of the same smart and hardy stuff.

Rob and Seth came to a cove that looked like a thousand others along the coast. Fog rolled in off the sound.

"We'll wait here." Rob hunkered under the overhang of a granite outcrop at the edge of the shore.

Seth squatted next to him. "Why did you agree to spy?"

Rob didn't have to think long. "Apples."

"Apples?"

"Jack Simcoe's Rangers cut down the orchard my grandfather planted. When I was young I climbed those trees to look out at the world. Every autumn baskets of apples lined the hallways. The smell of them filled the house. We children strung apple slices on thread, and our father hung them to dry. In the coldest days of winter we ate them baked into pies and cobblers. We spread apple butter on toasted bread. We drank them as cider."

"You're risking your life for apples?"

"No. I'm doing it so the British can never have the authority to ride roughshod over us. So they cannot destroy or take what we have labored to produce. I'm doing it so they can never treat us as vassals."

"The bloodybacks say that we and they are the same people," muttered Seth, "but they are mistaken."

Rob thought of the toll this struggle was taking. His father moved through the house like a shade now, rarely speaking. Samuel Townsend had no choice but to tolerate Jack Simcoe's presence, but he was furious with Rob for his friendship with John André. Rob said nothing about the charge from General Washington that required it. Involving members of his family would put them in danger.

Rob was weary of politics. He was sick of war. He wanted to be free to love. He wanted to ask Seth about his sister. He wanted to ask how Kate had behaved as a child, what foods she favored, and what books she read. He wanted to know everything about her, but if he called on her he would have to keep secrets from her. He was sure that if Kate found out he was gathering intelligence she would despise him for it, and he could not blame her. He would have to keep it secret from her just as he hid it from his father. Spying was contemptible work, deceitful, treacherous, dangerous, and worst of all, ungentlemanly.

He would not admit to himself that the thought of wooing Kate frightened him. His life was drab, true, but it was predictable. Love was not predictable. It was chaotic, troubling, and more unnerving, in its way, than spying.

To keep warm Seth paced up and down the narrow beach. Rob looked out at the thick fog until his eyes lost focus. The lap of the water and the whine of the wind blurred to an undercurrent of sound. He stood at the edge of existence.

He shook his head to clear it. He wondered if he had mistaken the meeting place. He began to fear that the British had finally caught Caleb. He was about to tell Seth that he would have to hide in the barn for another day when he heard a muffled thump out in the mist. The sharp prow of a whaleboat sliced through the fog like a blade through clabbered milk, and its keel grated on the gravel. The eight crewmen shipped oars and splashed ashore, hauling the boat with them. They were all big, but one blocked out more starlight than the others.

"You are late." Rob spoke in a hushed voice.

Caleb Brewster shrugged shoulders that looked like overstuffed luggage. "We had to dodge a man-o-war."

One of his crew spoke up. "He wanted to board it. Only the promise of mutiny dissuaded him."

"We could have taken it easily. It had but a skeleton crew."

Getting angry with Caleb Brewster was a waste of effort, but sometimes Rob couldn't help it. "Do not mix pleasure with business, Caleb."

"Harrassing British shipping is business, Rob."

"You know what I mean."

"Then let's get to the business of delivering the sprat to Connecticut."

Caleb waved the men back to the boat. "We'd best move along. The king's crud might have spotted us." He winked at Rob as though narrow escapes were the best fun. "In fact, I'm fairly certain they did."

Caleb Brewster had hunted whales off the coast of Greenland. He had joined the Continental Army as an artillery lieutenant two years ago. When his enlistment ended he took command of a fleet of whaleboats prowling the Devil's Belt of Long Island Sound. He had boarded and captured loyalist merchant ships, plundered caches of British stores ashore, and participated in countless tavern brawls with friends and foes alike, but he had not taken to the discipline of soldiering.

Seth was the one who took up a sentry position on top of the rocks. He underhanded a stone at Rob to get his attention and gestured toward the south. He jumped down to the beach and as he ran past Rob to help launch the boat, he muttered, "Horses."

He threw his musket and haversack into the bow and clambered in after it. Caleb and his crew splashed into the water, climbed aboard, and took up their positions at the rudder and oars. Rob waded out to shove the prow around so it pointed away from shore. He could hear the hoofbeats now, and he started at a trot down the beach in the opposite direction from home. When he looked back over his shoulder the fog seemed to take an eternity swallowing the boat.

The muted creak of the muffled oarlocks faded away as the horsemen arrived. Rob sprinted for the inadequate cover of a few stunted oaks.

"Halt."

Rob ran faster, the sand sucking at his sodden boots. He clawed his way up the bank as shots whined around him. He felt the warm breath of one on his cheek.

"Please, God . . ." he continued the banter he had carried on with the

Deity since he was a child ". . . no holes in my hat. I cannot explain a bullet hole in my hat without resorting to untruths."

Running at a stoop he followed the thread of a cowpath across the marsh. In the moonlight he felt as exposed as a beached whale. He heard the hoofbeats grow louder and then splashing, whinnying, and men swearing.

Rob climbed the bluff and reached the shelter of the sycamores. He looked up at the moon snared in the trees' bare branches. It had slid farther toward the western horizon than he would have wished. And he would have to make a wide circle to throw the patrol off his trail. The sun would rise before he reached home.

He wondered how he could explain his mud-caked state. Young Seth Darby was a Quaker who had gotten the hang of prevarication, but Rob could not do it. But then Seth had gone for a soldier.

Once one accepts a commission to commit murder, Rob mused, lying must follow as a natural course.

God would provide a solution to his problem. All Rob had to do was trust Him.

"OH MY! LOOK AT THIS SORRY SPECTACLE." SALLY AND ALMY stood at the small window of the upstairs room while Kate tried to see around their voluminous nightgowns.

"I cannot think who looks worse," Sally said, "Rob or Molly."

Molly? Rob was arriving shortly after daybreak with someone named Molly? Kate was stunned by the fury and despair that wracked her.

"She's so filthy how can you tell who it is?" asked Almy.

"Because she's missing half of her right ear."

Filthy? Half an ear? What sort of woman had Rob taken up with?

Kate squeezed in between them and looked down into the yard. "Molly is a cow!"

"Of course. What did you think she was?"

Almy pounded on the door connecting their room with the maids' quarters under the eaves. "Betsy, Lizzie, help us dress. Quickly now."

They shrieked and laughed as they splashed cold water on their faces. They gargled, spit, and rubbed their teeth with their fingers. They rooted through trunks throwing chemises and petticoats around, exchanging pockets, ribbons, and waistcoats, and deciding which dresses to put on. They ended up wearing each other's.

Lizzie seemed especially rushed. Her hands shook as she helped pull the chemise over Kate's head.

"Is thee well, Lizzie?"

"Very well. Only taken with a chill." She whispered, "Betsy pulls the covers off me when she sleeps, though she swears she does not."

"What's this?" Kate picked a piece of straw from the midnight thicket of Lizzie's hair.

Lizzie took it and blew it so it floated away in a cloud of her breath. "It must have escaped from the ticking while I slept."

Even though they were in a hurry and their country frocks were simple, dressing took time, especially for Almy. She insisted on wearing her whalebone corset and stomacher. Betsy laced it up the back, recruiting Lizzie to help her pull it tight. Betsy tied on the false rump carved of cork and arranged Almy's skirts over it. Almy would not leave until Betsy had pinned each curl in place, while Sally and Kate crossed their arms on their chests and drummed their fingers on their arms.

"You never know," Almy reminded them, "what gentlemen one might encounter at the foot of the stairs."

When they all were presentable they flowed in a cascade of wool lawns, worsteds, and shalloons down the narrow stairs. Lizzie stepped on Kate's skirts the whole way.

They found Jack Simcoe writing at his desk. "Your servant, ladies." He stood and bowed. "Captain André will join us later. He does not agree with Poor Richard about early to bed and early to rise. He says he is healthy, wealthy, and wise enough already."

Rob sat wrapped in a blanket in front of the corner fireplace with his knees almost in the flames. His mud-caked boots steamed on the hearth. His wet hair was clean and a tub of filthy water sat in a corner.

His face was haggard with exhaustion, but he smiled sheepishly when he saw them. "Good morrow."

"Cousin, you look like something the cat dragged in," said Almy.

"What happened?" Sally took his hand. "You're cold as ice."

"I heard Molly lowing and found her mired in the bog beyond the pasture. Had a bit of a time getting her out."

"Warm yourself, then join us," said Sally. "Jack has agreed to tennis if you will play."

"I'm returning to the city this morning."

Almy and Sally surrounded him. "You can't. You mustn't."

Lizzie hurried in with a mug of hot brandy. When she leaned down to hand it to him no one saw the look that passed between them. Kate was too distraught to notice the smile on Lizzie's face when she went humming upstairs to straighten the shambles in the sisters' room.

Kate stood aside feeling forlorn. Rob would not look at her, and she chided herself for being such a fool as to imagine he cared for her. He wrapped the blanket more tightly around him, nodded to them all, and went upstairs to pack his saddlebags for the trip back to the city.

Two of Simcoe's Rangers stamped the mire off their boots and came in to report. They were weary and spattered with mud. They had seen a boat just before moonset, they said, and had chased a man until they lost him in the bog.

"Which way was he headed?"

"East."

Simcoe pushed back from the desk and paced, his hands clasped behind his back, a scowl scudding in across his thick brow. "There are traitors at work, mark me. And I will ferret them out."

"Oh la, Jack," said Sally. "They were smugglers, I'm sure. They're more plentiful than seagulls along this coast."

There was no doubt that Jack Simcoe was smitten with Sally, but in this instance his smile was as sincere as Stork Withers's beauty mark and padded calves.

"Of course you're right, dear lady."

A FARMER PUSHED HIS BARROW ACROSS THE RUTTED FIELDS, stopping to pick up rocks heaved to the surface by the winter's frost. He was about to turn back when he saw the leather packet half dragged from the crevice between two boulders. He threw it on top of the heap of stones and trundled back to his stoutly built house with the glazed Dutch tiles and gambrel roof.

He carried it inside and opened it up. He couldn't read English, so he folded the parchment back up and wrapped it neatly in its oiled cloth and leather. He laid it on a shelf among the delft plates and meerschaum pipes, pewter flagons, and a Bible. He put a few more logs on the fire. He tamped tobacco into his favorite pipe, lit it with an ember, and sat on a bench in the fire's light with the Bible open on his lap. It was written in Dutch.

Twenty-four

Wherein Rob accepts employment with the Devil's tout,
but lacks the nerve to call on an angel

WHOEVER CREATED THE FICTION THAT COCKS CROWED ONLY at daybreak didn't know poultry. Roosters cock-a-doodle-dooed whenever the mood struck them. The sound of their crowing in Rivington's print shop might have seemed odd to passersby, but it always struck Rob as appropriate. James himself resembled a rooster.

At fifty-five he was small and sleek, and he favored ruffled shirts and claret red velvet waistcoats trimmed with gold lace. He had restless eyes, a nose like a half-opened barlow blade, and a triangular pout of a mouth. His kettle-belly cast a shadow over skinny legs clad in buckskin knee breeches that fitted him as snugly as they once had fitted the buck. He did not stroll, he strutted. He chased the ladies of all ranks and stations, and he was not what anyone would call a modest man.

Rivington's printing press was as big as a rhinosaurus, and bolted to the floor and braced at the ceiling besides. Rob didn't trust Rivington any farther than he could throw that libelous contraption, but he couldn't help liking him. James Rivington was a self-serving, mendacious, sychophantic libertine. He was also affable, educated, and funny. As Hercules Mulligan observed, Jemmy Rivington's hypocrisy was so sincere it fair warmed the cockles of the heart.

Rivington had sent one of the city's urchins to fetch Rob, but he always entered the print shop cautiously after hours. He once had walked in on James and a bow-legged beauty bare-arsed and entangled atop bundles of the *Royal Gazette*. James also turned loose the most belligerent of his fighting cocks in the evening to bullyrag anyone with a mind to pilfer. James had named him General Allen after Ethan Allen. Like his namesake the rooster was large, scarred, uncouth, and as dirty and disheveled as a feather duster. Rob could imagine him demanding, as Ethan Allen did of the British commander at Fort Ticonderoga, "Come out, you damned old skunk, or I'll sacrifice the whole garrison!"

Rob opened the door to Rivington's shop and peered inside. No feathered fury rushed to challenge him. The place was empty of the typesetters, pressmen, stonemen, clerks, printer's devils, and delivery boys who rushed around when an issue of the *Royal Gazette* was being peeled off the tympan, page by page. The hulking press itself filled the center of the room. The sturdy oak stands for the type cases, galley trays, composing sticks, and inking stones ranged around it.

On the tables portly brown bottles of ink and the big, stuffed-leather inking balls lay among the packets of freshly printed lottery tickets, billets, handbills, legal forms, and galley proofs. Bundles of the large sheets of paper called "double elephant" lined up against the back wall. They were wrapped in coarse brown paper made from the manufacturer's vat dregs. Drifts of paper trimmings swirled around Rob's feet when he entered the shop.

James kept his fighting cocks downstairs in wicker cages next to his wine racks. From the cellar came the sound of their bickering. The two roosters named Ethan Allen and Benedict Arnold made the most noise. They maligned each other with such fervor that Rivington referred to the basement as Fort Ticonderoga, the place where the two originals had fallen heels over helmets into loathing for each other.

In a side room James sold musical instruments as well as equipment for badminton, tennis, and fives, cricket, bowls, backgammon, and dice. Lining the pressroom were shelves holding green bottles filled with the Grand Cordial Elixir, British Oil, and Dr. Turlington's Balm of Life that he advertised in his paper. A heap of rags filled a corner. James bought them at a pittance from the children who scrounged the city for them. He then resold them for a larger pittance to the papermaker whose noisesome mill fouled Collect Pond three-quarters of a mile to the north.

He also had recently bought a half-interest in the Merchants' Coffee House at the docks. Hercules said Jemmy Rivington had so many enterprises going that one day he would sell himself to himself. Rob countered that the sale would never happen. Jemmy would ask an exorbitant price for himself then indignantly refuse to pay it.

Rob called up into the stairwell leading to the second floor. "James."

"Ascend, my boy." Rivington's accent was distilled aristocracy. His father, grandfather, and greatgrandfather had served as the Church of England's official publishers in London, which James found reason to mention often.

When Rob reached the landing he stood aside to let pass a tall fellow, all knobs, angles, and loose ends. The man gave his lopsided grotesquery of a smile and touched the rolled vee of his tricorn brim with fingers whose ends either bent at right angles or were missing the final joint. Rob turned to watch him bounce down the stairs, his long, faded black coattails flapping after him. He slammed the outer door behind him.

Rob went into the office and sat in the salamander slat-back armchair James offered.

"You're probably curious to know what brought Tunis Birdwhistle here." Rivington set a bottle of Madeira and two glasses on the small table between them.

Rob shrugged. "It's not my concern. I only know him from the coffee house."

"He had a business proposition." James settled into the enfolding curves of a morris chair and propped his gleaming, turkey-leather shoes up on the papers scattered across an old trunk. "He says he has found a source for the same paper the rebels use for their money, and the British will buy all the Continental notes he can print. They plan to distribute them to the king's loyal subjects in Connecticut to pay their taxes, thus devaluing the rebels' currency."

"They've found a way to devalue something that is already worthless. How enterprising of them." Rob added this news to the information he would pass along to Abraham Woodhull.

Rivington shrugged. "The point is they will pay handsomely for the forged notes."

"And Birdwhistle wants to use your equipment."

"Yes, but my press won't print from copperplate engravings."

Rob could tell that the missed opportunity weighed on Jemmy. He changed the subject, nodding toward the cellar door. "I see that General Allen is confined to quarters down in Fort Ticonderoga."

"He is recruiting resolve for a battle with Clinton's champion tomorrow." James poured a glass of Madeira for Rob. "I purchased the general from that lad who came looking for you at the coffee house last fall, and I must say he's a scrapper."

"The general, you mean?"

"Yes. And how do you know the boy?"

"He delivered a message from a business associate in Setauket." Which was true enough. Rob did supply Abraham Woodhull with goods.

"I have a proposition for you." James held his own glass up to the window. The sun shining through it created dancing patches of crimson light on the wide planks of the oak floor. "I am so occupied with my new duties at the coffee house that I could use your services as a correspondent for the *Gazette.*" James saw Rob open his mouth to decline. He held up a slender hand with fingertips discolored by ink and tobacco. "Yes, yes, I know. You members of the Quaking sect worship truth as your god. And you think that truth is as much a stranger to the *Royal Gazette* as the Almighty is to the Hottentots."

"Jemmy, you lie like ten epitaphs."

"Truth, my dear fellow, is a matter of timing. What was true yesterday may prove false today. And any base-metal exaggeration that I print tomorrow might alchemize into a twenty-four-carat fact the day after."

"Like the thirty-six thousand Russian Cossacks who will arrive at any moment to fight alongside the Hessian and British troops? Or your story of the assassination of Benjamin Franklin in Paris?"

"That was not a lie, my boy, but wishful thinking. And if I print it often enough it might very well become true. However, if Dr. Franklin dies in Paris it will most likely be of the French pox. I would say that a jealous husband might kill him, but while the French are capable of envy they aren't civilized enough to experience jealousy."

Rob knew that James Rivington hadn't always been so stridently in favor of the Crown. Several years ago he had vowed to print both sides of the issues, but his lack of bias in the patriots' favor had stirred up the Sons of Liberty. They had hung him in effigy and sacked his shop. He had taken ship to England just ahead of their tar pot and feathers, and a ride on the fence-rail hackney. When the British retook the city he returned in triumph with a commission as the king's printer, a new press, and a set of fine Caslon type. He had been blasting the American rebellion ever since.

"What would you expect of me?" Rob asked.

"I need someone to report on the social doings in New York. You could do what you already do, engage the officers in conversation when they come into the coffee house. Glean from them the news of their goings and comings. I'm sure the feminine readership will devour that information with great interest. You may write the truth, the whole truth, and nothing but the truth, unless of course, it is unflattering to the gentlemen in question. I'm short of funds, but I can assure you meals and beverage."

Rivington was always short of funds. Hercules said he would be the wealthiest man in America if he didn't fling his funds by the fistful into the whirlwind of whores and horses. But even free meals would be helpful for Rob. He had paid informants from his own pocket when the guineas that Abraham brought ran out, and he had little chink to jingle now. One more reason not to woo the fair Kate Darby. Who would want to marry a pauper when she was surrounded by wealthy aristocrats?

Rob savored the warm glow of the Madeira while he thought about the offer. One would need more than Ben Franklin's magnifying spectacles to find a flyspeck of truth in the *Royal Gazette,* but writing for it would provide a perfect excuse to gather intelligence.

Rivington broke the silence before it became uncomfortable. "Speaking of liars, have you heard about the latest argument between Ethan Allen and Benedict Arnold?"

"You mean the men, not the fighting cocks?"

"Yes. General Allen once asked General Arnold where he was going. 'Why, to Litchfield,' Arnold replied. 'Oh, you damned liar,' exclaimed Allen. 'You tell me you are going to Litchfield to make me think you are going to White Plains, but I have made inquiries, and I know for a fact that you are going to Litchfield.'"

Rob laughed. "Alright. I'll start tomorrow." He shook his head. "I imagine Satan bears a family resemblance to you, Jemmy."

James smoothed the velvet waistcoat taut over his burl of a stomach. "Not so. Sir Henry Clinton is a close friend of the Devil, and he tells me Old Scratch is not nearly so handsome as I." He refilled Rob's glass. "Lying is an 'abomination unto the Lord,' my boy, but a very useful device in times of trouble. I suggest you get the hang of it."

THE TINKLING OF THE BELL ON THE DOOR OF ROB'S DRY goods shop and the arrival of three Royal Welsh Fusiliers startled Abraham Woodhull so badly he dropped two quires of paper onto the floor. The fifty sheets of creamy vellum scattered.

Rob made a shopkeeper's bow to the soldiers. "Excuse me, gentlemen, I shall be right with you."

He helped Abraham pick up the sheets, counting them silently as he did so. When he reached thirty-six he slipped in a piece of paper that looked as blank as the others but wasn't. He added the rest of the stack under it.

Abraham was beginning to pant, and he turned so pale that Rob worried he would topple over in a faint. His hands trembled too badly to hold on to the paper, so Rob took it from him. He thought it best to distract him and get him out of sight.

"Abraham, would you fetch the bolt of bottle-green baize? These gentlemen have come to fetch it for a billiard table."

With one last anxious look at the paper Abraham scuttled for the storeroom door. Rob couldn't blame him for being terrified. This was the first time he had written his weekly report with the invisible stain that Caleb Brewster had ferried across the sound from Washington's headquarters in White Plains. Abraham had smuggled a vial of it into the city under his hatband. He had hidden the bulge with the red cockade he wore on his hat to show he was a loyal subject of King George.

The plan was to put the report in a specified place in the quires. Then if Abraham was searched on his way home, as he almost certainly would be, the sentries would not find a suspicious sheet of blank paper. When he reached home he could pull out the thirty-sixth page and send it off. But neither Abraham nor Rob believed the stain would work. They both feared the words would slowly appear under their horrified gaze, exposing their crime to everyone.

The Fusiliers watched Rob wrap the quires in rough brown paper and tie the package with string.

"I want for stationery myself," said one of them. "What's the tariff?"

Rob could feel sweat forming under his collar. This was all the paper he had in the shop and soldiers thought nothing of taking what they wanted. Rob frantically auditioned pretexts to slip the thirty-sixth sheet out of the stack if they demanded the paper.

"The gentleman has purchased this lot, but I can get more tomorrow morning at the Fly market. I'll sell it to you for what it costs me, ten shillings a ream."

Not that it mattered what he charged them. The officers rarely paid for anything. Rob had taken to delivering their bills to their commanders. The majors and colonels didn't settle their own debts either, but at least some of them required their men to, eventually. Hercules had the same problem collecting from his army customers. He said his shoes had gotten into such a habit of going to one particular officer's quarters in search of payment, that he had to change them for another pair whenever he wanted to walk anywhere else.

Fortunately this lieutenant was more agreeable than most. "I'll come back tomorrow then."

Abraham returned with the cloth and his composure. On their way out, the Fusiliers passed Almy and Kate coming in. Kate had the same affect on Rob that the Fusiliers had had on Abraham. He clasped his hands behind his back so she would not see them trembling. He would have stammered a greeting, but Almy didn't give him a chance.

"You wretched man, why haven't you called on us?" She buzzed about the shop inspecting everything, and leaving Kate and Rob looking everywhere but at each other. "It's already warm for April." Almy flapped her hand in front of her face. "Have you any fans, cousin?" She spotted Abraham. "Is that Woodhull? What brings you away from the farm and how is your father?"

Abraham opened his mouth to answer, but she was already exclaiming over the Spanish shawls.

"Good morrow, Friend Darby." Rob bowed to Kate. "This is my colleague, Abraham Woodhull of Setauket, Long Island."

Abraham bowed. "Miss Sally Townsend has told me about you. She was effusive in her praise, but you're lovelier than she painted."

Kate's cheeks flushed. "She is too kind in her assessment." She held out her hand, and Abraham made a crisp bow over it.

"And my wretched cousin Rob said nothing to you about Kate?" Almy looked out from among the hooped petticoats hanging in a far corner. "You see, Kate, I told you he was as shy as three church mice. And when are you going to move out of that musty belfry in which you roost, Robert?"

"I prefer the top floor, dear cousin. Only God is above me there. He's an active fellow but quiet."

Kate smiled. Almy laughed merrily and made one more circuit, in case she had missed anything. With Kate in tow she blew out of the shop as abruptly as she had entered. She left a calm behind her, like the eye of a hurricane, or the aftermath of a cyclone. Rob stood transfixed, trying to analyze the expression in Kate's eyes when she looked back at him on her way out. Was it wistful or peeved, polite or indifferent?

He waited two days so he would not seem forward. Besides he needed to gather enough nerve to call on an angel. When he closed the shop at two in the afternoon on the third day he went to his belfry, as Almy called it. He filled the basin and washed. He found a pair of stockings with no holes in them and polished his old shoes, although that was like trying to groom a pair of mangy dogs. He put on his best shirt, breeches, waistcoat, and coat. He combed his unruly hair and tied it back with the luxury of an eelskin. He brushed off his old beaver tricorn.

He arrived at the opposite side of the street from the Buchanan house as half a dozen officers were leaving. Kate bid them good-bye from the steps, but she did not see Rob. He peered over the piles of lettuce and carrots in a produce wagon as a lieutenant, his plumed helmet under one arm, bent over Kate's hand and kissed it. Kate went inside and the lieutenant passed close to where Rob stood. The man was solid. He was handsome. He gave off the unmistakeable bouquet of money and breeding.

Rob turned around and headed for the coffee house.

Twenty-five

Wherein William Cunningham reels in;
Rob takes up residence with alligators

JOHN ANDRÉ'S HIGH BLACK RIDING BOOTS WERE A WONDER and a mystery. Rob's own shoes always had filth from the streets on them, no matter how often he cleaned them. John kept his boots polished to a satiny gloss that stopped tastefully short of garish. His boots existed in another world, an elusive Eden where the streets were not awash in offal and mud. Some few fortunate individuals were privy to the secrets of elegance. John André was one of them. Rob was not.

John tilted back in his chair and rested those twin black marvels, crossed at the ankles, on the corner of the table. He and Rob watched William Cunningham, the provost marshal of New York's teeming prisons, lumber into the Merchants' Coffee House.

His appearance must have prompted André to say, "You know, in England we place all our emphasis on breeding."

Rob passed him the pot of coffee. "We think breeding is entertaining here in America too, but we engage in other activities as well."

André threw his head back and laughed. They both watched Cunningham and his convoy of officers who hadn't grown to despise him, which meant they must have just stepped off the transport from England.

Cunningham was a hulking man in a powdered wig that looked as if cattle had trampled it. His coat always had a line of stains that André called the tears of the tankard, the whiskey that he had spilled down his front. His filthy shirttails hung from under his rumpled black coat and his gray wool stockings sagged. His shoe soles had worn down so badly that they tilted like rowboats shipping water. He was always drunk and unsteady on his feet. Taken all in all he reminded Rob of an overloaded rag-picker's barrow lurching over cobblestones.

John André arched one of the eyebrows that a female admirer had, in a flight of overwrought doggerel, compared to a dove's wings. "Do you know the difference between a misfortune and a calamity?"

"No, I don't."

"If William Cunningham fell into the East River, that would be a misfortune. If someone pulled him out, that would be a calamity."

Rob laughed. It felt good. It felt more than good. He hadn't laughed since the last time he had talked to John André over a month ago. "They say that if Will Cunningham shakes hands with you, count your fingers afterward."

"He claims to be a self-made man . . ." André drawled, ". . . which relieves the Almighty of a burdensome amount of blame."

Rob decided to mention what bothered him most about the provost. "Cunningham allows inhuman conditions to exist in the prisons."

"Allows inhuman conditions? My dear friend, he perpetrates them." André shrugged.

Rob knew that John's superior, Sir Henry Clinton, could relieve the suffering of the American prisoners of war if he wanted. He also knew Clinton would sneer at the notion. The only member of the human species for whom he seemed to hold genuine affection was his adjutant, John André, recently promoted to major.

"I do wish Cunningham would do something about the smell from his jails." André raised his voice so the provost marshal could hear him.

Rob poured some of the bitter coffee into his saucer and sipped it. The hardest part of this job was holding his tongue when he wanted to denounce all the officers for the smug, arrogant, elitist curs they were. He liked John André, but even he wore that certainty of aristocratic superiority like a snake's skin. Rob realized that by saying nothing he was throttling truth like the unwanted runt of the litter.

Something was afoot with the British. Rob could sense it. He should introduce himself to the newcomers and gather what information he could over a pot of coffee laced with brandy, but he missed seeing Kate, and he felt so sad and discouraged with life that the effort was beyond him right now. Anyway the best source of intelligence was smiling at him from across the table. But that charming, gregarious, talkative source was not likely to divulge anything.

One afternoon, after General Clinton had put André in charge of intelligence, Rob had heard Jemmy Rivington question him about the army's plans. André had looked around to make sure no one was listening. "Can you keep a secret?" he had asked in a hushed voice. Jemmy had leaned forward eagerly. "Why yes, of course." André had grinned at him. "Well, so can I."

What was it Poor Richard wrote in his almanac? Three may keep a secret if two of them are dead.

"I heard the news of Peggy Shippen's marriage to Benedict Arnold," Rob said.

"Ah yes. When I frequented her parties in Philadelphia I observed that she had set her sights on marrying a title and turning heads at the Court of St. James, poor deluded little snippet."

Rob didn't generally ask personal questions, but he had become curious about how others dealt with the churlish cherub called Love.

"Did news of her marriage disappoint you?"

"No. Nor did it surprise me. Arnold is the most powerful man in Philadelphia, and a hero besides. The genuine item. I was at the Battle of Saratoga. He was splendid to watch. Too bad he chose the wrong side. Peggy went after him and she netted him." John raised that eyebrow again. "They say Philadelphia is a carnival of idleness, dissipation, and excess, which should suit Miss Shippen. Speaking of Philadelphians what of the lovely, flame-haired Kate with the sea-change eyes?"

Robert thought bitterly of his last month avoiding Kate, skulking and sulking, as his cousin Almy put it. He had been sleepwalking through the misery of his days when joy resided but a few blocks away.

"My current prospects do not underwrite wooing."

"What of the dry goods shop? Customers throng there. One would think you're giving merchandise away."

"We are." Rob's grin had little humor in it. "We're beginning to show a profit but most still buy on credit. And the war has disrupted shipping so that we can never be sure if goods will arrive here or if they will bedeck some pirate's wench in Martinique."

André's smile turned almost wistful. "We are both in the wrong business, Rob. We should take to the open sea as privateers, you and I."

Rob pretended to consider it, then shook his head. "Too many lice."

André glanced toward the door. "Speaking of lice . . ."

Rob looked up and saw Henry Clinton come in, trailed by a shoal of officers and their mistresses. André referred to mistresses as "wives in watercolors" because they were easily washed away. Clinton himself had Miss Blundell, his butler's daughter, securely fastened to his right arm. The women's high-pitched laughter curdled the mood in the room, but not even Jemmy Rivington had the nerve to remind the commandant that women were not welcome here.

André swung his boots off the table and stood up. He took the sword he called Old Cheese Toaster off the back of the chair, put the leather sling over his head, and straightened the sword at his side. He ran his fingers through his dark curly hair and adjusted his shirt cuffs to show a precise one inch below his coat sleeves.

"The duty of pleasure calls."

Rob stood up too. "I was about to leave anyway."

Clinton and Cunningham together represented too much evil for Rob. He wanted to ask John how he endured serving as adjutant to such an odious example of the species, but he knew the answer. For all his easygoing manner, John André was ambitious. He used his charm for advancement.

Maybe, Rob thought wryly, he is more of a Quaker than I am and can see God even in Clinton's dark soul.

When Rob took on the job of supplying Abraham with information he changed his lodgings so as not to endanger his former landlady, Abraham's sister. As he climbed the narrow stairs, he crowded against the wall to make way for the junior officers coming down. In a rattle of sabers they brushed past without noticing him. He continued up another flight to the attic he called his aerie. Anyone else would describe it as a musty garret, frigid in winter and sweltering in summer, but Rob liked it.

He would stand at the window and stare through the filthy glass at New

York's forgotten country, the angular landscape of rooftops and chimney pots. His favorite time was late afternoon when the setting sun washed the roofs in a pinkish-gold light. He felt relief here, away from the stridency of humanity in the tenements and streets below.

Rob was beginning to assume a slight stoop because he could only stand upright in the center where the slope of the roof was highest, but he had lined the low side walls with books in unruly stacks. His spare coat, waist-coat, and breeches, and his two extra shirts hung on pegs, with his good pair of shoes lined up on the floor under them. He had a pine-frame bed-stead with a rope lattice supporting a thin mattress. A pallet was rolled up against the wall for Abraham to sleep on when he visited. Two chairs, a long table, a few pegged shelves, and a trunk completed his estate.

He had the attic to himself, away from the six or eight junior officers who had taken over most of the lower floors. Although, he thought with wry irony, they noticed the cockroaches more than they did him. He came and went as if invisible. He had made his home in the nest of blessedly inattentive alligators.

He had locked the door when he left, but now it stood slightly ajar. Per-spiration formed under the queue at the back of his neck. Maybe the offi-cers had noticed him after all. With his heart racing he took inventory of what they might have found if they searched his belongings. He couldn't think of anything damning, so he opened the door and walked in.

Abraham Woodhull was writing at the table. He gave such a start he al-most fell over backward. Quill pens and papers scattered.

" 'Tis only me, Abraham."

Abraham put his hand to his heart. He had turned pale as a collar stock. Abraham was always nervous, but Rob had never seen him this agitated. While Abraham picked up the papers, quills, and the vial of invisible ink, Rob shaved tea from a compressed brick of it into a cup. He took the ket-tle from the embers in the small fireplace, poured hot water onto the leaves, and handed the cup to Abraham. Abraham's hand shook so badly the tea sloshed over the side.

"I've been found out," he whispered.

"Are you sure?" Rob sat down across from Abraham. They leaned for-ward until their noses almost touched with the tea steam writhing between them.

"When last I was in New York Black Jack Simcoe and a gang of his thuggees ransacked my house in search of me. They stole what they pleased and almost scared the life from my father left there alone." Abraham began pacing. "If I did not fear God and the law I would kill that son of a bitch Simcoe."

"How did he know about you?" Rob felt a cold helping of dread in his own chest. If the British had discovered Abraham's activities they might also know about his informant in New York City.

"Our contact in Connecticut did not receive our last communication in time."

"The one warning them about a raid across the Sound?"

"Yes. Lord Rawdon's men made a night attack on an outpost of Second Dragoons. They captured a letter from General Washington there. The letter spoke of the invisible stain, but they did not capture the liquid itself."

"Was your name mentioned in the letter?"

"No." The tea had a calming effect on Abraham. He closed his eyes and inhaled its fragrance.

"If your name was not mentioned, why did Simcoe come looking for you?"

"Wolsey returned on parole from Connecticut and made it his first order of business to inform on me."

"John Wolsey has had a quarrel with you for ten years, ever since that dispute over the milch cow. He knows you do not hold with the king, but does he know about your activities as an intelligenser?"

"I don't think so."

"If Simcoe had found anything damning, you would be in chains now."

Abraham drew a sigh up from his depths. "Simcoe is demanding restitution to the Crown for my treasonous attitudes. We have no money, Rob. I cannot pay what he asks."

"I'll explain to John André that Wolsey is taking revenge on you for an old quarrel. I'm sure he'll call Simcoe off and lift the fine."

"I would be grateful." Abraham hands still trembled so badly that the papers he sorted rustled like dry leaves. "I have another favor to ask."

"What is it?"

"This affair has compromised me. I beseech you to take over the operation here in New York and to write the weekly reports yourself." Abraham hurried on before Rob could object. "Because the enemy now knows about the stain, you must write between the lines of ordinary letters, or on the blank leaves of books or pamphlets. Either I or Austin Rowe will collect them."

The request took Rob by surprise. "Ask someone else, Abraham. I do not want to be in charge."

"The commander in chief himself has suggested that if the British become suspicious of me I should recruit a replacement. You are well positioned and a Friend besides. People do not suspect deception from Quakers. You're perfect for the office."

Rob shook his head. The idea of writing reports that the commander in chief would read unnerved him as much as spying.

"General Washington says the agent must be sharp-witted. He must be critical in his reports and not a mere gossipmonger. Your abilities are far superior to mine in that regard, Rob."

"Aye. I have as much wit as three folks—two fools and a madman."

"You must do it."

"My business occupies me. I cannot devote more time to this."

"You will have to quit the dry goods shop. This business will consume every waking hour." Abraham shook his head wearily. "And most of your hours will be waking. I am acquainted with anxiety the likes of which no one can imagine who has not walked in my shoes. Many times there has been not the breadth of a finger betwixt me and death."

Rob chuckled. "Do not think to begin a career as a recruiter, Abraham. Not even the greenest yokel would take the guinea from your drumhead."

"I believe you should know what the charge entails. Your handwriting will be on the letters. You will be accountable."

Rob sat silent for a long time. The store had begun to show profit, and business increased daily. Rob dared to think he could approach Kate Darby again with marriage in mind if some rich young officer hadn't snapped her up already.

"I know you have the interests of our beloved and plundered country at heart, Rob."

"Why does the commander in chief want us? From here to Setauket and then back to Washington's headquarters is over a hundred miles. Surely he can find a more direct route."

"No one has been able to get intelligence across the Hudson with any re-liability." Abraham laid the tips of his fingers on Rob's forearm. He was a reserved man and it was as compelling a gesture as if he had fallen on his knees, clung to Rob's legs, and rusted the buckles of his shoes with his tears. "We can work to end this cruel conflict but without you we are lost."

Rob sighed. He understood how the fox felt when the baying hounds had cornered him, and the pink-coated fops were hallooing and what-ho-ing in the distance. "Who else is swimming in this pot of porridge?"

Abraham hesitated.

"I have to know on whom my life will depend." Robert gave the wry smile that sent a ripple of humor across his dark eyebrows. "After all, hanging is the worst use a man can be put to."

"Of course. Of course." Abraham was chagrined that Rob might think he didn't trust him. "Our old friend Ben Tallmadge has taken the name John Bolton."

"Ben Tallmadge is Bolton?" Rob smiled. "I should have guessed."

"He has stationed dragoons every fifteen miles along the Connecticut coast to relay messages to Washington."

"How do the reports reach him?"

"Caleb and his men row them across the sound."

"Brewster?" Robert cocked one dark eyebrow.

"He knows that coastline better than anyone, and since last October he has performed his duties without failing."

"He has courage enough, but I question his judgment."

"The only man to see the reports besides Bolton and Washington is Alex Hamilton." Abraham steered the talk away from Caleb. "I sign my corre-spondence 'Samuel Culper.'"

"Sounds like culprit."

Abraham allowed himself a shadow of a smile. "It's the name of a dis-tant cousin. You must choose a false name too. For your own safety neither Washington nor Tallmadge want to know your identity."

Rob realized that even though the commander in chief did not know who he was, he was counting on him. He saw his prospects with Kate crumble. He could not make amends and court her, tend to his dry goods business, and run the entire intelligence operation. And what if he were caught? The woman he loved would have the privilege of seeing her suitor hung, and even, God forbid, might be arrested herself.

Rob knew with equal certainty that he could not refuse a request from the commander in chief.

"I will endeavor to collect and convey the most accurate and explicit intelligence I possibly can." He smiled ruefully. "I suppose I shall call myself Samuel Culper, junior."

Twenty-six

Wherein Lizzie sweeps herself under the carpet;
Rob writes what he can't read; Seth delivers a cypher

THE FLOW OF BLOOD IN THE TRANSLUCENT MEMBRANE OF A
frog's foot left King George's head forgotten in an upstairs room. Almy
Buchanan's guests gathered around the solar microscope set up by the parlor window. Oohing and aahing they took turns peering at lice, pregnant
fleas, hairs from their own heads, and the veins in the foot of that unhappy
frog.

As the daylight faded they released the frog into the gutter. They collected their hats and cloaks, and put on the masks that shielded them from
the summer sun and the city's foul air. They strapped on the high wooden-
soled pattens that would lift their hems out of the mud and garbage. Most
of them left in laughing groups, but Sir Henry Clinton swam against the
current. He bounded up the wide, marble staircase two steps at a time.

Lizzie could guess where he was headed. Everyone knew he was dally-
ing with his butler's daughter, but Sir Harry had time on his hands and one
woman could hardly suffice. His itinerant trysts were a favorite topic among
the servants in most of the mansions of New York. As the guests rippled
through the front door, one of Clinton's aides escorted a powdered and
painted pair of romps up the back stairs.

When Lizzie went upstairs to fetch Almy's set of tortoiseshell combs, she could hear the two women laughing next door. She tiptoed across the turkey carpet in the darkening room to retrieve the combs from the trunk by the fireplace. On the way she glanced at the settee in a corner of the room. King George's head looming in the shadows there made her jump.

The head sat propped up in the angle between the back and the arm of the settee. A blow had dented the king's nose. The gold paint had worn away, and the lead underneath had tarnished. His bulging eyes harbored a doleful and accusatory look. He stared at Lizzie as though she were responsible for his troubles since the New York mob dismembered him while celebrating in July of 1776, three years ago.

That same month the rebels had carted the king's torso and horse to Litchfield, Connecticut. Laughing lasses, glistening with perspiration, had pinned up their skirts, rolled their sleeves, and melted George down for bullets. The head didn't make that journey. A British raiding party sneaked through the American lines, stole it, and buried it. It kept company with moles and earthworms until the British army reoccupied New York and dug it up. It had been making the rounds of Tory mansions ever since. Loyalists exhibited it at their parties as a sample of American ingratitude and treachery.

Lizzie crossed herself as she passed it. She opened the trunk, found the rosewood box with the combs inside, and put it into her pocket. She was about to leave when she heard John André's voice coming from the cold fireplace nearby. She bent over to peek into it. The fireplace opened at both the front and the back, and Lizzie could see the candle-lit room beyond. She put her hand over her mouth to keep from giggling. This must be what Cook called the Half-Crown Chuck Office.

The two women were naked except for their wigs and their gartered stockings. They both lay tits-up on the floor, facing André and Clinton. They lifted their rumps until their weight rested mostly on their shoulders. They supported themselves in that position with their hands in the small of their backs. They spread their legs as far apart as they could. One of them had taken off her pubic wig and dangled it from her toe. Without the merkin her mons was as bald as a billiard ball.

John André and Henry Clinton lounged in chairs set next to each other about six feet away. The women giggled while the two men lobbed coins into the most available of the women's orifices.

"I say," said Clinton, "do hold still."

"Mine has underbrush," grumbled André. "I should receive a handicap."

Lizzie was about to leave when the conversation turned interesting.

"I have written to the lady," André said.

"You flattered her vanity, I trust."

"I told her my respect for her remained unimpaired by distance or political broils. And I offered to obtain for her in New York cap wire or gauze or needles, any gewgaws or notions she might require."

"Secrets for sewing needles." Clinton snorted. "A bargain, what?"

André fanned himself with a letter. "That correspondence may have prompted this communication from Gustavus."

"What does our new friend Gustavus have to tell us?"

"Nothing we don't already know."

"How much does he ask for information we already know?"

"Ten thousand pounds sterling. In coin, of course. He can't very well flash the Crown's pound notes in Philadelphia."

Sir Harry snorted. "Tell him to contact us when he has something of value to sell." He turned so his face was in profile in the candlelight. He had taken off his wig, and in his skullcap he reminded Lizzie of the vultures she had seen on the battlefield after Monmouth. "Have you found out anything about those miscreants who are ferrying intelligence across to Connecticut?"

"Not yet, Sir Harry."

"I know they're in contact with traitors here in the city. Damn their eyes and every other part of them."

John André glanced at the fireplace, and Lizzie pulled back out of sight. She started to leave, but she heard the other door open and close and footsteps approaching. She spun in place, looking for somewhere to hide. The trunk was full, and she could not bring herself to crouch behind the sofa with King George's head on it.

She lay down on the carpet, pulled the edge over her, and rolled toward the sofa, trundling herself up in it as she went. As soon as she did it, she regretted it. Of course a rolled carpet would look suspicious. And it was so dusty she felt a sneeze gathering force. She maneuvered one hand to her nose and pinched it closed. She squeezed her eyes shut too, on the premise that if she couldn't see whomever was coming, he couldn't see her.

The door hinges creaked, and light from a candle spilled across the floor. In the silence that followed, Lizzie imagined John André standing in the doorway, sweeping the room with the same amused gaze he used when entering a ballroom. She imagined him taking in the lumpy roll of carpet in front of the sofa. His footfalls started toward her.

When André looked behind the sofa his boots paused so close to Lizzie's head that even through the stifle of dust and mildew she caught a whiff of the soot and tallow used to blacken them. He continued around the room. She heard him open the trunk and then let the lid fall shut.

Sir Henry called through the fireplace opening. "Did you find anyone?"

"No. Must have been the wind blowing the drapery."

Lizzie waited until André and Clinton left, and the giggling women gathered up the coins and decamped. She unrolled herself from the carpet, stood up, straightened her skirts, and gave a mighty sneeze.

She stood irresolute in the middle of the dark room. She knew she should tell someone about what she had heard, but whom could she trust in this city of double dealing and divided loyalties? Then she remembered who had helped Seth escape from Oyster Bay. She would notify Rob Townsend. Maybe he would know who Gustavus was.

THE LATE JUNE AIR COLLECTED LIKE HOT ASHES IN THE attic. Rob tied a bandana around his head to keep sweat from falling onto the almanac and went back to writing on the book's blank endpapers. The quill pen moved across the paper in the loops and strokes of letters, but the words faded away almost as soon as they appeared.

The ink that Rob and Abraham called the "sympathetic stain" had taken getting used to. Mistakes soon faded until they were as invisible as the rest of the text, and Rob couldn't read what he had written. The brother of New York's chief justice, John Jay, had invented the stain in England, and no one knew how he did it. The British knew about it, but they didn't have the developer that made it visible when brushed across it. Neither did Rob.

He could not jot down military details as he heard them from officers in the coffee house. He dared not risk noting them in ordinary ink later on, for fear someone would see them. He had to memorize the names of ships and military units, the numbers of men in each, the names of their officers, their movements, the amounts of supplies they were laying in. Then he had to write them in words he couldn't see, along with his assessment of what it all meant. And he had to do it knowing that his reports would be read by the man he admired most in the world.

A tap at the window behind him startled him so badly he almost spilled the ink. He stoppered the vial, swept it and the almanac into a market basket, and threw his dirty stockings and small clothes on top of them. With shaking hands he set out the ordinary ink and a half-finished letter to his sister Sally, and went to the window.

Gleaming white teeth in a soot-blackened face grinned at him from beyond the filthy glass. The spectre wore a knit cap and held a chimney sweep's long-handled brush. Rob was about to tell him that he didn't need a sweep's services when he recognized him. Seth took off his coat and flapped it to shake out some of the soot.

Rob knocked out the rod wedged between the top of the lower sash and the frame above it. He raised the sash a few inches but could not move it further. Seth put his fingers under the sash, gave it a jerk, and raised it with ease. He had a harder time squeezing his six foot two inches and two hundred and fifteen pounds through the small opening. When he had unfolded himself inside, he stood with his cap in his hand. The tousled curls that brushed the ridgepole were a deep auburn instead of flame red.

"What happened to your hair?"

"Walnut stain. Otherwise I look like a barn on fire. Calls attention. Alarmed citizens have thrown water on my head to douse me."

Rob poured water from the ewer into the basin and handed him a towel. Seth washed his face and hands.

"On the way here some lack-wit insisted I scour out his chimney." Seth surveyed his filthy clothes. "These are General Wayne's duds. He'll swear up a breeze when he sees them."

Rob spoke in the low voice that had become second nature. "You're too big to climb down chimneys."

"I couldn't very well tell Sir Blockhead that, could I? I thought they would have to haul me out of there with a block and tackle." Seth took two shillings from his pocket and bounced them in his palm. "He tipped me a brace of hogs though."

"A hog being a shilling?"

"Too right."

Always the good soldier Seth went to the door and looked down the hallway, then checked the stairwell. He returned and prowled the room, stooping under the low pitch of the ceiling. He picked books off the tops of the piles and leafed through them.

"How did you find me?" asked Rob.

"I was told by a certain nut-brown wench who has my heart sewn up as tight as a defunct seaman in his hammock."

Rob wanted to ask about the brown wench's mistress but could not, Seth might let slip how much his sister despised him.

"How did you get here?"

"I impersonated an ivy bush, twined up a trellis, and skeltered across the roofs."

Rob laughed. The thought occurred to him, not for the first time, that Seth would make a first-rate brother-in-law.

"That's not what I meant."

"I left camp at White Plains before day-peep yesterday."

Seth dumped the contents of his canvas satchel onto the table. With his pen knife he ripped out the stitching in the false bottom. He reached into the opening and held out a thin memoranda book.

"What is it?"

"A dictionary of code. Each name or place or object is assigned a number. Major Tallmadge wants you to make a copy of it and give it to Samuel Culper, senior, when next you see him."

"How many of us will have one of these?"

"711, 721, 722, and 723."

Rob ran his finger down the list. Numbers 711, 721, 722, and 723 were George Washington, John Bolton or Benjamin Tallmadge, and Samuel Culper Senior and Junior, Abraham Woodhull and himself. 731 stood for man, 355 for lady, 727 was New York, and the last number on the list, 710, meant zeal.

"What route did you take?" Rob asked.

"Across King's Bridge, though we boys call it Liberty Bridge."

"Did no one stop you?"

"Several times. I pre-pre-pre-tended to, to, have a stu-stu-stu-stutter.

They gave up trying to question me and let me pass." He shook his head. "The route is shorter, but too well guarded and perilous for regular trips."

"The route though Connecticut is dangerous now too."

"Too right. The bloody cowards."

Rob knew whom he meant. General Clinton had ordered the former New York governor, Colonel William Tryon, and his Seventieth Foot to harry the Connecticut coast. Tryon had scores to settle and he exceeded his orders. He and his men killed civilians, assaulted women, and sacked and burned a dozen towns, all in an effort to coax Washington to come after him.

"The commander was hard put to sit still while they murdered innocents." Seth stowed his things back into his satchel. "If you had not warned him that it was a ploy, Clinton would have lured him into his trap."

Seth sat on the sill and threw a long leg over it. Before he ducked his head and levered himself outside, he turned and grinned wolfishly. "Mad Anthony Wayne's boys will create a diversion of our own before long."

Rob watched Seth bound, surefooted as a goat, among the steep roofs. He carried the chimney sweep's long brush like a halberd. He made Rob feel old at twenty-five.

No wonder Anthony Wayne had threatened to come to Long Island in search of him. Seth was strong and bright and off-handedly brave. He had youth's devil-may-care attitude, but even so, he was willing to die for his country. He and those like him, Rob thought, made the country worth dying for.

Rob prayed to God that no ill came to Seth while he and the rest of General Wayne's boys created their diversion.

Twenty-seven

Wherein Seth falls off a cliff;
Kate and Lizzie have a bitter experience in the Sugar House

NIGHTFALL DID NOT BRING RELIEF FROM THE JULY HEAT. The bayonet affixed to the barrel of Seth's rifle added to the weight of it, but he wasn't burdened with ammunition. As Sergeant Seth Darby slogged with an unloaded rifle toward battle, he had stockings on his mind. He wore his last pair, and the black water of the marsh had soaked them. He doubted they would survive the experience, and the prospects of acquiring another pair were scant. His friend Spitz worried about something more sinister.

He went leaping off through the water, whirling and stamping and splashing. *"Gott im Himmel! Schlange!"*

Seth resisted the urge to do some leaping himself. "What's *schlange?*"

"Snake."

"It's not snakes. It's sedge. Marshgrass."

"It is snakes, I am sure." Spitz whirled again and peered into water that would have been opaque even if Captain Charles Darragh's pocketwatch didn't read eleven o'clock at night.

Darragh glanced back at them. "Keep quiet. They'll hear you."

They'll hear us anyway, Seth thought.

He was relieved that General Wayne hadn't assigned him to the dog-killing detail. Wayne said killing them was necessary to discourage them from alerting the British who were stationed in the redoubt atop a promontory jutting into the Hudson River. As it turned out, the racket of twelve hundred men splashing through the marsh made barking dogs irrelevant.

Anthony Wayne slogged along in front of his assault party. He had picked the biggest, strongest, most seasoned men, and he insisted that all the riflemen mount bayonets. He said he never wanted to see the skewered body of a boy who had not a blade to defend himself when the enemy overran his position. And he did not distribute ammunition.

If no one had any ammunition, he reasoned, no one could fire an early shot and alert the British, but Seth knew better. Seth knew that the general still brooded about the massacre by bayonet of his men at Paoli two years ago. He intended to take revenge with the weapons that General Grey had used, blades.

The plan made Seth uneasy. He had come to terms with shooting men at a distance. The idea of looking them in the eye while he stabbed them in the gut unsettled his own vitals. Still he would do what he had to do. His country and his comrades were counting on him. And if there were no comrades Seth would have followed Mad Anthony Wayne into hell barefoot.

About midnight Seth and the others reached the base of the promontory. The full moon was not their ally. It made them plainly visible, and it lit the abatis, a barrier of felled trees with sharpened branches pointing outward. Beyond that loomed the gray rock face of the precipice called Stony Point.

British heads lined the redoubt on top of it. "Come on, you rebel dogs," they called down.

"Basimecu!" Spitz shouted the most useful of the French phrases he had learned from Baron von Steuben. It was the Americanized version of *baise mon cul.*

Captain Darragh shouted a translation. "Kiss my cooler!"

The British opened fire while Seth and the others raced to the abatis. Seth slid sideways among the sharpened limbs with shot splintering the wood around him. He freed a coattail caught on the last spike, put his head down, and started up the steep incline. In a rain of lead he clawed at the rocks and bushes, trying to keep close to Anthony Wayne.

When the general went down with blood streaming from a scalp wound Seth and Charles Darragh rushed to him. They draped his arms across their shoulders, and half led, half carried him up the slope.

Seth was only vaguely aware that he was yelling at full volume. He shouted as though the noise could drive bullets away like stray curs. As though the sound of his voice formed a shield against lead. All the troops shouted as they ran. Instead of gunfire the British were confronted with a wall of noise advancing up the slope.

Seth and Charles paused when they reached the crest. The other men stopped behind them and grew quiet. Wayne wiped the blood from his eyes and looked back over his shoulder at them. He made a high, broad sweep with his arm.

"Let's go forward, lads!"

With a roar the troops swarmed over the breastworks. The ferocity of their rush overwhelmed the defenders, and the fighting spilled out of the fort and raged across the promontory. Men brawled with bayonets, knives, halberds, hatchets, and tree limbs, with teeth, fists, feet, and fingernails. By ones and twos and then in groups the British soldiers began to surrender, shouting, "Quarter, brave Americans, quarter."

As Seth prowled the perimeter of the promontory he saw Spitz trotting toward him. He yelled a warning, but the grenadier behind Spitz swung his musket by the barrel. Seth heard the thunk as the stock connected with Spitz's skull. Spitz dropped and the soldier raised his bayonet to finish him.

Seth couldn't see how close the man was to the cliff's rim. He raced at him and hit him with a force that knocked the two of them over the edge and out in a graceful arc. The ground's disappearance confused Seth, and he kept running, his legs churning air. His trajectory landed him in the water beyond the rocks at the promontory's base.

Seth rose, sputtering, to the surface with his rifle still in his hand, but he stared into the iron eyes of at least two dozen cyclops, British issue. At the other end of the musket barrels stood British soldiers in three whaleboats. They pulled Seth into one of them, took his rifle, and tied his wrists behind him with the lieutenant's red sash.

"Look lively, lads," said the lieutenant. "I reckon the rebels shall give us a send-off shortly."

The soldiers pulled on their oars, and the sergeant at the rudder steered

them toward the British sloop-of-war anchored in the middle of the
Hudson. The sergeant happened to be with the quartermaster corps, and
he was not happy. He muttered about the loss of one hundred sixty thousand pounds worth of stores, not to mention the five hundred or so of the
king's men captured or killed.

Seth sat cogitating with three or four pistols trained on him. He me-
thodically catalogued everything he knew about British prisons. He wondered into which one they would put him. He had heard reports about all
of them. All the reports were bad.

He knew four things for sure. He would escape from wherever they put
him. He would live to see the British tuck tail and sail home in defeat. He
would see his family. He would kiss Lizzie again.

THERE WAS NOTHING SWEET ABOUT THE LIVINGSTON SUGAR
House. The old refinery stood near the blackened ruins of Trinity Church,
but it was as ungodly as it was bitter. The stone building rose five stories
high. The heads of American prisoners of war jammed every small, barred
window. They stood with the shortest in front and the tallest behind, each
man trying to breathe fresh air. While they were about it they lowered baskets and shouted requests for food at passersby, but most people gave them
a wide berth.

All of New York stank, but the stench from its six prisons had longitude
and latitude, magnitude and attitude. No one went near any of them unless
impelled by love, avarice, or an armed guard. Love drew Kate and Lizzie
there.

Kate held a lavender-scented handkerchief to her nose and mouth.
Lizzie led a sway-backed gray piled with sacks and baskets. Kate's mother,
Rachel, did not want even Almy Buchanan to know that Seth had been
captured. Almy's husband Thomas was a prominent Tory. Word that he
had connections with a rebel soldier would put him and his household's
welfare in jeopardy.

Pale and thin Rachel Darby had gotten dressed and walked to the pawn-
broker's shop. While Kate hovered anxiously around her she had arranged
to turn over her family's possessions as security for a loan to buy food and
clothing for Seth. Then she had gone home and taken to her bed again.

Now as Kate and Lizzie walked through the debris of the refinery's loading yard they stared up at the windows. They were so intent on looking for Seth's red hair among the shaggy, matted heads that they almost collided with an open cart and its canvas-covered load. Lizzie screamed when the cold, rigid fingers of a protruding hand brushed her arm. She scrubbed at the spot with her apron hem.

"I pray you halt, good man." Kate stepped in front of the greasy individual who led the pony by the bridle. "I would look for my brother among these unfortunate souls."

"Ye shan't find any souls here, miss. They's all gone to a better place." He crossed himself and spat. "Or a worse one."

He did not say that no matter what the destination of the dead men's souls, their shreds of clothing would go to the paper mill. Nor did he mention that he would split the profits from the sale of those rags with Provost Marshal William Cunningham.

Kate circled the cart, trying to find the faces that went with the tangle of bare limbs. She gently moved aside one emaciated body and lifted an arm so she could see the person under it. She glanced at Lizzie and shook her head. Seth wasn't here.

"Can't dally, miss." The cartman jerked the canvas back in place and squinted up into the kiln of the early August sun. "Have to pitch 'em into the potter's pit afore they grow much riper."

"Kind fellow, do let us pray for their souls."

Kate and Lizzie knelt in the dusty yard. The cartman took off his hat and shifted from one foot to the other. His pony twitched his ears to rattle the flies. When they stood up the cart rumbled away and Lizzie untied the two pack baskets. They each shouldered one and staggered under the bulk of the extra sacks. Kate rapped hard on the big oak door.

The disruption of trade with the West Indies had quieted the works here. The sugar houses were important because they distilled molasses from sugar cane, and molasses was the basis of rum. When the guard let them in they picked their way through the rubble of old troughs, boiling kettles, bricks, and barrel staves. They followed him up flight after flight of stairs. He did not offer to carry any of their load. The air grew hotter the higher they climbed. When the refinery had been in operation temperatures in the distilling rooms reached 140 degrees. It felt that hot to Kate now.

"We keep the incorrigibles up 'ere," the guard confided. "Them what's tried to escape. General Ethan Allen himself was confined 'ere. I knew 'im personal. A scrapper, 'e were, and mad as a hatter, but I got on well enou' wi' 'im."

On the fifth floor the guard held up a sand glass. "Five minutes."

"Ten." Kate looked him in the eye.

He shifted his gaze. "Ten it is, but not a heartbeat longer."

He searched through all the goods in the packs. With a look that was part defiance and part apology he pulled out a jacket and a twist of tobacco and set them aside for himself. He opened a padlock the size of Almy's lapdog and cracked the door wide enough for them and their bundles to squeeze through. He slammed it shut after them, slid back a small shutter in the door and poked his pistol barrel through it.

Kate gasped in horror and regretted that she drew in so much of the foul air doing it. Lizzie moaned and kept a tight grip on Kate's arm. They stood with their backs against the door and stared at more misery than they would have thought possible.

The room extended the length and breadth of the upper story, but humanity packed it. Those who couldn't defend space near the windows sat among the sick who lay side by side in the middle of the room. Kate could not tell the young from the old. They all resembled skeletons with matted beards and hair. Most wore filthy rags but some were almost naked.

The room grew silent as everyone stared at them. Kate had a sudden terror that these desperate creatures would attack her. She imagined them swarming over her and the guard not able or willing to do anything about it.

"Kate! Lizzie!" Seth jumped down from the keg he had been standing on to reach the upper part of a window.

He shuffled through the crowd with shackles clanking around his ankles. Lizzie ran to meet him, and the men parted to make way for her. He picked her up, whirled her around, and kissed her. He did the same for Kate. He looked better than the others, but then he was one of the most recent to arrive.

Lizzie noticed the stripes on his sleeve. "They made you a sergeant, Seth."

"Aye, much good it does me." He grinned at Kate and shook a foot to jangle the chain. "Would that thee were a rum kate, dear sister."

"A rum kate?"

"A kate is a picklock," said Lizzie.

"And a rum kate is a devilishly fine picklock." Seth grinned.

"We can only stay a short while, Seth." Kate glanced at the door and imagined the sand pouring into the bottom of the glass on the other side.

"Then tell me news of Mother."

"She sends her love but she is not well. The doctor says she must not leave her bed, or she would have come with us."

"Why took you so long to send us word?" Lizzie clung to his hand.

Seth ducked his head in chagrin. "I thought to deliver myself to thee instead of a letter."

"Thee tried to escape?" Kate imagined the guards shooting at him as he dangled from a window or sprinted across the yard.

"Several times but the bloodybacks are fast on their feet."

"Tell me what thee most lacks," said Kate. "We'll return tomorrow with it."

"We lack everything that keeps body and soul alive." Seth gestured around him. "We fear to eat the food. Cunningham puts arsenic in it so he can continue collecting the pitiful rations of those who die."

"That cannot be so."

"Yes, it can."

"I shall talk to John André," Kate said. "He'll arrange parole for thee." Seth shook his head.

"Yes, he will. John is my friend and Clinton dotes on him. He'll do whatever John asks."

Seth glanced at the guard's baleful eye at the narrow window in the door as he rummaged in the pack. What did thee bring us, sister?"

Before Kate could answer he lowered his voice. "There is one thee must seek out, Kate. If he cannot help thee, mayhap thee can help him."

"How so?"

"Lizzie knows."

Seth turned to face the prisoners, and Kate realized that they had been staring at the baskets the whole time. Seth was only seventeen, but the American officers were housed at the provost prison where Cunningham had his headquarters. As a sergeant and a veteran with three years' service, Seth outranked just about everyone among the able-bodied. He called half a dozen names and the men lined up in front of him.

"They're corporals," he told Kate. "I've put each one in charge of a company of men. They shall distribute the food and clothing."

"Seth, thee must perform Christ's miracle with the loaves and fishes to feed everyone here."

"We shall give first to those most in need."

He unpacked the stoppered jugs of milk and cornmeal mush, the bacon, sausage, dried beef, and loaves of bread. He inhaled the fragrance of the loaf. "This is Cook's work, isn't it?"

"God bless you, miss." The men crowded closed and some stretched out their hands.

Kate reached out and touched their fingers with her own. "We women will do all we can. May the Almighty keep you in his care, for without his divine aid, all assistance is vain."

Seth had started handing out the food and clothes when the door flew open and slammed against the wall. Wiliam Cunningham reeled in, a bottle in one hand and his iron ring of six-inch-long keys in the other. An escort of guards with pistols flanked him.

"Whoreson curs! By God's eyelid, you shall enjoy no pampering here."

He kicked the baskets, scattering the contents. When the men scrambled to recover what they could he waded into them and flailed about with his key ring. The iron keys did considerable damage. "Damn your blood, you black-hearted rebels."

In the uproar Kate saw Lizzie take a pin from her hair and something else too, and slip them to Seth. Kate almost panicked. If Cunningham discovered it, he might lock her and Lizzie in here.

"You!" Cunningham turned on her. "You strumpets are the damndest rebels. And a nuisance besides."

"Strumpets!" Kate's panic gave way to fury. She planted her hands on her hips, narrowed her eyes and jutted her chin. Even her hair seemed to expand and stiffen with indignation.

Lizzie knew the signs. Kate was about to lose her temper. Lizzie grabbed her arm and pounded on the door. The guard grinned after them as Lizzie dragged Kate down the hall.

"You will answer to God, Will Cunningham," Kate shouted. "God will see to you."

Twenty-eight

Wherein Sir Harry says no;
Lizzie has news; Kate says yes

"OUT OF THE QUESTION!" SIR HARRY CLINTON WAVED A HAND dismissing Kate.

The sentry moved forward to escort her out, but she planted the worn soles of her shoes and would not move.

"He is a good boy. He does not deserve such inhuman treatment. Even animals do not use each other so."

"Animals do not commit treason." Clinton glared out from under brows that hung like thatch over his puffy eyes. "Good boy or not, he is most damnably misled to take up arms against his sovereign."

"God is our sovereign."

Clinton swept his ice-eyed gaze over Kate's hair, pulled back and pinned into a knot, her apron of homespun tow, and Almy Buchanan's old dress. The dress once had been dark green but had now faded almost gray, except in darker strips where Kate had cut the lace trim off of it.

"Do not think, madame, that your gender and heretical religion allow you to spout claptrap." With his hands clasped behind him Clinton paced behind his desk as though propelled by his outrage.

"Your brother was captured in an assault on His Majesty's forces. He is neither an officer nor a gentleman, and therefore not eligible for parole.

Frankly, miss, your brother and his kind are not worth the powder necessary to blow them up. They deserve whatever ill befalls them. And if one
Quaker can oppose His Majesty I must wonder if his sister has involved
herself in treachery too."

"I love God, not politics."

"Then confine your activities to those mumbo-jumbo meetings you people conduct."

Kate wanted to tell him that his troops stabled their horses in the meeting house, but he must know about it already.

Clinton gave two abrupt waves of his pudgy fingers, as though flicking
away a fly. Fighting back tears Kate walked out of the room ahead of the
guard. André had gone off somewhere, leaving Sir Harry Clinton her only
recourse. Now he had destroyed her hopes of seeing Seth freed.

Lizzie waited outside with the old gray horse and a load of supplies for
Seth and his comrades. The look on Kate's face told Lizzie that she hadn't
been successful. The two of them led the horse up Broad Way toward the
Sugar House. The guard who had escorted them on their first visit met
them at the door. He held his Brown Bess across his chest, barring entrance.

"I can't allow you in, miss. Orders from the provost marshal. And besides, you cannot see your brother anyway."

"Why not?"

"Someone smuggled in a hairpin." The guard raised his eyebrows and
glanced at Lizzie. "Your brother used it to open his irons. He also got possession of a blade and cut away the window frame from around the bars.
The provost marshal thinks it was baked into a loaf of the bread you carried in. He ordered your brother to the Cellar."

Lizzie gave a small cry and dread clenched Kate's heart. They both had
heard about the Cellar. It was a wet, windowless, suffocating, pestilent,
rat-infested pit. More prisoners went down there than ever came back up
alive. Cunningham's Cellar had joined the Devil, wild Indians, ghoulies,
ghosties, and long-leggitie beasties as a threat to New York's disobedient
children.

"I pray you then take a letter to him."

The guard was a peach-cheeked farm lad from England's west country.
Cruelty was not in his nature but neither was insubordination. "'Twould
get me stripes if caught."

"This is all I have." She held out a shilling, and he pocketed it. "Will you see that the other men receive these things? And will you deliver bread and porridge to my brother? I swear you will find no blades hidden in them."

He shrugged again. "I'll do what I can."

"God will love you for your kindness."

Kate helped Lizzie unload the horse and saw that her hands were trembling. She put her arm around her while the guard moved everything inside. When he closed the door behind him Lizzie began pacing the perimeter of the stone walls, searching for an opening to the dark vault beneath.

"Seth, can you hear me?" She looked ready to dig the ground away from under the walls with her fingernails. "Seth!"

Kate saw the sentries approaching with their muskets leveled. She took Lizzie's arm. "Come away."

"They will kill him, Kate." Lizzie began to sob. "I will never see him again."

"They cannot kill him." Kate put a hand on Lizzie's cheek, trying to calm her, although she didn't feel calm herself. "God has already brought him through the Valley of Death."

Lizzie wrapped her arms around herself as though to try to confine her despair. "There's a Jack in the cellar."

Kate glanced at the Sugar House's thick stone foundation. Jack who? Then she realized what Lizzie was talking about.

"Thee is with child?"

Lizzie nodded.

Kate took the gray's bridle with one hand, and with her other around Lizzie's shoulders, she led her past the guards. Outside the gate Kate held Lizzie in her arms while she cried. Kate wanted to cry too, but she was too furious for tears.

The rage that shook her was new to her. Not when the mob burned her family's house, not when she saw the dead at Monmouth had she experienced hatred this intense. A mob had no face, and neither had an army; but in William Cunningham and Henry Clinton, evil had taken human shape. No matter what her people taught her, Kate could not detect any trace of God in these men.

Lizzie set out for the lower end of Manhattan at such a fast pace that the old gray broke into a lumbering trot at the end of his lead. She did not step aside for the red-coated soldiers who had to move out of her way. She didn't hear them swear at her. She almost overset the mussel monger's cart and forced dray wagons and their drivers, clenched fists waving at her, into the gutters. Kate hurried to keep up with her.

"Where are we going?"

"To Townsend and Oakman's dry goods shop."

Kate stopped in the roadway and stood as stiff as a milepost. She told herself that Rob Townsend was the last person she wanted to see, and herself replied that, other than Seth, he was the only one she wanted to see. The fact that he didn't want to see her grieved her more deeply than she would admit.

"Why?"

Lizzie led the gray back to where Kate stood. She ignored the carts and dray wagons, the barrows, sledges, and foot traffic that surged around them. She and Kate and the horse stood like boulders in the stream of traffic.

"Seth said to go to the man who might help us."

"Who is he?"

"Townsend."

"Rob Townsend?"

"Yes."

"What has he to do with Seth?"

"Ask him."

SCARLET UNIFORM COATS. CRIMSON CALICOES. CLOGS OF claret red Moroccan leather. Vermillion taffetas that rustled and squeaked when handled. New York was the only city in the colonies where the loyalists could live freely, and it had gone mad for red. Rob stood in the doorway leading from the storeroom and considered the irony of his situation. He was a dove-drab Quaker presiding over the gaudiest stock of gewgaws in the city.

The stock had become so popular that yesterday Rob had had to hire another clerk. The shop swarmed with officers and servants sent to fetch ordered goods. Macaronis huffed snuff and lisped "I say" and "Look you here" over the walking sticks, shoebuckles, and eelskin hair ties dyed cherry red. Women tried on hats and gloves and shoes. They fingered the shalloons and pullicats, the poplins, serges, satins, sarcenets, and lute strings, the silk ferret, caddis ribbon, and Brussels lace.

Most of them did more browsing than buying, and few of them realized what a serious business obtaining these fripperies was. Rob could remember where in the wide world each item originated. He knew how much cajolery, luck, shrewd bargaining, and mulish determination had been required to get them here. Speculators and smugglers made the job more difficult. As Hercules Mulligan put it, the town was clotted with villains and sharps enriching themselves.

Abraham Woodhull thought the shop was taking too much time away from Rob's more important work. He had come to tell Rob so, but as long as he was here he couldn't resist looking around.

The cost of everything in New York had quadrupled, including the rent for Rob's room. Rob contended that he had to continue working here. He could not collect intelligence if his landlord threw him onto the street.

Two matrons took the pasteboard box of cotton rumal kerchiefs that Rob had fetched from the storeroom. In exchange one of them slipped him a piece of paper with numbers on it. They would mean nothing to anyone else, but Rob knew they represented the troop strength of the unit under the command of the colonel quartering at her house.

Cotton cloth was rarely seen, and the two women knotted the scarves around their necks and turned to show them off, looking coquettishly back over their plump shoulders.

"And where do these come from, Mr. Townsend?" The plumpest one fluttered her lashes at Rob.

"India. They're quite durable." Rob saw no reason to mention that in India, members of the sect called thuggees used these diaphanous handkerchiefs to strangle their victims.

When Kate strode through the door with Lizzie behind her, Rob hoped she intended to browse for trinkets like everyone else. He feared she had come to demand to know why he had not called on her. Behind her, Lizzie grimaced and made gestures that Rob was too shaken to interpret.

Kate's forward momentum backed him through the doorway and into the storeroom. He was not prepared for the question she fired like cannon shot. She used the form of address reserved for strangers.

"What have you to do with my brother?"

Some harm must have come to Seth and she blamed him for it. He could only stammer. "Has something happened to him?"

"The British have imprisoned him in the Sugar House."

Rob stared at her with his mouth half open. If they had caught Seth spying they would surely hang him. Rob remembered him as he had seen him last, raising his chimney sweep's brush in salute, then bounding off across the rooftops. Rob wanted to drop to his knees and beg Kate's forgiveness, and Lizzie's too, for abetting Seth in espionage. He knew he couldn't have stopped the boy, but he felt responsible anyway.

"On what charges?"

"He was captured at the raid on Stony Point."

Rob let his breath out in a relieved gust. They hung spies but not prisoners of war. "Have you talked to John André?"

"He's not in the city."

Rob came alert. Where was Clinton's new deputy adjutant general, and what was he up to?

"You did not answer my question." Kate continued to crowd him, angrier than he would have expected of her. "When we visited him he said to come see you."

"Me? Why?" Rob wanted to box his own ears. Why did he turn into a gibbering idiot whenever Kate Darby came near?

"That's what I want to know. He said perhaps I could help you."

"Help me?" There, he did it again. What was wrong with him?

Kate lost what shreds of patience remained and she stamped her foot. "Cunningham is starving the prisoners. He's poisoning them. Seth needs help. Why would he say that I might help you?"

Rob knew but he could hardly talk about it here.

Kate didn't give him a chance to answer anyway. "They have taken him to the Cellar."

"Oh, dear heaven." Rob noticed the pair of lieutenants peering into the storeroom and he put the bland smile back on.

The officers were probably looking for goods that hadn't been uncrated yet, but Rob felt the cold breath of his old friend fear on the back of his neck. He took Kate's elbow and steered her toward the front door. Lizzie followed at the usual servant's distance of three paces. Rob nodded to the lieutenants as he passed them, and when he spoke to Kate his tone was jovial.

"Let us see what soup Phoebe Fraunces has conjured up today."

"How can you speak of trifles when men are dying in the city's prisons?" At least Kate had sense enough to keep her voice low.

"I'll explain everything." Rob beckoned to Woodhull. "Abraham, we're going to Black Sam's. Won't you join us for some of Phoebe's soup?"

"I'm feeling peckish myself." Abraham bowed to Kate. "So good to see you again, Miss Darby."

Rob saw the gray waiting outside. He called to one of the children hovering nearby, alert for any financial opportunity that might present itself.

"Zachariah, take this horse to the Buchanan house." Rob tossed him thruppence.

Kate tried to storm off with the horse, but Rob held her arm in a grip so tight it shocked her. Robert Townsend, she began to suspect, was not the man she had thought him to be.

SPYING WAS A DEVIOUS, DISHONORABLE BUSINESS, AND ROB was ashamed to admit he engaged in it. He started at the beginning, though, and he left out no detail. The story was long and involved, and by the time he had included Seth and Lizzie's part in it, he had drained a tankard of Black Sam Fraunces' thick ale.

He rested his elbows on the damask tablecloth and leaned forward. "Does thee follow me?"

"I do follow thee." Kate stared solemn as an owl at him. "But I must tell thee frankly, if I thought I could find my way back, I would."

Rob had expected reproach. He stared at her for a moment, then he laughed so hard that men in the noisy long room across the hall looked in his direction.

"I have put all of our lives in thy hands by telling thee this," Rob said.

"I will not betray thy trust."

Phoebe Fraunces and Lizzie carried in trays with bowls of oxtail soup, decanters of wine, and baskets of fresh-baked bread.

Kate watched her leave and gave Rob a quizzical look. Rob nodded. Phoebe and her father too were passing along information they heard from the British officers who ate and drank there. Lizzie returned with a pitcher of ale and listened intently while she poured it.

"I can be of assistance in this." Kate was ebullient. She had felt so help-less, but here at last was something she could do to help end this war and free Seth and the others. "All sorts of people visit the Buchanans. And they're used to Lizzie and me wandering the city every day, shopping at the market, going to the prisons, taking food to Canvas Town."

"No. It's too dangerous an undertaking for a woman."

"Lizzie and Phoebe have been helping you."

"They are of the class that British officers do not notice."

Abraham spoke up. "If she carried the codebook to Oyster Bay I could take it from there. And she could bring back a supply of the ink."

Rob glared at him but Kate leaned forward, her eyes sparkling. She looked ready to head straight to the Brooklyn ferry.

"Absolutely not. Jack Simcoe is still at my family's house."

"I could leave it at some agreed-upon place." For a novice Kate had got-ten the hang of deception quickly.

"The sentries are checking every man who takes the ferry," said Abra-ham. "They went through everything I had. They even made me take off my shoes. A woman could pass more easily."

Rob's scowl intensified. "Out of the question."

Lizzie spoke up. "I could carry it."

"No, Lizzie." Kate was adamant about that. Not only was Lizzie carry-ing Seth's child, but Kate knew that she would rather stay in New York than go where Seth was not. "Thee knows what snobs the British are. They would be more suspicious of a servant than the friend of a family like the Buchanans."

"I will not allow thee to involve thyself."

"If thee does not let me join with thee I will gather information anyway. I will look for some other way to get it to the Americans."

The idea of Kate acting on her own horrified Rob. She was smart, no doubt about it, but she had no idea how treacherous this city was. "What if thee must lie?"

"Has thee lied?"

"Not yet. I pray God that the necessity will not arise."

Kate was so eager to start she said something so brazen that it would have mortified her under other circumstances. "Thee must pretend to court me. Then thee can come to the house, and none will suspect thy true purpose."

That sounded like an excellent plan to Rob, but he had a nagging thought. Over the past several months he had enlisted the help of trusted friends and respectable citizens to collect information for him. They in turn had recruited others to bring them news to pass along.

Rob didn't know how many people were involved. He didn't know the sources of much of his intelligence, and many of the sources didn't know him. He felt like he was trying to keep the reins untangled on a twenty-horse team while driving full tilt over broken terrain at night.

What would happen to the venture if his heart took command where his head had always led?

Twenty-nine

Wherein Kate meets an old friend and enemy;
Tunis Birdwhistle finds what he didn't lose

"THIS SHOULD PROVIDE FOOD AND LODGING IF NIGHT FINDS thee distant from Oyster Bay." When Rob put the bag of coins in Kate's hand she felt the sting of a shock from his fingers.

Benjamin Franklin, Kate thought, wasted his time with kites, keys, and the copper coils of his Kissing Machine. He should have looked for electricity in the touch of lovers.

Not lovers. Kate corrected herself. She was not anyone's lover. She could not imagine ever being anyone's lover. Still something mysterious sparked as real as electricity between her and this quiet man who had turned out to be something else altogether.

Kate had come to Rob's lodgings to collect the codebook, but she crossed the threshold as hesitantly as a stray cat. She stood near the door and looked around. So this was Robert Townsend distilled, his world condensed to an attic room furnished as simply as a monk's cell.

Rob closed Kate's fingers over the small sack of coins and left both hands there, his long fingers covering hers. His touch sent shivers through her. She leaned against him and rested her cheek on his chest. He put his arms around her and stroked her hair.

"I beg thee to reconsider, Kate. I can pay one of the Dutch farmers on the flyboats to carry the book to Huntington Harbor. Abraham can retrieve it there."

"That's too risky a plan. Besides Anna Strong rides alone from Setauket to the prison ship near the Brooklyn ferry, and Setauket is twice as far as Oyster Bay."

"If ill befalls thee, I cannot live in this world."

"We all are in God's hands." The linen of Rob's old shirt, worn from countless washings, felt warm and soft against Kate's cheek.

She heard the muffled beat of his heart, steady and comforting. She was in God's hands. She was in love's arms. Good would prevail. Kate was sure of it.

KATE WONDERED IF PEGGY SHIPPEN ARNOLD'S BOUTS OF insanity were contagious and could lie dormant like malarial ague. If so, she wondered if she had caught madness from Miss Shippen in that long-ago place called Philadelphia. How else to explain her presence here on the first ferry of the morning? What had seemed a reasonable plan over wine in the back room of Black Sam Fraunces's tavern now stood unmasked as arrant lunacy.

The sentries' red coats flashed like poppies among the mud-colored homespuns of the merchants and farmers in the village of Brooklyn. The old gray's hoofs clopped on the stone steps as Kate led him up to the landing.

Kate walked to the end of the line of passengers. With shaking fingers she smoothed her skirts and the linen pocket fastened underneath them. The thin memoranda book inside the pocket seemed to have swelled like a waterlogged mattress ticking.

Abraham Woodhull had ridden the ferry too, but he pretended he didn't know Kate. She wished she could talk to him. He was usually in such a state of barely contained terror that he wouldn't have given much reassurance, but at least she would have had a companion who understood her own fears. She reminded herself that she was never alone. God was always with her. She closed her eyes and breathed a prayer. It calmed her.

Kate saw Abraham take off his shoes and hold out his arms. He looked small and woebegone as the two soldiers searched him and his saddlebags. By the time Kate arrived at the sentries' post, Woodhull had disappeared into the stable where he kept the horse. The hostler there didn't know that the monthly livery bill was paid by George Washington.

"Good morning, miss." The soldier touched two fingers to the brim of his helmet.

"Good morrow to you." John André had returned to New York and Kate held out the pass he had written for her, along with a cheerful letter to Jack Simcoe.

"Have you anything to hide?"

"Of course." Kate flashed him a mischievous smile. "Don't you?"

"That I do." He laughed. "But some villain has been sending intelligence out of the city. I must look in your saddlebags."

"Certainly."

When he finished he apologized for the inconvenience and wished her Godspeed. She rode away exhilarated. For the first time since this war started she was doing more than enduring it.

She passed the church in the center of the village of Brooklyn and the neat Dutch-gabled houses and kitchen gardens surrounding it. She set off into the rolling countryside where heath hens, quails, and doves called from the fields and pastures. A few miles east of the ferry landing, Wallabout Bay took a bite out of the coastline. In the middle of it four ships rode at anchor. The ships looked abandoned, but more men were crowded aboard now than when they had served as troop transports.

The mud flats stretched inland for half a mile, and the tides had uncovered bones left in shallow graves there. Hundreds of boards stuck up from the hill beyond it. They served to show where more corpses were located so that later burial details wouldn't uncover them by mistake. Two whaleboats sat beached with their bows in the mud. Five bodies lay in a line nearby. Several prisoners dug in the boggy soil while guards watched.

Anna Strong climbed onto the farm cart parked near them and guided the horse toward the road. Kate knew that talking to the wife of a man accused of spying would arouse suspicions, but she could not pass by without saying something. She reined the gray off into a meadow and let him graze.

"God keep you," she called out as the wagon pulled onto the road.

"And you." Anna Strong looked Kate in the eye as she passed. She seemed like a woman accustomed to following a plow, solid and unadorned.

Kate wanted to share the lonely road with her. She wanted to ask how her husband fared. She wanted to tell her about Seth. Instead she waited until the cart had lumbered around a bend before she set out again.

At midday she reached Flushing and stopped at an inn to eat. As soon as she walked in she wished she hadn't. Tunis Birdwhistle sat with some farmers at a table near the door. He raised a tankard in greeting and graced her with the leer that served him as a smile.

He didn't seem the type to keep company with farmers. Rob was probably right about him. Like other speculators in New York, he was buying large quantities of produce and beef here on Long Island and driving up market prices in the city.

Kate found a seat at the end of a long table on the far side of the room. The serving maid seemed to take forever bringing the boiled pork and cabbage, a basket with slabs of Indian bread, and a pot of blackberry jam. Kate could hear Birdwhistle's laugh above the hum of conversation, and she ate as fast as she could without appearing rushed.

"Law for me, Kate Darby, what in God's green creation brings you here?"

Kate looked up into Nan Baker's steady blue gaze. "God willing, a visit to a friend in Oyster Bay."

Kate wanted to ask Nan why she had taken the dead ensign's letters from her pack after the battle at Monmouth a year ago. She wanted to ask what had happened to them, but it didn't seem prudent.

"Did you find your brother?"

"I did." Kate moved over so Nan could sit next to her on the bench.

"And is he well?"

"Well enough for being a prisoner in the Sugar House."

"I'm so sorry to hear that, dear Kate." Nan put her hand on Kate's and squeezed it. "Are you living in that smelly bedlam on the other side of the East River or out here in the hinterlands?"

"My mother and I are lodging with Thomas Buchanan and his family."

"Ah." Nan nodded, and Kate realized she had passed the Tory test. Few people were more loyal to the king than Thomas Buchanan. "I have just come from your fair city of Philadelphia a week past."

"How fares my fair city?" Kate smiled through the memories of what she had lost and left there.

"Well enough. I went to the headquarters of the military governor. That dunderhead, Benedict Arnold, is in charge, you know. His wife grows ever more deranged, and he's in high dudgeon because the bastard assembly they call Congress censured him for his shady financial dealings. Forestallers are extorting prices higher there than in New York. General Arnold, they say, is the worst of the lot. I heard mutterings about hanging him in effigy."

"Is travel difficult to and from Philadelphia?" Now and then Kate entertained the notion of returning to the city.

Nan laughed. "I should say. We had to wait three days on that desolate shore at Sandy Hook for a boat to bring us to New York. The rain soaked us and the sun burned us until we looked like scalded chickens. And all the while hiding from enemy scouting parties."

Kate didn't usually pry into other people's affairs, but now it was important to find out everything she could about Nan Baker. "You had a companion on the trip?"

"An acquaintance."

The expression on Nan's face didn't change, but Kate sensed a shift. Nothing was visible, but the look in Nan's eyes went from open to closed, like one of those newfangled Venetian blinds that Almy had just had installed in the parlor windows.

Kate was awed. Nan had walked into the lions' den, the headquarters of the American military command in Philadelphia. Kate appreciated her nerve, even if she couldn't admire her duplicity. If Nan had been waiting for a British boat to rescue her from Sandy Hook last week she must still be spying. Kate knew, though, that she wouldn't expose her. The Americans probably would not hang a woman, but they might. And besides, she owed Nan a great debt.

TUNIS BIRDWHISTLE HAD JUST SEALED THE PURCHASE OF the farmer's entire crop of corn and beans. Now he sipped tea with his two permanently bent fingers projecting at a genteel angle from the handle of the cup.

The farmer's house was as neat as Birdwhistle would expect of a Dutch-man. The floor was sanded, the hearth was swept, the covers neatly laid out on the big bedstead with the bolsters arranged just so. Only one thing looked out of place. On a shelf, sticking out from behind some plates and the Bible, Birdwhistle saw a bedraggled leather packet tied with a stained red silk cord.

When the farmer left the room to relieve himself, Birdwhistle sauntered to the shelf. He slid the package under his belt and made sure his coat cov-ered it.

Thirty

Wherein Abraham misses his appointment;
Kate learns that she is a 355 and discovers one of God's better ideas

SALLY TOWNSEND WAS A HOUSE DIVIDED. ALONG WITH JACK Simcoe's shouted orders to the servants, the baying of his hounds outside, and the clatter of packing, Kate could hear her sobbing in her room at the top of the stairs. Jack and his rangers were leaving, and he declined to tell Sally where he was going or if he would return.

She had encouraged his courtship in hopes he would let slip information she could pass along to her brother. In the process she had become used to Colonel Simcoe's attentions and the luxuries, like tea and silk, that he provided. She had even developed a taste for his doggerel since it was usually in praise of her.

Kate knew she should take this cup of tea upstairs and comfort Sally, but she paused in the doorway to the front parlor that Simcoe used as an office. She could see papers on the desk across the room. While the colonel bellowed at the stable boys outside, she walked the narrow path between the trunks and satchels, and the scattered clothes, boots, saddles, weaponry, and tack.

Holding the cup and saucer in one hand, she shuffled the papers until she found Simcoe's orders. His Queen's Rangers and the Bucks County Volunteers were to take ship for Perth Amboy in the Jerseys in October. Under that was a letter. She scanned it quickly.

There is one Bruster who commands a number of whail bts out
of Norwalk which pass over almost every night to Long Island.

She was so intent she almost didn't register the sound of boots aproaching. She stepped away from the desk just after Simcoe's aide's nose arrived in the doorway, but a fraction of a second before his eyes did.

"Good morrow." She held out the cup. "Would you like tea?"

The aide stuffed the papers into a leather wallet before he nodded a greeting and took the tea. "I must insist that you do not come in here, Miss Darby." He glanced up at the ceiling through which filtered Sally's sobs. "Perhaps you could be so kind as to go upstairs and distract Miss Townsend."

"Of course." Kate nodded and went upstairs to retrieve her saddlebags and say good-bye to Sally.

She and the gray reached Setauket late that afternoon. She hadn't intended to come here, but Rob had warned her that these things rarely went as planned. Rob had also told her that Tories made up about half the population on Long Island. The ratio was higher in New York, but being anonymous there was easy. In a village like Setauket it was impossible.

This was where Abraham Woodhull lived and relayed secret information that would ruin him if discovered. Abraham had not impressed Kate before, but he did now. She had the feeling she had been transported into some other world where people she knew, like Rob and Abraham, Lizzie, Seth, and even Sally Townsend, were not whom she had thought they were at all.

Setauket was just as Rob described it, with a Presbyterian meeting house on one side of the village green and an Anglican church across from it. British soldiers had smashed the stained-glass windows in the meeting house and stabled their horses inside. They had fortified the building with the dead, or at least their epitaphs. They had surrounded the church with a wall made partly of gravestones they took from the cemetery.

Beyond the green lay the field where the loyalist militia held their

monthly musters. Drilling was thirsty work, and it was probably no coincidence that the militia mustered near Austin Roe's tavern. Kate stood in the
doorway and waited for her eyes to adjust to the smoke and the gloom.
Conversations hushed and everyone turned to look at her.

She kept her voice steady. "Is Austin Roe here?"

"Austin," someone shouted, "A prime dell asks after you."

A general roar went up. "Roe, you hound. Have you been sniffing
about?"

Kate felt her cheeks heat up. So much for staying inconspicuous.

An old man sitting on a stool by the door tugged at her sleeve. "Austin's
in the storeroom yonder." He pointed his chin at the rear of the tavern.
"Someone's been sucking the monkey back there."

"Sucking the monkey?"

He pulled his already sunken cheeks in further. "Drawing wine out of
his casks with a reed."

Kate assessed the territory she would have to cross to get to the storeroom. This was muster day. The tavern was full of men, most of them
wearing at least part of a uniform of the loyalist militia. One of them
jumped onto a table and raised his flagon.

"To the enemies of England! May they have cobweb breeches, porcu-
pine saddles, hard-trotting horses, and an eternal journey."

The huzzahs buffeted Kate like a gust that had been swilling stale beer.
She felt as though her own journey had been eternal. She wanted to sit in a
corner with the only good thing about being a Tory, a cup of hot tea.

She made her way through the crowd and peered into the storeroom beyond. Inside, a tall man was tapping the sides of the kegs with a barrel
stave. He didn't look happy about the sound they made.

"Are you Austin Roe?"

"Yep." When he straightened up he looked as slender, front to back and
side to side, as the stave.

Kate handed him the token Rob had given her. It was a brass button that
matched the ones on Austin Roe's waistcoat. "I have a delivery for Samuel
Culper."

Austin forgot about the hollow ring resonating from his kegs of rum. He
lit a candle and beckoned Kate to a closet, then through a hidden door in the
back of it and down a narrow corridor to a small, windowless room with

three or four stools scattered about. Kate could hear the faint rumble of conversation, and she figured she must be behind the tavern's big fireplace.

"Sound does not leave this room." He rapped lightly on the brick wall with his bony knuckles, but he also kept his voice low. "You must be the three-five-five that Abraham mentioned in his letter."

"Three-five-five?"

"It means 'lady.' He wrote that you were an acquaintance who could help him 'outwit them all.'"

Kate handed him the codebook. "Abraham was supposed to retrieve this at Oyster Bay. I understand you will know what to do with it."

"Abraham was robbed."

"Sally Townsend told me. She said three men ambushed him near Huntington. He fears Jack Simcoe set them on him and has men watching him yet. I feared he would not come back for the book."

"He was shaking like laundry in a brisk breeze when he came by here. Said he was going home to protect his father, in case Simcoe decided to raid his house again."

"While I was at the Townsends' I saw orders sending Simcoe's Rangers and the Bucks County Volunteers to Perth Amboy in October."

"We wondered where he was going. Abe can add that to his report."

"I saw a letter too, warning Simcoe about someone named Bruster."

Roe chuckled. "The Redcoats have known about him for a year or more. Can't catch him, though the good Lord knows they've tried." Roe glanced at the stone wall as though he could see the taproom on the other side of it. "If I leave here now there are those as would wonder why. I need you to deliver a message to someone out at Strong's Point."

"To whom?"

"Anna Strong."

And so Kate added another person to the list of those who were more than they seemed. The Strongs were celebrating when Kate arrived. Anna had prevailed on her Tory relatives to arrange her husband's release, but his safety was in jeopardy on Long Island. She told Kate that Caleb Brewster was coming that night to take him and the children across the sound to Connecticut. That explained the Bruster mentioned in the letter on Jack Simcoe's desk. Anna was staying here though.

When Kate left Anna she was hanging out laundry, but the line was stretched between two trees at the top of a bluff overlooking the sound, and the clothes weren't wet. Anna explained the system. From the other side of the sound Caleb checked the clothesline with a telescope. The black petticoat warned that British patrols were on the lookout for him. The number of white linen sheets hanging next to it indicated which cove to use for his landing.

As the old gray plodded back to the ferry Kate wondered who else was keeping secrets. She would mention to Rob what Sally had stopped sobbing long enough to whisper to her. She said that on his last visit, John André had hinted to Jack Simcoe that he was working on something important. Something that would end the war, Sally said, and ensure a British victory.

Maybe Robert could find out what it was. Then she began to worry. While she was away what if someone Robert trusted informed on him? She imagined returning to his room and finding it bare, with no trace of him. She imagined trying to find him in the prisons. She imagined him hanged.

She knew a canter was beyond possible for the gray, but she kicked his sides to get him to at least break into a faster walk.

ROB WOULD HAVE SPENT EVERY DAY AT THE FERRY, STARING across at Brooklyn, but that would have aroused the suspicions of the soldiers who stood guard there. So he paced in his room until he wore a track in the floor. He was pacing on the afternoon of the fourth day when he heard the quiet knock on the door. He yanked it open so fast he found Kate with her hand raised to rap a second time.

He pulled her to him and closed the door. He wrapped his arms as far around her as they would reach, and held her like he never intended to let her go. He started to tell her how lonely he had been and frightened, but she cradled his face in her hands and kissed him. The ferocity of it left them dizzy and bewildered and jubilant.

Kate had never kissed before. She decided it was one of God's better ideas. She would thank Him for it later.

She stopped kissing Rob long enough to say one word. "Yes."

RACHEL DARBY'S ROOM WASN'T COLD, BUT SHE SAT WRAPPED in a quilt stuffed with goose down. Her big chair had high, encircling arms and a canopy to protect her from the noxious night airs. She was so thin that she looked like a child in it. Lizzie had brushed her hair and pinned it up, but her eyes had sunken into dark hollows. Kate stood in front of her with her arm brushing Rob's. He caught the tips of her fingers hidden in the folds of her skirt. Cook, Lizzie, and Almy stood behind them.

"So this is the young man thee has told me so much about, Kate." She looked Rob in the eye. "Will thee care for her?"

"I pledge all my affection and estate to protect her and provide for her." Rob wanted to add ". . . and make her happy," but that sounded like hubris to him, and he did not dare throw Fate any temptation that might wreak havoc on happiness.

"We want to announce our banns, Mother, but there is no longer a Meeting where we can do it."

Rachel smiled. "Cook and Lizzie and Almy are of the world, but they are family for all that. This looks enough like a Meeting to me. I pray God will consider it so, given the circumstances." It was a long speech and it left Rachel panting. She waved a hand for them to proceed.

Rob turned to face Kate and held both her hands.

"I, Robert Townsend, do take thee, Katherine Darby, to be my wedded wife, and I promise with God's help to be a loving husband until death separates us."

As Kate repeated the vow she heard Cook snuffling. Cook had taken her aside in the kitchen earlier and delivered her view on matrimony. "More belongs to marriage, Miss Kate, than four bare legs in a bed."

If Kate and Rob had declared their union in the Quaker Meeting there would have been no celebration, so they didn't miss it. When they left the Buchanan house they were happy to walk hand in hand in a city that had not changed, but would never be the same for them.

Thirty-one

Wherein Cook goes eye-to-eye-to-eye-to-eye with Thomas Buchanan;
Seth's situation gets worse, and better

COOK'S KINGDOM ENCOMPASSED THE KITCHEN, THE PANTRY
and the scullery. Until today she had never invaded the front house, much
less the parlor where Thomas Buchanan conducted his business. Wielding
her ladle like a scepter, she came as close to leveling a baleful stare at him as
her devil-may-care eyes allowed. The household servants hovered in the
narrow back corridors and leaned over the rail of the stair landing, listening. Across the entryway Kate and Lizzie watched from the west parlor.
Lizzie's child had begun to create a bulge under her apron and that was
causing the fuss.

Kate wondered if Cook would deliver a rap with the ladle on Thomas's
head as she had to Seth when he was young. She looked irate enough, although with Cook that was hard to distinguish from her usual expression.
Thomas seemed not so much angry or intimidated as confused. Nothing in
his experience had prepared him for a menial who bolted her bailiwick.
Besides, a staring contest with Cook always disconcerted.

"If you turn that child out into the cold, I shall go with her." Cook
shook the ladle at the curtain of snow falling outside the window.

"Go then and be damned. There are a thousand and a thousand more in
New York who would step lively to take your place."

"Thomas!" Almy rushed into the room as Cook stomped out.

Almy carried her conical tin powdering mask in one hand and her mirror in the other. She wore pinned around her shoulders the piece of muslin that protected her linen chemise from spilled flour. With his rat-tail comb stuck into his own hairdo and his powder bag in one hand, Almy's wig dresser chased after her. He collected the pins and wool pads as they tumbled out of her half-finished coif. One end of a roll made of a stuffed cow's tail had come loose and hung down Almy's back. As soon as she stopped he tried to fasten it back into place, but she shooed him away.

Almy wanted to discuss this without everyone in the household listening in, but she was too overwrought to keep her voice low. Kate and Lizzie could hear her clearly.

"You cannot discharge Cook."

"Yes, I can. And that brown trollope too. I'll not be feeding the servants' by-blows."

"We cannot maintain our social position without help."

"Our social position is what concerns me."

Almy let loose her cascade of a laugh. "As if anyone in our circle cares a fig what the servants do. The antics of our high-class belles give more than enough fodder for gossip." Almy took a practical tack. "Reliable help is hard to find, and good cooks are impossible to replace."

"Nonsense. I can engage both in Canvas Town any day."

"You can canvas Canvas Town from one end to the other, and you will not find anyone else who can prepare roast veal the way you like it."

That stopped Thomas in mid harangue. Cook performed some abracadabra with the veal that brought it to the table moist, unscorched, and exquisitely garnished with parsley and sliced lemons. Cook's veal alone made the Buchanans the envy of New York society.

Almy pursued her advantage. "As for servants, Lizzie is 'nation honest. You know very well that anyone you hire will likely steal the lint from our pockets."

Thomas knew when he was bested. He cleared his throat and harumphed. "Then the father must pay for the brat's upkeep."

"We shall worry about that when Lizzie's time comes."

Lizzie had not named her baby's father, but she had confessed to Almy that he was an American soldier imprisoned at the Sugar House. Almy wasn't about to tell her Tory husband that. On her way back upstairs with her wig dresser trailing her, she stopped at the west parlor. Lizzie was crying and Almy put an arm around her.

"There, there. You know what they say. A woman cannot become a lady of fashion until she has lost her reputation. Don't fret yourself. No one is leaving here." Almy winked. "That odd fellow, Birdwhistle, brought beef yesterday, which he offered to us for a mere king's ransom. Tell Cook I said to give you some to take to your soldier."

Lizzie dropped into a curtsy. "Thank you, mistress."

"Tell Betsy to give you my old blue wool cloak for yourself, child, and half a dozen blankets to take to the prison."

"God's blessings on thee, Almy," said Kate.

Almy glanced out at the white landscape. "Law for me, I never knew it to start snowing halfway through November. Here it is December and it shows no signs of stopping. The prisoners must be freezing in that dreadful place."

Thee does not know the half of it, Kate thought.

Kate and Lizzie set out, following the beaten tracks between the snowdrifts. They could not be sure that Seth would receive any of the food, or the letters they included, but they went almost every day anyway. Now and then someone smuggled word out to them that Seth still lived.

When they reached the Sugar House they always went first to the snow-covered heap in the yard. They brushed the powder off with their mittens, uncovering the bodies stacked like cordwood. The broken panes of the prison windows had not been covered when summer ended. Most of these men had died of cold or starvation or the bloody flux, but some had obviously contracted smallpox. Kate moved the bodies aside to see the ones underneath.

She and Lizzie breathed a prayer of thanks when they didn't find Seth. As they did each time, they knelt in the snow and prayed for the souls of the dead, and for the living too.

KATE SHIVERED AND STAMPED HER FEET, TRYING TO GET feeling back into them. She and Lizzie and Rob stared up the street leading to the ferry.

"We should have gone to the prison." Lizzie paced a trough in the snow deep enough to expose the garbage frozen to the cobblestones. "Are you sure he's coming?"

Rob tried again to reassure her. "There's often a crowd there. We'll have a better chance to talk to him here."

The three of them had waited since early morning, and now the merchants were returning from their noon meal at the coffee house. Rob opened his greatcoat, gathered Kate and Lizzie into it, and held them close.

Lizzie's teeth chattered. "Tell me what Phoebe said."

Rob repeated what he had told her a dozen times already. "She said she heard a captain of the guard mention they were transferring prisoners from the Sugar House today and bringing them to the ferry. He said the big, red-haired rebel would be among them."

Rob didn't repeat it exactly as Phoebe Fraunces had heard it. The officer had actually said they would be rid of that carrot-topped troublemaker once and for all, and the Devil take him.

"There they are!"

Lizzie left the shelter of Rob's coat and slogged through the snow toward the horse-drawn sledge rounding a corner. Kate and Rob ran after her. Kate moaned when she saw the prisoners. Would she even recognize Seth?

The shivering men stood shackled to each other and packed together like herrings. They squinted in the glare of the sun on the snow. Filth had stained them and the shreds of their clothes to shades of dark brown. Their long hair and beards had felted into tangled mats. Most wore no shoes.

"Seth!" Lizzie paced alongside the sledge. "Seth, where are you?"

One gaunt figure jostled his way to the back. Since they were all chained together at the ankles, the others had to shift so Seth could reach out to Lizzie. She ran to keep up and handed him a bundle of clothes and a pair of shoes tied with twine. Rob and Kate threw two more bundles at his feet. One contained blankets and the other food.

Kate called to him. "We will keep petitioning Clinton for thy release, Seth."

"What of Mother?"

Kate hesitated. How could she tell him that his mother was dying. "She prays every day for you," she shouted.

The guard tried to make his way back through the press, but men moved to block him. He swore and struck at them with a club.

"I love thee, Lizzie." Seth knelt in a rattle of chains so he could reach out and touch the hand she held up to him as she ran. "I will hug thee again. I swear it before God."

Lizzie opened her cloak so he could see the bulge under her apron. Then the horses pulled the sledge away and she fell sobbing into the snow. Kate knelt next to her and put her arms around her. Rob had never felt so helpless and enraged, not even when Simcoe's Rangers cut down his family's apple orchard. At least where Simcoe was concerned, Rob had had some revenge. Thanks to Kate finding Simcoe's orders last fall, the militia in New Jersey were ready for him. They had shot his horse out from under him and taken him captive. Rob wasn't the only one who hated him. New Jersey's governor said it would be best for Simcoe's safety not to grant him parole.

Like most acts of revenge it served little purpose though. Seth was still a prisoner. He had become as thin as a rail, and his hair had turned white. Rob hadn't recognized him.

Rob had included something extra in the bundle of blankets he threw to Seth. He prayed that the lad found an opportunity to use it.

CONDITIONS AS BAD AS ANYTHING HELL COULD OFFER HAD not broken Seth. The sight of something lovely, of Lizzie and Kate, almost did. He stared at them, kneeling dark and forlorn against the unbroken expanse of new-fallen snow. Then the sledge turned a corner and Seth hunkered among the swaying prisoners. He put his head between his knees and wept.

The date was December twenty-third and when the Sugar House guards came for him and the others, Seth had dared to hope that Clinton had granted them a Christmas pardon. When he saw the ferry landing ahead he knew there would be no pardon. The men around him also realized where they were headed. They pleaded with the guards to turn the sledge around and take them back to the Sugar House.

Seth didn't. He was elated. The Sugar House was built of stone and bricks. A ship was made of wood. Seth intended to gnaw his way out of it with his teeth if necessary.

During the ferry ride Seth divided up the things in the bundles and passed them out among his friends. He kept a few items for himself, including the sewing kit that Kate had given him. He found Rob's compass and smiled. This was Rob's way of telling Seth that he knew the ship wouldn't hold him. Rob was giving Seth a tool to help him get his bearings when he escaped.

On the Brooklyn side the soldiers marched the shackled men the three quarters of a mile to Wallabout Bay. Along the way they passed the hundreds of crude grave markers and the bones uncovered by the tides. Dogs and pigs skulked off, and buzzards and gulls rose from the corpses left unburied.

Three whaleboats waited for them. Four prison ships were moored in Wallabout, but the whaleboats broke through the thin ice and headed toward the *Jersey*. The hulk looked ghostly floating on gray water against a gray sky and with snow falling in a veil around it. Seth knew he wouldn't see the outside of it again until he escaped, so he studied everything about it.

Chain cables held the Jersey at its moorings so the ship wasn't likely to change orientation. Seth made a surreptitious check with the compass and noted in which direction it pointed. The rudder hung unhinged. Of the rigging, only the bowsprit remained and a derrick for taking on water. The portholes had been boarded shut. Two tiers of openings, about twenty inches square, had been cut in the sides. Seth figured he could've squeezed through if they each hadn't had a pair of iron bars set into the frames at right angles.

Once aboard, the guards unlocked the manacles. With cat-o'-nine-tails and belaying pins, they drove the prisoners down the ladder into the abyss of the 'tweendecks. Clutching the things he had kept from the bundles, Seth descended into stench and a clamor of cries and moans. When he reached the bottom he put his other hand to his heart where, under his ragged shirt, he carried the few of Lizzie's and Kate's and his mother's letters he'd been able to preserve.

He stood hunched under the low ceiling and waited for his eyes to adjust. The barred openings let in the wind, and the temperature in the hold hovered around freezing. At least a hundred living skeletons sat or lay elbow-to-elbow. Two cut-down barrels served as privies, and they had overflowed. Seth would not have believed that anything could smell worse than the Sugar House, but this beat the Cellar all to tarnation, as Lizzie would say. The guards upended a bushel basket at the hatch opening and men fought for the wizened apples that showered down on them.

Seth headed for the area with the fewest people. When he got there, he saw why it was sparsely populated. Maggots crawled over the crust of smallpox sores that covered five of the men lying on the filthy floor along the wall. He laid his new blanket nearby in a beam of light from the opening in the hull just under the ceiling. He made his first order of business testing the bars. They held firm.

He sat cross-legged on the blanket and ran his hand over the thick wool. Bless Lizzie and Kate and Almy. Their gifts of food and clothing had kept him alive since summer.

Seth took inventory of the items in his bundle. He set aside a red bandana, a white handkerchief, and a dark blue shirt with a long tail from which he could tear a piece. With a needle and thread from the sewing kit he began making a small American flag to replace the one the guards had taken away in the Cellar. They had beaten him when they found it on him.

A man crawled over to him. "Could I have the use of that there needle?" He was almost naked. He must have realized that a needle was an odd request from someone with nothing to mend. "I mean to inoculate myself against the pox."

Seth wrapped the handkerchief and bandana in the shirt and set them on the blanket. "I'll help you."

He spent the afternoon taking festered matter from the victims' sores and scratching it into the skin of the men who lined up for it. By the time the light faded, some were calling him Doctor and some were calling him Captain. Many of them came to him with problems he was powerless to do anything about except nod in sympathy.

When the light grew too dim to see, Seth rolled up in his blanket. Lice crawled over the floor in such numbers that they crunched under his new shoes, but he didn't worry about rats. He figured that the few not eaten by now would have learned to avoid the 'tweendecks.

Seth went to sleep to a lullabye of groans and cries and curses. He woke up to shouts. "Madman with a knife!"

Someone had gone lunatic. It happened often, even in the Cellar. Everyone scrambled to get out of his way except Seth. He knocked him down, wrenched the blade from his hand, and slipped it into the waist of his breeches at the small of his back.

He returned to his blanket, but he didn't sleep. He had a warm blanket, new shoes, a knife, and a compass. God was merciful, and practical too. At first light he would check every window opening in the ship's hull. He would find the one where the wood was the most rotten. He would start cutting away at it.

To put himself to sleep he silently recited the Declaration of Independence. He had carried a broadsheet copy of it with him until the guards took it from him at the Sugar House. They had said it would prove useful in the privy.

It didn't matter to Seth though. He had memorized all of it. It had become a sort of prayer for him. It had calmed him and cheered him in the worst of times.

When he came to the line ". . . that they are endowed by their Creator with certain unalienable rights, that among these are life, liberty, and the pursuit of happiness," he stopped to think about it. His own life and liberty were precarious right now. As for happiness Seth remembered what Benjamin Franklin had had to say about that. The Declaration of Independence only guaranteed the pursuit of happiness, Ben wrote. People would have to catch up with it themselves.

Seth went to sleep thinking of Lizzie and the child she carried. That made him happy.

Thirty-two

Wherein Kate and Rob embark on a fool's errand;
Seth abandons ship

ROB HAD MADE A MARK FOR NOON ON THE SILL OUTSIDE HIS window, but the panes themselves served as a clock as the sun arced across the soot-grimed glass. Kate looked out from under the heap of blankets and checked the sun's position. The day would start fading soon. She burrowed back into the cocoon of warmth she and Rob had created in the garret.

Rob put his arms around her, and she lay with her cheek against his long-tailed wool shirt. He rubbed her back to warm her, and she was astonished to find that something as elusive and simple as contentment could be so intoxicating. She ran her palms across the twin hollows at the base of his spine and along the taut curves beyond them. No explorer setting foot on a new continent after a long, lonely voyage could feel happier than she. She had always resisted the carnal thoughts that would distract her from God, but occasionally she had tried to imagine what love felt like. Her imagination could never have come close to this.

Kate wished she could halt the sun in its arc across the window. She wished she could stay here with Rob forever. She wished they didn't have to get up and slog through the drifts of snow on what was almost certainly a fool's errand.

"Tell me again how Dr. Franklin proposes to produce more daylight?" she murmured.

"He doesn't propose to produce it, but to set clocks an hour ahead in springtime so that there is light later in the day in the warm months."

"But why? Most people don't know what time it is anyway, or care."

"Just a fancy of his, I suppose. One never knows when Franklin is being serious or having a tug at your leg."

"Like his sundial that fires off cannons to mark each hour?"

"Yes."

"By his reckoning, the clocks would be set back in the winter, is that right?"

"Yes."

"That means it's an hour earlier now."

Rob kissed the top of her head. "It's time to go."

They put on almost every article of clothing they owned. Then they walked to Sir Henry Clinton's headquarters and stood in the icy wind until a fleet of sleighs arrived with brass bells jangling. A gaggle of party-goers disembarked and swept past them and up the broad marble steps. The heavy doors swung open to admit them, spilling out light and music and warmth. Kate took Rob's hand and pulled him after her as she ran up the stairs to slip in before the doors slammed shut.

The guests milled in the vast entry hall shedding wool cloaks and long surtout coats, hats, gloves, muffs, scarves, and galoshes that they handed to the waiting servants. Some of them scattered to the inner rooms. Others joined the officers and their ladies on the curved marble stairs leading up to the ballroom.

Doorways opened onto the entry and hundreds of candles lit the rooms beyond them. Kate and Rob could see fires roaring in the hearths in all of them, including the one with a long table covered with platters, bowls, tureens, and chafing dishes.

"So this is where all the beef roasts went," muttered Rob.

"And the firewood," added Kate.

Every tree in New York had been cut down. Hundreds of cords of wood stood stacked along the Long Island shore for British ships to load, but the rank-and-file soldiers shivered in their flimsy, unheated barracks. The poor burned whatever wood they could steal. Some of the middling

wealthy had resorted to chopping up furniture. Soldiers guarded the public buildings and the barrels and crates at the waterfront, even the wharves
themselves, to keep them from being taken apart and stolen.

Rob knew before they left his rooming house that this was a bad idea,
but now it seemed a really bad one. Clinton did not care about his own soldiers' lives. He certainly would not care about an enemy.

"They will not discuss anything with us while they're celebrating
Christmas," he said.

"We have to talk to them tonight."

Rob knew that. He was the one who had reported to General Washington that Clinton and André and sixty-five hundred of their men would
take ship in the morning before the river froze solid. The war had moved
to a warmer clime, and Clinton and André were headed for South Car-
olina. Clinton had turned the military command over to the German general Wilhelm von Knyphausen. In twelve hours John André would leave,
and Kate and Rob would lose the only friend who might be able to set Seth
free, or at least arrange for his transfer back to a prison in the city.

A lieutenant hustled toward them. He would have had the same look on
his face if the party guests had tracked dog excrement in on their shoes.

"If you're looking for dole, go 'round to the servants' entrance."

"We wish to speak with General Clinton."

"His Lordship will grant no audience tonight."

"Then tell Major André that his friends Rob Townsend and Kate
Darby are here to see him."

"He will not see you. You must leave."

Kate smiled sweetly at him. "I will leave after I speak to John."

She gathered her skirts and coat and cloak around her and sat on the
floor in the middle of the entry hall. People collected in the doorways and
on the stairs to point and laugh.

"I say." The lieutenant looked at Rob. "I say, good fellow, do take her
away."

Rob shrugged. "I am a Quaker and may not force anyone to do what he
or she will not."

"What's this about?" John André pushed to the front of the onlookers.

"God keep you, John!" Kate stood up. "I must speak with you."

André led them to the back room that served as his office. He closed the door behind him. Kate started to make her plea for Seth, but André held up a hand.

"I know that your brother has been taken to the *Jersey*, Kate."

"Then you will ask Clinton to grant him pardon or parole?"

Kate was so eager she almost pushed the paper and quill across the desk to him. When she glanced at the inkwell, she noticed a letter next to it. It was addressed to someone named Gustavus.

André dropped a sheet of paper on top of it. "I cannot recommend either pardon or parole."

"Why?"

"Your brother did more than take up arms against his king and country." André lowered his voice. "An informant reported seeing him at the Merchants' Coffee House last fall."

Rob felt the bottom drop out of his stomach. He feared the look on his face might betray himself, and Kate. Had the informer seen Seth deliver Abraham Woodhull's first message to him at the coffee house? Probably not, Rob decided, or he himself would have been in the provost prison right now, or hanged and providing rations for worms.

A slow thumping began above the ceiling. The rhythmic squeak of bed ropes accompanied it. Rob used the distraction to rifle through his memory. Who in the British pay had snitched on Seth? Was it Rivington? Or was it Birdwhistle, the lop-faced hobgoblin Rob had met on the stairs at Rivington's office that day? Birdwhistle worked at the coffee house when he wasn't counterfeiting, speculating, forestalling, smuggling, prevaricating, and double-dealing. Maybe he and Rivington both had reported Seth to André.

"Someone is having a happy Christmas." André glanced up at the ceiling where the bed's beat was quickening. "What is it your Poor Richard says? ' 'Tis easier to keep holidays than commandments.' " His brief smile radiated amusement and apology for the impropriety upstairs. Then he returned to business.

"The informant said your brother was selling chickens at the coffee house. One wonders why a rebel soldier would dress like a farmer and peddle poultry where his enemies gather."

Kate stood stunned. To deny that Seth was a spy would be to lie, so she said nothing.

"You are a loyal subject of the king, Kate, and neither you nor Rob would stoop to deception. But I know that Seth was spying, and others suspect it." André didn't have to say that one of the others was Henry Clinton. "Seth's lucky he wasn't hanged."

André put his slender hand on Kate's. She remembered that hand arranging gowns and wigs for the Mischianza, and she was suddenly aware of how shabby and moth-eaten her mitten was.

"Because you are a dear friend, Katie, I will tell you something I should not. I paid the informant an extra shilling not to carry that piece of information about your brother any higher, but to leave it with me alone."

John didn't mention that he had made the deal sweeter, or more bitter. He had said that if Clinton found out about Seth, he would arrange for Birdwhistle to be found floating, bunghole upward, with the dead dogs and aged sauerkraut in one of the old defensive trenches.

Kate had resolved not to cry. Tears were undignified. They were the sort of ploy Peggy Shippen would use, but they rolled down her cheeks anyway. She struggled to keep her voice steady.

"If Seth perishes in that terrible place, John, our mother will die of a broken heart."

"He's strong. He's clever. He'll not perish." John reached for the inkwell and started writing.

For a few moments Kate thought she had persuaded him to write out a parole for Seth. He sprinkled sand on the wet ink to dry it, then shook it off. He rolled up the paper, warmed the end of a stick of red wax over a candle, and dripped it on the seam to hold it closed. He pressed his ring into the wax, and handed the paper to Kate.

"This pass will get you by the officer on duty at the ferry. You can continue taking food to Seth."

So, André knew Kate had been visiting her brother at the Sugar House. Rob wasn't surprised. Clinton had not made him his deputy adjutant general in charge of intelligence only because he doted on him.

Kate took the pass with a trembling hand. "I thank thee, John.

Above them the bed's performance reached a crescendo. It skipped an ecstatic foot or more across the ceiling, shuddered, and fell silent. André looked toward the door and the faint sound of music beyond. That delectable smile—charming, affectionate, self-effacing, and bold—lit his face more be-guilingly than a hundred candles.

"Excuse me, but Sir Henry becomes agitated if I am more than a few minutes from his sight." He rolled his blue eyes, and Rob could only imagine what a trial it was to serve as Henry Clinton's closest confidante. "I must rejoin the *mobile vulgus*. The mob, as you Yanks say. Rob, you've delivered goods to this house. You know the way out."

"Yes."

"Then I will bid you both Godspeed until we see each other again."

"May God grant you a safe voyage, John," said Kate.

André shook Rob's hand. He put his arms around Kate and hugged her to him. He stepped back, but kept his hands on her shoulders with a grip so strong it surprised her. He stared into her eyes.

"I am deeply sorry for your brother's plight, sweet Kate, but have a care. Do not let Seth draw you into intrigues that may cost you your life."

André headed, whistling, toward the front of the house. Rob put his arm around Kate's shoulders and walked with her down the back hall. On the way Kate glanced into one of the rooms. In the dim light from a whale oil lamp she saw a tattered object on a sideboard. She slipped inside.

"Kate," Rob called softly after her. "What are you doing?"

She held up the mouse-gnawed, water-stained leather package. Rob didn't ask for an explanation until they reached the street.

"What is it?"

"I don't know. I found it on a dying soldier and assumed it contained letters to his family. I thought to see it delivered, but someone took it from me after the fight at Monmouth. And now here it is again."

"Did you also see the letter on André's desk?" Rob asked.

"Yes. Do you know who Gustavus is?"

"No. Lizzie overheard André and Clinton talking about him months ago. He lives in Philadelphia and claims to have information to sell. Lizzie said they didn't think of it as having any significance. She thought a woman was involved too. I've been trying to find out who they are."

"With John André gone, there is nothing we can do about it here." Kate thought about old friends in Philadelphia who might know something.

She could send a friendly letter to Ned Whithers, the one Lizzie called

Stork. As for contacting Peggy Shippen Arnold she was well connected but too skittish by far. Skittish was an understatement. Cook said Peggy Arnold was as unpredictable as a cat hot-footing it across embers.

Kate had a contrary thought but dismissed it. Peggy was too flighty for treachery, and her husband was a hero of the American cause. They could not be the ones Lizzie had heard Clinton and André talking about.

They climbed the steep stairs to the room that had become Kate and Rob's haven. They lit a lamp and their breath formed clouds in its feeble light as they unrolled the parchment. They laid the four pages out on the table and weighted the corners.

They were in remarkably good condition, considering all they had weathered. Rob ran his fingers over the spidery writing. Thomas Jefferson's draft had many words crossed out with corrections written above them, but the opening line read as he had originally composed it.

" 'When in the course of human events . . .' "

SETH PREPARED FOR HIS THIRTY-MILE HIKE THROUGH A snowstorm by stripping naked. The wind whistled and moaned around the *Jersey*'s hull. Snowflakes blew into Seth's face when he grasped the iron bars and tugged. He had spent three weeks cutting the wood away from around them, and they came loose in his hand. The prisoners gave a collective sigh, but no one cheered. Cheering would bring the guards and their belaying pins.

Seth stuck one of the bars into the bundle of his clothes. He handed the other to the Massachussetts shoemaker who had kept watch for him. The shoemaker had come up with the idea of hiding the wood chips in the privy barrels. It wouldn't do to leave them lying around, inside or out, where the guards might spot them.

The shoemaker was barefoot, but so were seven of the twelve men coming with Seth. Most of them were half-naked besides, in spite of the fact that Seth had parceled out his clothes until he had few left for himself. But at least they might be strong enough to face the ordeal on the other side of the hull.

Seth had lost fifty pounds, but he still inhabited a large frame made of sturdy bones. He put his head through the opening. It would be tighter than he had expected. He pulled back into the hold.

"Can you fit?" the shoemaker whispered. Everyone knew that if Seth could get out, they all could.

"Yes." Seth could make no other answer. He had to fit.

He put his arms through, and then his head. The shoemaker locked his fingers to form a step for Seth's foot and heaved him upward. Seth's shoulders wedged, and he twisted to position them on the opening's diagonal. The rough wood rubbed his skin off and drove splinters into his shoulders and arms, but slowly he wriggled through.

He landed in the four-foot-deep drift that nuzzled up against the hull. His bundle of clothes flew through the opening. Shivering, he put them on. He checked his coat pocket for his compass. Then he held out his arms and grinned up into flakes spiraling down to caress his face. He gulped lungfuls of the fresh air. He wanted to shout with joy, and dance like a bear in the deep snow. Several hours of daylight remained, but the snow formed such a dense curtain that Seth and the others would be invisible from shore. Once they walked thirty feet from the ship no one aboard would be able to see them either.

When everyone was out Seth led them from the stern to the starboard midships. He put his back to the hull. Ahead of him lay the frozen river, a highway to freedom. To avoid British-held territory he and the others would have to walk up the middle of the East River and Long Island Sound, then across to Greenwich or Stamford in Connecticut.

Seth knew that he would end up carrying the weakest of the men in the group. He figured he would lose some fingers and toes to frost. He leaned into the north wind and the driven snow and took the first step.

He wondered how long the guards would take to discover that the hold held thirteen fewer prisoners. Seth remembered the woodcut in the copy of *Poor Richard's Almanack* that he had pored over as a child. It showed a bumpkin setting out on a journey on a sunny day with a walking stick in one hand and a sack slung over his shoulder.

"He's gone," the caption read, "and forgot nothing but to say farewell to his creditors."

Thirty-three

Wherein the Lord giveth, and He taketh away;
Seth jumps from the fire into the frying pan

COOK SWUNG THE MAUL IN A POWERFUL ARC. THE CRACK OF splintering wood shattered the stillness of the morning. "Wrecking a perfectly sound garden fence to bake bread," she muttered. "I never saw the like."

"Almy's right." Kate used a crowbar to pry the broken pickets away from the crosspieces. "If we don't use the wood, some poor soul will take it while we sleep." Kate would have been willing to let the poor souls have the wood but for two reasons, her invalid mother and Lizzie's infant son, born just before daybreak.

"What has this world come to?" Cook warmed to the task, leaving a row of smashed fence pickets in her wake.

The destruction seemed to cheer her. She gave each picket a name. She started with what she called the Unholy Trinity—George Washington, John Adams, and Benjamin Franklin, whom she referred to as the Old Goat. She claimed that Franklin had pinched her bottom once when passing on the street in Philadelphia. She said the French could have him for all she cared.

She went on to smash Henry Clinton, General Knyphausen, and William Cunningham. She included the Marquis de Lafayette, and Louis XVI, the king she called Louie Says. She threw in the entire French nation for good measure.

Cook was furious with the rebels for starting this war. She was furious with the British officers for fiddling while the rest of the city had nothing to burn. She was furious at the starving, shivering masses who stole everything they could lay hands on. She was beyond furious that Rachel Darby was dying and that Seth could not see his newborn son.

Kate stacked the wood onto the sled. She pulled and Cook pushed the load through the canyon they had cleared in the five-foot-high snowdrifts. On the way to the kitchen door they passed the vacant woodshed. Cook eyed it like a cow fatted for slaughter.

She shook a finger at it. "You're next."

They also passed the sleigh that Thomas Buchanan had driven back empty from the country yesterday. The farmers insisted that the British quartermaster had bought all their cordwood. Thomas had come roaring into the kitchen and thrown his purchases—a bushel of sprouting potatoes and a smoked ham—onto the brick floor. "Quartermaster my arse! Plundermaster, more like. Is this how those loyal to the king are served?"

The officers formerly quartered here had left for Charleston with General Clinton, and they took their privileges and perquisites with them. At least their going meant that Kate and Rachel could move one floor down to where the rooms had fireplaces. And Almy had agreed to let Cook and Lizzie share Kate's room, so long as word did not get out that her houseguests were sharing accommodations with servants. New York's high society would tolerate any pecadillo but fraternizing with menials.

Almy intercepted Kate on her way upstairs. "Squire Triple-Chins has dropped anchor and wishes to board you."

She led Kate to the drawing room door. The two of them peeked in at the portly man sprawled in the embrace of Thomas Buchanan's big chair. His tier of chins rested on his ruffled cravat, and he snored like a bulldog with asthma. Almy and Kate fled across the entryway and into the west parlor. Almy giggled. Kate did not.

"What's he doing here at this hour?" Kate whispered.

"Mayhap after calling on you yesterday, his passion for you forbid him sleep."

"He's sleeping now." Kate was mortified not so much that her father had decided to arrange a marriage for her, but that he had thought so little of her as to send this antique. The man was at least forty years old.

"Your father's letter says he is wealthy and a Quaker and a man of business in Jamaica besides."

"I am married to Robert, Almy."

"Your father doesn't know that. And Rob sees so little of you that he's probably forgotten." Almy raised a hand as a shield against Kate's indignation. She looked as contrite as she was able. Almy did not feign contrition well. "I know. I know. You have tarried here to tend your mother and to help me while Lizzie was great enough with child to produce a calf."

Kate started off toward the stairs.

Almy called after her. "What shall I say to Sir Triple-Chins when he wakes up and finds himself careened and Kateless?"

"Tell him that I am flattered by his attentions, but all the ingots of the Incas would not induce me to make him my husband."

Almy laughed. "Always the diplomat, dearest Katie."

Kate carried an armload of the wood upstairs to her mother's room. Lizzie sat in a chair by the hearth, holding her son. Cook was trying to coax Rachel Darby to eat some rice gruel. Kate built up the fire and sat on the edge of the bed that Cook had warmed. Cook twisted her hands in her apron and hovered next to Lizzie.

Rachel Darby lay with her head and shoulders propped up on pillows. Kate reached under the covers to hold her hand.

"Lizzie and Seth's child are here, Mother." Kate kissed her on the forehead.

Lizzie held her infant so Rachel could see him. Kate leaned down to hear what her mother murmured.

"She says he's beautiful."

"We desire you to name him, Mistress Darby," said Lizzie.

A smile fluttered across Rachel's pale lips. She tried to raise her hand to touch the baby. Lizzie laid him in the curve of Rachel's thin arm.

"Isaac," she murmured. "Laugh."

"Isaac Laugh?" Lizzie asked.

"Do you mean you're laughing like Abraham and Sarah, Mother?"
Rachel nodded.

"Abraham and Sarah laughed in disbelief when their son Isaac was born," said Kate. "Because Abraham was a hundred years old and Sarah ninety. They never thought they would see a child born to them."

"Then Isaac he is," Lizzie said.

"We have other news, Mother. One can cross the East River on horse-back now, and yesterday I rode to Brooklyn with provisions for Seth. The soldiers at the ferry have become quite amiable. They told me that Seth escaped from the *Jersey* more than two weeks ago."

"The guards at the ship never told us." Lizzie was more than indignant. "They took the vittles and duds we brought, and they kept as mum as a chopping block."

Rachel raised her eyes in a prayer of thanks that Seth had escaped, then she went back to gazing at the baby.

Kate didn't mention that the sentries at the ferry couldn't tell her what had happened to Seth. They only knew that he and twelve other prisoners had made their escape in a snowstorm.

While Kate talked she saw the light go out in her mother's pale blue eyes. She put her hand on her heart, next to the sleeping baby, and felt no beat. She closed the eyes that held no more life now than two marbles. Cook sobbed and Lizzie lifted the child and rocked him in her arms.

"The Lord giveth," Kate said, "and the Lord taketh away."

Cook, ever a good Anglican, murmured the Lord's Prayer.

Rachel died at forty years of age. Kate continued holding her mother's hand. She stared at her face, with the smile still on her blue-tinged lips, until Rachel's fingers grew cold and night summoned the light from the room.

SETH WISHED THAT THE CREATOR HAD DESIGNED COWS WITH sled runners. Or he wished that He at least had equipped this particular cow with them. Seth trampled the shoulder-high drifts as best he could, but his feet had no more feeling than two lumps of lead. He floundered, lost his balance, and fell back into the snow. The cow stared down at him with what looked like sympathy in her big brown eyes, or at least curiosity. Her drool froze in a rope that came just short of hitting his face. He got to his feet using her front leg and bell collar to haul himself up.

He had found her lowing in a shed at a plundered farmhouse and had scavenged hay for her from the shed's loft. In return she had become devoted to him. He didn't know how she had escaped the foraging parties, but he tied a lead line around her neck and he thanked God for her. He knew his comrades would too. An American deserter had told him what to expect at the encampment at Jockey Hollow, but Seth figured life there would be a lark compared to the *Jersey*.

Seth had no difficulty finding the Continental Army. A line of plat-forms twenty-feet high held fires to serve as beacons. Snow-covered log huts and brush lean-tos covered the hillsides like tumuli. On the open pa-rade ground a man was being lashed on the bare back for desertion. It all looked familiar to Seth.

As he led the cow through camp he turned down offers of a gold watch, three farms, a foundry, and the hands of various sisters. A few men tried to take her by force, but Seth still had the iron bar from the *Jersey*. He snarled at them with a ferocity that made them reconsider playing hound to his wolf.

He limped into the camp of the Pennsylvania Line and found several of his old comrades huddled around a roaring fire. They were gnawing the bark off sticks of river birch while their belts and cartridge boxes came to a boil in a brass kettle. They didn't recognize Seth under his prison pallor and thatch of wild white hair and beard, but they were happy to see anyone who arrived in convoy with a cow.

Spitz was the first to realize who he was. He threw his arms around him and showered him with German, then English. "You saved my life, my friend. Und I t'ought you vas dead!"

"And I thought you would have left when your enlistment was up."

Spitz pulled at his beard, a habit he had when about to wax philosophical. "God and I both once knew why I re-enlisted, but now God alone knows."

The rest of the Pennsylvanians were more interested in the cow. She looked back at Seth as half a dozen of them led her away. Seth wondered if he would be able to eat whatever part of her they served up. He thought he probably could.

He began to shiver, and his bones felt like they were turning to slurry as exhaustion from his long journey through the frozen countryside took over. Kind people had sheltered him along the way, and he had come across isolated outposts of American soldiers, but more often than not he had slept in hayricks or dens in the snow. Two days ago a doctor in one of the villages had offered to cut off his frozen toes, but he knew he still had a long way to walk and he declined.

He curled up in his blanket as close to the flames as he could get without igniting himself. He thought that if he were to die, fire would be a good way to go. He felt as if he had never left here. He went to sleep to the lullaby of the same complaints he had heard at Valley Forge, only more bitter. The winter of 1776 in Valley Forge had not been nearly this long or cold.

No pay for more than six months. Threadbare uniforms. Illnesses of devilishly inventive and hideous misery. Simple, stark starvation. Supply wagons stuck on snow-packed roads. Greed and thievery among those provisioning the army. Inferior arms and little ammunition. The usual squabbling among the officers. John Adams was right when he said, "I think we shall never take a fort until we shoot a general." And there were desertions. A lot of desertions. Worst of all, the civilian population wanted this expensive nuisance of an army to go away.

"The citizens would be happier with a plague of locusts in their midst," said one of the men. "Locusts only live a season."

Seth didn't sleep long. Prison had conditioned his reflexes, and he came instantly awake when he felt someone removing his shoes. He leaped on the culprit, one hand squeezing the man's windpipe and his iron bar raised to smash his skull. The force of his attack carried the thief backward into the dirty snow with Seth on top of him.

"Easy, lad." Anthony Wayne grinned up at him. "I wanted to see what condition your paws are in."

Seth wrapped up in the blanket with his bare feet sticking out so Wayne could inspect them.

"We thought you had given up the ghost when you went over that cliff at Stony Point." Wayne studied the three blackened toes for more time than necessary so no one would see the joy glistening in his eyes.

"They will find it hard work to kill me," said Seth. "I have been a guest of Billy Cunningham."

"Not many of the ranks walk out of that son of a bitch's grasp."

"I'm like one of those two frogs that fell into a pail of milk, sir. One frog gave up and drowned. The other kept kicking until they found him the next morning floating on a pat of butter."

Wayne chuckled. "When Spitz said you were killed I felt like I'd lost a son." Wayne looked at the misery around him and shook his head at the quantity of greed and folly loose in the world. "Why did you come back?"

Seth thought of the charred brick shell of his family's house in

Philadelphia. He thought of his beloved Lizzie among the enemy in New York where he could not reach her. He thought of the bleak, burned, and plundered country through which he had tramped.

"I had nowhere else to go." He shrugged. "I thought surely things would have improved, with winter providing a chance to rest and recruit."

"Improved!" Wayne threw his head back and guffawed.

Seth realized how much he had missed that laugh. It carried even over cannon fire.

"Did you hear the story about the young fellow who went out for a ride on his horse?" Wayne asked.

Seth shook his head.

"He came to a stretch of ground that looked boggish. He called to a country clown who was ditching and asked if it was hard at the bottom. 'Ay, ay, it's hard enough at the bottom, I'll warrant you.' So the cove rode in and the horse sank to the saddle skirts. The young gallant whipped and spurred. He cursed and swore, but the horse kept sinking. 'Why you whoreson rascal,' he shouted. 'Didn't you tell me it was hard at bottom?' 'Ay,' the clown answered, 'but you are not halfway to the bottom yet.'"

"No matter how bad the circumstances, sir, we have our honor."

"That would be a fine thing if only we could serve honor hot on a platter with potatoes and gravy. All our hopes now ride on Lafayette."

"Is he still in France?"

"Aye. Washington has paced a trench in the floor, waiting for him to return. If Lafayette can't convince King Louie to send us men and ships, we are finished."

"So, we are depending on one despot to rid us of another."

"My boy, you have summed up the entire situation. And because of the French despot's excesses, France's economy is a shambles. I shall be surprised if Louie agrees, even for the chance to bugger the Brits." Wayne nodded toward the officers' tents. "Come along. I'll have my striker heat water, and we'll cut your hair and shave you. You look like Father Christmas on famine rations."

Seth tried to pull his shoes on, but once free of them, his feet took the opportunity to swell up like aggrieved puffer-fish. Wayne pulled a pair of thick wool stockings from his haversack and held them out. Seth received them like a sacrament. He put them on and carried his shoes. He had long since learned not to leave unattended anything as valuable as shoes.

As they passed among the officers' quarters, something on a trash heap caught Seth's eye. He picked it up.

"One of Colonel Tallmadge's dragoons brought it in," Wayne said. "That fellow Brewster carried it across the sound from Long Island. Tallmadge was away so the dragoon turned it over to Major Hamilton."

"Caleb Brewster is still at large?"

"Yep. He's the only one of that Culper lot who doesn't bother with a false name. The bloodybacks know about him, but he slides through their grasp like a greased pig."

Seth untied the cord and opened the weatherbeaten leather wrapping.

"Do you know what this is, sir?"

"No. Alex Hamilton said it was of no value."

"May I have it?"

"Certainly. I reckon some of the men would have found it soon and thrown it into the evening stew, along with their boots."

General Benedict Arnold gave a curt salute and stumped past in the high red shoe he wore to compensate for the leg shortened by his wound at the battle for Saratoga.

Wayne waited until he was out of hearing. "The hero of Saratoga hasn't changed either. Still in high dudgeon about being passed over for promotion. Still begging for a command."

"Isn't he the military governor of Philadelphia?"

Wayne shook his head. "He's bankrupt. He's been accused of speculating. A court-martial convicted him of using army equipment for transporting personal goods, which is the least of his transgressions. They withheld his salary and ordered General Washington to reprimand him. And then there is his rib . . ."

"Peggy Shippen?"

"Exactly."

"What of her?"

"These are troubled times and when the pot boils, the scum floats uppermost." Wayne flashed him an oblique look. "My advice is to steer well clear of the shoals of Mrs. Arnold."

"I was acquainted with her in Philadelphia, but she will have nothing to do with the likes of me."

"That's good luck for you then."

Benjamin Tallmadge had gotten word of Seth's arrival and was waiting for them. He grinned, pumped Seth's hand, and thumped him on the back in a show of more elation than anyone had ever seen from him. When Seth finished his account of the past six months Wayne gave him several gills of rum to take his mind off the fact that the surgeon was about to separate him from three of his toes.

Afterward Wayne said he could sleep on a cot in his tent, but Seth preferred to join his comrades. The surgeon bandaged Seth's feet. Wayne gave him another pint of whiskey, a twist of tobacco, and two more blankets. Seth limped back in triumph with them to the camp of the Pennsylvania Line. That evening he and his old friends devoured four pounds each of beef charred on the outside and bloody in the middle.

From the corner of his eye Seth saw James Coleman about to light his pipe with a familiar-looking piece of parchment crumpled into a roll. He snatched it before the corner of it reached the flames of the evening fire. He rounded on Coleman.

"Do not take my things." He smoothed it out and put it back into the leather wrapping.

James looked chagrined. "It has no purpose but as tinder."

James would think so. It already had writing on it, so he couldn't use it to forge the discharge papers that he sold to prospective deserters.

Seth fell asleep that night spooned with Spitz and James by the fire, inside a cocoon of blankets. He held the packet in his arms instead of his rifle. He missed his rifle and wondered where it had ended up. He missed it less than he missed Lizzie, but he mourned its loss anyway. He had slept with his rifle more nights than with Lizzie, and his fingers had absorbed the feel of every sleek curve and straightaway of it. He remembered how the hard iron took on the warmth of his body under the blankets at night.

Still God had been good to him. His feet were too numb from cold to hurt much. He had come home to his comrades. He was a free man. This war would not last forever. When he saw Lizzie again she would hold up his child for him to kiss. He would put his arms around both of them and never let go.

Thirty-four

Wherein Rob is forced to volunteer; Jemmy Rivington proposes a duel to the death with sausages and mistakes Kate for a zebra

RIVINGTON ALWAYS FOUND A SHELTERED SPOT TO SIT, EVEN on a redoubt exposed to the early March wind squalling off the Hudson. He laid down a satin cushion stuffed with goose down and parked himself in the lee of an artillery piece with his back against the wheel and his forearms resting on his knees. He watched Rob and Hercules and a hundred other members of the Loyalist Volunteers pickax large rocks into smaller ones and haul them to the top of the wall. Rivington continued his story, although most of New York had heard it.

"Her husband arrived at the coffee house," he said, "brimful of wrath and cabbage. He cut quite the dash in his dress uniform with its tin and tinsel. He stood as stiff as if he had stowed his ramrod up his arse. I had been forewarned that he intended to call me out and so had prepared. I observed that as I was the challenged party, I had the choice of arms. He clicked his heels, snapped a bow, and concurred. I went to the kitchen and returned bearing aloft a tray holding my weapons." Rivington paused for effect. "Two large sausages.

"'One of these has rat poison added to the ingredients,' says I. 'The second is perfectly sound. Let His Excellency do me the honor of choosing whichever he wishes to consume, and I will eat the other.'" Rivington shielded his pipe from the wind, lit it with his flint, and drew in a lungful of warm smoke. "Needless to say the poor cuckold thought better of his plan."

"And well he should," Hercules put in. "If he challenged every rake-shame who shagged his fair shackle he would not find leisure to bugger his striker."

"When his wife goes to her reward," Rivington said, "her epitaph shall read, 'At last, she sleeps alone.'"

"And did you hear of the letter threatening to kidnap Benedict Arnold's wife for money?" asked Hercules. Rob and Jemmy shook their heads. "General Arnold penned this reply, 'Sir, I don't have much money, but I'm mighty interested in your proposition.'"

"The hero of Saratoga," added Rivington, "has had to give up his stables and move out of his mansion. I hear he and the missus are living in a chicken coop."

"Now, Jemmy," said Rob, "surely not a chicken coop."

"Arnold's wife has put him in such reduced circumstances that he would willingly pick up a farthing from a pile of dog shit with his teeth." Rivington knew dozens of the jests circulating around New York about Benedict Arnold and his wife. In fact, he had made up most of them. "They say that before Miss Shippen married the Hero she made a full confession of her past affairs. What courage that took. What honesty! What a memory!"

Rob chuckled. Jemmy might not pull his weight on work details, but he made the time pass more quickly.

Now that March of 1780 was well along, the ice on the river was melting, but General Knyphausen was still certain that the attack he had been expecting all winter would come any day. Washington's false reports of troop strength heightened his anxiety. If anyone doubted that Knyphausen was worried, he had only to note that James Rivington had been included in the sweep of civilians conscripted into the newly formed Loyalist Volunteer militia. A commander would have to be anxious indeed to expect the editor of the *Royal Gazette* to defend the city against anything deadlier than a cutting remark. Hercules Mulligan said that putting Jemmy Rivington in a uniform was like strapping high-soled clogs on a cat and expecting it to execute the manual of arms.

The recruiters had drafted Mulligan too, but at least he profited from the excess of anxiety. The twenty-six hundred recruits kept him busy altering the uniforms they had to buy with their own funds. Rivington had ordered Hercules to fit him out in a full rigging of gold braid, ribbon, sashes, tinsel, and ruffles for his captain's uniform. Rivington had discovered what the lowest-ranking soldiers had known for centuries. A uniform was like honey to ants when it came to women.

Rob himself had discovered that there was nothing voluntary about the Volunteers. The proclamation called on every man from seventeen to sixty to report for duty, including Quakers. Hercules was sympathetic with Rob's plight. He suggested that Rob put on a frock from his shop's inventory and pass himself off as a fishwife.

Since mid-February he had to wear a uniform, carry a musket, drill three times a week in the snow, and stand shivery sentinel outside houses where regular army officers were quartered. He hated it. The fact that everyone else had to do it didn't make him feel any better. According to Abraham Woodhull, word of it had reached his father, and Rob knew that this would make reconciliation almost impossible.

By four o'clock the wind had stilled, and Kate's arrival signaled time to stop work. She carried a pail of chicken and turnip soup smothered in dumplings.

"Thunder and oakum," Rivington roared. "I'm as peckish as a shark."

Kate shrugged out of the straps of her old camp basket and unpacked it. She spread an oiled cloth in the shelter of the battery and set out bowls, cups and spoons, the soup pail, a hunk of farmer's cheese, a golden-crusted loaf of Cook's bread, and a pot of tea. The four of them sat cross-legged on the cloth and made a picnic on top of the ramparts with a view of the Hudson and the craggy cliffs of the Jersey shore.

When they had eaten, Hercules and Jemmy doffed their hats, bowed to Kate, and headed off toward home with the rest of the Volunteers. Rob and Kate sat under a blanket with his arm around her shoulders and watched the show of colors in the western sky.

Kate handed him a book. He read the title by the slanting light of the setting sun.

"*'The Turkish Spy: Observations Upon Occidental Manners by Oriental Visitors.'* I've been looking for this. Where did you get it?"

"I spent the afternoon wandering among the book stalls."

A paper fell out from between the pages. Rob unfolded it. "This is a bill of lading."

"Oh, yes. I went to the docks this morning. Last week I took one of Cook's curatives to a stevedore's wife in Canvas Town. Her husband promised to obtain a list of provisions for the British commissary. Ten thousand rations, I believe. And he says that six victualing ships are on their way from Cork."

"Dearest Kate, you must not go to the docks. It's dangerous at any time, and to gather intelligence there is too perilous."

"But you always say that if we know what supplies they're laying in, we can speculate about their numbers and intentions."

Actually Kate liked the waterfront, at least when the breeze was blowing in off the water. The smell of tar and spices, aromatic woods and brine intoxicated her. When she stood on a pier and gazed out at the forest of masts, she wondered what it would be like to take ship to the West Indies. She imagined walking through the door of her father's office in Jamaica. And she realized that he did not know yet that his wife had died.

"I was there only a few minutes," she said. "I clerked at the shop, and when it closed I delivered the ribbon that Colonel Becker's wife ordered. I took more of Cook's kitchen physic to the stevedore's ailing wife in Canvas Town, and I looked for wool yarn at the Fly market. Then I went to the booksellers' shops."

That had been the best part of the day for Kate. She had wandered among the stalls heaped with books until her feet hurt. Then she had sat on the floor in a corner, reading.

When night fell and the temperature dropped they knew they should go home, but they lingered. From the ramparts' heights they watched the gibbous moon, looking like a polished pewter spoon, rise over the rooftops.

"I bought yarn to darn the holes in your stockings," Kate said.

"You know my philosophy of holes and stockings."

" 'A hole is an accident of the day,' " she recited, " 'but a darn is premeditated poverty.' "

Rob blew on the curls around her ear to set them dancing. They were as wispy as the clouds along the horizon had been, and the same red-gold color. Kate laughed and shoved him so hard he toppled over. She pounced on him and tickled his ribs. They rolled in the blanket until they were wrapped up tightly together. They kissed, oblivious to the fact that the British sentries could happen on them in their rounds. They lay there a long time, too happy to move.

The world had become a series of partitions for them, like the bulkheads of a ship, or the chambers of a nautilus shell. The outermost was England, France, and the lands beyond them. Then there was the wide ocean, and the American-held territory surrounding New York. Inside that was the city itself, sealed off from the rest of the country. Then there was wherever the two of them happened to be—Rob's room or his shop or this rampart. Next was the encompassing warmth of the blanket. At the center of it all beat Kate and Rob's hearts, fortified against the storm of war around them.

JEMMY RIVINGTON LOOKED POSITIVELY PROLETARIAN IN THE leather apron that covered him from chin to knees. His typesetter had taken ill with ship's fever, and James was putting together the next edition of the *Royal Gazette*. He didn't mind. It reminded him of when he was a much younger man and did this on a regular basis in his father's shop. He enjoyed the process of laying type in rows to build words, images, opinions, and passions the way a mason constructed the courses of a stone wall.

He had come to the obituaries.

On Monday afternoon the spirit of that facetious,
good-tempered, inoffensive convivialist Mr. John Levine
ascended to the skies.

He was so absorbed in sending off amiable old John Levine with a fitting tribute that he didn't hear the door open.

He started when Tunis Birdwhistle said, "Good day to you, Squire."

"Good day, Birdwhistle. What are you selling today?"

"Information, Squire."

"For the *Gazette*?"

"Nay, Squire. This titbit is not for publication. I know of a woman who is spying for the rebels."

"Why are you telling me?"

"I have not been able to contrive an audience with General Knyphausen, and I can't speak enough of that heathenish Deutsch gibberish to converse with his lackeys. You have contact with the Hessians. If you deliver the report, you can take a percentage of whatever they pay for it."

"And who is this spy?"

"The Quaker wench who resides with the Buchanans and has taken up with Townsend."

"Kate Darby?"

"The very one. I saw her alone in an inn on Long Island. Her presence there seemed strange to me, so I have kept an eye out for her since. Two days ago I watched her collect information from one of the hirelings at the dock. I tried to follow her to see where she delivered it."

Misfortunate Kate, Rivington thought. Her reputation and her life have become a commodity in this huckster's hands to be sold to the highest bidder.

"And where did she deliver it?" he asked.

Birdwhistle exhaled an onion-and-garlic gust of exasperation. Kate had not meant to be sneaky, but she had led him on a merry chase through New York's narrow streets and alleys.

"She went first to Colonel Becker's quarters."

"But Becker is true blue."

"How can we be sure? In any case, from there she meandered like a drunken alley cat all over the city. I lost her in the booksellers' shops. One minute she was wandering among the stalls, and the next she was gone. She's slippery as a larded eel, she is, but I'm fly to her lay."

"Do you suspect Townsend too?"

"I think he's too much the rustic to conspire, but the jilt could be fooling him as well as Thomas Buchanan and John André and God alone knows who else. I think she's the one carrying intelligence out of the city."

"All right. I'll pass along your suspicions, and I'll pocket half of the informer's fee for my trouble."

"That's too much."

"Take it or leave it."

Birdwhistle mumped and muttered, but Rivington stood firm.

Jemmy continued humming to himself and arranging type for an hour after Birdwhistle left. Then he washed his hands and hung the leather apron on a peg. He put on his coat and hat and strolled to the Coffee House. He found Rob interviewing officers about their elaborate plans for the celebration of King George's birthday.

Rivington took him to a quiet corner. "Tunis Birdwhistle thinks your lady is a spy."

"What gives him that idea?"

"He says he saw her collecting documents from a navvy at the docks. He wants me to play the snitch with Knyphausen."

"Do you think she's a spy?"

"Of course not." Rivington rolled his mantis eyes at such a preposterous notion. "If I hear hoofbeats I suspect horses, not zebras. Miss Kate is a zebra. She's a Quaker, and hardly up to the duplicity of espionage. But you must keep your wits about you. Birdwhistle would sell his mother . . . if in fact he ever had one. I contend that he is the end result of a rattlesnake's indiscretion with a fireman's ladder."

"What do you advise?"

"Go about your business, both of you. Do not do anything that might excite Birdwhistle's zeal to serve his king and his own interests." Jemmy started to leave then turned back. "Do you have a few guineas about you? I shall give them to Birdwhistle and tell him it's his bounty for turning informer. That way he will think his message has been delivered and he will drop the matter. I would pay it myself but I'm short of funds."

Rob gave him the coins and held his tongue. Jemmy did not spend his money wisely, but no purpose would be served by pointing out that what maintained one vice would bring up two children. Besides, a few guineas added up to a trifling tariff for the favor Jemmy had done him.

When Rob left the coffee house he used all his will to keep from sprinting up Wall Street to his lodgings. Sprinting would have proved difficult anyway. He would have had to charge through the press of traders haggling in front of the Merchants' Exchange. He would have had to bowl over the urchins, dogs, pigs, sailors, laborers, soldiers, artisans, women of high degree and low, and the bewigged gentlemen and their servants, the catch-farts, all of whom crowded the narrow streets.

When he reached the boardinghouse he followed the beckoning bouquet of seared mutton up the stairs and into his room. Kate sat on a stool at the small fireplace. She was frying thin slices of spring lamb in butter and flour with half a lemon, half an onion diced, a blade of mace, and a bundle of sweet herbs. She added gravy and an anchovy minced. The aroma was headier than a jolt of rum.

Rob grabbed her and hugged her to reassure himself that no one had come to arrest her while he was absent. He held her away from him so he could look at her, then he pulled her close again. He rubbed his hand over her back and shoulders and lovely posterior, trying to make contact with as much of her surface as he could.

He ran his fingers through her hair, dislodging the pins and setting it loose from its knot. He wound both hands into the curls and kissed her.

"Dearest Kate, thee is light and gladness to me."

"What has happened?"

"I am quitting the operation. We are not gathering any more intelligence. I am not writing another report."

"Why not?"

"Birdwhistle saw thee at the docks. He wants Jemmy Rivington to tell Knyphausen that thee is an intelligencer."

"What should I do?"

"Nothing. If thee behaves differently thee will raise suspicions. Jemmy doesn't believe it's true, but he says we must be careful."

"We can't stop. General Washington and Colonel Tallmadge are depending on us."

"Dearest, the war has moved south. Seth has escaped from the *Jersey*. And now that the river is no longer a frozen highway for attacking rebels, old Knyphausen and the rest are taking their ease. The officers occupy themselves plotting what fireworks they'll have for the king's birthday and deciding whether to serve pheasants' tongues or roasted plovers at the banquet."

When Rob finally let Kate go she served up the lamb ragout. Kate knew that once Rob made up his mind he did not change it. If he said he would not gather information anymore, he meant it. But she worried about what would happen if they stopped supplying General Washington with intelligence. And she wondered who Gustavus was and what mischief John André had been up to before he left for Charleston. Whatever it was, she reasoned, surely it had blown over in his absence.

Thirty-five

Wherein the last-ditch stalwarts mutiny; Lafayette rides to the rescue;
Benedict Arnold finally has something to sell

WHEN BENJAMIN FRANKLIN SIGNED THE DECLARATION OF independence he said, "We must all hang together or, most assuredly, we shall all hang separately." But this, Seth thought, was not what he had in mind.

The eleven men accused of desertion stood in a line in the long shadow that the afternoon sun threw outward from the gallows platform. They couldn't have asked for a prettier day to be strangled to death. Irises bloomed in the bogs. Birds trilled in the May warmth. The empty stomachs of the assembled army growled in unison like snare drums.

No one believed the execution order would be carried out, and a cheer echoed among the surrounding hills when Benjamin Tallmadge galloped up with a reprieve from General Washington. He read out ten names, and then cantered back to the rear of the formation. A few quick heartbeats passed before Seth realized that he hadn't heard James Coleman's name.

James had not deserted, but he had forged discharge papers for those who could pay for them. He had forged quite a lot of them, but he was no coward. He had served his country through thin and thinner.

He walked up the steps to the gallows platform and he surprised Seth by how nonchalant he looked up there, like an actor on a stage. He behaved as though after two years of being deprived and ignored he was pleased to

have everyone's attention. He tugged on the rope and informed the hangman it wasn't strong enough and the knot wasn't right. He adjusted the
noose, and waved away the black cloth hood. Before he put the rope
around his own neck he made a short speech.

He told the soldiers to obey their officers, and to love their country. He
lectured their commanders not to give their men cause to desert. The officers didn't look happy about the scolding, but what could they do about it?
They were already hanging him.

The executioner pulled the lever to drop the trapdoor. James had been
right. His weight broke the rope, and he landed in a heap on the ground underneath. The men cheered and then groaned as he walked back up the stairs
and waited until someone brought stouter hemp. Seth watched through a
fog of tears as the second rope held, but the new noose failed to throttle
him. James kicked wildly and clawed at the rope while his face swelled
up and turned purple. The hangman grabbed his boots and hung on them
to speed his demise, but long minutes passed before James's body went
limp.

The groans from the spectators turned to shouts. Seth didn't see who
threw the first rock, but more followed it. The hangman ran for cover in a
hail of them. He was lucky the ranks had no ammunition.

The soldiers dispersed to their camps, but the men from Connecticut
gathered on the parade ground. "We are going in search of food," their
leader shouted. "Who will come with us?" A regiment fell in with them
and then another.

Their captain waded in to make a prisoner of the troublemaker and
found himself facing the business end of a hundred bayonets. Anthony
Wayne rallied his men. They were just as hungry as the mutineers, but with
their empty weapons leveled, Seth and the other Pennsylvanians surrounded them. Wayne persuaded them to return to their huts, but they
kept their weapons close by all night. They muttered at their country, their
government, their officers, and finally at themselves for staying here and
starving for an ungrateful people who did not care what became of them.

As Seth sat at the evening fire he hummed an old ballad to himself. It
was one that Lizzie sang softly in her husky voice while she spun yarn.
Lizzie's singing was the only music Seth had ever heard in his father's
house, and she did it when neither Rachel nor Aaron Darby were around.

It was one of the many things he loved about her and for which he gave thanks to God on a daily basis.

> *There are twelve months in all the year,*
> *As any man will say,*
> *But the merriest month of all, I hear,*
> *Is the merry month of May.*
> *With a link a down and a day*

The song took thirty or more verses to tell the story of Robin Hood saving three men condemned to hang for poaching deer. The last one went,

> *They took the gallows from the slack*
> *They set it in the glen,*
> *They hang'd the proud sheriff on that,*
> *And releas'd their own three men.*
> *With a link a down and a day*

" 'And released their own three men,' " Seth sang softly. " 'With a link a down and a day.' "

A train of supply wagons arrived the next afternoon. A distribution of rations mollified the men somewhat, but Seth wondered if the salt pork and Indian corn had averted disaster or merely postponed it.

SETH STOOD AT ONE OF THE SENTRY POSITIONS SCATTERED in a chain north along the road from the encampment. He hoped that none of the officers came to inspect because Spitz had left his post to go check the snares he had set in the woods near an abandoned farm. When he returned Spitz hoisted aloft a skinned creature, lank and bloody. It looked like a hare, but it could have been a cat. Seth didn't ask.

"I found this." Spitz held out a leaflet. "Though it will not taste so good in the kettle."

The broadside showed men in British uniforms, but they weren't drilling or fighting. They were carving a huge roast of beef.

"You are neither clothed, fed nor paid," it read. "Your number is wasting away by sickness, famine, and nakedness . . . This then is the moment to fly from slavery and fraud."

The hair stirred on Seth's arms. Hundreds of these had appeared in the encampment this morning, like toadstools that had sprouted in the night. Who had scattered them? What traitor walked unrecognized among the patriots? Seth preferred to think that loyalists from the surrounding farms had left them.

"Do you think they will build that bridge?" Spitz stuffed the rabbit into his haversack.

"It's just rumor."

Still the rumor had sprung up the day after James Coleman died dancing on the gallows. Seth had a feeling that wasn't a coincidence. Someone must have told the British about Coleman's final performance. The British, according to the grapevine, were planning to build a bridge from New Jersey to Staten Island to make it easier for American soldiers to cross over to the other side, literally.

Seth heard shouting from the road ahead as a small procession approached. Leading it was twenty-two-year-old Marie Joseph Paul Yves Roch Gilbert du Motier, the Marquis de Lafayette, followed by his shadow, his black servant James, who was dressed almost as splendidly as his master. There was no mistaking the marquis. After almost a year in France he was still tall, gawky, and thin enough to support pole beans. He rode a black stallion and he wore a spanking new blue, white, and gold major-general's uniform. He nodded his powdered, sausage curls at the cheering men who lined the road and waved their boiled leather helmets.

Seth had never noticed before how shabby his headgear was. Our helmets, he thought, look like dogs run over by a quarry drag.

He wondered what the marquis thought of this gaunt army to which he had returned after more than a year of hobnobbing with royalty. Many of the men went barefoot. What was left of their uniforms had faded to gray. As parts of them wore out, their owners had replaced them with whatever articles of clothing they could find or patch together out of rags and blankets. They saluted Major General Lafayette with pikes, rusty muskets, spontoons, halberds, even hatchets. With a grin stretched wide under his long thin nose Lafayette saluted every one of them back.

Seth had never felt so proud. These soldiers were the best, the toughest, the most dedicated to the cause of liberty. And he was one of them.

General Washington rode his old white charger to meet Lafayette, and no father and son ever embraced with more joy. Maybe that wasn't surprising. A British bullet had killed Lafayette's father the year his son was born, and Washington had no male children. The two men had liked each other from their first meeting three years ago.

Besides, Lafayette's high spirits were contagious. He had campaigned tirelessly at home for the Americans' cause, and from his triumphant look he must have been successful. He and Washington rode off together so Lafayette could deliver his report in private.

Lafayette had persuaded Louis XVI to send a fleet of ships and six thousand troops, but Washington had expected three times that many. The British could field thirteen thousand troops in the north and twelve thousand in the south. Washington's own force stood at perhaps seven thousand ill-equipped men, and while his officers could estimate how many of those were able, they couldn't say for sure how many were willing.

Washington called his most trusted commanders to his headquarters to discuss what to do next. Anthony Wayne, Benjamin Tallmadge, and Alexander Hamilton were among those who attended. General Benedict Arnold had made the journey from Philadelphia to plead for an active command, and Washington invited him to join them too. Tallmadge pointed out that they were at a disadvantage now. Those spies who had been of service to them in New York, he said, had stopped reporting. He said he would press them to take up the cause again.

While the generals and colonels argued for this plan or the other, Lafayette kept quiet. He did not mention that King Louis and his foreign minister had left a bolt-hole for the commander of the French forces. Should the American army look like it was about to indulge in one of its famous retreats Count Rochambeau was to trundle his men back aboard the warships and sail for the West Indies.

Lafayette did not share his king's skepticism. He arrived with grand plans to recapture New York, move on to take all of Canada, and then head south to capture Charleston. Once he saw how few soldiers Washington had, though, and how many of them didn't even have shoes, he realized that invading Canada would have to wait.

For the next two months he rode from Philadelphia to Newport. Like an itinerant evangelist he filled lecture halls and gave rousing speeches. He cornered colonial governors and assemblymen and badgered and shamed them into contributing funds and supplies. The loaded wagons began to trundle in. When he returned, Washington gave him command of a regiment of twenty-four hundred men. Lafayette outfitted them at his own expense, and their gaudy new plumes and uniforms and brass were as easy to spot in the sprawling encampment as lupines and goldenrod blooming in a mud puddle.

Benedict Arnold, however, did nothing after that meeting except wait for word of General Clinton and Major André's return. He was back at the encampment around the middle of June when he heard that the two British officers were on a ship headed for New York.

Benedict limped to his tent and laced the canvas door shut behind him. He lifted the false bottom from his campaign trunk and took out the cardboard template underneath it. He thought a long time before he laid the template over a sheet of paper, picked up a quill, and wrote his report inside the hourglass-shaped opening cut in the cardboard. Not only did he have to blend the message into innocuous sentences on each side of the opening, but he had to substitute many of the words for other words and numbers that John André had sent him as a code.

It was a complicated process, and Arnold's hand shook with impatience. He had a lot to say. He told Clinton about the six French warships, several frigates and troop transports, and six thousand men headed for Newport, Rhode Island.

His most important news was that Washington had promised him a command. Washington had been apologetic about it. It wasn't an active unit. It was garrisoned only to keep the British from penetrating north along the Hudson River. In Washington's opinion it was a post beneath a man of Arnold's zeal and courage. But if Arnold consented, he could take charge of the Highlands, the line of fortifications on the cliffs overlooking the river. The citadel itself was called West Point.

Arnold couldn't wait to let Clinton know that for the right price he would surrender it and its garrison to the British. He and Peggy could live in comfort when the British took control of the country again. Most important of all, his lovely, golden-haired wife would be pleased. He tried not to think about how his lovely, golden-haired wife might be occupying herself in Philadelphia in his absence.

He addressed the letter to John Anderson, the name André used. When he finished he signed it "Gustavus." He folded it, sealed it, and slid it inside a slim book of poetry.

He had seen Nan Baker in camp. Her presence was such a fortuitous coincidence that it seemed the best possible omen. She would see that his letter reached André. He sent his aide, Ned Withers, to find her and tell her he wanted to purchase a jar of pomade from her.

Thirty-six

Wherein Rob and Kate get back into the game;
General Rush 'Em Boys drops anchor

NEW YORKERS LIVED TO REVEL. ROB OBSERVED THAT IF AN earthquake were to level the city, its inhabitants would hold a fair in the rubble to celebrate the event. King George turned forty-two on June 4, 1780, and Sir Harry and his officers put on quite a show. They set off fireworks at the battery at the southern end of Manhattan Island. They paraded with prancing horses and a military band up Broad Way. They attended a lavish feast and ball to which the common folk were not invited. Undaunted, the common folk were still concocting festivities of their own six weeks later.

Like magic, a raree-show appeared in the middle of July in front of Trinity Church. Throngs gathered to watch the jugglers, puppets, and contortionists, the conjurors and musicians. Sharps hid peas under walnut shells and challenged the gullible to find them. The owner of Toby the Sapient Pig loudly claimed he could read minds for tuppence. Women hawked eggs boiled in brine, sweet pastries, roasted oysters, and lamb pies with slices of pancreas and testicles for added savor.

Rob and Lizzie, with her baby riding in a sling on her hip, wandered off to see the two-headed calf, but the sound of chirping drew Kate to a wicker cage of sparrows. The tout reached in and grabbed one, knotted a string around its leg, and fastened the other end to a buttonhole in his latest mark's coat. The sparrow tried to flutter away, but fell back when he reached the end of his tethe.

"Mumble-sparrow here, good people. Threepence a try." While the tout tied the mark's wrists behind his back, he kept up a steady patter. "Gather 'round. Bite the head off the bird and win a shilling."

Kate watched, horrified, as he put the bird's wing in the man's mouth and he began trying to chew his way up to the head. The sparrow didn't hold still for it. To the crowd's delight he flapped his other wing in his tormenter's face and pecked at his lips until he drew blood. At last the bird bested him. The man went off wiping his mouth on his sleeve and another fool stepped up. Kate slid smoothly in front of him.

"You think to test your skill, little lady?"

"No. I should like to purchase your birds."

"They're not for sale."

"I'll give you two quid for the lot of them, and the cage too."

"Can't sell my livelihood, now can I?"

"Yes, you can. Two quid is all I have, but I'll add this." She took the gold ring from her pocket. It was one of the thirty that she and Almy had bought to present as gifts to those who attended her mother's funeral. Her mother would approve of using it for this.

She could see him running a mental finger down the plus and minus sides of his ledger. By the end of the day these birds would be dead anyway. Two quid was likely more than he would net, and he wouldn't have to stand here making himself hoarse all day. He could take the coins and slope off to soothe his throat at the nearest tavern.

He bit the ring to see if it was gold, then he waved a hand at the cage. Kate picked it up and hurried off before he changed his mind. She found Rob waiting while Lizzie and her baby sat for a portrait. With scissors the artist cut their silhouettes from black paper. Lizzie continued to face straight ahead, but she swiveled her eyes in Kate's direction.

"This is for Seth."

"It will surely please him." Kate didn't remind her that they had no idea where Seth was, or if he lived at all.

"Townsend! I've been looking everywhere for you." Austin Roe was as thin as ever, but he had to slide sideways to make his way through the crowd. Usually Austin was as unperturbable as Abraham Woodhull was high-strung, but today he looked agitated. "Mulligan said I might find you here." He doffed his hat and swept it into a limber-legged bow. "Miss Darby, what a pleasure to see you again."

Kate nodded. "And you, Austin. How fares our friend, Abraham?"

"He is ailing, but he sends his regards."

Neither Rob nor Kate asked what had caused Austin to leave his tavern in Setauket and come to New York in Abraham's stead. The reason was almost certainly something they shouldn't discuss in public. Kate felt a low-lying hollowness that gave the term "pit of her stomach" new significance.

She didn't want to hear what Austin had to say. She wanted to tell him to go back to Setauket and leave her and Rob in peace. These past two months had been the happiest she had ever known. God had given her the rarest of gifts, an ordinary life. She breathed a prayer of thanks each morning for it.

She missed her mother and she worried about Seth, but she loved waking up beside Rob each morning and keeping company with him at the shop. She enjoyed bantering with the customers without wondering who was a Tory and who a patriot. She went to the docks and the markets with a carefree heart and a clear conscience. She didn't have to look over her shoulder, except to watch for pickpockets.

She took care of her new nephew when Almy gave parties and Lizzie had extra work to do, which was often. He had become a favorite at the shop, and his smile was the best kind of sorcery. In the evenings Kate and Rob went to Black Sam Fraunces's tavern for supper. They attended lectures on the motion of the earth and how the moon's phases affected the tides. They saw a demonstration of artificial thunder and lightning that had the audience gasping.

They wandered among the book stalls. They read to each other in a quiet spot they had found by the water at the far end of the bowling green where swallows darted at dusk. It was close to General Clinton's former headquarters in the Kennedy mansion, and so no garbage was allowed to be dumped there. In nearby Canvas Town touch-me-nots, lamb's quarter, and pokeweed rioted in the ashes. Wild grape, poison ivy, and fragrant cascades of clematis draped the charred beams and chimneys.

Kate had expected something would happen to upset the apple cart, as

Cook often predicted. General Clinton returned to New York a few days ago, full of piss and vinegar after his victory at Charleston. Kate feared he would bring trouble with him. And now here it was, and bad enough to rattle Austin. With a trembling hand Kate opened the cage door and let the sparrows fly free. She kissed Lizzie on the cheek.

"Will you be alright?" Lizzie whispered.

"We are always in God's care."

AUSTIN ROE PACED, AND HE WAS NOT A PACER. HE HAD paced for two days. The garret was sweltering, which didn't help his state of mind.

The French fleet had been spotted off the coast days earlier and was due to arrive in Newport, Rhode Island, at any moment. General Washington needed to know if the British intended to attack them. If they did he didn't have men enough to stop them, but he had other options. From his summer headquarters in Bergen County, New Jersey, he wrote Benjamin Tallmadge. He asked him to revive the correspondence with the Culpers, both junior and senior.

"If the younger cannot be engaged again," he wrote Benjamin, "you will endeavor to prevail upon the older to give you the movements and positions of the enemy upon Long Island, and their numbers." He asked for a report on provisions, wood, and forage, as well as cattle being bought so he could gauge the strength of any intended campaign.

Tallmadge had ridden to Fairfield, Connecticut. He found Caleb Brewster in his favorite tavern and impressed on him the need for speed. Caleb had rowed the message across Long Island Sound and delivered it to Austin, since Abraham was too ill to make the trip from Setauket.

Austin had ridden hard. He didn't know it, but he had kept just ahead of the British informant on his way to tell Clinton about the fleet's arrival. In the two days since Austin's arrival Rob had contacted his informants and gathered the intelligence Washington needed. The best contact was Kate's friend, the stevedore.

Without telling Rob what she was up to, Kate had delivered a bolt of chintz to the Kennedy house. She took the opportunity to get lost in the back corridors and found a memorandum from Clinton to John André. In it he mentioned Huntington Harbor as the anchorage from which he would launch his attack.

Rob found the vial of invisible stain at the bottom of his trunk and now he wrote steadily. Austin paused in his orbit to stare at the words fading away behind Rob's pen.

"Did you say that the British are lading forage and wood?"

"Yes."

"And that they plan to embark six thousand troops on Royal Navy transports?"

"Yes."

"Austin . . ." Kate patted the bench next to her. "Bring thy aft end to an anchor."

Kate was much happier than Austin. The crisis that concerned General Washington was brewing in Newport, a hundred and fifty miles away. She and Rob could easily obtain the information he needed from the people they already knew. Best of all Benjamin Tallmadge had sent word that Seth was alive and well.

Austin was soon up and pacing again. "They will search me, Rob."

"I know."

"I saw the guards at the ferry confiscate a ream of paper that a merchant carried. They were probably looking for the kind of invisible ink that can be seen with the application of heat. How shall we disguise this report?"

Kate reached up and caught Austin's sleeve as he ankled past. "Dear friend, it is difficult enough for him to concentrate when he can't see what he is writing. You are impeding the work." She pulled him back down onto the bench and tried to distract him.

"Abraham told us he was disheartened when he heard that Washington thought he lacked heart and nerve for the work."

"Disheartened? I should say! He was humiliated. I saw the letter Abraham wrote to the commander. He apologized for costing so much trouble and expense for little or no purpose."

"But that's not true. He and Rob provided useful information every week for two years."

"You know Abraham. He's as nervous as a cat locked in a room with a large and enterprising dog."

"I should think he would feel vindicated now that the commander has come to him for help."

"I reckon he does."

"It's done." Rob turned the paper over and began writing on the other side with regular ink. He used good stock, and the ink didn't bleed through.

Austin and Kate stood next to him to watch. His neat hand was plainly visible now.

New York, July 20, 1780

Sir,

I rec'd your letter by Mr. Roe, and note the contents. The articles you want cannot be procured, but as soon as they can be, I will send them to you. I am your humble servant,

Samuel Culper

Rob addressed the letter to Colonel Benjamin Floyd of Brookhaven, Long Island.

"Are you mad?" Austin barely remembered to keep his voice low. "Floyd is a Tory all the way down to his toenails."

"Maybe he is and maybe he isn't, but it doesn't matter."

Kate understood what Rob was up to. "Floyd will never see this, Austin."

The light dawned in Austin's spaniel eyes. "What a blockhead I am." He hit his forehead with the flat of his hand. "The sentries won't suspect a correspondence with a loyal subject of the king. Damned clever of you, Townsend."

Kate took the rolled portrait of Lizzie and her child from her trunk. Lizzie had tied a yellow ribbon around it and included a letter inside.

"Austin, would thee do me the favor of seeing that Benjamin Tallmadge receives this? He will know where to deliver it."

IN HIS CRAMPED QUARTERS ABOARD THE *DUC DE BOURGOGNE* anchored in Newport's harbor General Rochambeau took considerable time putting on his most resplendent bib and tucker. He had come, after all, to save an entire nation from the tyranny of his old nemeses, the British. It would not do to dress as though for a stroll to the market for bread and cheese.

He spit on his handkerchief, polished a spot of tarnish on his brass gorget, and hung the big crescent on his beribboned chest. He blew on the snowy egret plume to fluff it before he set the helmet squarely on his powdered curls. Sweat had already begun to collect under those curls in the moist July heat.

I have seen fifty-five summers, he thought. I am too old for this.

As he crossed the deck to the rope ladder thrown over the side he returned the salutes of the miserable remnant of his command. Once seated in the bow of the whaleboat he glanced up. Heads lined the taffrail. They weren't looking at him but staring toward land.

Rochambeau didn't blame them. Bad weather had extended the voyage, and he had had to put everyone on half rations of wormy beef and moldy hardtack. The salted meat created a terrible thirst, but the barrels of drinking water in the hold contained mostly scum. Worst of all, the casks of red wine had been drained dry. Without wine his men grew restive.

Rochambeau crossed himself and muttered a quick prayer asking God not to smite any more of his people. He had started with less than five thousand soldiers instead of the eight thousand he had been promised. And now almost two thousand were sick as dogs with scurvy and dysentery. On the long, turbulent voyage he had watched too many corpses lowered over the side to the sharks that had trailed the boat most of the way.

Mon dieu, he thought. We shall all be glad to disembark this floating pesthole.

On the short trip to shore in the gathering dusk he kept a nervous eye out for British sails. If the British attacked, his troops were too few and too weak to put up a defense.

He rehearsed the few words of English he had prepared. He had brought an interpreter for the rest of his address to George Washington and his cadre of officers, the assembled dignitaries, and townspeople. It would be helpful, he thought, if le marquis de Lafayette had managed to teach General Washington some French. He wondered if there would be a band, and just how execrable their attempts at music would be. And he braced for the interminable speeches of welcome and gratitude.

The sailors dragged the boat onto the beach, and Rochambeau and his six highest-ranking officers disembarked. He saw no band. No assembled dignitaries. No townspeople. And certainly no George Washington. The welcoming committee consisted of a ladder-ribbed hound wolfing down a dead seagull. With the gull in his mouth and his tail between his legs he scuttled off at the men's approach.

To the barking of dogs Rochambeau and his retinue clanked along Newport's deserted main street. The tread of their boots echoed between the walls on either side. All the houses and shops were shuttered. All the doors were closed.

Rochambeau's first thought stirred the hair on the back of his neck. What if old animosities lingered from when the Americans had fought alongside the British against the French twenty years ago? What if Rochambeau's allies intended to mow down their rescuers from the loopholes in the shutters? And why would townhouses have loopholes in their shutters anyway? What sort of barbaric country was this?

When no one opened fire on him Rochambeau wondered if some plague had killed the inhabitants. He was relieved to see a figure approaching in the gathering darkness. The man was staggering. Maybe he was ill too.

Rochambeau held a handkerchief soaked in clove-water to his nose in case the fellow was afflicted with whatever had laid waste to the town. He motioned for his interpreter to come forward.

The young man launched into a confused exchange with their first American acquaintance, and Rochambeau realized that the boy had greatly exaggerated his ability to speak English. At least he discovered that the local was merely drunk and not carrying pestilence about in his pockets.

He also found out that no one had told the townspeople of the fleet's arrival. They thought the French had come to invade them. With graphic gestures he explained that they had locked up their daughters to save them from the lustful horde of Frenchmen who, everyone knew, were as lecherous as goats.

Rochambeau made a note to tell the good people of Newport that he would hang any man of his who touched one of their daughters. From experience he knew that would have two beneficial effects. It would dispel the worries of the townsfolk, and it would inspire the women to pursue his men with a single-minded fervor. When it came to aphrodisiacs none proved so powerful as impediments.

The man motioned for them to follow him. The procession passed through town to a wretched-looking building on the outskirts. A pungent heap of oyster shells and clamshells guarded the entry. Someone had painted "The Lusty Oyster" and a leering bivalve on a shingle over the door. The door itself was tied on with rope instead of hinges, but once inside Rochambeau found welcome enough.

A dozen or more topers sat on stools in the smoke-thick room lit by a few guttering oil lamps. Decades of soot had blackened the low beams of the ceiling, and the aroma of tobacco permeated the wood. The serving wench put a tankard of beer in the American's hand as soon as he walked through the door.

"What did you say your name was?" Rochambeau's new friend asked.

"Jean Baptiste Donatien de Vimeur, comte de Rochambeau."

"Rush 'Em Boys?"

"*Non.*" The savior of America enunciated carefully. "Row-sham-bow."

The American raised his tankard for attention. "Lads, meet Mr. Rush 'Em Boys." He waved the tankard and christened Rochambeau's new name by spilling beer down the front of the count's uniform. "Him and his chums here are Frogs."

That got a laugh loud enough to shake soot loose from the beams. In the seventeen years since the last war, stories of hungry French soldiers wading into ponds and dining on the hapless amphibians had reached the status of legend. A favorite subject of speculation in the taverns was whether or not the Frenchmen turned their long, Gallic noses up at snails and salamanders.

The older men passed the rest of the evening regaling their visitors with tales of how many Frenchmen they had killed in that last war. Fortunately Rochambeau understood none of it and his interpreter could make almost nothing of the Yankee dialect. Rochambeau listened and nodded and smiled in the way that charmed everyone in his own country. It worked here too.

Thirty-seven

Wherein Seth revisits Fothergill's Folly; George Washington
tells another lie; Gustavus's cauldron comes to a simmer;
Peggy Arnold puts on a performance; Lizzie says good-bye

AT NIGHTFALL SETH CLIMBED DOWN FROM THE CORN HEAPED in the cart and thanked the farmer for the ride. As he ghosted through the hamlet of Flatbush he did not expect a welcome, nor did he want one. He especially did not want the sort he had received the last time he had passed this way, a patriot mob intent on trying him with Charles Lynch's law.

He walked to the farm called Fothergill's Folly. It looked the same as when he had stayed here two years ago. He knocked on the door. Usual Fothergill opened it and stared at him with no recognition in his eyes.

Seth hadn't seen a mirror in a long time, much less one that would show more than his chin whiskers. He forgot how thin he was. The white hair had changed his appearance too and so had the horrors he had endured. Even if he could have seen himself, he would not have realized how extraordinarily handsome and exotic all that hardship had made him.

Seth's striking looks did not affect Fothergill. He eyed him suspiciously.

"I bring a message from a mutual friend." Seth held up page twenty-three ripped from a book.

Fothergill left and returned with a copy of *Plutarch's Lives*. He opened it to where page twenty-three should have been. Seth laid his there. The two torn edges matched. Fothergill nodded and Seth followed him inside.

From the false bottom of his knapsack Seth took a pouch containing papers. He didn't waste time with pleasantries. The faster he could get away from here the better, and it wasn't the British or the Tories he feared. He wanted to ask Usual where his surly nephew lurked, but thought that unwise.

"Here are orders for an attack on New York."

"Are these from the commander in chief?"

"In his own hand."

"Did he give them to you himself?"

Seth could tell that the awe in Usual Fothergill's eyes was an interloper. He would have bet that nothing short of a calling card from God would impress the man, unless it was a chance to shake George Washington's hand.

"No. I received them from his aide. Washington's instructions are for you to deliver them to the nearest British outpost. Tell them you found them by the side of the road where a careless courier dropped them."

It seemed a weak ploy, but it had worked before.

"How many troops does he say he's got this time?"

"Twelve thousand."

Usual chuckled but the laugh sounded rusty. It hadn't gotten much use in the past five decades. "Going to fool the bloodybacks again, is he?"

"With your help."

"I assume this has something to do with the fleet of Frogs just arrived up there at Newport."

News, Seth thought, travels quickly in this backwater.

"Yes. He intends to draw Clinton back to New York so he won't attack the French."

Usual tore out another page of *Plutarch's Lives* for Seth to take to General Washington as a token for the next messenger. He smoothed page twenty-three and replaced it reverently in the book. Then he insisted that Seth sample his latest batch of wine. Seth had the sense this time to merely sip Usual's elderberry witchery.

Seth and Usual discussed politics and Goodwife Fothergill darned stockings by the fire's light, but neither of their comely daughters appeared. Maybe they had married bumpkins from neighboring farms, but Seth wouldn't have been surprised if Chastity Fothergill had gone to New York to shake her heels. Wherever the two of them were, Seth wished them happiness. He was not a vain person, but he had a feeling Chastity would have recognized him at the door tonight.

" 'TIS HOT AS GUINEA AT NOONDAY, IS IT NOT?" THE PROSPECT of silver clinking in his pocket made Tunis Birdwhistle jovial, in a funereal sort of way.

John André didn't bother answering. He left behind the heat of the last day of July and followed Birdwhistle into a tunnel near the Hudson River. Birdwhistle unlocked an iron grate, and they descended the steep stone steps. The temperature plummeted. Water dripped from cracks in the brick walls. The vault at the bottom of the stairs was so cold John shivered.

"This is the last of it, Your Excellency." Birdwhistle held his torch up to illuminate the heap of sawdust and straw in the far corner. "They cut it from the Hudson in February, well to the north of the city. It's pure as new moonlight, it is."

"For what you're charging, it had better be." John pulled back the straw and brushed away the sawdust. When he touched the ice underneath, his fingers stuck to it. "And the saltpeter?"

John could have obtained that from the army's own supplies, but Birdwhistle was faster and raised no bothersome questions about using government stores for personal purposes. John knew Birdwhistle had no doubt acquired the saltpeter from some enterprising artillery sergeant anyway.

"I can deliver it this afternoon along with the ice."

Birdwhistle held the torch high to light the way back up the stone steps. "If you don't mind my asking, Your Excellency, what do you need ice and saltpeter for?"

John did mind his asking, but a man like Birdwhistle was essential when dirty work needed to be done. If he hadn't offered his services when Clinton arrived in New York, André would have had to recruit him.

"Iced cream."

"Iced cream?"

"Yes. The general is fond of it."

"Adding gunpowder to cream. What will they think of next?"

"The saltpeter mixed with ice makes the cream freeze faster."

"Can't say as I've ever tasted iced cream."

I'm sure you haven't, John thought.

Making it was a costly and laborious process, although John had no idea what the process was. He couldn't even have found the kitchen in the house where he quartered, much less say what went on there. He only saw the fruit-and-liqueur-flavored confection when it arrived at the table, freshly turned out from a fluted mold and adorned with mint sprigs. His mouth watered at the thought of it.

When he get back to headquarters John went to Clinton's office on the second floor. Sitting on the general's desk was the toy the French called *le incroyable.* John was sure Sir Harry hadn't left it there. He wasn't the sort to play with anything that he couldn't bed or bet on.

André took the yoyo outside and gave it to the first urchin who passed by. The girl had never seen one, so John fastened the string's loop around her finger. Standing behind her and holding her hand in his, he showed her how to reel it out and coax it back. She made a hasty curtsy and headed on the run for Canvas Town to show her friends.

John didn't know who had left the yoyo on the desk, but he understood the message. He knew something Sir Harry didn't. He knew that the general's officers had taken to calling him Lord Yoyo. Sailors had brought the toy from the Philippines where it had been popular for two hundred years. Yoyo was the Tagalog word for "come back," and as far as Clinton's officers were concerned, that described him.

His first act when he returned to New York a month ago was to cancel the offensive that General Knyphausen had already launched against New Jersey. That was no mystery to anyone who knew Clinton. He could not tolerate someone else getting credit for anything.

Then he loaded his army and all its equipment onto transports and sailed up the Hudson. Loyalists assumed he intended to occupy the length of the river, thus dividing the colonies so he could strike a death blow. However, he got fourteen miles upriver and stopped long enough to burn and pillage the local farmers. He returned with their cattle and chickens milling around on the ships and never engaged the enemy. Jests spread about the trouble and expense Clinton incurred to put meat on his table.

New Yorkers had always despised him. That foray made him a laughing-stock. The ridicule ran over onto his officers like the dye from a new red shirt in a washtub of white linens.

In his latest maneuver Clinton had rushed six thousand troops onto transports again. This time he sailed in the opposite direction, determined to conquer Rochambeau and his men at Newport. He got as far as Huntington Harbor. Two days later he ordered the ships to turn around when he received word of Washington's plan for an offensive on New York.

The attack didn't come. George Washington, the officers grumbled, had diddled them again. And Rochambeau, who had won the hearts of the people of Newport by now, had his men digging fortifications with the butts of their Charleville muskets. Clinton had lost the chance to catch them with their proverbial pantaloons down.

Clinton didn't care. Indifferent to criticism and ridicule and the disapproval of his officers, he went back to his hectic schedule of brandy, bawds, cockfights, horse races, and faro. André was the only one who knew why the general had no interest in leaving the comforts of his mistress's arms to seek out the enemy. John unlocked the top drawer of Clinton's desk and took out the letter that a trusted courier had delivered from Philadelphia. It was addressed to John Anderson, the name André had used for this correspondence for a year.

He found Clinton playing euchre with three lieutenants. Clinton liked to gamble with junior officers because they were less likely to try to beat him. André figured by interrupting the game he was postponing the day these men would have to sell their commissions to repay their debts to their commander.

André gave a conspiratorial lift of the eyebrow. The general pushed back his chair and pocketed his chits. He and John went outside to the grassy plot along the water where they could talk freely.

John gave Clinton the letter, but it was in code that only he could read. Clinton handed it back.

"What does our old friend, Gustavus, have to say?"

"He accepts your offer of twenty thousand pounds."

"He damned well should. That's almost four guineas for each man he surrenders to us."

"He agrees to the advance of five hundred pounds instead of the one thousand pounds he demanded."

"What about his request for indemnification? Why should we guarantee him ten thousand pounds if he fails to deliver?"

"He says he will waive that."

"Half a loaf is better than none, eh?" Clinton threw a rock at a gull on a wharf post. "If he requests a meeting send a trusted agent in your stead. Don't get any more involved with him than you already are. Traitors are like wives who diddle their husbands. What's to keep them from cheating on their lovers too?"

"He says he'll deal with no one but me. The prize is worth the risk."

And given what this war was costing the crown, André thought, twenty thousand pounds was a bargain. He wondered how long pretty Mrs. Gustavus would take to run through that amount and leave lint in the bottom of her husband's wallet. Still, once this wretched little misunderstanding was over, John could enjoy Peggy's company again. Perhaps she and he could take up what she coyly called her flute lessons where they had left off.

"All in all, this is a grand country." Clinton interrupted his thoughts. "When we take it back we shall divide it among us."

André nodded, but he thought about something Seth Darby had said when he had visited him in the Sugar House. André had told no one about the interview, not even Kate. He thought it would have distressed her to know that her brother was so obdurately disloyal to the king he had turned down a chance to get out of prison. André had promised Seth freedom in exchange for joining the British army. He had even offered to buy Seth a commission as an ensign.

He had pointed out to the boy that they were all countrymen, after all, and that when this rebellion was put down, those loyal to the crown would receive favors and land. André remembered Seth's answer. "The only land in America that a British officer shall ever hold will measure six feet long by two feet wide."

PEGGY SHIPPEN ARNOLD SCREAMED. SHE HURLED THE GOOD china at the wall. A disinterested observer would have admired her stamina. Her fits were taxing, and this was her second of the evening. She had thrown one earlier while dining at the Morris's house. A friend arrived there with congratulations and the news that General Washington had assigned her husband command of the light cavalry.

Peggy's performance then had been less tempestuous, but more dramatic.

She had collapsed on the floor, sobbing that such a strenuous command would open his old war wound and reinfect it. It would kill him, she wailed. Her friends tried to reassure her that the post was more fitting for Benedict Arnold's courage and abilities than West Point, but she would not be consoled. Now, at home, she had more to shriek on the subject.

"He promised West Point to us." She stamped her feet, threw more crockery, and screamed again. She kept screaming.

Her husband tried to calm her, but he was as ineffectual as always. Arnold's fearlessness had made him a hero at the battles of Quebec, Valcour Island, and Saratoga. He had led his shivering, desperate troops into a Canadian winter through terrain, weather, and privation that would have turned back a lesser man. He had defied authority and placed his soldiers in the forefront of fighting. He could lead a charge into a hail of enemy fire without flinching, but his beautiful twenty-year-old wife's "spells," as he called them, reduced him to stammering helplessness.

"My dearest dumpling, General Washington thinks command of cavalry has more honor than an out-of-the-way garrison like West Point."

"I don't care a damn what he thinks!" By now Peggy's face had turned as red as a boil, and she panted like a spaniel in labor. She began pulling the sheets and bolsters off the bed and ripping them with her teeth. A flurry of goose down floated around her.

Benedict had never seen her this frantic. He feared she would suffer an attack of apoplexy and die. As much distress as she caused him, he could not bear the thought of living without her. Whenever he entered a room with her dainty hand on his arm he felt himself the envy of everyone.

"Do not fret so. I will remind him that my wound was acquired in the service of my country and that it prevents me riding with the cavalry."

Peggy calmed a bit. "Do you think that will dissuade him?"

"Of course. Washington took my part when those damned ingrates passed me over for promotion and then subjected me to that mockery of a court-martial."

"He did promise us West Point."

Arnold smoothed her glossy golden hair. "Yes, and you shall have it." He went to the door and shouted. "Withers!"

Ned Withers hustled down the hall. "Yes, sir." He had exchanged his macaroni clothes for a lieutenant's uniform.

"Some fresh air would benefit Mrs. Arnold. Accompany her on a walk."

Arnold had another reason for wanting the command of West Point. It would take his wife far from the gay social life of Philadelphia and the attentions of a certain dashing scion of the powerful Livingston family.

ROB FOUND JOHN ANDRÉ IN A FAR CORNER OF THE MER-chants' Coffee House. He sat with his chair balanced on its hind legs and his anthracite-bright boots resting on the corner of the table. He was playing his flute softly. As Rob got closer he recognized the song. "Three merry boys, three merry boys, three merry boys are we, as ever did sing in a hempen string, under the gallows tree."

When John saw Rob he swung his boots off the table, stood up, and did a few jig steps to his own music.

"You're full of vim and vinegar today." Rob sat down and John resumed his seat across the table.

Rob reckoned that the devilish twinkle in John André's eyes these days meant he was either in love, or plotting something dire. Rob would have bet on the latter. André may have been the best-looking officer in the British army, but he remained remarkably unattached. Or rather he was attached to a different woman every time Rob saw him. And Rob saw as much of him as he could.

He hoped that André would mention Gustavus in conversation, and give some hint as to who the man was and what he did. Besides that, Rob liked to spend time with John. He was more entertaining than even Jemmy Rivington and Hercules Mulligan.

"Did you hear what John Wilkes said to Lord Sandwhich?" John asked.

"Wilkes. Is he the fellow they keep throwing out of Parliament and into jail for criticizing the king?"

"That's the one."

John fluted a few bars of "Rule, Britannia" then went on with the story. "'Wilkes,' said Lord Sandwich, 'you will die either on the gallows or of the pox.' 'That,' replied Wilkes, 'must depend on whether I embrace your lordship's principles or your mistress.'"

Rob chuckled. "How goes your poem?"

"The one about Anthony Wayne's expedition? I have six stanzas completed, but I think I shall end with twenty or more. Rivington will have to print it in installments in the *Gazette*. I'm calling it 'Cow Catcher.'"

With two thousand men General Wayne had tried to reduce the British blockhouse at nearby Paulus Hook, but his light artillery did not have the heft to breach the walls. Wayne's dragoons drove off the loyalists' cattle instead. André was composing an epic satire about it.

Five refugees 'tis true were found
Stiff on the blockhouse floor;
But then, 'tis thought, the shot went round,
And in at the back door.

With a wink, André recited the last verse of his poem.

And now I've closed my epic strain,
I tremble as I show it,
Lest this same warrior-drover Wayne,
Should ever catch the poet.

"It seems this war will die of consumption," said Rob. "Consuming the enemy's cattle."

John laughed and answered a bit too quickly. "Nay, my friend. The rebellion will end suddenly, in a whimper."

A waif arrived with a message requesting Rob's presence at the Buchanan house. Before Rob could tip him sixpence André flipped a shilling into the air.

Rob said his farewells and found the Buchanan household saying theirs. Even Cook was crying, and Thomas Buchanan hovered in the background. He had taken more than a liking to Lizzie's son, Isaac, and he could often be found carrying the baby around the house on his shoulders. In the privacy of her kitchen Cook allowed as how the child would make a philanthropist of the old ogre yet.

Lizzie had put a few belongings into Kate's pack basket and rigged a sling to carry Isaac on her chest. She had received the first letter from Seth since he escaped from the *Jersey*. She bounced Isaac on her hip and waved it at Rob.

"His regiment has been assigned to West Point. He says he is one of General Arnold's Life Guard. And he has proper quarters near the general's house, and regular rations. He says we can be together."

"Lizzie is determined to go to West Point." Kate was distraught. Losing her dearest friend was bad enough, but to have her beloved nephew go too was almost more than she could bear.

"West Point is seventy miles away," said Rob.

"I have put aside my wages, and Mrs. Buchanan has kindly given me money for expenses. Mr. Buchanan has arranged passage with a fisherman as far as Peekskill. And Seth says the American army has set up sentry posts all along the river. I can travel from one to another."

"Even so, bands of brigands roam that region," said Almy.

"If need be I shall grime my face and knot my hair in elf's tresses. Dirty as an ash cat, I shall play the madwoman." She tilted her head and crossed her eyes. "We shall all be together again when this is over." Lizzie kissed Kate on the cheek. "In the meantime God will care for us. You always say so yourself."

Thirty-eight

*Wherein Seth dodges Peggy's attentions; Benjamin Tallmadge thwarts
Benedict Arnold; Kate goes out on a roof*

EVERY MAN WHOM SETH KNEW, AND MOST OF THOSE HE
didn't, would envy him today. Peggy Shippen Arnold had singled him out
to escort her and her maid on their daily outing. She looked particularly
ravishing sitting sidesaddle in her riding costume, a long deep-blue velvet
skirt and close-fitting jacket that showed off a waist Seth could have encir-
cled with his hands. She had partly unbuttoned the coat to show the ruffles
of her starched white linen shirt. She left the shirt open far enough down to
give a glimpse of the alluring abyss between her breasts. She had pinned a
rosette of blue grosgrain ribbon to the front of her white beaver hat.

The only one who didn't envy Seth was Ned Withers. General Arnold
usually assigned Ned to Peg-tending duty, and he knew better than anyone
except Arnold himself what it entailed. He had warned Seth to be careful.

Peggy, he said, was charming only so long as nothing upset her. She had
a nervous disability, he said. And when it took possession of her, she would
blurt out whatever was on her mind.

"I knew her in Philadelphia too," Seth had reminded him.

Ned had rolled his eyes. "She's worsened since then."

So Seth was ready for anything, but the day passed pleasantly enough.
The three of them rode among towering spruce and hemlocks, and along

spectacular cliffs. Peggy led him to an outcrop near a waterfall with a view
of a mist-shrouded gorge lush with greenery. Even in mid-August the air
was crisp in the Highlands.

The maid laid out a damask cloth on the grassy height, and they shared
a picnic of cold venison cutlets, stuffed pigeons, bread, cheese, strawberries
and cream, and wine in crystal goblets. Seth had eaten roasted pigeons before in the army, but only when he could snare them himself.

Peggy talked about the idyllic days of the British occupation in Philadelphia as though Seth had shared the good times with her. She reminisced
about the parties, balls, and concerts. It didn't seem to occur to her that Seth
had not been invited to any of them, or that even if he had been, his Quaker
beliefs would have kept him from going.

The more wine she consumed the more flirtatious she became, but Seth
didn't take it personally. He realized that pretty Peggy was bored and she
was lonely. She was, as Cook would say, a walleye-out-of-water here in the
hinterlands. She missed presiding over a drawing room brimming with
belles and sallow aristocratic lieutenants. She longed to ride in a carriage
again. And no matter where she was she craved the attention of every man
who crossed her path.

After a while Peggy's chatter blended with the noise of the waterfall.
Seth pasted a dutiful smile on his face like a handbill on a wall, but his
thoughts strayed to Lizzie. He was better off now than he had been since
he joined the army, but in a way he understood how Peggy felt. He was out
of place here as a member of General Arnold's Life Guard. Standing sentry duty and running errands was not his idea of a soldier's life.

Each day he waited for a letter from Lizzie. Each day he imagined
Abraham Woodhull carrying it from New York to Setauket, and Caleb
Brewster ferrying it across Long Island Sound. He imagined Brewster
passing the letter to the Second Dragoons who would ride in relays to deliver it to Major Tallmadge. Tallmadge would see that it arrived—muddy,
tattered, perhaps with a hoof mark or two on it—at Seth's tent.

Seth knew he should thank God for his good fortune to be sheltered and
fed, but every night he went to sleep with an aching heart. Maybe Spitz was
right. Maybe the human condition consisted of higher and higher levels of
ingratitude.

Peggy tapped the tip of Seth's nose with her fan to get his attention. She snapped the fan open with a flick of her wrist and peered over it at him. "Ned Withers says you have a sweetheart, Seth Darby, and you a mere boy for all that white hair."

Seth was determined not to discuss his personal affairs with the commandant's wife, even if he had known her for most of his life. Besides, he knew what her reaction would be if she discovered he had fathered a child on a serving girl, and a negro at that.

"I'm only two years younger than you, Mrs. Arnold."

"La, call me Peggy. We are such old friends. And speaking of old friends, tell me of your sweet sister, Kate. We were the closest of chums in Philadelphia, you know."

That was news to Seth, and he reckoned it would be news to Kate too.

"How does your sister amuse herself in New York?"

"I don't know. There is no post between here and there. I have received no letter from her in a long time."

"I find it hard to believe that you haven't found a way to write to your family and your sweetheart. You're such a resourceful boy."

"I'm not so resourceful as that."

"And your father? Is he still in Jamaica, that preferred destination of bankrupts? I hear Jamaica is sickly as a pest house and hot as hell."

"I don't know where my father is."

"Oh la, I should hope he's still in the Indies."

"What do you mean?"

"Smuggling goods to the British—I'm sure that put him in line for a ride on the Liberty Boys' rail."

"He never smuggled goods to the British."

"That's not what my father says. Aaron Darby would load his ships with timber and pitch and set sail from the Philadelphia docks. He would arrange for them to be captured by British cruisers lying in wait in Delaware Bay. They loaded the cargo onto their own boats and sailed to New York. Your father's associate, Thomas Buchanan, sold the things there and saw that the money made its way back to your father's till, after he took his percentage, of course. Even after Friend Darby got to New York there were those who would do him harm because of it."

"That's not true." Seth fought to control the temper that he and Kate had both inherited along with their red hair.

"It is true, but who can blame him? In war people do what they must."
Peggy's laugh was like a dessert fork lightly tapping a crystal goblet. She
had practiced it until she achieved that effect. "But enough about war. I
prefer to emulate the ladies who are too wise to wrinkle their foreheads
with politics."

Seth's own forehead began to ache and throb. He was relieved when the
sun sank behind the trees and the air turned chill. At last he could return
Peggy to her infant daughter who spent far more time with her wet nurse
than her mother. Seth knew what these outings really were, a method of
separating Peggy from the daily activity of General Arnold's command.
She had a way of getting into the middle of things and distracting everyone.

They returned to the estate known as Robinson's Farm on the east side
of the Hudson, across from West Point and a couple miles downriver. Bev-
erly Robinson was an old friend of George Washington. He was also a
Tory, but so gracious and amiable that he got on well with his lodgers, the
Arnolds. The hundred picked men of Arnold's guards lived in tents and
barracks around the house.

Ned Withers met them at the stable. "Sergeant Darby, someone is waiting for you at your tent."

"Who?"

"A visitor. Two visitors, actually." Ned took the reins of Seth's horse.
"I'll see to your mount."

Seth walked to the tent he shared with Spitz. He pushed back the flap
and froze with his mouth open. Lizzie and the baby lay asleep on his cot.
The hems of Lizzie's skirts were heavy with mud and the soles of her shoes
had worn through. Her face in sleep looked like an ebony angel's.

Seth sat on his heels next to them. He held his son's tiny hand in his and
studied him. The child's perfection took Seth's breath away.

He lay down behind Lizzie and pulled a blanket up. He cupped his
body along the length of her back and put his arm around her and the
baby. He fell asleep with his cheek resting in her hair, her fragrance filling
his lungs and her warmth penetrating his bones.

Tomorrow he would kiss her 'til the cows came home. Then he would
take her and their son to meet General Wayne.

————

THE SCENE IN THE ARNOLDS' BOUDOIR THAT NIGHT WAS NOT so serene. While Peggy was picnicking with Seth, Benedict Arnold had received a letter from Benjamin Tallmadge. He limped from one end of the room to the other, his big red shoe thumping rhythmically with each step.

"He would not give me the names."

"But you told him you needed them?"

"I wrote that the safety of this garrison depends on good intelligence of the designs of the enemy. I said I must request to be informed who his agents are in New York, as I wish to employ them for the same purpose."

"Are you sure Tallmadge knows who the spies in New York are?"

Arnold stamped his foot the way his wife did when she was peeved. "Of course he knows. He mentioned them when we all gathered to hear Lafayette's report on his return from France last May. Now he says he gave his people a solemn pledge not to reveal their identities. He says not even General Washington knows who they are."

"And after you offered his dragoons all those horses. The ungrateful wretch."

"I have already asked Lafayette and another general officer for the information. I dare not pursue the matter further."

"I've heard rumors that Seth Darby has gathered intelligence in the city in the past. Perhaps his sister provides it to him. She's a deep one, she is, and she's well placed in a loyalist household."

"You did not suggest your suspicions to her brother . . ."

"I'm not such a fool as that."

But curiosity was working its wiles on Peggy. She decided to write Kate a letter and send it by way of her old friend, the Philadelphia crockery merchant. He could deliver it on his next business trip to New York. Whether Kate was spying or not, Peggy wondered what she was doing. She envied Kate's proximity to the society that swirled around the British command, and she wondered if she was spending time with John André.

Peggy also wondered if she could persuade Kate to put in a word for her with her handsome, aloof younger brother. After all, time was heavy on Peggy's hands, and she could use some diversion. Seth Darby looked like he could be quite diverting if he put his mind to it.

THE GERMAN GUARDS AT CLINTON'S HEADQUARTERS IN THE
Kennedy mansion all knew Kate by now. She helped them with English
whenever she delivered goods there. Much of what they wanted to know
led her to think they were very lonely. Today she taught them to say, "You
are very beautiful. May I call on you sometime?"

She left them practicing, and smiled her way through the delivery entrance. She had timed her arrival an hour before a feast in the banquet hall.
She knew from watching Cook work herself and Lizzie into a frenzy on
similar occasions that no one would pay much attention to her. Also André
and Clinton would likely be dressing for the affair.

Kate gave the package containing dance slippers to the downstairs maid,
but instead of leaving she slipped into the back hall and up the servants' stairs
to the second floor. With her cloak wrapped around her she ghosted down
the dim hallway to the room that John André used as an office. She could feel
her heart beating as she shuffled through the papers on top of the desk. She
replaced them as she had found them and looked through the drawers but
uncovered nothing useful.

She crouched in front of the locked drawer. Alert for the sound of anyone approaching she took a pin from her hair. She closed her eyes, and using the tips of her fingers to orient herself, she probed the lock with it. Seth
had taught her to do this when they were children and wanted to taste the
sweets that Cook had locked in the pie safe. Kate had spent a good deal of
her childhood wracked with guilt for that thievery. She never thought that
the skill would prove useful later.

She opened the drawer and found André's codebook and a letter. In the
dimming light she decyphered the letter, dated September fifteenth. It was
from Gustavus and addressed to John Anderson, merchant. It instructed
Anderson to come to Dobbs Ferry around midnight, September twentieth.
Gustavus said he would provide Anderson with a reliable escort to take
him to a safe place where they could meet. Gustavus added that Anderson
should wear a disguise.

Kate felt her blood chill. She still didn't know for sure who Gustavus
was, but she knew now that John Anderson was John André. Dobbs Ferry
was at West Point. It sounded very much as though Gustavus meant to betray the citadel.

With shaking hands she replaced the papers and closed the drawer. She realized that she had learned to open a drawer's lock, but she did not know how to lock it again. She heard the distant mumble of men's voices in the hall. She opened the window and looked out.

Old virginia creeper vines enlaced with the English ivy around the window. People had gathered on the bowling green below to enjoy the evening breeze off the water and the cooler September air. Kate feared some of them would notice her and report her, but she had no choice.

She crawled out the window. Her first instinct now was to reach the ground, but she thought better of it. With her cloak floating out around her, she found footholds where the vines intertwined. She pulled herself up around the dormers of the third story and climbed onto the slate shingles of the roof. She crouched, panting, behind a chimney pot.

She was too far away to hear Sir Henry Clinton complain about servants who left windows open and let in the noxious night airs. Clinton walked to the hall to call for someone to take care of it, but John went to the windows. When he leaned out to close them, he paused to look at the bowlers and folk out for an evening stroll on the green below.

On the roof Kate wanted to hurry home with her news, but she knew she had to wait for darkness. Once her heart stopped pounding she savored the exhilaration of being so high above everything. Looking out over the city and the ships in the harbor she thought about the consequences of what she had just read.

When Lizzie said she had heard André talking about sending needles and lace to an agent in Philadelphia, Kate had assumed he meant Nan Baker with her peddler's pack of sewing notions. But Nan had gone south with her husband's artillery unit more than six months ago.

Kate concentrated on the puzzle. The knowledge that John Anderson was John André gave her a chill that had nothing to do with the September breeze blowing in off the water. She still did not know for sure who Gustavus was, but if her suspicions were correct, they might explain the letter she had gotten several days ago from Peggy Arnold. When the merchant delivered it to the shop, along with the china Rob had ordered, Kate had wondered why Peggy would bother to write her.

"You most fortunate of creatures," Peggy had written in her round, childish hand, "to dwell there at the bright center of the universe. Such a gay life you must lead while I suffer alone and friendless here in the wilderness."

Peggy had asked wistfully about John André. She had mentioned Seth who, she said, had turned into quite a winsome brute. She added that he had shown a want of sense in taking up with a negress, but he always was a heedless boy. Kate was glad to see that Lizzie had made it safely to West Point, but she had been puzzled by Peggy's final comments. "God willing, I will see you ere long, and we shall have a party. West Point is not important now, but soon it will become so."

Maybe heights were prime places for epiphanies. After all, Kate smiled at the thought, Moses had received the Ten Commandments on a mountaintop, not a bowling green. She thought about what had brought her to perch, like a crow in a cloak, on the roof.

Four years ago she had been less than the sunshine patriot that Thomas Paine wrote about. She had been no patriot at all. She had begun this work in anger at how the British treated Seth and the other prisoners. She had continued out of love for Robert. Now she did it because liberty had infected her as surely as smallpox. It had made her immune to a life governed by the likes of Henry Clinton.

As darkness fell, the watchmen lit the street lanterns and they twinkled like fireflies in the narrow canyons of the city. A breeze rang the changes on the blocks and tackle, the pulleys and halyards of the ships' rigging. By now Clinton and André and their guests must have gathered for supper. Kate started down the vines, her toes searching for purchase. She saw that the windows had been closed, and she prayed that John would think he had left the drawer unlocked by mistake.

Rob would be frantic with worry, but this was worth the risk. If Gustavus was Benedict Arnold, he had total control in the Highlands, with no other generals around to check up on him. If he allowed the British to capture West Point and the other forts, they could cut off any chance of Washington's army in the south receiving recruits from New England. The war would be over. The British would throw Seth into prison again, and what would happen to Lizzie and Isaac? What would happen to all of them?

Kate had to get this information to Benjamin Tallmadge as quickly as possible.

LIVING PEOPLE WERE MUCH MORE OF A NUISANCE TO TRACK down and sell than dead ones. Tunis Birdwhistle shifted from one shovel foot to another, waiting in the echoing entry of the Kennedy mansion for the subaltern to return with John André. He had been waiting for over an hour. He could hear the sounds of laughter and the chime of silverware and crystal from the banquet hall.

Coincidence had nothing to do with his being on the bowling green where he could watch Kate climb out of the window of André's office. He had shadowed her for months, whenever he hadn't anything more lucrative to occupy him. General Knyphausen had done nothing about the report on Kate that Birdwhistle had sent him by way of James Rivington last spring, but what could one expect from a Hessian? As far as Birdwhistle was concerned, they all had sauerkraut for sense.

Now Clinton was back in charge, and Major André was handling intelligence. Birdwhistle had information that would certainly interest them, and it would be worth several guineas at least. If they had granted him an interview when he first knocked on the door, they could have caught the Quaker strumpet cowering among the chimney pots. He worried that someone else might have sighted her scrambling up the vines, but if they had they hadn't bothered to report it and beat him to the bounty.

André finally appeared. "What do you wish to tell me, Birdwhistle?"

"Shouldn't we go somewhere private, Your Excellency?"

"This will do. No one is about."

"Well, Your Excellency, I saw the Darby chit shinning out of your office window not more than an hour ago."

John burst into laughter. "Kate Darby?"

"Yes, Your Excellency."

"Climbing out my window?"

"Yes, Your Excellency. The very one. She climbed to the roof using the vines."

André could hardly stop laughing enough to speak. "I think you must be mistaken."

It was a sign of André's breeding that he was courteous to underlings, even one as far under as Birdwhistle. He did not call him a liar. He did not say that he was falsely accusing someone to earn a bounty, but he thought it.

"I'm not mistaken, sir. And it's not the first time. I saw her obtaining documents from a navvy at the docks."

"She clerks at Oakman and Townsend's shop. She has reason to go to the docks frequently."

"She's a spy, sir, I would bet my life on it."

"And hers," said André. "No one else has come to me with the news that my window is leaking young women. Do you have witnesses?"

"No, Your Excellency."

"The bowling green was crowded this evening yet you tell me that no one saw Miss Darby but you."

"I suppose they didn't, but I did. I, Tunis Birdwhistle, swear it on my honor, sir."

André chuckled at the absurdity of "Birdwhistle" and "honor" spoken in the same sentence. "Next time you accuse Miss Darby of a hanging offence, bring proof."

André turned on his polished heels and went back to enjoy the rest of his meal. It would be the last one he ate in New York City.

Thirty-nine

Wherein John André meets his match in Benjamin Tallmadge;
Peggy puts on the performance of her life;
Tunis Birdwhistle has news for Benedict Arnold

IF JOHN ANDRÉ HAD LEFT HIS SHINY BOOTS IN MANHATTAN, he might have lived to see his thirty-first year. Benedict Arnold convinced him to wear civilian clothes for the trip back to New York, but when he left the Tory house where he and Arnold had their meeting, his high black boots gleamed below his long riding cloak. He carried a pass written for John Anderson and issued by General Arnold.

The loyalist guide Arnold had engaged for him turned back at the bridge across the Croton River, the southern limit of American-held territory. From here André was on his own. On the other side of the river lay the Neutral Ground, and fifteen miles beyond that the first of the British outposts. When John crossed the river his anxiety vanished. He was enjoying the magnificent scenery and humming "Yankee Doodle" when three men blocked the road in front of him.

While one kept his old matchlock pistol leveled at him and a second brandished a musket the third requested his watch, his cloak, and the money in his pockets. Then they told him to hand over his boots. Maybe if the boots had been scuffed and worn down at the heels they would have let him keep them. Or maybe not. In any case when John pulled off the left one the packet of papers fell out.

The men couldn't read. The sketches of the fortifications in the Highlands and the dispositions of troops meant nothing to them until John offered to pay them a hundred guineas to let him go. They weren't bright
enough to wonder where he would get the hundred guineas since he didn't
have them on him, or to consider why he should pay them anything once
he was free of them. They hadn't intended to take him prisoner in the first
place, so the idea of a reward for setting him free intrigued them. They began to suspect that they had not landed any ordinary fish.

The Neutral Ground was plundered on a regular basis by men of strong
political leanings or none at all. These three could have belonged to one
of the loyalist gangs the locals called Cow Boys, but André's luck had run
out. They were Skinners, the marauders who deemed themselves patriots.
For them patriotism was not the last refuge of scoundrels, but the first. With
visions of a bounty dancing in their heads they took John and his stocking
feet to the nearest American outpost.

The text of the papers was in André's numeric code, but the colonel in
charge was smart enough to realize what the sketches were. He was filling
in for the regular commander and none too sure of himself, but he got
busy making decisions left and right. He sent off a report with an express
courier to notify General Arnold of the capture of a man named John Anderson. He dispatched another messenger with the plans and sketches from
André's boot.

General Washington was enroute to West Point for an inspection tour
of the defenses, and the messenger's orders were to intercept him and deliver the confiscated papers to him. The colonel decided not to give the
three Skinners a reward, and he made them return André's boots, watch,
cloak, and money. He issued them each two gills of rum, hailed them as
patriots and heroes, and sent them grumbling on their way.

It did not occur to the colonel that the commandant of West Point could
be involved in such treachery. His last decision was to send the prisoner
and a guard detail to the Robinson house for General Arnold to deal with.
André thought the damning documents were going with him, which
meant that he and Arnold might yet be able to figure a way out of this. He
was like the rabbit in the old folk tale, begging the fox not to throw him in
that briar patch. He set off north with a lighter heart than when he had arrived. Then his next round of bad luck landed.

By chance the Skinners had brought André to the post near the Connecticut line where Major Benjamin Tallmadge was assigned. By the time Benjamin and his muddy, saddle-sore detachment of dragoons arrived on Saturday night, the colonel had made all the decisions he was going to that day. So when Benjamin suggested he make a few more, and at least one that reeked of insubordination besides, the colonel wasn't interested.

He briefed Benjamin on what had happened and Ben recognized the name John Anderson. General Arnold had written asking him to provide an escort of dragoons for his business associate, Anderson, should he need it. Benjamin had also received a letter from Culper, Jr., warning that treachery was afoot, though Robert Townsend could not say exactly what it would be. The more detailed information that Kate had discovered was still enroute, but Benjamin smelled a pair of rats. If this Anderson fellow was an associate of Arnold's, then the hero of Saratoga was involved up to his periwig in perfidy.

Benjamin leaned across the colonel's desk. "Arrest General Arnold." He was a serious fellow anyway, and this crisis had distilled that quality to a ferocious intensity. "I will take responsibility for it."

"Are you mad?" The colonel leaped up as though the front of his trousers had caught fire. "I will do no such thing."

"Then send a message to the guards to return here with Anderson. Send another to intercept the courier before he can alert General Arnold to the situation."

Those were two suggestions too many for the colonel's overtaxed faculties. "The commandant must be kept informed."

"The commandant may be a traitor."

"We don't know that."

Benjamin took a deep breath. Why did that old misanthrope, Samuel Johnson, have to be right so often? He was the one who said: *It must have taken him a great deal of pains to become what we now see him. Such an excess of stupidity, sir, is not in Nature.* "Then at least bring Anderson back here."

The colonel pondered that for what seemed an eternity. "All right. I will send a man to instruct the guard to return with the prisoner."

André and his guard had gotten ten miles from Arnold's headquarters when the messenger caught up with them and turned them around. As soon as Benjamin saw the prisoner, he could tell by his posture that this was no mere businessman. He still insisted his name was Anderson, but as the hours dragged by, the rate of his pacing increased. Benjamin decided to rattle him some more.

He made himself comfortable in a chair by the fire and watched the man march to one end of the room, turn in precise military fashion, and repeat the route to the other wall.

"Mr. Anderson," Benjamin said, "the colonel sent your handiwork to the commander in chief."

André stopped abruptly. "Washington?"

"Yes."

That had the effect Benjamin was looking for. André dropped onto the edge of the other chair and looked at Ben. "I am John André."

Benjamin almost let his jaw drop. He almost said, "Good Lord." He almost stood up himself and started pacing.

The famous Major John André. Harry Clinton's adjutant general in charge of intelligence. Benjamin's counterpart. His nemesis for four years. Finally Benjamin did say it. "Good Lord."

MARCHING A SMALL CIRCUIT WAS WHAT SETH HATED MOST about guard duty outside General Arnold's quarters, but today he was too excited to stand still anyway. General Washington was coming for breakfast. Lizzie had borrowed a flatiron and pressed Seth's uniform while he polished his brass buttons. She had convinced him to give Washington the draft of the Declaration of Independence if he got a chance.

Seth had put the papers into a metal dispatch tube and carried it in his haversack. Now he listened for the sound of hooves. A hundred and sixty horses made a lot of noise, and that's how many members of the Light Horse were riding with Washington and Lafayette. Two of the commander's aides had already arrived to tell Peggy Arnold that the general was on his way. Peggy, not surprisingly, was still in bed.

When Seth finally did hear hoofbeats they were coming from behind him. He whirled and saw General Arnold round the corner of the house and head straight for him. Seth dove out of the way and rolled. As he brushed himself off, he watched Arnold race his horse to the high embankment by the river and guide him down the trail on the other side. He was headed for the boat landing at the foot of it.

Ned Withers ran outside. From the upstairs bedroom came wailing. It sounded like Peggy Arnold had caught her fingers in a mousetrap.

"What's happening, Ned?"

"The general says he's going to West Point to arrange a reception for the commander in chief."

"He's in a tearing hurry."

"A courier arrived. Whatever message he brought has rattled the general."

From upstairs Seth could hear Peggy screaming, "No! General Arnold will never return. He's gone forever. They have put hot irons on his head."

Seth looked anxiously off in the direction from which General Washington and his entourage would come. This, he thought, is a very bad time for her to have one of her spells.

Peggy's outbursts continued throughout the morning. Seth was about to go off duty when Ned called to him.

"The doctor wants you to try to calm her down."

"Why me?"

"You've known her since she was young."

"So have you."

Ned gave him a wry smile. "But I am not you, my dear friend. I never have been and never will be."

Seth went upstairs and opened the door cautiously. Peggy sometimes threw things when she was in this state.

Mrs. Arnold occupied a bed ringed by the doctor, three bewildered majors, and a colonel who was an old friend of her husband. Peggy wore only a loose-fitting morning gown that had a way of becoming looser as she moaned and sobbed and thrashed among the covers. Strands of her long blond hair formed a silken curtain across her face. Seth had to admit that she had never looked better, and he couldn't help entertaining the uncharitable notion that she probably thought so too.

Seth was still standing by the door wondering what to do when he heard Alexander Hamilton and General Washington in the hall. He had seen the commander in chief at the worst of times, at Valley Forge and at the miserable encampment at Morristown, but he had never heard such anguish in his voice.

"Arnold has betrayed us. Whom can we trust now?"

So that's what this was all about.

"I'll go after him," said Hamilton.

The door opened and Washington came in. He dropped his saddlebags and went to the bed. The general filled up any room he occupied, and there was no mistaking him, unless one was Peggy Arnold in the midst of a spell.

"Are you going to heap hot irons on my head?" She pulled the covers up to her chin and stared wide-eyed at him. "Are you going to kill my child?"

No amount of reassurance could calm her, but while she had everyone's attention, Seth took the metal tube from his haversack and slipped it into General Washington's saddlebag. He would write the commander a letter telling him who had put it there. Maybe it would bring him some comfort in the days to come.

When Washington saw that his presence was not helping the situation, he collected his saddlebag and left. He had a lot more on his mind than Mrs. Arnold. The doctor motioned for Seth to stay, then he and the other men filed out.

As soon as the door closed Peggy heaved a huge sigh and fell back on the pillows with her hair spread out around her. She waved Seth forward and he approached as cautiously as he would an unexploded mortar shell.

She had instantly become calm and lucid, which didn't surprise Seth at all. "What will happen to me, Seth?"

"I don't know."

"All these theatricals are tiring."

She closed her eyes and began snoring lightly. Seth eased out of the room.

Washington saw that Peggy got her wish and gave her and her child an escort back to her family's house in Philadelphia. No one believed that she had had any part in her husband's treachery, but she was not popular there anyway.

In spite of the letters Clinton wrote to General Washington in an effort to save John André, he was condemned to death on the gallows. During the ten days he was a captive, André charmed everyone. Alexander Hamilton and several generals pleaded with Washington to spare him, but he would not relent. When André died on the second day of October, 1780, Benjamin Tallmadge, Anthony Wayne, and a lot of other men wept. So did Seth.

When Kate and Rob heard of it, they both cried. Rob could not imagine going to the coffee house and not seeing his friend's cheerful smile and his black boots on the edge of the table.

As for Benedict Arnold, if he had expected a hero's welcome among the British he did not get it. The other officers despised him and no one trusted him. Everyone, Sir Harry Clinton most of all, wished that the Americans had hanged Arnold and that John André had escaped. When he walked New York's streets in his scarlet general's uniform, people turned away from him. When he attended social functions, no one spoke to him.

One person was glad to see him though. Tunis Birdwhistle knocked on the door of a mansion near the bowling green soon after Arnold moved in. He had heard that the American turncoat wanted to know who was spying for the rebels in New York. For a price Birdwhistle could tell him the name of one of them. She had escaped him twice, but he would snare her the third time.

ROB USHERED OUT THE LAST CUSTOMER AND LOCKED THE door. He walked around the shop selecting things that he and Kate would need and putting them into traveling bags. Arnold's defection had terrified him. He had visited all the people who had gathered information for him and told them he would not be asking for their services any longer.

He persuaded Kate to go with him to Long Island until it seemed prudent to return to New York. The Townsends' house in Oyster Bay would not be safe, but Abraham arranged for them to lodge at Anna Strong's farm near Setauket. Kate had gone to the Buchanans' to collect the rest of her clothes and say good-bye to Almy and Cook.

Rob whirled when a key rattled in the lock and James Rivington let himself in. He closed the door behind him and locked it again. His face was ashen.

"They have taken Kate, Rob."

Rob thought his heart would stop beating. And then he wished it would. "Who?" But he knew.

"The provost. Billy Cunningham. Clinton has charged her with spying. They arrested Hercules too, but he's merely Cunningham's favorite suspect whenever sculduddery is afoot. He'll talk his way out. He always does."

"Which prison did they take her to?"

"The *Jersey*."

Rob swayed and Jemmy put out a hand to steady him. He led Rob, as dazed as a sleepwalker, into the storeroom, where they couldn't be seen by anyone looking in the big windows.

"The Brooklyn ferry is too dangerous," Jemmy said. "They may be on the lookout for you there."

Rob heard the voice but not the words. His ears rang. His breath caught in his throat, and he gasped for air. His hands shook as if palsied, and the trembling spread to the rest of him until his knees let him down, none too gently. He slid down the wall to sit on the floor.

"Rob, listen to me." Jemmy crouched so he could look him in the eye. "I know a Dutch farmer at the market who will take you in his produce boat when he returns to Flushing in the morning. You can go to the Fly Market after dark and sleep aboard it tonight."

"Kate."

That was all Rob could say. It was all he could think. Pretty Kate. Pretty ember-haired Kate. Kate whom he loved more than life.

"We'll get her out, Rob, but there's nothing you can do here. Take yourself to safety, lad, so she'll have someone to come back to."

Jemmy Rivington had told a lot of lies in his life, and this was one more. But he had learned that people often would rather hear a lie than the truth. He felt sure that Rob would prefer this lie to the ugly truth that Kate would not be coming back.

Believing that she would return was easy. After all, the British didn't hang women. But Henry Clinton excelled at vindictiveness. He was enraged that Washington had hanged John André, the only person in the world Clinton cared for. He wanted revenge, and Kate's was the one name for whom a witness would swear guilt.

The best Jemmy could wish for her was that they hanged her soon. Winter was coming. The less time she must spend in the horror that was the *Jersey,* the better.

Wherein Kate receives good news and bad news and good news

LIEUTENANT PATRICK RYAN PAUSED IN FRONT OF THE GUN-
room door to tug the wrinkles from his crimson wool tunic and adjust his
expression. If he smiled too broadly when he entered, Miss Darby would
think General Clinton had relented and signed a pardon for her. Rumors
of a reprieve made their way to this cabin at the stern of the ship from time
to time, and Lieutenant Ryan could not bear to see hope kindled in her
eyes, then snuffed again.

Patrick did have good news for her though. It was treading on his
heels and breathing on the back of his neck. The captain in charge of the
Jersey had ridden up the coast with some of Clinton's officers to hunt anything remotely digestible. He would run up bills in Long Island taverns
and shops that he had no intention of ever paying. In his absence Patrick
took the liberty of inviting aboard the women who had brought food,
books, and clothing to the landing for Kate every week for the past three
months.

He rapped his knuckles on the door.

"God keep you." That gentle voice was what compelled Patrick to stay
on duty here after the weekly rotation of his guard detail to a more agreeable assignment.

Hell, Patrick thought, would be a more agreeable assignment than the *Jersey.*

At least German soldiers had come aboard this week. They and the British seamen were less brutal than members of the loyalist militias. For the loyalists this war was personal. The rebellion had made refugees of their families. It had dispossessed and impoverished them. It had killed loved ones. They took revenge however they could. Their cruelty to the prisoners sickened Patrick, but the problems were too vast for him to fix, even if he had had the authority.

He stayed on here to protect Kate. He told himself that he couldn't abandon a woman to the horrors of this place. He did not admit that he stayed so he could see her burnished copper hair and serene, sea-green eyes each day. He did not admit that sitting with her, discussing passages from the Bible he had given her, left him feeling more at peace and, at the same time, in greater turmoil than he had ever experienced. He longed to put his arms around her and comfort her, but he did not dare.

As Patrick wrestled the key into the rusty lock he heard a squeal of impatience from the good news shifting from foot to foot behind him. He put his shoulder to the door and shoved it open in its warped frame. He intended to greet Kate as he did every morning, and announce the arrival of her friends, but Almy had another plan. She pushed past him and charged through the narrow doorway. Patrick was a solid six feet tall and fourteen stone, but when Cook jostled by after Almy the bulk of her hip knocked him off balance.

Almy and Cook rushed to Kate and flung their arms around her, enveloping her in their long wool cloaks. The three of them stood together, swaying as though buffeted by a storm of grief and joy. They kissed and sobbed and laughed, and kissed again. Then Almy turned a beguiling smile on Patrick. The vapor of her breath condensed in the icy room.

"Dear Lieutenant Ryan, won't you accompany us for a promenade on the quarter deck? Kate looks quite peaked. The fresh air will do her a world of good."

"The air is freezing up there."

"Well, it's little better in here." She nodded to the cracks in the planks through which the wind blew. "And where are the blankets we brought for Miss Darby?"

"Do not blame him, cousin." Kate held tightly to Almy's hand. Since the soldiers dragged her away from the Buchanan house that terrible day this was the first contact she had had with anyone she knew, much less loved. She didn't intend to let go. "I sent the blankets to the men imprisoned below. I asked to be allowed to tend to them, but my petition was refused."

"Perhaps a stroll topside would be of benefit." Patrick bowed and offered his arm to Kate. Almy and Cook followed them into the narrow passageway and up the steps to the small deck high at the ship's stern. The wind blew across it, whipping Kate's cloak around her thin body. Even here, even with the wind, the stench from the lower decks unsettled her stomach.

For a moment Patrick wondered if Almy Buchanan had some scheme to help her friend escape. He wished she did. He wished a boarding party of rebels would swarm over the taffrail, point their muskets at him, and demand he surrender Kate. He would miss her company, but at least he would not have to watch her grow thinner and more hollow-eyed each day. He feared that death would arrive for her before a pardon did.

Patrick looked over the rail but was disappointed to see no whaleboats loaded with a rescue party. Almy took his arm.

"Lieutenant, do tell me the names of those vessels." She chattered to him as she led him to the other side of the deck for a view of the four other prison ships.

He glanced back, half expecting to see Kate disappear over the rail, but she stood with the Buchanan's servant, the one they called Cook, and gazed toward shore. He turned his attention back to Almy who kept up a stream of conversation. Patrick was no fool. He assumed Mrs. Buchanan was distracting him so her servant could deliver messages in private to the prisoner, but as long as whatever she told Kate alleviated her misery Patrick didn't care.

"Can you see him, Miss Kate?" Cook nodded in Rob's direction. "He's standing there on the hill. Among the grave markers."

"Yes!" Kate wanted to shout for joy. She wanted to wave her arms over her head. She wanted to call to him, but all she could do was throw back the hood of her cloak so he would see her more clearly.

Cook spoke quickly in a low voice.

"General Arnold sailed for Virginia with British troops two weeks ago, and good riddance. With him no longer stumping about looking for folks to imprison, Mister Townsend thought it safe enough to return to the city. He has not come calling at the Buchanan house, though. If you ask me, not seeing you there is more than he can bear. He does not pass time at the coffee house, either. Phoebe Fraunces says he has gone for a ghost and speaks to no one. She says he takes the Brooklyn ferry each morning and stands on that hill, staring at this ship."

"Please ask Phoebe to tell him I pray every day to God to protect him." Kate knew she could not write to Rob nor he to her. The guards here would inform on anyone they suspected of collusion with her.

When Kate spoke she did not take her eyes off him, standing on the windswept crest of the hill and surrounded by the scattered bones of prisoners.

"And Seth and Lizzie and the little one?"

"We have had no word of them, Mistress Kate. General Arnold believed that spies in New York exposed his treachery. He was determined to root them out. We're all as skittish as ash cats, we are, and not even Miss Almy has been able to send letters out of the city or receive them." Cook snorted. "Mr. Buchanan still quakes when he thinks of those soldiers barging into his house looking for you."

They heard Almy come toward them with Patrick in tow. "Law for me, the dear lieutenant is right," she called out. "The wind up here would freeze hell's hinges."

When Kate pulled her hood back in place, she left her hand up next to her face, palm out, for several beats of her heart. It was the only sign of recognition she could give Rob. She wiped the tears from her eyes and turned away from the rail. She did not want the lieutenant to join her there and see Rob. Almy was keeping him distracted. She linked an arm through Kate's elbow and chided him.

"She's dwindled to kindling, lieutenant. Do you not deliver the vittles we bring?"

"I do but she sends it, along with the blankets, to the prisoners below."

Kate went to his defense. "The good lieutenant offers to share his own rations with me, but I cannot eat them while others starve."

"You have to eat, Kate. What good is a pardon to a corpse?"

Seeing Rob created such an ache to be with him that Kate gave in to a moment of hope. "Dear cousin, think thee Clinton will grant me a pardon?"

"Of course. General Washington and his officers have sent numerous petitions and so have our friends here in New York. Even my husband has written Clinton. With that dreadful beast Arnold gone, the general will see that this is all a hideous mistake."

Almy knew that Clinton was still furious with Washington for hanging John André, but she could not believe he would do the unthinkable. He was the most spiteful man Almy had ever met, but even he would not send a woman to the gallows for so petty a cause as revenge. Still, when Almy and Cook left Kate, they both sobbed and held her as if they would never see her again.

KATE STOOD UP WHEN PATRICK OPENED THE GUNROOM DOOR. His face was haggard and his eyes red-rimmed. He had received word of the execution six hours ago, and he had paced the quarterdeck in the February frost since then. He could have excused himself from this, but he knew his would be the last and only friendly face Kate would see.

"Is it midnight?" Kate asked.

"Yes." Patrick paused until he could speak without faltering. "Know this, Miss Darby, if I could take your place I would, and gladly."

The commander of the ship was following the army procedure of hanging prisoners in secret at midnight. The usual policy was to haul the unsuspecting victims from their sleep and march them away, but Patrick had come to tell Kate as soon as he heard about the order. The two of them had prayed together.

Even then he could not believe that General Clinton would allow the execution to take place. In case he did, Patrick had asked to be allowed to bury her. He would see that she was interred properly in a churchyard, even if he had to do it at night and swear the other men on the detail to secrecy. He would tell no one where her body lay, except the fellow who came to stand on the hill every morning. He wanted to ask Kate about him, but was too shy.

Patrick slumped onto the stool and put his face in his hands. Kate laid a hand on his shoulder. One of the last duties of the dying, after all, was to comfort the living. "I am in God's care, dear friend. The worst cannot harm me, nor can it harm thee."

But Kate's hands trembled. It wasn't death she feared, but the manner of dying. She asked God to forgive her for doubting His mercy. She gripped the Bible tightly as she followed Patrick out of the cabin, down the passageway, and through the door in the ten-foot-tall barrier erected to keep the prisoners away from the crew's quarters. Beyond it was the upper gun deck, where the crew had assembled. Above her arched a black sky glittering with stars. The magnificence of it brought tears to Kate's eyes.

Kate knew she could not bargain with God, but she wished she could. She would ask Him to let her lay her head on Rob's shoulder and feel his arms around her one more time. She would ask Him to let her tell Rob how happy he had made her and that she loved him more than life.

As a gallows the guards had rigged the derrick that brought water casks aboard. The long wooden arm and the noose hanging from it were silhouetted black against the stars. Even at this hour Kate heard the cries and moans of the prisoners below.

She closed her eyes and concentrated on her prayers while the captain read the charges. One more time he offered her clemency if she would divulge the names of her fellow operatives. She shook her head. The seaman assigned hangman's duty took her arm and steered her under the noose.

Patrick stepped forward and handed her his red sash. He struggled to keep his voice steady. Giving in to his grief would not help her now. "Do you want me to tie it?"

"I thank thee, but I can manage it."

Kate stooped so she could wrap the sash around her ankles and tie it in a knot. It would keep her legs from kicking in an unseemly way as she strangled. Dancing on air they called it. She was aware of the irony. She had never danced before and that was one of her very few regrets. She did not regret the work that had brought her here.

The hangman held out the black hood to cover her head, but she smiled at him and waved it away.

"I would rather see God's creation."

Patrick recited what he could remember from the Book of Common Prayer.

Into thy hands, O merciful Savior, we commend the soul of thy servant. Acknowledge, we beseech thee, a sheep of thine own fold, a lamb of thine

own flock, a sinner of thine own redeeming. Receive her into the blessed
rest of everlasting peace, and into the glorious company of the saints in
light.

The hangman followed the ancient custom of kneeling on one knee to ask her forgiveness and her blessing.

Kate gave it, then looked around at the half dozen sleepy guards. "I pray that God will bless you all. I pray this war ends soon and that you may go home and live in peace with your families gathered around you."

She didn't recognize her own voice. She felt as though she had left her body already and was watching from somewhere above. Then the hangman put the noose around her neck and she registered the weight of it and the scratch of the rough hemp.

When the hangman and two others hauled on the rope, it squealed as it rubbed along in the derrick's big wooden tackle. It made so much noise that Kate did not hear Patrick groan. She felt the noose tighten around her throat and the deck fall away from under her feet. A prickling started in her toes, as though electricity were surging up from them. She fought for breath.

Points of light flashed like sparks behind her eyes. The world went black, then blindingly bright. A feeling of love as vast as the far-flung stars washed over her and soaked through to her marrow.

She remembered her first sight of Rob at the docks. She remembered standing with him under the stars at Oyster Bay. She remembered the first time they made love. She remembered every moment she had spent with him. She remembered everything.

Afterword

Very little is known about the operative referred to as 355, the Culpers' numerical code for "lady." She is mentioned in two letters from Culper, senior, but never identified. It is believed, however, that she was the only member of the ring whom the British arrested, imprisoned aboard the *Jersey,* and hung as a spy. Much of what we think we know about her is based on speculation and inference. A favorite theory is that she was a member of a prominent Tory family in New York.

Not long after 355's execution, an officer left the British army and asked General Washington for sanctuary because, as Washington wrote, "He was ordered to do what no gentleman should." The assumption is that he had to preside over 355's execution. It has been suggested that he fell in love with her while she was a prisoner. Historians have also linked her romantically with Robert Townsend, some going so far as to call her his common-law wife. Next to 355's identity, that is one of the busiest realms of speculation.

After Benedict Arnold went to Virginia with his command of British soldiers, Robert Townsend began transmitting information again and continued to do so until the end of the war. Some sources claim that 355 had his child aboard the prison ship *Jersey,* but that's fiction. Robert did give his name to a boy born after 355's death, but the mother was his housekeeper in New York. The general assumption is that he fathered the child, but Robert's brother, James, also lived in the apartment. Some speculate that Robert took on the responsibility for the boy's education even though James was the father. Given what we know about Robert Townsend's character, that's a likely possibility.

After the war Townsend returned to the family home in Oyster Bay. He lived there with his unmarried sister, Sally (Sarah), until his death in 1838. Today the house, now called Raynham Hall, is claimed to be the most haunted place on Long Island.

Robert never spoke of his activities as an intelligencer. His identity was kept so secret that Washington himself did not know who he was. The discovery that Robert Townsend was Samuel Culper, Jr., did not come out until 1930, when a comparison of Townsend's and Culper Junior's correspondence proved they were the same man.

Abraham Woodhull, aka Samuel Culper, Sr., went back to his farm in Setauket and served as a Suffolk County judge.

Benjamin Tallmadge became a merchant in Litchfield, Connecticut. In 1783 he married Mary Floyd, the daughter of William Floyd, a signer of the Declaration of Independence. Benjamin served in the House of Representatives from 1801 to 1817. He died at age eighty-one.

Austin Roe ran his tavern in Setauket until 1798 when he moved to Patchogue and opened a hotel.

Congress gave the Culpers' whaleboat captain, Caleb Brewster, a pension for his gallantry in action. After the war he commanded a revenue cutter used to apprehend smugglers around New York.

Fraunces' tavern, still located in Lower Manhattan, became American headquarters, where Sam and his daughter Phoebe happily served Washington and his staff. The tavern was the scene of an emotional ceremony when Washington bid farewell to his officers.

When George Washington entered New York on November 25, 1783, he did not visit Robert Townsend because he had no idea he was the man who had been such a great boon to the patriot cause. He did go to see Hercules Mulligan and ordered a complete civilian wardrobe from him. Mulligan added "Clothier to Genl. Washington" to his shop's sign and prospered as a result of it.

The commander in chief also called on James Rivington. Witnesses claim he gave Jemmy a bag that clinked. It's possible that the most strident Tory in New York was also a double agent. When the Americans took over New York, Rivington apologized for his pro-British propaganda in the *Royal Gazette*, but a victim of his libels accosted him in the street and beat him up anyway. His paper, renamed, lost subscribers, and his generosity landed him in debtors' prison when people whose bills he'd guaranteed defaulted. He died in poverty on July 4, 1802.

One of the more colorful participants in the war, Baron von Steuben, also spent his last years in poverty. Congress eventually paid him a small fraction of the eighty-five hundred dollars it owed him. It gave him the balance in Treasury Certificates at six percent interest, which did not bring even ten cents on the dollar. In 1794 at the age of sixty-four he died of a stroke in a two-room log cabin in New York State. The U.S. Army used his manual of arms for many years, and he was an early proponent of the U.S. Military Academy established at West Point in 1802.

The character Nan Baker is based on Ann Bates, the most successful spy operating for the British. Poverty-stricken and in poor health at the war's end, she petitioned the Crown for the pension promised her. She wrote, "Haid I doon half as much for the scruff of mankind, I mean the Rabls, I should not be thus left to parrish." She eventually received her pension.

New York's infamous provost marshal, William Cunningham, was arrested for forgery in London in 1791 and sentenced to hang. Just before his death he is said to have written a confession. "I shudder at the murders I have been accessory to, both with and without orders from the government, especially while in New York, during which time there were more than two thousand prisoners starved by stopping their rations, which I sold."

Estimates are that up to eleven thousand five hundred Americans, mostly men in their twenties and thirties, died in British prisons. In the years following the war, building projects around Wallabout Bay uncovered countless numbers of bones of those who died aboard the prison ships. In 1792 the citizens of Brooklyn resolved that the bones be collected. A crypt containing them, and a monument to the Prison Ship Martyrs, stands in Fort Greene Park, Brooklyn.